Treachery

Who can I trust
Who can trust me

Sequel to the novel A FALL TO THE TOP

By

Noel Primrose

ISBN: 978-1-916981-98-0

This book is dedicated to my family and friends, including those no longer with us; all of them have contributed in one way or another to the very happy and rewarding life I have enjoyed.

I'll also take this opportunity to extend a special welcome to Great Granddaughter Heidi Grace, who recently joined the Primrose Clan.

PROLOGUE

The prologue is based on the pages ending the final chapter of A
Fall to the Top, published in 2022, my first book. It lays out the
final scenario leading to this novel. Jack Somerton's friend and
parliamentary colleague, Foreign Secretary Alan Croudace, has
agreed to accept the Prime Ministership until a permanent
successor can be found, at which point he will step down and
resign as a Member of Parliament. Somerton, this novel's central
character, is engaged in conversation with a mysterious scientific
genius known as Jupiter. Pressed by Somerton, Jupiter has agreed
to reveal his identity and is speaking.

*'My name is Josef Svetinsky; I was born in Russia, I was a
little known, rather unimportant scientist working in a remote
research establishment in Siberia. Quite by chance, I discovered
a means of accessing data held on computer systems throughout
the world. I developed a massive quantum computer which
monitors every research computer on this planet on a 24/7 basis
- their knowledge is my knowledge. I devised a series of
algorithms to identify any discovery or innovation that could
further my knowledge. I then went on to develop and extend this
capability to a level I never dreamt was possible.*

*'As my knowledge increased, I found a way of taking this
knowledge and embedding it, via neural pathways, into my brain.
As time went on, I found that subjecting my brain to these
transfers gave it the capacity to advance the natural evolutionary
processes. In effect, I stole knowledge from scientists throughout
the world and became the genius I am now, a super-genius in
fact. I can use a similar process to improve the intelligence of
chosen humans to whatever extent I choose.'*

*'So why didn't you make the skills and knowledge you
possessed available to Russia, your own Motherland? Why come
to the United Kingdom?*

*What seemed like a genuine look of sadness crossed Jupiter's
face. 'For no other reason than I came to believe the Communist
regime would not use my knowledge for peaceful purposes; in
fact, quite the opposite. I was sure it's aim would have been*

world domination. It would have been a world of death and destruction; a world of dictatorship and all the unhappiness and inequality that would result. Think of me what you will, but that is not the kind of world I aspire to. Earth is a truly beautiful planet, one that I love and want to preserve.

'I needed a new platform to work on; a country of historical importance that believed in democracy and diplomacy. It had to be one which had global influence, one that would be respected and trusted by the rest of the world. In my judgement, the United Kingdom is one of the few that meets those requirements. Strong leadership was also a requirement and Mr MacKinnon provided that. Through him, and those close to him, I set about my aim to promote a peaceful and just world.

*'Obviously, I had to have an ally; without one, my powers are, to a large extent, unusable. I needed someone I could trust, and through whom I could seek to deliver my ideals. It had to be a politician with access to power and resources; one who could act on the world stage, such as Colin MacKinnon. Also, though far from perfect, the United Kingdom probably engenders more trust than most nations. Frankly, that's why I need you or somebody like you. I sincerely hope that you will accept my offer of a partnership. I firmly believe that the best way, **the only way**, to ensure peace on this planet of ours is to have the deterrent and control opportunities provided by my satellite system, TS2 as it is currently known.'*

Jupiter, Josef Svetinsky as he now was, paused, a look of sadness, almost pain, crossed his face. 'There was just one difficulty, one that seems to be unresolvable; ironically the processes that served my brain so well, all but destroyed my body's immune system, hence my need to live in a controlled environment. Someday, maybe I'll find an answer to this unfortunate side effect and lead a normal existence, but sadly not yet. That's my history, Jack, now it's up to you. Do we have a partnership or not?'

Somerton was facing a huge dilemma, ambition and caution pulling in different directions. 'How do I know if you are telling me the truth? You could be spinning me a well-rehearsed yarn for all I know?'

Jupiter nodded, 'Absolutely, I could indeed be doing just that. It's up to you to decide whether you believe me or not, and, whether we can work together in harmony. The choice is yours and yours alone to make. I accept that it's a big decision and fully understand your concerns, but at the end of the day it's a decision for you to make; no-ne can make it for you. I suggest that we end this conversation now and I leave you to give the matter further thought. When we next meet, I will want an answer to my proposition, a simple yes or no. Should you accept my offer, our priority will be to launch TS2.

'What happens if I say no?'

Jupiter shrugged. 'I don't think you will, but if you do, I will take my offer elsewhere. By the way you were right when you told Mr Croudace that it might be risky to attempt to gain access to my laboratory; the result would be catastrophic; it would be like Chernobyl revisited. One final thing, if you tell Mr Croudace, or anyone else of our partnership, my offer will be withdrawn; for now, he must not learn that I still exist'.

Before Somerton could respond, Jupiter disappeared from the screen. He sat deep in thought for nearly an hour then reached into a desk drawer for a bottle of St Magdalen. It's time for a sip of your favourite malt Jack, you're going to be famous.

Jupiter's laboratory.

Jupiter entered a little used priority code into his secure communication system; it brought an immediate response. The figure on the screen wore a military uniform. 'Go ahead.'

'I have spoken to Somerton and await his decision. I'm almost certain he will be prepared to enter into a partnership. When he does, I'll encourage him to convince Croudace that Jupiter is no more and I'll urge an early launch of TS2. He appreciates that the UK needs the telecommunications capacity it provides, and his military background virtually guarantees that he will place great value on the deterrent facilities TS2 provides.

'I intend to contact him again in 48 hours and will report to you as soon as he informs me of his decision. He'll accept our offer, I'm sure of it.'

'Give him 24 hours and make sure he says yes.'

CHAPTER 1

National Research and Security Centre.
The UK's National Security Advisor, Jack Somerton, close friend and confidant of Alan Croudace, the Prime Minister, slumped back in his office chair, his thoughts in a turmoil. The decision he had to make, and make quickly, would determine his future, that of his country, and perhaps the world, for decades to come. In the aftermath of Colin's Mackinnon's assassination, only a few days before, Croudace had been chosen as his Party's leader, and accordingly the UK's Prime Minister. Somerton shuddered as he thought of the events flooded his mind; he could picture himself, eye to a telescopic rifle sight, pulling the trigger, a lifeless Mackinnon falling to the ground. The images would haunt him for the rest of his life, Colin Mackinnon, his friend, his comrade in arms, the UK's Prime Minister, dead, murdered, and his finger had pulled the trigger----the ultimate act of treachery.

And here he was again, contemplating a decision that would involve betraying his closest friend and political master, Alan Croudace, Prime Minister of the United Kingdom. *What kind of a friend are you, Jack?* In a nutshell it was a simple choice of what came first, friendship or country; for Jack there could only be one answer. In his heart he knew the answer to his own question, he just didn't want to answer it, at least not yet.

His deliberations were interrupted by a knock on his office door; currently he didn't have a PA to welcome or deflect visitors, maybe that would have to change.

'Come in.'

The door swung open immediately, and Eric Barker, one of his security supervisors, made his way in, his expression serious, his hands cradling a bundle of files.

Somerton's heart sank a little further. He really didn't want any distractions, but security was his responsibility, and he had to deal with whatever came along. Forcing a smile, he pointed at a nearby chair. 'Grab a seat Eric and tell me what gives.'

Barker, a no-frills Mancunian, shook his head. 'To be honest I don't know for certain Jack; I'd welcome your advice. We've been tracking suspect on-line terrorist activity of this lot for the last few days, and I've put them on Red Alert, but I just can't decide on whether they present genuine threats or are fakes planted to keep us busy. Our intelligence guys and our police are already overloaded, and I don't want to create another fruitless operation if I can avoid it.'

Somerton nodded, a sigh escaping his lips. It was a problem faced by security personnel since time immemorial. 'You've taken the right approach; I'll take a look. I presume it's those ISIS bastards; they're as clever with technology and deception as we in the West are nowadays. Somerton slammed the desk with the palm of his hand. 'Damn it, it's all so fucking time consuming.'

Barker gave him a wary look, 'It's our job, Jack, and it's a rewarding job; we've saved hundreds, maybe thousands, of lives over the years.'

Somerton felt chastened, Barker was right, 'I'm sorry, it's one of those days, ignore me. Put the files down, I'll go through them and get back to you. In the meantime, I have a job for you; I want you to carry out a detailed check on an individual called Joseph Svetinsky.' Somerton spelled out the name. 'He's a Russian scientist from some years back; I want to know his background and where he ended up. And Eric, do it discreetly please, meaning don't involve anyone else.'

Barker looked at Somerton quizzingly, inviting explanation, 'A defector, Jack?'

'A need-to-know basis Eric, even I'm not party to all the facts.'

'Understood Jack, I'll get right on it.'

After Barker had gone, Somerton made a start on the security files, Red Alerts had to be given priority, time consuming though they were. He used his top-level security clearance to access US, NATO and Interpol files, checking and re-checking every conceivable intelligence avenue open to him. In the end he concluded that two were definite fakes, the other doubtful but possible. He buzzed through to Barker and invited him to join him.

Somerton waited for Barker to settle then invited him to give his take on the three suspects.

'Testing me, Jack?'

Somerton grinned, 'Got me in one Eric, so let me have your views on each suspect.'

Barker lifted a file, glanced at the title then locked eyes with his boss. 'I reckon this one is a fake al-Queda effort.' He reached over and picked up another file, 'Same verdict this one, a good fake but a fake nevertheless.'

'Two out of two, Eric. A good start, anything you want to add?'

Barker pursed his lips, 'As I said, they are good efforts, it took a lot of time and effort checking them out but I'm pretty sure they're not the real deal.'

'And then you thought you would pass them across my desk and check out my judgement?' Somerton raised an eyebrow.

Barker grimaced, 'Not really test you Jack, we know how good you are, know the contacts you've got; I just wanted to be absolutely certain we'd got it right and not start off by pointing you in any particular direction. I was checking out our judgement not yours.'

Somerton nodded. 'Hmm, I can see that I'll have to keep on my toes with you lot. So, what now?'

'Despite our conclusions regards the fakes we remain on full alert; the two principals involved are known to us; the Egyptian could well be planning a terrorist attack, and these are pure window dressing to put demand on our resources.' Barker was referring to al-Queda's leader Ayman Al-Zawahiri.

'Spot on Eric, put a tag on these guys but I see no need to alert our intelligence colleagues. And on to the third file, your thoughts please.'

'I'm not really sure Jack, we haven't been able to find a link to any known terrorist group, but the suspect converted to Islam a few years back and regularly attacks the West in his utterances. There's been a change of focus in recent weeks, more talk of the need to take action to further the Islamic cause and citing the advances being made in Afghanistan under Taliban rule. There haven't been any untoward purchases that we've been able to track down, nor any records of firearm ownership. But worryingly he has accessed bomb-making websites recently. Now, that could be curiosity, but it could be intent.'

'And your recommendation Eric, given how hard pressed our intelligence services and police forces are?'

Barker nodded, 'I take the point you're making Jack but, hard pressed or not, we need to keep an active watch on this individual. We should notify the intelligence guys and get the local police force to discreetly check him out. I'm pleased to say that, as it happens, the local Imam is not an extremist.'

'That's the right answer Eric, do exactly as you suggest and keep me advised of any developments. Anything else you want to raise? If not, that's all for now, keep up the good work. I'll be heading off shortly, it's been a long 24 hours one way and another.'

Barker nodded and waved a goodbye as he headed back to his workstation.

Somerton's thoughts returned to his conversation with Jupiter, now Joseph Svetinsky, voicing a question to himself. *There's a thought, how should I address you now that Jupiter has ostensibly flown the nest? Maybe I'll opt for Joe in remembrance to your long time ago dictator Joseph Stalin. No, keep it simple Jack, Jupiter he is, Jupiter he'll stay.*

Somerton spent the next hour mulling over a range of scenarios, reaching few conclusions, though one did keep cropping up. If he wanted to be a major player, or any kind of player for that matter, in the world of politics he had to get elected to Parliament and only one person could help him achieve that goal, Alan Croudace. He had already mentioned the prospect to Alan, but it was time to follow up that conversation and show his friend that he really was serious about becoming an MP.

Croudace's private mobile rang out for several minutes and Somerton was about to ring off when the line opened.

'Hello Alan, how goes the day?'

'Busy Jack, very busy. In fact, I was about to head off to a meeting for which I'm already late. What can I do for you?' He glanced at his watch, 5.15. 'I'll have to keep this short, Jack, I really am pressed for time.'

'Sounds like I've called at the wrong time. I can try again later, it's a personal matter.'

'Out with it, Jack and I'll help if I can.'

'Have you managed to do anything about my candidature for Colin's constituency?'

'I've never quite come to terms with the thought of you being an MP, Jack, but I have put your name forward. That's all I can do, thereafter it's the constituency party that decides who it wants to represent it, so no guarantees. You're up against stiff competition in Reggie Marsh.'

'Never heard of him, what makes him so formidable?'

Croudace sighed, 'I don't want to sound a note of pessimism Jack, but he has three advantages; first off, he lives in the constituency, second, he was Colin's local representative and advisor, and thirdly, if the foregoing isn't enough, he's the local party chairman's prospective son-in-law. Reggie got engaged recently to Sir Isaac Meyer's daughter Debbie; they get married next year.'

Somerton let out a whistle, 'Fuck it, he is going to be hard to beat.'

'As it happens, I'm attending the constituency meeting tonight and I will strongly endorse your candidacy. I'm hopeful I can get your name on the voting paper, but that's about all I can promise.'

Somerton felt downhearted but didn't let it sound in his voice, 'It's the best you can do Alan and I appreciate it.'

'Look Jack, I really must go, but on a completely different note, I'm finalising Colin's funeral service arrangements with Chloe and Her Majesty tomorrow. I take it you still want to say a few words?'

'Of course, just a few, heartfelt and meaningful.'

'I was sure you would. One last thing before I hang up, have you heard anything from Jupiter?'

'Not a dickie bird, he's gone I reckon, though I can't be sure. I'd like some further discussion about Colin's funeral arrangements, tomorrow if you can fit me in.'

'Talk to Jess about a time slot, she'll fit you in, I'm sure. That's it, I'm off.'

Before Somerton could respond the call was terminated. He wasn't looking forward to the funeral and it was now less than two weeks ahead; it would be a day he'd remember for the rest of his life. A State Funeral, gun carriage, Westminster Abbey, Her Majesty, hordes of dignitaries, and of course Joe Public lining the route. His friend's last outing, Colin Mackinnon's last port of call.

The handset barely replaced, his mind flooded again with thoughts, ideas, plans, sketchy options, all half-baked, all swimming in and out of his thoughts relentlessly. *Fuck it Jack, get a grip, get your fucking act together.*

He clasped his hands and leaned back in his chair, nodding to his own thoughts; time was running out; he had to formulate a way forward and he would do his best thinking away from the work environment, at home in the company of a bottle of malt whisky.

CHAPTER 2

Somerton's Apartment
It was just after 6pm when Somerton parked his car in the underground car park serving his apartment block; pangs of hunger manifested themselves and he realised he hadn't eaten since breakfast. *Damn.* He wasn't in the mood for cooking and in any case the fridge was nigh on empty; a takeaway from the local Indian didn't appeal either but a smile took over his grumpy countenance when the solution hit him - *treat yourself Jack, pay a visit to Firenza.* Firenza was a family run Italian, less than ten minutes' walk away.

Arriving at the restaurant he made his way in through the dark green heavy door, looking round for a table as he entered; there was plenty of choice, at this early hour he was the sole diner. The manager, Toni Fusco, caught sight of him immediately and welcomed him with a beaming smile, reaching his hand forward, shaking Somerton's with genuine warmth. 'Signor Somerton, how nice to see you, it's been a while since you honoured us with your presence.' Ten years in England had done little to lessen his southern Italian accent.

'Sorry about that Toni, call of duty, too many long days at the office; we've had to step up our security surveillance of late. Sadly, takeaways and home deliveries have prevailed for most of the last month. I have missed visiting Firenza I can assure you.'

Fusco smiled sympathetically, 'I understand. Follow me, your favourite table awaits you.' He led the way over to a quiet corner with low level lighting and bade Somerton to make himself comfortable before clearing away one of the two place settings.

'Now what can I get you Mr Somerton, the menu, a bottle? Your wish is my command.' Fusco bowed with a flourish.

Somerton smiled, 'You can begin by dropping that Mr Somerton stuff and call me Jack for a start. I know exactly what I want, my mouth is watering at the thought. So, I'll skip the menu and the wine list and settle for a large glass of your best dry white and an old favourite of mine, your seafood risotto with lobster if I remember rightly.'

'Of course, Mr Somerton, sorry, Jack, and I'll bring you a bowl of olives in the meantime.'

Within seconds it seemed, Fusco returned with the olives and some bread sticks.

'Grazie Toni.' Somerton's attempted Italian accent fell well short of authentic, but Fusco smiled politely. 'Oh Toni, whilst I remember; you don't have any problems these days, I hope? The sort of thing I can help you with?' A year or so back Toni had been threatened by a local hoodlum looking for protection money and it had come out in conversation with Somerton, who had duly phoned a friend, who had in turn phoned a friend, and the problem had gone away.

An anxious look momentarily crossed Fusco's face but was quickly replaced by a smile. 'No problem, Jack, everything's good since your intervention. I see the thug from time to time; he crosses the road when he sees me coming. He limps very badly now, almost drags his right leg along.'

It was Somerton's turn to smile, 'Oh dear, let's hope he limps for the rest of his life, sounds like he's got problems with his knee. Maybe that will keep him out of mischief.'

Fusco shrugged, 'I hope so. I'll go and hurry your meal along.'

'Thanks Toni, I won't linger over my meal, got some work to do; I want to get home early.'

Somerton's apartment, two hours later.

A showered and refreshed Jack Somerton settled down in his favourite chair clad in a comfortable full-length turquoise velvet dressing gown, ready for bed, just as soon as he unscrambled his thoughts and sorted out a semblance of an action plan. He poured himself a large Speyside malt, Glen Moray on this occasion, took a sip and reached for his notebook and pen. He liked lists, liked to see where he was headed in black and white. *So, what's first up, Jack? Jupiter, Joseph Svetinsky, who are you....do I believe you or not? Are you genuinely altruistic and only interested in a better world for the benefit of mankind? Surely you want some*

*sort of reward, some sort of recognition, some personal benefit;
I can't believe you don't.*

Somerton paused his ponderings and took another sip of the
malt. *How much leeway do I give you.? How can I even go into
partnership with someone I don't really know and can't trust?
There has to be a partnership, Jack. Without one, TS2 and the
power it could bring to the UK won't happen. Conclusion; go
along with Jupiter for now, build trust, but find a way of getting
the upper hand, a credible sanction. The trouble is Jack, at this
moment in time, you don't have a credible sanction.*

*Next question; can UKTS2 deliver, live up to its design
capabilities? Conclusion; there has to be an early test, a tough
one, maybe more than one. Hold on Jack you're getting ahead of
yourself, UKTS2 is still on the ground. Come what may, you must
persuade Alan to launch; that has to be your number one
objective when you meet up with him tomorrow.*

Somerton returned to his malt and savoured the amber liquid
as it flowed over his tongue. *'And power Jack, power. You need
to take a step up the ladder. As Head of National Security, you
have some influence, but the real power brokers sit in the House
of Commons, or better still, around the table in the Cabinet
Office. You have to get yourself elected. And to do that you have
to get yourself selected as a Conservative Party candidate,
ideally for Colin's old constituency.*

Somerton knew that whoever stood would get elected; it was
a Conservative stronghold. In a general election, Jupiter had
shown he could tamper with the on-line vote but selecting a
constituency candidate involved old style pen and paper. *You
need to tip the odds in your favour Jack, but how? Right at that
moment he didn't know, but a way had to be found.*

He took another sip of whisky and reached for his burner
phone.

'Hello Mike, how goes the day?'

'It's gone well up to now, Jack, but you don't often phone at
this time of night, so is my peace about to unravel? My guess is
you want something done and done quickly?'

'Not much gets past you Mike. I want you and Eddie to carry
out some research for me, discreetly and quickly.'

'Nothing new there, Jack, so who is the target.'

'Targets plural Mike. Find out all you can about Sir Isaac Meyer, chairman of Colin's old constituency committee; ditto his daughter Debbie and her fiancé, Eddie Marsh. It's really urgent.'

'Noted. I take it you don't want me to find out if they are all churchgoers and do good deeds?'

'I'm interested in everything you can find out, but anything than can inflict damage would further my cause.'

'I'll get onto it tomorrow. Anything else?'

'I think that's enough to be going on with Mike, sleep well.'

'You too Jack.'

Somerton drained the last of the malt and stood ready to retire to bed when he recalled what Alan had said about having a residence in the constituency. *Another item for your list Jack.*

He made a note to contact a couple of estate agents first thing in the morning and jotted down his requirements. Two ensuite bedrooms, kitchen, dining room, lounge, office space, furnished or unfurnished. Preferably a flat on the top floor of a smallish tower block served by two lifts with allocated parking for two cars.

He took a couple of steps towards his bedroom when his inner voice spoke to him. *And what about the risks Jack, or is it all blue sky where you're headed? And who are the risks? Friend and foe alike?*

Somerton sighed and sat back down. There were lots of minor risks that just had to be dealt with as and when they arose. His mind was buzzing again, he needed to clear them away or he wouldn't sleep. *So, who presents a risk Jack, put a name to them? First up has to be Jupiter, the genesis of this whole situation but also the lynchpin of success. And there was Vladic, currently in gaol, the poor sod scapegoated for killing Colin. A small risk, but a risk nevertheless. And finally, his close friend and ex SAS colleague, Alan Croudace.*

Somerton shuddered at the thought of Alan being filed in the risk category, and a serious one at that. As Prime Minister, only he had the authority to authorise the launch of TS2, and currently he was opposed. Even when he left office, he could go public about its capabilities if he chose to. *Alan, Alan, why do you have to be so fucking difficult?*

CHAPTER 3

Next day, Somerton's apartment

Somerton rose at his usual time, 6.30am, went through his usual exercise regime, showered, dressed then sat at his kitchen bar to enjoy a simple breakfast of cereal and a slice of toast, bolstered by a large mug of strong black coffee. Not that he needed support for an adrenaline rush, his thoughts were already on fire.

Easy things first Jack; estate agents the first port of call. A quick internet search gave him the names of two companies operating in Colin's old constituency. Fletchers of Harrow, and Mason, Sheldrake & Co. Somerton gave both a description of what he was looking for, furnished or unfurnished and stressed the urgency, offering to meet, preferably that afternoon or tomorrow morning at the latest. Both companies promised to email him details of several properties immediately and confirmed that they could arrange early viewings.

Now, do I phone you Alan to enquire as to how last night's constituency meeting worked out, or do I wait for you to phone me? Somerton ruminated for a few seconds then opted to wait for Croudace's call. *I want you relaxed and amenable Alan, and with time for the vital, potentially contentious discussion he knew would ensue.* The decision was barely made when he changed his mind. *On second thoughts best if I phone Jess and book a face to face.*

'Jessica Tate speaking, who's calling please?'

'I'll give you one guess Jess, and I'll be heartbroken if you don't get it right.'

'Hmm, well now, sounds a little like Paddington Bear. How can I help you Mr Somerton?'

'I know he's up to his neck, but could you squeeze me in for a face to face with Alan, it's urgent, today please if possible?'

'He's asked me to avoid setting up any meetings this week and I'm afraid I can't put you through, he has a couple of Middle East dignitaries with him. Can I tell him you phoned and, in the meantime, seeing as it's you, book you in for 3pm? You will have to get your business done quickly; he has another meeting lined up for 3.30.'

'Jess you're a treasure, let's go for that, see you at 3pm sharp.'

'Look forward to seeing you Jack, is there anything I should prewarn him about?'

'I suspect he'll guess; last night's constituency meeting and Colin's funeral are on my agenda plus a brief mention of security matters. If anything crops up in the meantime and we can't meet, text me, I'll be out and about.'

'Will do, bye for now.'

Somerton checked his emails, pleased when he found that the estate agents had forwarded the rental details he'd requested. There were ten in all, six from Fletcher of Harrow and four from Mason, Sheldrake & Co. He immediately rejected seven, all detached houses despite having specifically asked for an apartment in a small tower block. Houses were a no-no for him; he didn't want a garden to look after and didn't want people gaping through his windows. That left three that met his requirements, all fully furnished.

He was about to examine them in detail when his mobile buzzed, a text from Jess confirming his meeting with Alan. He replied with a simple, thumbs up emoji.

Two of the flats were outstanding, both exquisitely furnished, both coincidently from Fletcher of Harrow. *Brilliant, that simplifies the viewing arrangements.* He phoned the Agent, introduced himself and requested viewings of two properties one in Gibraltar Heights, the other in Harrow View. There was only a short walk between them which made it easy. *Your lucky day Jack.*

A meeting with Guy Fletcher, presumably the owner or his son, was arranged for 1pm at Gibraltar Heights; no directions were required.

Don't forget the day job, Jack. Somerton opened up his laptop and accessed the NRSC website to check his emails; quickly scrolled through around thirty, pleased when he found nothing of immediate concern. That done he typed in his security code and perused the current alerts, relieved to see there were no new red flag incidents. One item was of interest though, a request from Eric Barker to meet up. Somerton smiled, *let's hope you have some info for me about Joseph Svetinsky.* He glanced at his watch as he logged out. 12.15, time to be making a move; he was cutting it fine if he wanted to get to Gibraltar Heights on time.

Gibraltar Heights

A smartly dressed young man strode forward, hand outstretched, as Somerton got out of his car.

'Guy Fletcher, pleased to meet you Mr Somerton.'

Somerton nodded and took the offered hand, 'Fletcher? Do you own the business?'

A shake of the head. 'Maybe in due course; my father set up the agency nearly fifty years ago, he's still involved but a light touch nowadays. Shall we head for the penthouse? It's gorgeous, I'm sure you'll like it.'

'Who owns it?'

Fletcher shook his head, 'I've honestly got no idea; we administer the apartment on behalf of an overseas investment company based in the Bahamas; Chinese, I believe.'

Somerton's heart sank a fraction. *Chinese, they usually have plenty of loot. They won't be happy bunnies if I try to negotiate a reduced rent, but I'll try.*

Fletcher strode forward to the semi-circular three-step entrance where he tapped in the access code, then pushed open the glazed panelled door, motioning Somerton to make his way in. The entrance hall was large, well decorated and adorned with modern art paintings; a stairway and lift well were situated to the left and a corridor ran straight ahead to the ground floor apartments. Somerton took in the scene appreciatively. 'That's a bonus.'

Fletcher raised an eyebrow. 'A bonus, what exactly?'

Somerton smiled, 'Two lifts, I like exercise when I feel like it, but don't enjoy climbing twelve floors at the end of a hard day when I find the single lift that serves the building has broken down.'

Fletched nodded, 'I can empathise with that situation, I've experienced it a time or two and in buildings much taller than this. If you decide to take the apartment, you'll be given a code to enter that allows direct lift access to the penthouse floor.

Similarly, there's a transmitter that will summon the first available lift and give you priority going down.'

Somerton smiled, 'I like the sound of having priority, and security looks good at first sight; I like the CCTV cameras inside and out, and the door intruder alarm. The building seems to be fairly secure?' He looked closely at Fletcher, raising an eyebrow, looking for reaction and a response

Fletcher nodded. 'The security installed is first class. Sounds like you are well versed in security?'

Somerton grinned, 'Just a bit.'

'Do you mind if I ask who you work for.'

'Not at all, I work for Jack Somerton.'

Fletcher took the hint, didn't press further and made his way over to the lift; he knew he would get the answer to his question if Somerton chose to rent. Arriving on the top floor, the two men got out and strolled down a short, covered external passage to the solid oak door to the penthouse.

Fletcher produced a key, 'The door is secured by a top grade, Chubb locking system operated by key or door pad or both together if you want.'

A comprehensive guided tour followed with Fletcher pointing out all the features; the whole apartment lived up to the descriptions in the brochure. The rooms were spacious, the kitchen, laundry and ensuite facilities were all at the luxury end of the spectrum. The furnishings and curtains were tasteful and immaculate. The views were far reaching and the centre of London was less than 15miles away. Looking round Somerton could see the M1 to the North, the M4 to the South, the M25 and Grand Union Canal to the West as were the various rail networks. But despite all the traffic activity not a whisper penetrated the triple glazed windows.

Fletcher followed Somerton's gaze and remarked, 'Quiet, isn't it? The windows are triple glazed to the highest standard, no heat loss, no heat gain. You have solar and gas heating, air conditioning if you require it. The rent includes all maintenance and energy charges, but the tenant arranges their own domestic services.'

Somerton nodded, 'It's impressive but it's expensive at £8,000 a month.'

Fletcher nodded, 'Good things usually are Mr Somerton, and of course **you** asked for a viewing.'

Somerton was prepared for the response. 'I did indeed, but I've also ascertained that it's currently unoccupied and has been since you first advertised it three months ago with immediate occupancy; that's a loss of £24,000. I won't deny that I like the apartment, but my best offer is £6000 a month starting from the earliest date you can produce the contract. I'll pay the rent six months in advance.'

Fletcher shook his head, 'I couldn't accept an offer as low as that, I'll have to phone my client.'

'Go ahead, I'll wait in the kitchen. Join me when you have an answer.'

Five minutes had passed when Fletcher returned. 'Good news, my client will accept £7,000 a month, a substantial discount.'

Somerton shook his head, 'Sorry, you'll have to do better than that. Tell you what, I'll split the difference. £6,500, with twelve months rent in advance, take it or leave it, my final offer.'

Fletcher nodded, 'You drive a hard bargain Mr Somerton, I'll have to consult my client again.'

Somerton shrugged, 'You know where I'll be.'

Ten minutes later fletcher returned to the kitchen. 'We have a deal, Mr Somerton; £6500 per calendar month, twelve months in advance, with occupancy as soon as the paperwork is signed. And, of course, subject to satisfactory references. My client took a lot of persuading, you've got yourself a bargain'

Somerton nodded. *Only assuming I get on the ballot paper for this constituency otherwise it's money down the proverbial drain.* 'No problem, my bankers are Coutts in The Strand and my referee is Alan Croudace.'

Fletcher smiled, 'The same name as the Prime Minister, you are joking?'

Somerton stared icily, 'His address is 10 Downing Street. By the way, I run the UK's National Security Service. Now I must go, I have a meeting with Alan at 3pm.'

The two men travelled down in the lift in silence, one wondering if it was all a hoax, the other thinking about getting Croudace to agree to launch the satellite system.

CHAPTER 4

Prime Minister's Office, Downing Street

Jess Tate glanced up from her screen as Somerton strolled into her office, 2.58pm. 'Spot on time as always Jack, and how are we today?'

'I'm good thanks Jess, and yourself?'

'Fine, I guess. Just managing to keep my head above water. It's been hectic of late, what with Colin's funeral arrangements and Alan's imminent departure.' She sighed. 'Added to that is the search for our next PM. Everybody seems to want to talk to Alan nowadays, and there's all the usual parliamentary business going on in the background. Between you and I, and I do mean you and I, I'm thinking of getting out when Alan makes his exit, a few years earlier than I planned.'

Somerton's face showed his genuine concern. 'I hope not Jess, you're one of the few people I trust to get things done in this building, and you know the top-level political scene like no other. If I get elected, and you want a change of scenery, please come and work for me, I'll match your present salary.'

Jess Tate smiled, taken completely by surprise with Somerton's offer. 'Do you really mean that Jack? I might just be interested.' She looked at him wistfully, 'In fact if I do decide to stay on, I'll be happy to take up your offer.'

Somerton smiled broadly. 'Damn right I do, I'll come and ask you on bended knee, I promise.'

She gave him a knowing look. 'You're stretching credibility to breaking point Jack, but I'm flattered, I hope you mean it.' She paused, a thoughtful look on her face, 'I think I'd enjoy working for you and, of course, whoever replaces Alan, could well bring their present PA with them. Can I take a rain check on your offer? See how I feel nearer the time? Now to business, you're not here to chat to me.' She buzzed through to Croudace, 'Jack's here Alan.'

'I'm ready for him, only urgent calls to be put through.'

'He's free Jack, go straight in.'

'I meant what I said Jess, truly.'

Their conversation ended when the door to the PM's office opened and a serious Croudace beckoned Somerton enter. 'Grab a pew Jack, let's get down to what brings you here.'

Somerton sat down, ramrod straight, eyes fixed on his friend. 'Personal matters first, as you might guess. What happened at the constituency meeting last night?'

Croudace shook his head, a touch of impatience showing. 'I would have phoned you Jack, there was no need to set up a meeting. I…'

Somerton bristled and interrupted. 'That's just one item, Alan, and you haven't phoned; there's also Colin's funeral in case you've forgotten plus an update on Jupiter. There's the outstanding UKTS2 issue. And what you pay me for, the lowdown the latest terrorist threat situation and, who knows, you might just have a security issue you want to raise with me.'

Croudace bit his lip and nodded his head apologetically. 'Sorry Jack, I'm a bit on edge. I still haven't come to term with losing Colin, I feel strangely guilty about helping to choose his successor.'

'Forget it Alan, we're both uptight, I understand. In any case you're his successor, even if only temporarily, and he'd have wanted you to be. Just tell yourself that someone has to replace Colin and you're acting on his behalf to choose one. It's a bad time for both of us but the old saying holds true, 'The king is dead, long reign the king. And I'm not without guilt as National Security Advisor.' He was offering his friend comfort, but he felt his stomach knot as his thoughts imaged his eye to the gunsight yet again.

'I guess you're right but that's not how it feels. The constituency party meeting went much as I expected; the chairman wanted to shoe-horn in his prospective son-in-law, and still does, but I persuaded the committee that Joe Public and the media would see it as blatant favouritism and it would be better to have at least two names on the ballot sheet. There was quite a debate, but I managed to persuade them to put your name down, though the chairman pointed out that I was the one showing favouritism to an old army buddy, one who had no connection to the constituency. However, I won the day and you're in the mix along with Reggie Marsh who, as I told you, is Sir Isaac's future son-in-law. He'll be lobbying furiously for Marsh and to be brutally frank, I don't think you stand much of a chance.'

'Who dares wins, Alan, I've faced tougher odds.'

Croudace pursed his lips and looked thoughtful. 'Hmm, no funny business Jack.'

'As if Alan! I promise you it will be a fair fight and all by the Marquis of Queensbury rules. I'm sure the media will have young Reggie in their sights though. The Press will turn his life inside out looking for something untoward. And I wouldn't be as keen on being an MP if you weren't standing down leaving me without the ear of the nation's leader. I don't suppose you've had second thoughts?'

'No way, not a chance. I confirmed my resignation at last night's 1922 Committee; and I've informed my own constituency chairman, there's no turning back now.'

Somerton shook his head, genuinely sad at the prospect. 'A big loss for parliament and the nation. Might I ask who is likely to succeed you?'

'It's not in the public domain yet Jack. Ken Ogilvie has thrown his hat in and has a lot of support, but my money is on a dark horse, Laura Taylor our Home Secretary. In fact, I'll be supporting Laura; it's time we had another woman at the helm; she has a lot of experience and determination. She knows what she wants and goes all out to get it, reminds me of Mrs Thatcher.'

Somerton shrugged. 'Don't really have an opinion, she's always come across as genuine and hard-working; the public like her and that's important. Ken's sound but lacks a bit of imagination and always seems to resist innovation. In fact, he gives the impression of being absolutely risk averse; a safe pair of accounting hands sums him up.'

Croudace nodded. 'I won't dissent from that analysis but sometimes a safe pair of hands is what the nation needs. Anyway, we'll see what the first ballot brings and with a few days to go there's the possibility of other nominations. So, what are you going to say at Colin's funeral?

Somerton's face clouded. From some guilt-ridden recess of his subconscious, the distorted words of a hymn formed in his thoughts. *Praise him, praise him, kill him, kill him*, 'You'll have to wait and see, but it will be what you would expect, praise for a much-loved colleague.'

Croudace nodded. 'I won't press you. Now have you got anything for me from our friend Jupiter?'

'Not a word from him, nothing at all; I'm pretty sure he's gone. I've tried speaking out loud to him in the office, we know he listened in on our conversations. I've tried online via a link Colin gave me when we were discussing UKTS2 but not a dickie bird.'

Croudace stiffened. 'You have a direct link to Jupiter, how come? I was never offered one.'

Somerton shrugged. 'Colin let me have one so I could check out some TS2 technical details. Incidentally, when I last went in, it brought up an alert showing 'connection not available'. *Lies, lies and more lies, Jack.* In effect the link doesn't work now, so it really does look like Jupiter has shut it down or it's lapsed in his absence. He's flown the nest if you ask me.'

Croudace pursed his lips, 'I reached the same conclusion initially, but it occurred to me that the NRSC is equipped with CCTV inside and outside the building and along the perimeter fence. That being the case, surely your guys would have picked him up if he left his laboratory?'

Somerton smiled, he had anticipated this scenario and had his reply ready. 'That's the same path my thoughts took Alan, but then I thought, with his expertise, it would be child's play for Jupiter to temporarily neutralise the security systems and leave us none the wiser. He was aware of your reservations about his integrity and, sadly, I reckon he decided to search out a partner elsewhere. A big, big loss, his scientific capabilities were a great asset to the UK. Thankfully though, our researchers are the best on the planet, and we don't really need Jupiter now.' Somerton smiled inwardly. *Hope you're listening Jupiter.* 'I will maintain a 24/7 watch Alan, but I think it's safe to assume that he's gone.'

'Fair enough, Jack; but inform me immediately if you hear from him. And that applies whether I'm still in this chair or not.'

'Of course, you'll remain my closest friend whether you're PM or not. Which leads nicely into the situation regarding TS2; I think it's time we launched. If it hangs around much longer, more and more questions will surface as to why not, and accusations made of money being wasted; it'll be seen as a white elephant, and that won't do the Party image any good.'

Croudace grimaced, 'I know. Ken Ogilvie has been muttering about a return on investment recently, but you know my concerns, Jack. In the wrong hands the system could be lethal.'

Somerton shrugged. 'Our views don't quite align in this instance Alan but let's look at the facts. He held up a finger. 'One, Jupiter is out of the picture. Two, very important, our existing telecoms system is on its last legs, and this just isn't affecting the national telephone system, it's impacting on national security capability, and broadband speeds in every aspect of government, public and business life. I'm absolutely convinced we should launch, preferably on the day Colin is laid to rest; it would be a magnificent tribute to our late colleague. And why not name the system in his memory? Constellation Mackinnon would be a worthy epitaph and legacy to a great man.'

Croudace hesitated, anxiety showing in his eyes, 'What if Jupiter is still around? What if he could still control the system from wherever he is?'

'You can't worry about him forever Alan; look at it this way. If he has set up elsewhere, he could build another system. And having worked with the UK, the so-called nice guys, and got nowhere, he might decide to set up with a country with a more tarnished reputation. Or maybe one who might be less squeamish about taking over the world, like our friends in the Far East or conceivably maybe even just across the pond.'

'All valid points Jack, but the risk remains a real one.'

'Forget it's global control capability, we need the telecoms. Tell me, are you prepared to ask Parliament to spend cash on a new system and accept the delayed benefits? Or are you going to walk away and leave the problem for your successor to solve? Can I suggest a compromise? You authorise a launch of half the satellites with the remainder to be launched following a review?'

Croudace sighed. 'You make a strong case Jack; OK, you've convinced me. I'll give the go-ahead to launch, with the first to coincide with Colin's funeral. I like the sound of a review; let's say six months hence. And I'll take up your suggestion about calling it Constellation Mackinnon'.

Somerton grinned broadly; he had won the argument. 'By which time you'll be sitting with your feet up at the fire or busy writing your memoirs. And you'll have left the problem in abeyance for your successor to deal with.'

'You're beginning to sound like a politician Jack; truly, I'm not passing the buck. As I see it, I'm safeguarding our nation in an uncertain situation.' He gave a wry smile, 'Although that said, I won't hesitate to bask in the praise that follows the launch and the benefits that flow from it. Just remember, my successor won't know about Jupiter, or the risks associated with the system unless you reveal the truth. Now I must call an end to this meeting unless you have security issues you want to raise?'

'Just one needs a mention, Alan.' Somerton briefed Croudace on the most recent terrorist threat, explaining that it remained under surveillance.

'Keep a close watch on it Jack, I don't want to make my exit against the backdrop of a terrorist attack.'

Somerton smirked. 'Tell you what, Alan, I'll play politics and build it up so you can claim to have foiled a major terrorist threat! I'll go now and leave you in peace.' Business completed, Somerton made his way out, not realising he had a broad smile on his face until Jess Tate remarked, 'You look pleased with yourself Jack; a good meeting?'

'Mission accomplished, Jess, mission accomplished. Don't forget our earlier conversation about being my PA if I get elected.'

NRSC next day.
Eric Barker intercepted Somerton on the way into his office, waving a sheet of paper and winking by way of introduction. The two men sat down and Somerton waited expectantly for Barker to begin.

'I've done some research on the Svetinsky guy you expressed an interest in. You wanted it done on the quiet so I haven't put pen to paper.'

Somerton gave him the thumbs up. 'I'm all ears Eric, what have you come up with?'

Svetinsky was born in Moscow. His father was a minor Communist Party official and made a bit of a name for himself generating misinformation and propaganda for the Kremlin. Joseph went to Somonosov Moscow State University studying computer sciences, graduated, followed up with a Masters, and finally a Doctorate in neural sciences. He was well respected and was placed in the Russian Academy of Sciences. His work isn't well documented but he was well respected and undoubtedly destined for a stellar future. However somewhere along his career path he badly upset the hierarchy and he was transferred to the Siberian Research Institute of Geology, Geophysics and Mineral resources. There is no record of how he spent his time at the Institute other than a brief note in their records to the effect that he failed to turn up one day and disappeared altogether without trace.'

'Disappeared.' Somerton echoed. 'That sounds ominous.'

Barker nodded. 'It does, given that Siberia is often the final resting place for Russian dissidents. His father however continued to work in the Kremlin and retired after a successful career. There's nothing on record about his relationship with his son. I could dig further but sooner or later my interest in Svetinsky would be spotted and questions would follow. I don't think you would want that.'

Somerton shook his head. 'You can park it for now, Eric, you've answered all my questions. Thanks for your efforts. Is there anything else you want to run past me?'

Barker shook his head. 'Nothing new, Jack. I'll keep you posted if anything comes up requiring your attention.'

Somerton reflected on what he'd just heard. *Interesting, it all seems to fit with Jupiter's account. Let's talk to the man himself.*

Somerton switched on his desktop and, when the screen livened up, tapped into his Jupiter link.

Jupiter appeared almost immediately, 'Mr Somerton, at your service.'

Somerton's face held no expression. 'I'm sure you know why I'm getting in touch.'

'Do I indeed? How could I?'

'Don't play fucking games, Jupiter, let's at least try to be business-like. I'm sure you listened in on my conversation with Alan, so you know that TS2 is going to be launched and I want to discuss next steps.'

'My, my, we are touchy. Have it your way Jack. You did well to persuade your friend Croudace to launch, although with only half the satellites in place, its efficiency and capability is greatly reduced; at best it will be 30% effective. We need full capacity if we are to achieve our goals. You…'

Somerton cut in, echoing Jupiter's words. 'Our goals? Our goals? I wasn't aware **we** had any goals.'

Jupiter didn't back down. 'Let's not replay the words of your deceased colleague. We either work as partners on shared goals, or we go our separate ways here and now.'

Somerton held his ground. 'Don't threaten me. I'm fully aware you can fuck off any time you please or at least you think you can; just bear in mind I can put guards all round this place 24/7 and stop you going anywhere. If I so choose, I could encase you and your laboratory in an overcoat of ready mixed concrete. So, let's get it straight right from the start. I decide on the goals; you will have an input but that's all.'

'Have it your way Jack, just try using TS2 without me and see how far you get, a press of a button is all I need to turn TS2 into a heap of scrap metal.'

Somerton nodded, 'I'll concede that's a powerful card you hold, but I have one or two cards of my own, like maintaining a roof over your head, air, water and electricity. And, of course, kidnapping young women for your entertainment.'

The Russian nodded, 'All of that is of course true, but I can monitor scientific progress around the world, further the work of your researchers **and** maintain the UK's lead in the world. By the way, I'm happy to suspend my requirement for female company.'

It was Somerton's turn to make a concession. 'I value your input Jupiter, of course I do, but the goals have to be mine, I have to set the targets. I very much welcome your decision about the girls. What brought this on?'

'Consider this, Jack, you won't always be in a position to identify the targets, that's one aspect of TS2 which I alone can operate. Let's stop arm-wrestling Jack, we both hold trump cards. Put them together and we have a winning hand, pit them against each other and we'll both lose out. Together we can make the UK and the planet a better place for all. As to the girls, let's just say that I have other priorities; put further abductions on hold.'

Somerton nodded. 'I'm pleased about the girls, thank you for that. As to politics, I'll always have the final say. As for TS2, I'll be coming up with a test as soon as the satellite system is operational. Having said that, if you come up with a proposal before I do, let me know.'

Jupiter smiled. 'OK Jack, have the final word. In the meantime, I will keep you posted on any threats, or perhaps I should refer to them as potential targets?'

This time Somerton made no riposte and was on the point of concluding the meeting when the man on the screen continued.

'I assume that it is still your ambition to become an MP and that you will be hoping to be chosen as a candidate for Colin's old constituency?'

'You heard what I said to Alan, so you know my ambition. I have that matter in hand, thank you.' Somerton knew there was more to come and sought to avoid saying anything provocative.

'When it comes to the election vote, I can help as you know, but I can be of only limited assistance in your quest to be the chosen candidate. However, you might want to access the birth certificate for Charlie Wilson, a boy born 13th April 2019, you might find it interesting.'

'And who exactly is Charlie Wilson?'

'That's for you to find out Jack.'

Before Somerton could respond the screen went blank. 'Bollocks!'

CHAPTER 5

Somerton's Office, NRSC : Thursday 7am

Somerton fished out his current burner phone, he changed them weekly, and dialled Eddie Black, relieved when he answered after four rings.

'Hi Jack.'

'Hi Eddie, have you and Mike made any progress with checking out our friends in Harrow?'

'Fuck me Jack, it's been barely 24 hours since you set the wheels in motion. We're nowhere near completing our enquiries.'

'I realise that, but this really is urgent; I need to wrap this up quickly, pull out all the stops.'

'We're doing all we can, but these things take time, you know that. Give us another 12 hours and we should be in position to give you a full run down.'

Somerton sighed, 'Fair enough, meet me tonight at the Grey Goose with all you've got, let's say 7pm. I need a plan of action Eddie, there's no margin for delay on this one.'

'Understood Jack, but don't get your hopes up too high; nothing untoward has come our way so far.'

'Don't dampen my spirits, Eddie; do your best, bring me some good news tonight. Bye.'

Somerton stroked his chin and pondered his next move. *Now then Jack, let's find out what we can about young Charlie Wilson, find out why Jupiter thought he might be helpful. Thank God for the Web.*

Somerton brought up the Registry of Births, Marriages and Deaths; his top-level security clearance placed very few limits on what he could access. A few seconds later he was looking at the child's birth record.

Charlie Wilson, a boy, born 13th April 2018

Mother; Tricia Wilson, Research Assistant, 18 Winterbourne Road, Harrow

Father; Reginald George Marsh, Research Assistant, Address; Not Known

Well, well, well, naughty Reggie. Hmm, I wonder if your future bride knows about this little legacy? Thank you, Jupiter, this revelation could be very helpful, very helpful indeed.

Somerton turned his attention to HM Revenue and Customs website and looked up Tricia Wilson. Her first and only job since 2016 was as Research Assistant for Harrow Conservative Constituency Association. She was still in their employ and working from home, address 18 Winterbourne Road as per Birth Certificate. A search of the Association's website produced numerous press cuttings and photos for the years 2016 to 2018. One photo in particular, taken in 2017, caught his attention; it depicted Colin MacKinnon and his wife Chloe at a summer BBQ surrounded by the constituency team. They were flanked by a young man, presumably Reggie Marsh, and three young women, one in her thirties, two in their twenties. Somerton studied the two younger women. *I wonder which of you two is the lucky girl, or is it the unlucky girl? Sorry Eddie, I'm going to add to your workload again.*

'Eddie, it's me. Have you got pen and paper handy?'

'Fire away.'

'Tricia Wilson, 18 Winterbourne Road, Harrow. I want photos of her, preferably with her kid; bring them with you tonight.'

'Christ Jack, I can't promise that; we've got too much on, as you well know'.

'You'll just have to work a miracle; I need those photos. Bye'.

Eddie Black shook his fist and threw his mobile into an adjacent armchair. *Sometimes you're a real bastard Jack.*

Mike Davies glanced across. 'What's wrong with you Eddie?'

'Not a fucking thing, except Jack wants me to get photos of some bird in Harrow for our meeting tonight, as if we didn't have enough on. Break off what you're doing Mike and I'll carry on here. This is the target. Try and get a photo of her with her kid if you can. He passed over his note, it's a Harrow address.'

Davies shrugged, 'Will do, expect the unexpected is par for the course in our game.'

Winterbourne Road

Mike Davies parked his car more or less opposite No18 Winterbourne Road, an average sized, detached, brick-built house with a small front garden, neatly bordered by a low wooden picket fence. Just for effect, he pulled out a street map and made a show of studying it, all the while glancing over at the window for signs of movement. He took out his mobile and took a couple of pictures of the house making sure he had a clear line of vision should Tricia Wilson fortuitously open the front door.....no such luck. He fingered his lapel to make sure the lens badge connected to the mini camera in his pocket was securely in place.

Time to move Mike, you can't sit around here all day. He got out of the car and strode purposefully across to No18, made his way along the entrance path and pressed the front doorbell. He waited a minute or so before knocking loudly on the door and allowed a minute or so to pass before knocking again with the same result. *Damn, no-one home, I'll have to come back later.*

'Can I help you?'

He turned and found himself facing a young woman standing at the entrance to a property on the other side of the road. A young boy was tugging at her hand, trying to pull her back to whatever activity they were engaged in.

Davies smiled, 'I'm not sure. I've been asked to give this letter to the owner in person; it looks like an official document of some kind. Are you the owner of No 18?'

'I saw you through my neighbour's window and wondered why you were so interested in my place. I do own No18 am but I'm not expecting anything official. Do you mind if I take a look at the envelope?'

'Not at all'. Davies shrugged, 'Hold on, I'll bring it across, your young man looks determined not to let go of you. Might I ask your name?' He crossed the road operating his lapel camera a few times in the process.

'Tricia Wilson, and this little brute is my son Charlie.'

Bingo! Davies nodded, 'Oh, that's not the name I have but it's the right address, No18 Winterbourne Crescent.'

Tricia Wilson smiled and shook her head, 'Ah that explains it, this is Winterbourne Road, the Crescent's right at the end.' She pointed to her left. Charlie grabbed her hand and tugged furiously, 'Mummy, come on, we're waiting for you, let's get on with our game.' His little face looked at her pleadingly.

'Just coming darling, I'm giving this gentleman directions.'

Davies smiled broadly, 'Thank you Tricia, I'll get on my way. I'm so sorry to have disturbed you.' He dug in his pocket and held up a £2 coin. 'My apologies to you, young man; here's a little present for you.'

The child's eyes lit up, but he'd been told never to accept presents from strangers. He looked from the coin to his Mum, his question obvious but unspoken. 'Go ahead darling, it's OK.'

'Here you are Charlie.'

The child's face lit up as he took the coin and held it up for his Mum's approval, gaining a gold star when he uttered a well-mannered. 'Thank you, Mister.'

Inwardly Mike Davies was smiling broadly, he now had a photo of the child holding his Mum's hand. *Fingers crossed the camera's done its job and Jack will be a happy bunny.*

Later in the Grey Goose Pub

Somerton, Black and Davies, assembled in the back room of the Grey Goose at Jack's request. The landlord, the enigmatic Andy Swift, had just grunted when Jack had asked to have the room for an hour or so, promising to add a tenner to the bill.

'Now what do you want to drink?' Andy enquired. 'If you want anything to eat, I can heat up a pizza or two or three?'

Somerton nodded, 'Sounds good, three pints of best and three pizzas, any sort will do.'

The trio chatted until Swift returned with the beers and carried on with general rambling until the pizzas arrived ten minutes later. 'Anything else?'

'We're good thank you, Andy. Leave us for a bit, we don't want anyone joining us. One of us will come to the bar if we need anything.' Andy nodded, and asked no questions, he knew the score.

Davies grabbed a slice of the nearest pizza. 'I reckon we should scoff this lot before we get down to business, First, because I'm ravenous, second I don't want greasy fingerprints all over the photos or paperwork.'

Somerton smiled, 'Point taken Mike, let's get tucked in.'

Twenty minutes later the pizzas were gone and the glasses half empty.

'All done?' Somerton enquired, 'Had enough?'

Eddie Black spoke up, 'Well now that you mention it, a cuppa and a slice of cake would be nice.'

Somerton grinned, 'Absolutely, treat yourself on the way home. Now let's see what you've got for me, starting with Sir Isaac.'

Davies pulled some papers and a couple of photos out of a brown envelope. 'Took these photos yesterday; caught him out for a walk in the park with his dog.'

Somerton scanned them briefly. 'A distinguished looking gentleman I must say.'

Davies nodded. 'I've checked out his history and there isn't a single blot on his character that I can find. His parents were war time refugees, and he attends the local synagogue regular as clockwork. He has a track record of promoting good race relations over the years and does a lot of fundraising for the local hospice.'

Somerton nodded, 'Sounds like an all-round good guy. What about the daughter?'

Davies reached into another envelope and produced two photographs of a pretty, young woman; one of her in a smart, tailored, two-piece light blue suit, probably a wedding outfit. In the other she was dressed in tennis gear, racquet in hand. 'As far as I've been able to find out, sweet, kind, thoughtful and loyal are the descriptors that turn up most. Doesn't seem to have anyone serious in her life before Reggie Marsh.'

Somerton shrugged, 'So, she's a pretty girl, quite demure by modern standards and there's very little sign of make-up. Doesn't come over as a party girl.'

Davies nodded. 'That sums her up I reckon. And, last but not least, here are the photos you wanted of Tricia Wilson and her little lad.'

Somerton compared these with those he'd found on-line earlier in the day. 'Here she is. This is a photo taken at a constituency BBQ a few years back; well done, Mike, these will useful for sure. What have you come up with, Eddie?'

'This is the young man in question, plenty of him on the local newspaper website. I accessed his Facebook history from his university days. Like his fiancé, he plays tennis. Unlike her he's a party animal, a real lady's man by all accounts. He's very right wing, and a touch arrogant judging by his utterances over the last few years.'

'Thanks for all that you two, you've done well. So where does that leave us? Does his bride-to-be, the demure Miss Debbie, know about the child? Does Sir Isaac know about the child? Does the local community know Reggie's fathered a child? I'll bet the answer to all three questions is no. We're done here; let me have a think about how we take this forward. I'll contact you later tonight with a plan of action.'

A few minutes later the trio was saying their goodbyes on the pavement outside the Grey Goose.

Two hours later
'Eddie, it's Jack. Listen up this is the plan……

CHAPTER 6

'Harrow Observer, Polly speaking. Who am I speaking to please?'

'Can I speak to the News Editor please?' Somerton attempted to disguise his voice with what he thought was a Scottish accent.

Polly persisted, 'It would be helpful if I could have your name, please.'

'Just put me down as an anonymous caller, hen.'

Polly breathed an exasperated sigh, 'And I suppose you won't tell me the nature of your call?'

'Wish I could Polly, but alas it's what we call, sensitive. You know what I mean'

'Very well, I'll ask Mr Collins if he'll speak to you. Hold the line please.'

A long, few minutes passed, with Somerton on the point of hanging up, when he was joined by a male voice. 'Dave Collins, duty editor, who am I speaking to?'

'As I told your operator, I'm an anonymous caller.'

'Your choice, but we might not be able to use what you tell us without knowing the source.'

'That's your choice, there are other newspapers.'

'Not in Harrow there isn't.'

'Cut the crap, the tabloids are on sale everywhere. Now, do you want my tip-off or not?'

Collins was irritated but news was his business. 'We've come this far, let's hear what you have to say.'

'Now we're getting somewhere, that's more like it, Dave. My call is about Reggie Marsh, you've probably met him in the course of your work. As you know he's hoping to be chosen to stand for Colin MacKinnon's old seat.'

'I know Reggie well, he's a decent bloke. What about him?'

Somerton paused for effect before replying. 'Got pen and paper handy?'

'Never go anywhere without them, fire away.'

'Note down the name Charlie Wilson, born 13th April 2018.'

Collins was slightly irritated, this revelation seemed unremarkable. 'So, what about Charlie Wilson?'

'Do your job Dave, I think it's called investigative journalism; you have two names Reggie Marsh and Charlie Wilson.' Somerton hung up.

Collins looked at his notes, screwed up the piece of paper into a ball and was about to chuck it into his wastepaper basket when the potential penny dropped.

'Janet,' he bellowed out of his office door, 'look sharp, I have a job for you.'

Seconds later a young woman cub reporter stood in front of Collin's desk, nerves tingling.

'Take this and find out what you can about Charlie Wilson; there might just be a story in this for you.'

Gibson glanced at the note. 'Charlie Wilson, he's only a kid?' She looked at Collins expectantly.

'Don't tell me what I already know, Janet. Get a move on, your feet are taking root. I'm out this afternoon so be in my office first thing in the morning with any feedback. One more thing, this is between you and me, no chat around the office.'

'Understood Mr Collins, I'll get right on to it.'

Later same day

Somerton's desk phone buzzed and he picked it up, 'Somerton.'

'Hi Jack, it's Alan.'

'What can I do for you, Prime Minister?'

'Nothing on this occasion; I just wanted to tell you that you'll get a letter sometime soon inviting you to attend a constituency meeting next Friday, 7pm, to put your case to be chosen as Harrow East's candidate for the by-election. As expected, you and Marsh are going head-to-head, there are no other candidates. I wish you luck, Jack but I don't think you stand much of a chance given Sir Isaac's personal interest and Marsh's previous service to the constituency. I'm currently looking around for another constituency for you; there are a few members thinking of retirement.'

'Thanks, for that Alan. I'm pretty well resigned to the fact that I won't be offered the candidacy, but I'll give it my best shot. It'll be good experience if nothing else.'

'I can't tarry, another meeting beckons; make sure you have a good breadth of knowledge about Harrow East, do your research.'

'I've already made a start, no worries on that front.'

'And before I go, you've remembered it is Colin's funeral a week on Sunday?'

'Not something I need to be reminded of, Alan.'

Saturday morning. Harrow Observer Offices

An excited Janet Gibson approached Dave Collins' office, the door ajar as always. She knocked gently and waited for a response.

'Yes', the voice was raised and slightly irritated as Janet entered. Collins had his back to the door and was typing furiously.

'It's me Mr Collins; with the information you asked for.'

Collins swivelled round in his chair, 'Come in Janet, tell me what you've found out about that kiddie. What's his name?'

'Charlie Wilson, Mr Collins.'

'That's it. Come in and sit down.' Collins nodded at a chair with a touch of impatience; he had other priorities requiring attention.

The young cub reporter, made herself comfortable, took a deep breath and began. 'Charlie Wilson, born 13April 2018; mother, Tricia Wilson. And this is where it gets interesting: father, Reginald George Marsh, previously advisor to our late Prime Minister and front-runner to replace him at the next election.

Collins was now sitting upright, attention fully focussed. 'Go on Janet, I sense you have something else to tell me, though I can guess what's coming.'

Gibson nodded her head eagerly, all nerves gone. 'Marsh is currently engaged to Sir Isaac Meyer's daughter Debbie, and he is the Chairman of the local Conservative Party.'

Collins shrugged. 'The whole constituency knows that, Janet.' Collins stroked his chin thoughtfully. There was a germ of a story but it wasn't all that exciting. 'Naughty Eddie, but these things happen.'

'That's not all Mr Collins. Tricia Wilson is a Research Assistant for the local Party and still works for them, though mostly at home.'

'And what do you think we should do with this situation, Janet?'

'Well, I assumed we would print it.' She felt a touch deflated; her Editor seemed to be less than enthusiastic.

Collins smiled. 'Don't worry, we'll use it, maybe even in this week's edition. We just need to come up with a decent headline and a good reason for running the story. Leave it with me for now Janet and I'll see what I can come up with.'

'Do you think I should do any further research?' The young reporter was desperate to maintain her involvement.

'Such as?'

'I could try to find out if he's still seeing Tricia Wilson and his child.'

'Hmm, there's a thought. OK. Drop whatever else you're doing and see what you can come up with before Wednesday's print deadline.'

'Mr Collins,' she was hesitant, but nothing ventured, nothing gained, 'if I find out something useful, do you think I might get a mention?'

Collins regarded her sharply, 'You want to see your name in print, is that it?'

'Only if you think I deserve it, Mr Collins.'

She held her breath, wondering how he was going to react, relieved when he smiled.

'Of course, you'll get a mention; and Janet, never be reluctant to ask. Your career is built on headlines. If you do the work, I'll see that you get the credit. Now off you go.'

Janet Gibson felt like skipping out of Collin's office but resisted the urge although the huge smile on her face betrayed her inner joy. She had what she believed was a trump card; her brother and Marsh played for the same football team and he might just have some insider boys' chat he would be prepared to share with her.

'Hello Billy, it's your darling sister, phoning up to see how life is treating you?' She'd gone to the women's toilets to be as far away from prying ears as possible.

'Hello kiddo, I'm very well thank you. It's not often you phone your big brother during the day, so what do you really want?'

'It's just as I said, I'm enquiring after your welfare.'

'I'm doing jolly well, not a thing to complain about in this whole wide world. So that said, what is it you're after? A loan?'

'No, I do not,' Janet Gibson replied indignantly, 'I've got all the money I need, thank you very much.'

'Lucky you, now are you going to tell me what it is you want from me, dearest sister.'

'Okay, you're absolutely right, I am looking for a favour; one that could help me get a promotion.'

'Go on, I'm listening.'

'You and Reggie Marsh play football together and I'm wondering if there is anything you know about him that would be useful to me? I'm doing an article on him.'

'Oh right, the Tory by-election candidate. Can't tell you much really, he's a reasonable midfielder, easy enough to get on with, doesn't talk politics unless you press him. That's about it.'

'He's engaged, isn't he?'

'I believe so, getting married later this year, not that he's sent out any invites to his wedding.'

'Does he play around? Is he a ladies' man?'

'Well, he's a good-looking bloke and has mentioned a few conquests. Here, hang on a minute. You're not looking for dirt on him, are you? Don't go quoting me about anything.'

'No-one will ever know about this conversation, Billy, I promise. Was he involved with anyone in the constituency office?'

'Well, he has boasted about a few dalliances in the past, likes to show off when he's had a drink, but I can't remember anyone in particular.'

'If I said the name Tricia, would that jog your memory?'

'This is beginning to sound a bit serious, Janet. I don't want to drop him in the shit.'

'I'll take that as a yes.' The young reporter felt a wave of excitement flow through her, she had struck it rich. 'Is he still in touch with her?'

'I think I've said too much already, I'm going to end this call.'

'Oh, come on Billy, this could really give my career a boost.'

'Well, he has referred to his *bit of extra comfort* when he's had too much booze and come to think of it the name Tricia does strike a chord. One last thing, though I fear I've said too much already, he doesn't hang around on training nights. We train every Monday and Wednesday after work, 6.30 to 8.30 and he takes off as soon as he's showered. Sorry but I have to go. No mention of this conversation, understand?'

'I promise, and next time we meet the drinks are on me. One more favour, could you text me this coming Monday night when he's heading off…please, my lovely, handsome, big brother?'

'Cut the bullshit. Just this once; I'm not happy with being a sneak, the guy's a teammate, I feel a bit bad.'

'Thank you, Billy, it's really appreciated.'

CHAPTER 7

Harrow Conservative Party constituency office. Saturday
Reggie Marsh sighed inwardly when Mrs Rankine pushed open the door and shuffled slowly into the office. It was five minutes short of 7pm closing and he'd had a busy three hours dealing with constituents; he'd had listened to enough complaints for one day. Added to that he felt weary after the morning's hard fought football match.

He smiled broadly to conceal his irritation; the 78 years old woman was a regular visitor. 'Mrs Rankine, how nice to see you again; do take a seat whilst I lock the door. You're my last customer.'

'Am I dear? I didn't realise it was so late.'

'The office has been open since 2pm and we close at 7pm; it's been a really busy afternoon. I'll be happy to get home and get changed; I'm going out tonight, dinner with my fiancée at her parent's home. Now what can I do for you, Mrs Rankine?'

'You can call me Dot for a start. If you're going to be my MP, we might as well get on first name terms. You're Reggie, aren't you?'

'That's right Dot, now how can I help?'

'You don't mind me calling you Reggie, do you? I mean I can call you Reginald if you prefer?'

'Reggie's absolutely fine, so….?'
Dot Rankine just stared at him blankly.

'Dot, tell me please, what brought you here on this chilly evening?'

'It is cold dear, isn't it? Again, she hesitated, searching for a word, or recall, only she knew. 'Why am I here, ah yes, I remember now, it's the noise Reggie. It keeps me awake when I go to bed.'

'Noise? Now what noise would that be?'

'The pub dear, every weekend, music blaring out till nigh on midnight. I go to bed at 10pm, it's just not fair on us older people.

It's so loud I just can't get to sleep. And the music's awful, all that modern stuff.'

'I see,' Marsh nodded sagely, 'you have my sympathy. Have you told the Council? Complaints about noise is their responsibility?'

'I tried to dear but got fed up hanging on the phone waiting for it to be answered. I eventually got through one day, but they told me the person who deals with noise was out. They said they would ring back but they never did. So, I thought I would come to you for help, dear. Mr MacKinnon would have sorted them. No bother.'

'And help I will Dot. What's your address?'

'16 Taylor Crescent, I've been there for thirty years.'

'And the name of the pub.'

'The Boar's Head dear, I'm sure you know it.'

Marsh nodded. 'OK Dot, leave it with me; I'll get a stiff letter off to the Council on your behalf.' He glanced at his watch, 7.15. *Could be worse, plenty of time.*

Thankfully Dot Rankine took the hint. 'Of course, you'll be keen to get away to see your young lady; when's the wedding?'

'Maybe later this year, we haven't set a date yet.'

'Well, I hope the sun shines for you on the big day.'

'Thank you, Dot. Lovely to see you. You go home and put your feet up in front of the Tele.'

Dot pushed herself unsteadily to her feet. 'I'll try to but I just hope the pub's not too noisy tonight. Saturdays are the worst. Now, make sure you win the election. Mr MacKinnon was a wonderful man; it'll be difficult for you following in his footsteps.'

'It certainly will.' Marsh took her arm, 'Here let me help you.'

'No need for that, I'm quite steady on my feet.'

'Of course, you are.' But he held on and gently guided her over to the door. 'You take care now; it's been lovely seeing you. I'll get that letter done and post it on the way home.'

'Thank you, Reggie, you are good but don't keep yourself late for your young lady. Bye now.'

'Bye Dot.' He gave her a wave and closed the door, putting an end to any further chat. *Thank God that's over, what an afternoon it's been.*

Marsh made his way over to his desk and began to tidy it, all the time thinking about what he would be saying to please his future father-in-law, Sir Isaac Meyer. His support was essential if Marsh was to secure his selection as the party's election candidate. His thoughts were interrupted by loud urgent knocking on the door. *Shit, who in Hell's name is that?* He waited to see if his visitor would give up, but the knocking persisted. Grimacing, he moved forward ready to point out the hours of business as shown on the notice fixed to the door.

In a split second his resolve faltered when he saw the young woman standing in the doorway; a very attractive auburn haired, green-eyed beauty. She stood around 1.7metres and wore a neat fur-cuffed suede jacket over a red polo-necked sweater and a mid-grey tweed mini skirt, short but not too short.

Marsh put on his sunniest smile. 'Hi, the surgery ended at 7pm but I can give you a few minutes if it's urgent.'

A smile lit up her face and she danced a few steps, 'It's urgent, that's for sure; I saw your light on and I have desperate need of a loo. I've been visiting friends and should have gone before I set off for home.'

'Oh sure, no problem, come in. The toilet is straight ahead.'

The young woman didn't linger and disappeared behind the corridor door leading to the toilet, leaving behind the scent of her perfume. Marsh was in the process of finishing some filing when she re-appeared some minutes later.

'Phew, that's better; sorry to have disturbed you.'

'No problem, in fact it's been a pleasure.' He was conscious of her eyes taking in his appearance, hoping she liked what she saw. 'Do you mind if I asked your name?'

'Not at all, it's Daisy Langton. And yours?'

'Reggie Marsh, at your service.' He gave a theatrical bow.

'At my **service**,' she echoed, 'hmm, I wish it were true. And what is your role here, Reggie?'

'I used to be Colin Mackinnon's researcher and constituency advisor and, until we elect a new MP, I'm dealing with constituents' concerns. If everything goes to plan, in a few weeks' time I'll be standing for election as Harrow East's next Member of Parliament.'

Her eyes widened, 'Really, I had no idea MPs could be so young and handsome; lucky old Harrow East.'

'Thank you, Daisy, I'm very flattered. Can I count on your vote?'

'Alas I don't live in Harrow. Wish I did; my vote would be the very least I'd offer you. Do you mind me asking if you have a girlfriend, or a wife for that matter?'

Her eyes were fixed on his. *Oh my God, she's flirting with me.* He just couldn't pass up the opportunity. He stepped forward, shaking his head, 'There's no-one special in my life, up to now, that is.' His face was inches from hers. It was one of those moments, his lips met hers, gently at first, then urgently. She pushed he body into his, a quiet groan escaping her lips. His pulse rate was going through the roof, he knew he shouldn't be doing this but…. She didn't resist as he backed her onto the desk, pulling up her skirt as he undid his belt and pushed down his trousers and underpants.

'Hold on,' Her voice firm, 'where's the condom?'

'Christ, I don't have one. Aren't you on the pill?'

'Of course, I am but I don't know you and I'm not taking any chances. It'll have to be a pleasure postponed, Reggie. Give me your telephone number and we'll arrange something more romantic next time. I'm not far away, Crawley, so won't be difficult.'

'I'd like that, sooner rather than later.'

'Me too, can I have your card?'

Marsh suddenly remembered how exposed he was and hurriedly pulled up his pants and trousers, his cheeks flushing with embarrassment. He stole another kiss then reached past her to extract a card from a box on his desk and handed it to her. 'Don't leave it too long, please, I think we could have some real fun.'

He glanced at his watch, 'I'm sorry I have to be going, meeting with the branch chairman.'

Daisy Langton smiled wistfully, 'I understand, you politicians are always in demand.' She jumped down from the desk and gave him a gentle kiss before crossing to the door and stepping onto the pavement where she turned and gave him a wave. 'Good luck with your erection, oops sorry, Freudian slip, meant to say election.' With a giggle she wandered off to where she had parked her car.

Marsh watched until the car turned into a side street, muttering to himself when he remembered he hadn't asked for a contact number.

The Meyer household
Marsh was nearly twenty minutes late when he pressed the doorbell. He had dressed fairly formally, a smart, but casual, jacket, tailored shirt and well-pressed trousers. Sir Isaac frowned on casual dress for dinner invites.

'Come in Reggie, you're late, dinner's nearly ready.'

'Sorry about that, I have to blame Mrs Rankine. She turned up at the last minute and I didn't have the heart to turn her away.'

Sir Isaac smiled and his irritation melted away. 'Ah, dear old Dot, a supporter of long standing. What did she want?'

'Nothing too serious, pub music keeping her awake when she goes to bed. I listened patiently and promised to take it up with the Council.'

Sir Isaac nodded, 'Good idea, pass to the Council; they can be the killjoys.'

Just then, Debbie Meyer joined them and threw her arms around his neck. 'Thought you were never going to get here, I've missed you.'

'I've missed you too, darling.'

Mrs Meyer stuck her head round the door, 'Come along you lovebirds, save the sweet nothings for later, dinner's about to be served.'

Minutes later they were all gathered round the dinner table, heads bowed whilst Sir Isaac said grace in Yiddish. That done he rose to his feet and moved over to the sideboard to retrieve a bottle of champagne from an ice cooler.

'Thought we would have some fizz and raise a glass to our next parliamentary candidate.'

Marsh gulped, 'A bit early isn't it, Sir? I mean the committee hasn't voted yet and the constituents haven't had a chance to vote. After all Somerton's an ex-SAS hero with a Military Cross, and a good friend of Colin's; that will appeal to many.'

Sir Isaac winked, 'It's in the bag, believe me. Think no more about it. Now let's get tucked into this lovely meal Mother's prepared for us.'

CHAPTER 8

Eddie Blacks's flat. Sunday

It was shortly after 9am when Eddie Black answered the doorbell, glancing up at the security screen as he went, smiling when he saw who it was. 'Come on in Rachel, you're bright and early.'

'Have to be Eddie, I'm meeting up with a friend in Sevenoaks at 10; we're off out for the day'.

Black raised an eyebrow, 'Heavy date, is it?'

'Well, I hope he's not too heavy, though it's a good earner so I'll take it as it comes.'

'You're looking fabulous as always; he's a lucky guy whoever he is.'

Rachel McNeil chuckled, 'He's not lucky, he's rich.'

'Don't you ever feel you want to get out of this game? Settle down, get married perhaps, maybe even have kids?'

'Don't go slushy on me Eddie, unless you're proposing. I'll carry on for another two or three years by which time I'll have a tidy sum laid by and then I might just cast my eye round for someone I could live with.'

'Good luck with your dreams, darling. Now, what have you got for me?'

She opened her handbag, brought out a small plastic bag and tipped the contents into her left hand. 'If the electronics worked, you'll have everything you want. I used an alias by the way, Daisy Langton.'

'I hope Marsh wasn't rough or anything like that?'

'Not at all, he just followed my lead and played his part to the full.'

'Can I get you a coffee?'

'No thanks Eddie, I really must get moving. Can't be late for my client.'

'OK, hold on whilst I get the cash.' Minutes later he was back with an envelope. 'There you are darling; you'll find there's £600 in twenties.'

'We agreed £500 Eddie and you haven't even checked out the product.'

'A wee bonus, it's good to have someone I can trust for jobs like this. Someone who won't gossip about what's she's been up to. Technology is my responsibility, I'm sure you made your contribution to perfection.'

'Thank you darling, it's nice to be appreciated. I'm off. If it hasn't worked, let me know. I'm sure I could arrange a repeat performance; I know for sure Reggie would be….shall we say… **up** for it.' She smiled impishly.

As soon as she had gone Black headed to what he called his office and booted up a processor that facilitated wireless extraction of what had been recorded by the microdot camera secreted in the brooch and ring Rachel had worn when she engaged with Reggie Marsh. The procedure only took a few minutes. *Hmm, you didn't hang about Rachel, now let's take a look at what we've got.*

It was all there from the doorstep welcome to the pavement farewell, everything needed to make life very uncomfortable for Marsh. *I hope your fiance, your mistress and your child don't suffer too much when this goes public, Reggie. But I've got no sympathy for you, you're an arsehole, plain and simple.*

'Jack, it's Eddie, I have a DVD and a selection of photos for you; what do you want me to do with them? I don't think you'll be disappointed with the product.'

'Brilliant. Make three duplicates of everything for starters; you hang onto the original. Drop the stuff off at the NRSC tomorrow, I'm there from 10am till 2pm.'

'Will do, Jack, see you tomorrow.'

Somerton punched the air; Master Reggie was in for a shock when the shit hit the fan. The Press had the soft stuff, but this was dynamite. *I feel sorry for you Debbie Meyer. You're going to be devastated when you see what your fiance has been up to; I feel really sorry for you but you're well rid of him. And the kid's Mum, what of her? I don't want to think about it. Maybe there's another way of getting you out of the way without too much collateral damage.*

'Eddie, me again, change of plan…….'

Monday

The weekend had dragged by; Janet Gibson couldn't wait for Monday to come and when it did every hour seemed like a lifetime. But the hands of time never stop. How ever slow it seemed, the day passed and at 8.30pm she was parked not too far from 18 Winterbourne Road waiting for Reggie Marsh to put in an appearance. Please be a good boy and go to training. The minutes dragged by, and she was starting to get worried when her phoned buzzed; her brother's text had arrived. 'He's on his way, time 8.48pm.'

Bless you Billy, I'll buy you a bottle of your favourite brandy.

It was just five minutes after the hour when she saw Marsh making his way along the pavement towards her. She risked taking a photo with the best camera the Observer had available, dropping it below the dashboard when he got nearer. He didn't give her a glance as he drew level and turned into No18 and walked briskly along the path to the door. The security light came on and Reggie Marsh was clearly recognisable; the camera was working overtime. He was in the process of putting his key in the lock when the door was opened by Tricia Wilson, son Charlie at her side. The child put his arms round Marsh's leg and shouted something. Meanwhile Marsh was embracing and kissing his lady friend. The woman eventually pulled away. Marsh lifted the child, then went into the hallway closing the door behind him.

Janet Gibson was beaming; she had her story, and it would be a headliner with photos to back it up. She had been told to take loads of photos and she had certainly done that. You're in for a big shock Reggie and you deserve it. I hate fucking two-timers.

Tuesday morning

Janet Gibson proudly presented herself in Dave Collins' office shortly after 8.30am. 'I've got it Mr Collins, it's all here on camera, photos of Reggie Marsh and the Wilson woman.'

Collins was impressed and gave her an approving nod. 'Well done, and might I enquire how you managed to catch Reggie in the act?'

Gibson blushed, 'Oh they're not actually doing it Mr Collins, it's just photos of them together, the child as well.'

'Relax, Janet. We wouldn't use photos of them having sex; we're not that kind of newspaper. The readers will draw their own conclusions. Let's go down to the photo lab and see what you have.'

Ted Small, the Observer's long time photography expert looked up in surprise when Collins and Gibson walked into his office without knocking.

'Morning, Ted. I've got an urgent one for you; print whatever's on this camera and bring copies to me soon as. I need them for tomorrow's print run if they're any good.'

'No problem, Dave, count on it as done.'

'I wonder,' Janet Gibson ventured somewhat nervously, 'if Ted could maybe put them up on the screen for us, Mr Collins. You could choose whichever suited best?'

'Good point, Janet. Can you do that Ted?'

'No problem, let's have the camera and we'll go next door to the lab.'

Minutes later three faces were studying a total of fifteen photos on a monitor screen. Ten minutes had passed when Collins ended their deliberations.

'Right, time to make our minds up; I reckon No13 is best for our purposes.'

Ted Small nodded, 'Agreed.'

'And what about you Janet?'

'I reckon it's between 12 and 13; 13 probably edges it. The kissing shot is good, but you can't see their faces.'

'Hmm, on reflection I think we'll use both. Thanks Ted, three copies of 12 and 13 please. Now let's go and leave Ted to do the technical stuff.'

On their way back to their respective desks, Janet Gibson summoned up her courage, it was now or never. 'Mr Collins do you think I could write this one up? I'd love to have an article in print, it would be a big step for me.'

Collins pursed his lips. 'I don't know if you've had enough experience Janet, this is quite a biggie. Still, you've got to start some time, and you have put in the work. Yes, go for it; let me have something in front of me for 11am.'

'Thank you, Mr Collins, I promise I won't let you down.'

CHAPTER 9

Conservative Party constituency office: Wednesday
It was just 10am, and Marsh had been at his desk for the past hour preparing for a clinic due to open in an hour's time. Suddenly the outside door pushed open and Sir Isaac stepped forward, an angry expression on his face.

'Sir Isaac…' Marsh didn't finish what he was about to say when he saw Debbie follow her father, her face tense and troubled. His eyes travelled between the two of them, 'What's happened? Mrs Meyer is all right? What…?' His voice trailed away; something was seriously wrong.

Meyer turned to his daughter. 'Close the door Debbie and bolt it.'

Marsh's stomach churned. *Trouble. I can feel it, something bad, I know it.*

'This is what brings us here Reggie, you cheating little toe-rag; explain yourself.' He thrust the midweek edition of the Harrow Observer into Marsh's hands. He gulped, there was no need to read the narrative, the banner headline was all that was needed **"HAPPY FAMILY?"** The two photos below the headline showed himself kissing Tricia, the other showed Charlie snuggling into his father. It was all there in black and white; denial wasn't an option.

He looked Debbie in the eye, registering the hurt and tears; he could see his nomination going up in flames. 'It's not what you think, darling, honestly. I love you and only you; I want my future to be with you. Let me explain, please.'

Sir Isaac interrupted. 'You can't explain something like this away, you have no future here or with my daughter. I want you to pack up right now and get out of our lives.'

Marsh looked at his fiancé pleadingly, 'Please darling, at least let me explain.'

Sir Isaac thumped the desk with his fist. 'I don't want your excuses, just leave.'

Debbie Meyer reached forward and put her hand on her father's arm. 'Please Dad, let him have his say. I do love him.'

'Very well. Go ahead Marsh but you're wasting your time; you're finished here.'

Marsh endeavoured to look and sound contrite. 'I'm sorry you had to find out this way darling. I've been trying to summon up the courage to tell you, but the right moment never quite came along. We were always so happy; I didn't want to risk damaging what we had in any way. I guess I was too afraid of losing you.'

He saw her face soften, *maybe I can still get out of this mess.* He was about to go on but Sir Isaac intervened, his anger unabated, the pain he knew his daughter was suffering bringing hatred to his heart. 'Get on with it, let's hear more of your pathetic excuses.'

Marsh knew Sir Isaac's ears were closed to anything he might say and fixed his eyes on Debbie's. 'It all happened four Christmases ago. I had too much to drink, walked Tricia Wilson home, she invited me in, and things got out of hand, Charlie's the result. We're not, and never were an item, but I just couldn't abandon my responsibilities to the child; it just wouldn't be right. So, after football practice, when it doesn't interfere with us, I go round and spend an hour with the child. Tricia and I are friends I guess, but nothing more than that, I swear.'

Meyer shook his head. 'All very pat, Reggie. So, Tricia just makes you a cup of tea and takes herself off, does she? The photo shows you embracing and kissing her, how do you explain that away?'

Marsh shook his head. 'It's nothing more than an arrival kiss, that's what she does with any friend.'

'So why don't you take the kid out for the evening?'

'Charlie's young, he doesn't like being away from his mother.'

He locked eyes with Debbie again. 'I'll stop seeing him. I'll do anything you want; I don't want to lose you. This should never have happened, but it did, and I can't change that. I should have told you and wish I had; I've failed, and I know it. There's been no-one but you since and never will be again if you marry me.'

Sir Isaac clapped his hands when Marsh finished. 'All very pat Reggie, you tell a nice story; you would have made a good MP. Do the decent thing and marry your son's mother.'

'I don't love Tricia, I love Debbie.'

Meyer shook his head, a sneer on his lips. 'Get out before I throw you out.'

His daughter touched his arm again. 'Dad, please, leave it to me now. I still love Reggie or at least I think I do. I need time to think about this. We'll go now. Don't call me Reggie. I'll call you one way or the other when I'm ready.'

'I understand, darling, please know that I love you.'

'Let's go home now, Dad; I've got a lot of thinking to do.'

Meyer shook his fist at Marsh. 'If she rejects you, you are finished here; either way you will not represent Harrow East. I'm sure the voters wouldn't want you as their representative. I'll be taking soundings in the constituency.'

After they'd gone, Marsh slumped in his chair, distraught, his thoughts bubbling as they pondered on the future. *There was nothing more he could do; it was out of his hands. Debbie seemed to have left the door open, but could her love overcome her pride? Then there was Tricia; no matter what he told Debbie, he still had feelings for Tricia and his son. And, even if Debbie sticks with me, will Sir Isaac stick with me? Or will he sack me and I'll be out of a job? Fuck, fuck, fuck.*

Constituency office Thursday evening.

Another long day had passed with no news from Debbie. Marsh was despondent; *surely, she would have come to a decision by now?* He had thought about phoning her, sending her flowers, going round to see her but her instructions had been clear; he had to sit it out. He tried to dredge up some optimism, *no news is good news, give her time, it's going to be OK.*

Not for the first time he glanced at the clock, ten minutes short of 7pm; he would be going home shortly. *But going home to what? More pessimistic thoughts, more television he couldn't concentrate on, another meal he couldn't finish, another night of disturbed sleep? Fuck, fuck, fuck.* On the other hand, home was where Debbie was most likely to phone him. Home was where he wouldn't be distracted by work or engaged with a constituent. *Yes, that's what she's waiting for.*

His thoughts were disturbed when a young man in his twenties rang the doorbell and stepped into the room.

'Good evening, how can I help you?'

'I'm Tommy Langton, Daisy's brother. She knew I would be over this way and asked me to drop off this envelope.' He walked forward and dropped it on the desk in front of March. 'She didn't say anything about a reply, so I'll not hang around. Nice to have met you, Reggie.'

Marsh shrugged, 'Yeah, sure, nice to have met you too.' Marsh tipped his forehead as his visitor departed, 'See you around.' With that Tommy Langton was gone and Marsh gave his attention to the envelope. *Hmm, weighty, intriguing. I wonder what you've sent me Daisy?* He sliced open the envelope with his silver letter opener, grimacing when he recalled it was a present from Debbie. He spilled the contents onto his desk, gasping when he saw the nature of the dozen or so photos. *Oh no, it can't be blackmail?!* He dashed over to the door and onto the street but there was no sign of his visitor or his means of transport. Marsh's hands were shaking, he felt sick as he made his way back to the desk. The photos left nothing to the imagination, it was clear what had taken place. There he was, centre stage, with his trousers and knickers around his ankles. Photos but no note! *What the fuck's going on? Maybe it's Daisy's idea of a joke?* He picked up the envelope and looked inside, there it was - a folded notelet.

Dear Reggie,

Firstly, my name isn't Daisy Langton and Tommy isn't my brother; both of us live miles away. I doubt if our paths will cross any time soon unless it becomes necessary.

I'm a close friend of Debbie and she's confided in me regarding your 'friend' Tricia Wilson. She asked me if she should still marry you. My advice is that it wouldn't work, you were bringing too much baggage to the marriage. She has doubts aplenty but still has feelings for you, so I took it upon myself to test you out. She's a good friend and a lovely girl, and I couldn't bear the thought of her getting hurt. Clearly, I was right; you're not the faithful type and she will be better off without you.

What next? Simple really. You are going to tell Sir Isaac that you've had second thoughts and it wouldn't be right to abandon your son whose existence would always cast a shadow on your marriage. He'll be so glad to get rid of you he'll give you a good reference.

Do what I ask and that will be the last you'll hear from me. If you don't, I'll send him the photos and maybe give him a call. Debbie bares her soul to me every night to talk about her feelings, so I'll know what's going on.

Marsh was devastated; Debbie would be out of his life, his nomination for Harrow East was a non-starter and he'd be out of a job. *What a fucking disaster. Take stock Reggie, be realistic, you're a survivor; what's the best you can make of this situation?* He had to face up to Sir Isaac and listen to his view on how to end his engagement to Debbie.

That done, he would have to go and see Tricia Wilson.

CHAPTER 10

Meyer residence Thursday evening.
The telephone rang and Sir Isaac rose from his seat and moved across. 'I'll get it dear. Hello, Sir Isaac speaking, how can I help?'

'It's Reggie, Sir Isaac. I wonder if I could call round and have a word, it's important.'

'There's nothing I want to talk to you about. I'm still hoping Debbie shows you the door.'

'It's Debbie I want to talk about. Please Sir Isaac, I can come round to your place, now if you'll allow me?'

'Very well, but make it quick, I've got commitments.'

Fifteen minutes later, Reggie Marsh stood opposite Sir Isaac Meyer in the latter's study; he wasn't invited to take a seat.

'Come right to the point, Reggie, I've got no time for you; Debbie hasn't smiled since we last met. I'm still praying she gets rid of you.'

Marsh took a deep breath. 'I'm truly sorry this has happened.'

'Truly sorry you got found out you mean.'

Marsh summoned up a pained expression and wrung his hands. 'You're right, I should have been honest with Debbie from the beginning, but I loved her and wanted her to love me, so I said nothing about my situation. I'm saddened, I'm ashamed and haven't stopped thinking about Debbie, Tricia too, and my son. I've been a fool; I've messed up big time and caused those I love unbearable pain. I wish I could turn the clock back, but I can't. I've reflected on what you had to say, and I think you're right.'

Meyer shook his head impatiently. 'Right? Right about what exactly?'

'It's best for Debbie if I take myself out of her life. She deserves better than me. My son would forever cast a shadow on our marriage; it would complicate issues if we were to have children.'

Meyer repressed a smile; he was going to get his way. Marsh was making his exit.

'You know my feelings, the quicker you get out of Debbie's life the better, but it's her you should be speaking to, not me.'

Marsh nodded glumly. 'I will do that if you wish but I thought it best to tell you first; I've got a letter for her. It would be tough on her doing it face to face.'

'You might be right, Marsh, she'll take it badly and face to face might make it worse.'

'I'm glad you agree Sir. I have the letter with me if you would be prepared to give it to her or I can post it if you wish.' Marsh took an envelope out of his pocket.

Meyer grabbed it. *In my hands, the little bastard won't be able to change his mind.* 'I'll give it to her; no need to delay this any longer than necessary. Now is that it? Are we done?'

'I wondered if you would be prepared to give me a reference? I realise you'll be reluctant, but I **have always**, done good work for Colin and the constituency over the years. If you were able to, I would move out of the area and take Tricia and Charlie with me; that way Debbie would never see any of us again. I was thinking of trying to get a job in Westminster, and in time try for another election opportunity.'

Sir Isaac took time to respond, wanting to keep Reggie dangling on tenterhooks. 'OK, you'll get your reference; now get out of here, we're done. You know the way.'

'Just one more thing, Sir. I'll go to the office tomorrow and put everything in good order for my successor. I'm really sorry our relationship has ended on a sour note; you taught me all I know about politics. Working with you has been a pleasure.'

Meyer made no effort to reply, his steely stare conveyed his feelings.

Later that evening.

Sir Isaac sat with his wife in the lounge, both trying to give a television programme their attention, both glancing repeatedly at the clock.

'She won't be much longer, dear, she said she would be home by 9pm.' Ruth Meyer could sense the tension in her husband; neither of them was looking forward to telling their daughter what had transpired.

'I hope not, I want to get this over with; she's going be devastated.'

Ruth Meyer raised a finger to her lips. 'I think I heard a car on the drive, it can only be her.'

They hear the front door open. Sir Isaac sighed resignedly. 'Off you go and make us all a cuppa, I'll start the ball rolling.'

'A stiff drink might be better. It'll all work out Isaac, I know it will.'

'Hello Dad, how's your day been?' His daughter smiled wanly and moved forward to give her father a hug and a kiss.

'It's been an eventful day, darling; take a seat, we need to talk.'

'Oh dear, that sounds ominous.' She sat down on the edge of the sofa and waited expectantly. 'Well, out with it, Dad, don't keep me in suspense.'

'Reggie called in this evening and left a letter for you.'

To his surprise his daughter showed not a sign of apprehension. 'Let's have it then, see what he has to say.'

'I know more or less what it says, and there's no easy way to tell you. He's breaking off your engagement and going back to his mistress and child.' To his surprise his daughter didn't burst into tears. She was saddened, he could see that.

'Oh well, I guess that saves me the trouble of doing it.'

Meyer was momentarily speechless. 'Sorry, did I hear you right? You were going to end it?'

She nodded, her eyes moistening. 'Yes, it wouldn't have worked. I want children and, if we had been blessed with them, Reggie's child being on the scene would have made things difficult, more so if I hadn't been able to have them. I think our marriage would have slowly crumbled with his ex and child in the background. I hope he's not going to stay in the area?'

Meyer was over the moon; he could hardly get his words out. 'No, no, not at all. He's going to try and get a job in London and take the Wilson woman and her child with him. In fact, he'll be out of the way after tomorrow; he has some tidying up to do in the office then he's out of our lives.'

'That's good, make sure you give him a good reference. I'd hate his future to be totally ruined. Right now, I'm going upstairs for a bath and to read his letter. I'll let you know what it says. I might shed a few tears but that will be the last chapter as far as I'm concerned.'

As soon as she'd gone, Meyer went in search of his wife. 'Good news darling, Debbie has taken it remarkably well.'

'I know dear, I was listening at the door. I've poured us a gin to celebrate.'

18 Winterbourne Road

Marsh was satisfied with the outcome of his meeting with Sir Isaac; a good reference alongside his experience meant he would have no problem getting a post in Westminster, the very heart of British politics. But there was one more bridge to cross. With Debbie out of the picture, Tricia could move centre stage along with his son. He rehearsed the spin he was going to put on the Observer article as he drove the short distance to Winterbourne Road.

Tricia's eyes opened wide when she opened the door and saw her lover standing on the doorstep. 'My God, Reggie this is a surprise, what brings you here? Not that I'm complaining.'

Marsh stepped in, closing the door behind him. 'You've seen yesterday's Observer?'

Wilson shook her head. 'I'm not big into local newspapers; I only see it occasionally and I haven't been out to catch up with the latest gossip.'

'We made the front page. You, me, Charlie, history, background, the full works. Disastrous timing, I no longer have Sir Isaac's support so won't get nominated for the by-election. I'm afraid our plan for me to get elected, and then break off my engagement to Debbie has been overtaken by events.'

'Gosh! How's Debbie taken it?'

Marsh gave her a resume of what happened between himself and Sir Isaac, painting the best picture possible to show himself in good light. He then fabricated a face-to-face meeting with Debbie. 'She's obviously not happy but I told her I had to stand by Charlie and had always worried he might cast a shadow on the marriage. I told her she would be better off without me. Debbie surprised me by saying she could cope with the situation; fortunately, we got lucky, in that Sir Isaac and Mrs Meyer both shared my viewpoint and brought her round to my way of thinking. I think in their heart of hearts they were both quite pleased; they had asked me from time to time would I give thought to adopting the Jewish religion and I'd declined. All's well that ends well and Sir Isaac is going to give me a good reference, tomorrow's my last day.'

'So darling, if you're agreeable, I'd like us to move closer to Westminster and I'll get a job as a researcher in the House; maybe find an opportunity for you to do some work from home. What do you think; will you come with me?'

Tricia threw her arms round his neck and kissed him. 'Of course, darling, it's what we were always going to do, it just brings it forward. Does this mean you'll be staying the night?'

Marsh smiled, 'You try and stop me. What's for dinner?' *That was a good piece of spin Reggie boy, you're definitely MP material.*

Somerton's apartment

Somerton's mobile buzzed; a glance showed it was Eddie Black.

'Hi Jack, I think your plan has worked.'

'How so?'

'Well, the photos were duly delivered, and Reggie boy immediately closed the office and set off. I followed him and he went straight to Meyer's place; he was there for around ten minutes. When he came out, he drove straight to his girlfriend's. I hung around for an hour, and he didn't put in an appearance; I reckon he's curled up in bed with her. End of story.'

'Thanks Eddie, fingers crossed you're right. The signs are good, but I won't know until I hear from Sir Isaac or possibly Alan. How much do I owe you for the delivery?'

'I got one of our young contacts to drop it off. £100 will cover it; he knows nothing of the background. Just why did you want it handled that way, Jack, you really let Marsh off the hook?'

'Oh, just keeping the collateral damage to a minimum. I figured the kid deserved a dad, Tricia Wilson a husband and Debbie Meyer can have a future with a man that might be true to her. I think maybe I'm getting soft, Eddie.'

CHAPTER 11

It was shortly after 8am when the phone rang. 'Good morning, Alan.'

'Morning, Jack. I'm just phoning to wish you luck with your interview, looks like you'll have a clear field.'

Somerton feigned puzzlement. 'Sorry I don't know what you're getting at, Alan; *a clear field,* fill me in.'

'Sounds like you haven't read the Wednesday's Harrow Observer, you really should give it a looksee, at least until you secure your nomination.'

'You're right as always, Alan, I should read the local press; it just hasn't come my way. So don't keep me in suspense, what gives?'

'Your competition, young Mr Marsh, has blotted his copybook. Remember I told you he was engaged to Sir Isaac's daughter? Well, apparently, he has a young son by a local woman and former colleague of his.'

'So what? He made a mistake however long ago. I can't see that it affects his eligibility to be nominated; still, if it makes it easier for me, who am I to argue? Must say though, the guy has my sympathy.'

'My goodness, that's very magnanimous of you Jack. Not at all the Somerton we all know and love. I won't criticise Sir Isaac, it's totally understandable, a father wanting the best for his daughter. Anyway, good luck; will speak to you after the interview.'

Somerton was smiling when the call ended; he had conveyed a good impression to Alan Croudace, just as he had hoped. His manufactured story line of the Marsh compromise and the fictional friend had been a smoke screen to minimise the risk of himself being accused of arranging the honey trap; Alan for one would have been suspicious. *Right Jack, get moving, you have an interview to go to.*

Harrow East Conservative Party offices.

Somerton arrived a few minutes before 10am and rang the doorbell. The door was opened within seconds by Sir Isaac Meyer who introduced himself and invited Somerton to follow him.

'Do take a seat Mr Somerton and I'll introduce you to the committee.' Somerton could feel himself being appraised from the moment he entered the large side room. As he took his seat at the large antique mahogany table, his eyes flicked around the photographs of previous Conservative Party prime ministers adorning the walls. He smiled and waved his hand in their direction, 'I'm certainly in good company.' There were a few smiles but no verbal acknowledgements from the two women and two men, none of whom would see seventy again.

Sir Isaac made the introductions and opened the proceedings. 'You're aware of why you are here Mr Somerton; I'd like you to tell us why you think you should be our next MP. I must make it clear that this committee doesn't choose the nominee. We simply put together the ballot paper, then it's up to members to cast their vote. We would be looking for votes to be returned two weeks today. The floor is yours Mr Somerton.'

Somerton launched into his presentation immediately, looking round the table catching everyone's eye in turn, judging reaction, approving or disapproving. He spoke for twenty minutes without notes, at the end of which he was confident he had covered key national and local issues. 'I'd like to end by saying why I want to be your next Member of Parliament. At its simplest, I want to follow in Colin MacKinnon's footsteps and carry on doing what's best for my country and this planet of ours. My interest in politics stems from serving under him, something I was proud to do. And more than that, I want to do all that I can to improve everyday life for the residents of Harrow East. He loved this constituency and often reminded me, and Alan Croudace, to consider the impact of political decisions on ordinary people, both locally and nationally.'

'Thank you, Mr Somerton, I'll go round the table and see if there are any questions but, before I do that, I have one for you. You are currently the country's National Security Advisor; do you intend to carry on in that role?'

Somerton had prepared for this question. 'I will serve my country in any way the Prime Minister asks me to but it is my intention to resign as NSA. Security is a 24/7 operation and must function effectively whether I am there or not. I have several colleagues who regularly deputise for me, and I have been training one of them to be my successor. Just as when I decided I would like to become an MP, I observed Colin MacKinnon, Alan Croudace and many others at close quarters, listening to their views and learning how the political machine works at first hand. If I am successful in gaining your nomination, and get elected, I will serve you well and promise never to let you down.'

Sir Isaac gave the slightest nod of approval and then invited the other committee members to ask their questions. Twenty minutes later it was all over, and Sir Isaac brought the interview to a close. 'Thank you, Mr Somerton, we'll be in touch one way or another. Now, unless you have any follow up questions, I'll see you out.'

Somerton smiled and rose to his feet. 'No further questions and I'm happy to see myself out. Thank you for interviewing me ladies and gentlemen.'

When Somerton had gone, Meyer addressed his colleagues. 'As I explained before Somerton arrived, Marsh has withdrawn his application and we're left with Jack Somerton, who, I have to say, seems a good candidate; but it's for you to decide. 'Rhoda, what's your view?'

'I liked what he had to say, I'm happy for his name to go forward.'

'And Margaret, what do you think?'

'I'm happy with him and I'll likely vote for him in the ballot.'

'Charles?'

'Somerton will get my vote; he came over well; we're lucky to have him.'

'Bill?'

'Somerton's fine, he ticked all the boxes and I'm happy for his name to be on the ballot paper. However, I don't like the idea of only having one candidate, the constituents will think it's a fit up by the committee.'

Meyer nodded. 'I agree with you, but we don't have a lot of time and the Observer article provides the background to Marsh's withdrawal. I guess I could contact the Party Chairman and take advice on our predicament. If Central Office chooses to put someone forward, can I get your clearance by phoning round rather than convening a meeting? All in favour of that proposal?'

Four hands were raised. 'Good, we are all agreed; I'll get on to that as soon as we pack up. And I formally propose that Somerton is included on the ballot paper. All in favour?'

Again, four hands were raised. Meyer smiled. 'Carried unanimously. My, my, we are an agreeable lot. Meeting closed.'

Having thought about the matter, Meyer decided to phone Alan Croudace rather than the Party Chairman. Their historic close friendship could lead to accusations of cronyism if Somerton wasn't seen to have competition.

Meyer phoned Downing Street and got put through to Jess Tate.

'I'm sorry Sir Isaac, he's in a meeting at the moment. I've got no idea how long it will last. The best I can do is ask him to phone you when the meeting is over.'

In the event it was over an hour before Meyer got his call. "Thank you for calling back Prime Minister. I know how busy you are. I won't take up too much of your time.'

Croudace surmised it was about the by-election and was only too happy to get involved. 'Nice to hear from you Sir Isaac, how can I be of assistance?'

Meyer explained the Marsh situation and how the committee was left with only one candidate and felt uneasy about proceeding on that basis. 'I stress that we are very happy to support Somerton's candidacy but would prefer it if we could give our constituents a choice. Our problem, in the time available to us, is finding another candidate.'

Croudace agreed without further discussion. 'Leave it with me Sir Isaac, I'll get on to the Party Chairman as soon as I put the phone down. I'll ask him to come up with another candidate and get back to you as quickly as possible.'

True to his word Croudace contacted Geoffrey Crowne immediately and explained the background to his request. The Party Chairman was understanding of his request. 'No problem, Alan. We always have a list of aspiring applicants. Now I'm going to make some assumptions; I take it you support Somerton, so we don't want strong competition; we want someone not too experienced and not too local? Would I be right in those assumptions?'

'I'll leave it to your judgement entirely Geoffrey, I'm entirely neutral.'

'Of course, Prime Minister, that goes without saying, notwithstanding the fact that you've worked with, and served with, your ex-SAS colleague Mr Somerton over the years. Leave it with me; I'll come up with someone and email you details within the hour.'

Geoff Crowne knew exactly who he was going to put forward; an old friend who he knew wouldn't be interested in a southern constituency but would value the canvassing experience involved. And, of course, doing the Prime Minister a favour might bring its own rewards in a future Cabinet re-shuffle.

Within two hours Sir Isaac had received an email offering up a candidate; one Will Wakehurst, born in Hull and currently resident in Sunderland, primary school teacher, married, no children, mountain climbing listed as his only hobby. *Couldn't be better, thank you Prime Minister. We'll explain in the ballot circular that Wakehurst was put forward at the last minute by the Party's Central Office following Marsh's withdrawal. It should be a landslide victory for Somerton. It won't look good if we don't interview Wakehurst though and time is short; alas I think we'll have to resort to technology and set up an on-line meeting.*

Meyer canvassed his committee members and with Wakehurst's co-operation the on-line interview duly took place later that evening.

Saturday morning

'Good morning, Jack.'

'Good morning, Sir Isaac, what can I do for you?'

'Let's drop the Sir stuff for a start, we're going to be working with each other for the foreseeable future. I'm just calling with an update on the situation. Ballot papers will go out to Party members tonight. Central Office have put forward another candidate but he's not local and as such won't attract much support. What I want from you by midday is the final version of your election leaflet. Make sure it encompasses anything you gleaned from your interview yesterday. What you come up with is entirely up to you.'

'Gosh, that doesn't give me much time.'

'It's all the time you're going to get. Your opposition is a Mr Will Wakehurst if you're interested.'

'I think I'll pass on further discussion and get on with preparing my campaign pitch.'

'Keep it short and simple, that's the only advice I'm going to give you.'

Somerton scratched his head, preparing an election ballot leaflet wasn't top of his skills list. *You must have seen dozens in the past, but in truth never gave them much attention.* He clicked his fingers. *I know someone who can help.*

'Jess, how's my favourite lady in all the world?'

Jess Tate smiled. 'Good morning, Jack, lovely to hear from you. Now what is it you want from me?'

'I won't flannel Jess, I badly need your expertise. As you know I want to win Colin's old seat and I'm in the process of trying to win local support. I need to prepare a canvassing leaflet and thought you could help. I presume Colin prepared some of these in the past?'

'A long time ago, Jack. He delegated that kind of thing to his constituency office.'

Somerton frowned. 'Of course, problem for me is I can't really call on that until I win the ballot. It's a bit chicken and eggish. I'm not sure where to go from here, I guess I'll have to cobble something up.'

'Leave it with me Jack, I'm sure I can sort out something for you.'

'Bless you Jess, it has to be with the constituency chairman by noon.'

'Bloody hell, that doesn't give me much time.'

'Sorry Jess, I don't have an option.'

'This is going to cost you a five-star Michelin dinner.'

'Pull it off and you can have one a month for the rest of the year.'

Tate laughed out loud. 'I might just hold you to that if my waistline can stand the strain. I'd better get on with it; fortunately, Alan's out for the morning.'

Somerton was on edge all morning, watching the clock and his computer monitor; becoming increasingly anxious with less than an hour to go. He breathed a huge sigh of relief when an email from Jess hit his screen. He read and re-read its contents, his spirits lifting. *Jess you're a gem, I think this candidate would win my vote.*

Ten minutes later Jess rang. 'Well, what do you think of it, Jack? It's the best I can come up with in the time available.'

'It's perfect, how did you manage?'

'It wasn't as difficult as I thought. I have access to Central Office files. All the canvassing leaflets are held in an on-line library, as are local committee meeting minutes and of course briefing notes sent to Colin about local matters. You can play about with it and put your stamp on it. I won't keep you talking but I will expect that dinner invite very soon.'

'You're a life-saver Jess; please give serious thought to being my PA. I'll be in touch soon about that dinner date.'

Somerton spent the next ten minutes tweaking Jess's draft then emailed it to Meyer, ten minutes short of the deadline.

Saturday afternoon.

Around 2pm, Somerton received a call from Sir Isaac giving his seal of approval and confirming that the ballot papers would go out that evening. He also suggested that Somerton gave a thought to raising his profile in the constituency.

There was only one person he could turn to for advice, Alan Croudace.

'Hi Alan, I need your advice, about what Sir Isaac calls "raising my profile in the constituency" and if the ballot goes my way, canvassing for election.'

'Well, he's absolutely right and the obvious routes are local newspaper and local TV interviews. Offer yourself up for those. As for canvassing we have specialists in Central Office who will advise you on that and will probably be in touch when the local ballot results are confirmed. When electioneering does start, you'll be dropping leaflets, visiting local interest groups, and standing in shopping malls etc. You'll be led through the process by our experts; they will produce a programme for you. We'll get some Party heavyweights to accompany you, I for one, Laura Taylor would be good and maybe Ken Ogilvie.'

'Phew, thank goodness for that; I'm feeling out of my depth, Alan.'

'Not a confession I ever thought I'd hear from Jack Somerton; you are doing fine, believe me. Now a routine question, anything from Jupiter?'

'Not a dicky bird, Alan; I will tell you if he gets in touch, I assure you. And what about your successor, any news on that front?'

'Not settled yet, but support for Laura Taylor is growing. Are you all set for tomorrow?'

Somerton knew he was referring to MacKinnon's funeral. 'I'm as ready as I'll ever be; uniform laid out, speech prepared, medals polished. I'm not looking forward to it. It's a black day I want over and done with.'

'I know how you feel; I wish I could wear my uniform, but as Prime Minister, I don't think it would be right. I'm not looking forward to the occasion either but it's an opportunity to make a fitting tribute to Colin and what he stood for. See you there, Jack, bye for now.'

CHAPTER 12

Colin MacKinnon's funeral. Sunday

Somerton awoke shortly after 6am; the funeral procession was scheduled to begin at 9.30am. As tradition dictated, the Duke of Norfolk, the Earl Marshall, was responsible for organising the event, the first State funeral since Winston Churchill in 1965. Members from the Houses of Lords and Commons who were invited would leave from the House, the Royals from Buckingham Palace, all carefully co-ordinated to arrive in order of seniority, Her Majesty last of all. The coffin would be borne on a gun carriage as befits a soldier.

The weather was kind; mild and sunny, with only an occasional small white cloud flitting across the blue sky. The route was lined by the public, the approaches to Westminster Abbey a solid mass of people wanting to pay their respects. For all its numbers the crowd was quiet, the mood sombre as people reflected on MacKinnon's career and untimely death. Heads bowed as the gun carriage passed, the hitherto silent crowd clapped in homage.

The Abbey was full, every seat taken; every corner occupied by standing groups. Giant television screens had been installed in parks and squares in the Capital and in other cities throughout the land for those who wanted to watch outdoors and share their grief with others. Record viewing figures would subsequently emerge for those indoors.

Practically every Head of State in the world was in attendance; such was the universal respect for MacKinnon. Those countries regarded as persona non grata, such as Russia, North Korea, Iran and a few African dictatorships were not invited. Somerton was seated in the front row, primarily because he would be making a verbal tribute.

The congregation rose as the Archbishops of Canterbury and Westminster led the SAS coffin bearers and Royals down the aisle, bowing their heads as the entourage passed. For a brief second Somerton caught Chloe MacKinnon's eye and saw the tears glistening then migrating down her cheeks. Dressed in black, as were the rest of the MacKinnon family, she and Abbi, her daughter emanated sadness and grief. Abbi still used a cane to help her stand; Somerton felt guilt envelope him, there was nothing he could do to banish it. He felt ashamed, Colin, Abbi, direct consequences of his actions, he alone was responsible.

The two Archbishops led the service and leaders of other religions made their contribution followed by a touching eulogy delivered by Alan Croudace. It was then the turn of Colin's granddaughter Maggie and grandson Murray to make their shared tribute, a moving mixture of joy, sadness and thanks for their grandfather. And finally, it was Somerton's turn to take centre stage; attired in full military uniform, he chose not to climb the short set of steps to the pulpit, opting instead to stand alongside his ex-comrade's coffin. Apprehension filled him and he feared words would catch in his throat; his eyes moistened as he began to deliver his final farewell.

Colin MacKinnon was my comrade-in-arms, a brave soldier. He was my colleague, my mentor, my Prime Minister but above all, he was my friend. In my eyes he was the greatest Prime Minister the United Kingdom has ever had.

He never shied away from making tough decisions whether on the battlefield or in the Palace of Westminster, and always in the best interest of this country he loved so much.

He never sought popularity, but never failed to gain it; the world is a poorer place without Colin MacKinnon. His loss has left a shadow on the heart of all those who knew him, most of all his beloved Chloe and his family. His loss is immeasurable, we will never see his like again.

Somerton placed his hand on the coffin before going on. *Colin, I will miss you till the end of my days. Tonight, I will look to the stars, as Constellation MacKinnon is launched and know, that somewhere in the sky above, your star will shine brightest of all.*

Colin, I salute you.

With that he turned and made his way back to his seat. Once again, his eyes were drawn to Chloe. Was it by chance? Was he seeking approval or just trying to imagine a forgiveness she could never confer? He wasn't sure. He felt his heart lift when she gave a wan smile and gentle nod.

The Service was ended by prayers from both Archbishops, the coffin raised by the SAS bearers and carried to the gun carriage, and then drawn by a military vehicle to Golder's Green crematoria. Only family, Croudace, Somerton and the SAS team had been invited to attend. An Army Chaplain said a prayer, Maggie and Murray, MacKinnon's grandchildren, each read a short poem, and finally the most moving tribute, the sounding of the Last Post by an army bugler as the coffin passed behind the purple velvet curtains.

The service complete, Croudace and Somerton joined the MacKinnon family to say their goodbyes. There was to be no reception; Chloe wanted the day to end with the Last Post.

'I still can't believe he's gone, Chloe.' Somerton was ill at ease, and had considering leaving, but felt he had to stay for a few minutes. 'The nation will never know his like again.'

'Thank you, Jack. Your words, and Alan's, brought some comfort to me and the family. You both knew Colin better than anyone; he would have valued what you said.'

Somerton nodded glumly. 'Might I ask what will happen to Colin's ashes?'

To his surprise Chloe smiled. 'We're having a piece of jewellery made for each of us. We will carry a bit of him with us wherever we go. The ashes that remain will be divided, half will be sprinkled in the Thames from the House and the remainder in Parliament Square Garden near Sir Winston's statue.'

'Was that something he requested?'

Chloe shook her head. 'No, he never spoke of death or what was to happen after he died; we as a family decided on the arrangements.'

'And what are your plans, Chloe?' Alan Croudace asked, his voice soft, concern showing in his expression.

'We're jumping ship, Alan. We are all heading off to the States for a year, maybe more, depending on how things go. We want to close the door on all that has happened in the past year, Abbi losing David, then Colin; it's left very deep scars. There are too many reminders for us over here; maybe a complete change will help the healing process. As you can see, Abbi is walking with a cane and that'll go soon, physically at least, she is getting back to something like her old self. As for the children, I'm hoping that the States will introduce a whole gambit of new dimensions to their lives.'

'I'm sure it will; it's a very different lifestyle over there. Where will you be staying?'

'We'll start off in Boston and after a spell there, maybe move to Washington; my Kennedy connections have put a house in Boston at my disposal. Similarly, when and if we choose to move to Washington, another awaits me. Both are small by their standards but, by ours, they are akin to a small stately manor house. And of course, there is the whole of the USA to see; we are all looking forward to getting away.'

'Sounds wonderful, Chloe. I wish you all every happiness. Hopefully you will return to the UK, but if not it's our loss, their gain.'

'Thank you, Alan. If you are ever over our way, please come and visit; that applies to you too Jack. Our door will always be open to both of you; and if you've got wives, or girlfriends, the invite applies equally to them.'

Somerton nodded, but the longer they talked, the guiltier he felt. It was time to go. 'Chloe, I'm sorry but I really must take my leave; it's a busy time for me.'

'Oh, of course, you've got an election coming up. Make sure you win, Jack, and good luck with your political career. Who dares wins, as Colin often reminded me. Right?'

'Who dares wins, Chloe.' Somerton took a few minutes more to say his goodbyes to Abbi and the kids then set off to his car.

Croudace also took his opportunity. 'I'll be on my way too, Chloe; let you get home and recover from the day.'

'Not long till you step down, is it? Strange to think about the three of you. Colin gone, you resigning, and now Jack seeking election; all change.' She shook her head sadly, her eyes filling with tears. 'Colin was very proud of you both, please don't forget to keep in touch.'

Croudace caught up with Somerton just as he was getting into one of the pool cars. 'Mind if we share a car?'

Somerton shrugged, 'Be my guest, though your security people won't like it.'

Croudace waved a hand dismissively. 'They can follow us. Are you all set for the election campaign?'

'Not quite, Alan, there's the little matter of the constituency ballot.'

Croudace waved his hand dismissively. 'A foregone conclusion.'

Somerton nodded. 'We'll see, I'm not tempting Fate. I am preparing though; I've drafted out a few speeches, formulated responses to a range of questions and brushed up on Party policies. Your advisers are joining me tomorrow to design my campaign, so I'll be in their hands.'

Croudace smiled. Take their advice, Jack, though you might not always agree with it; they're good at their job, I assure you. But, whatever else, be yourself, just as you have been all the years I've known you.'

Somerton laughed. 'I don't know about that; you and Colin have left your marks on me over the years. You've smoothed away some of the rough edges, I'm more accommodating than I used to be. I've almost accepted that I don't always know best. Well, at least not all of the time.'

Croudace laughed out loud. 'Somehow, I just can't bring myself to believe Jack Somerton has changed all that much.'

'What about you, Alan? How much longer will you be around?'

'I intend to step down the day after you take your seat in the House.'

'Any chance I could persuade you to stay?'

'Nope. It's too late anyway, the process of electing my replacement is under way.'

'And the winner is…..?'

'I honestly don't know, it's too close to call. It's entirely down to Members, I've got a single vote like everyone else. Any plans for tonight?'

'Nothing planned, except I will watch the satellite launch. After that I'll probably have an early night, unless there's something gripping on TV. And you, Alan, any plans? You're looking a bit weary if you don't mind me saying so?'

Croudace shook his head. 'No plans, I didn't even bring home any official papers to read. Like you, I'll watch the launch and then it's straight to bed.'

CHAPTER 13

As expected, Somerton romped home in the ballot to choose the Harrow East by-election candidate. His sole competitor, Will Wakehurst, secured less than five per cent of the votes cast. Sir Isaac wished Somerton well and promised to render him every assistance during the election campaign.

That's the easy bit done and dusted Jack; now for the main course.

Gibraltar Heights

The day following the funeral Somerton met with his campaign advisors, Ben Morrison and Alice Jansen, to agree an outline for the campaign programme. Croudace had phoned to tell him that they were the best available and, although their surnames differed, they were in fact husband and wife.

The couple arrived at 11am as arranged, introduced themselves, and got down to business immediately. Alice began the proceedings. 'We're here to help you put your campaign together and act as a link to Central Office. I warn you now, there will be times when effectively we will appear to be running the show and, in general, that's how it's got to be. I hope that sits well with you Mr Somerton?'

Jansen, a petite, slim, brunette searched Somerton's face for reaction; Morrison a lanky six-footer with a mop of unruly hair looked on without comment.

Somerton nodded. 'You're the experts, I'm new to this game, so lead on.'

Jansen shook her head, 'It's not a game Mr Somerton, electioneering is a serious business.'

Somerton hid his mild irritation. 'Whatever you say Alice, I'm not a wordsmith. We'll start by you calling me Jack. I suggest we move into the lounge; make yourself comfortable whilst I make us a cuppa. I assume you'll prefer coffee?'

Settled and munching on a biscuit Somerton referenced back to their earlier conversation. 'I'm reliant on your guidance but I need some clarification regarding your comment about 'running the show'. That's not altogether what I envisaged and wonder if you could expand further?'

Morrison nodded, 'I understand where you're coming from, but our aim is to ensure that your time is utilised to maximum effect and this involves negotiating time slots on TV and radio, and at events like local football matches, school competitions, shop openings and the like. We have to match up your commitments with the availability of the PM, Ken Ogilvie and Laura Taylor, all of whom have promised to accompany you on occasion. It's impractical for you to make the range of appointments involved so with all that in mind, it will appear that we are running the show and telling you what to do, and when to do it.'

Somerton scratched his head. 'When you spell it out like that, it makes good sense. Let's get started.' To his surprise, Jansen produced a calendar for the next six weeks showing his commitments to date. Somerton was taken aback at just how many slots were filled. 'Gosh, I'm impressed. You have been busy, thank you.'

Morrison smiled. 'You probably didn't give it a second thought but you made a very good impression with your tribute at Colin's funeral. You're ex-SAS and you're the National Security Advisor; all in sundry want a bit of you, Jack. You're in demand whether you realise it or not.'

Jansen cut in, 'Added to your engagements we will want a daily face-to-face session with you to provide feedback and brief you on any policy matters Central Office want you to headline in the course of the campaign. We will also be keeping tabs on what Her Majesty's Opposition has to say and giving you advice on how to respond.'

Somerton blinked, 'Christ, there's a lot more to be considered than I thought. I have prepared a number of speeches, my manifesto if I can refer to it as such; in effect what I hope to do for Harrow East.'

Jansen tutted and smiled, her tone verging on condescending. 'Best let us have a copy of any set pieces you have in mind; we'll check them out and give you some feedback. You haven't had a chance to study the programme yet, but your first engagement is tomorrow afternoon on local radio, followed in the evening by a slot on local TV. I'm afraid you aren't going to have much free time from now on.'

Somerton shook his head, 'I'm nearly speechless; I don't suppose you've got a list of what I should wear, perhaps my hair style or colouring?'

Morrison smiled. 'As it happens no. We've looked at lots of photos and we're happy with what we've seen; in fact, you're very photogenic. Don't be dismissive about appearance, some very famous politicians, including Prime Ministers have had voice coaching, choices of apparel and hair styling.'

Somerton was about to come out with a sarcastic rejoinder but let the urge subside. 'I guess I'll just have to get used to being a bit of a pawn for the next six weeks, but I must say it does seem to be a very intense campaign for what's supposed to be a safe Conservative seat.'

Jansen nodded. 'All true, but no seat is 100% safe and you're going to attract a lot of public interest as Colin's successor. Here in Harrow East, you'll be seen to be representing the Party nationwide. The media will pour over your every word, believe me.'

Somerton threw up his hands. 'Now you are beginning to worry me.'

Morrison laughed heartily. 'We are laying it on a bit thick; don't worry, I'm confident you'll win the seat, but we want you to win by a big margin.'

'Yeah, me too.' Somerton desperately wanted to do as well as Colin. *Make a mental note to tell Jupiter what result you're looking for, Jack.*

Jansen took over again, 'Unless there's anything else, that's all we have for now. Take a good look at the programme, raise anything you're not sure about and don't forget to email us those speeches. We'll meet again tomorrow at the Constituency office if that's OK with you? Shall we say 11am?'

Somerton acquiesced and with that the duo departed.

By-Election Campaign

Much to his surprise, by the end of the campaign Somerton felt drained; it had been a gruelling experience with its early starts, late finishes, never ending walkabouts, with and without leaflet drops, hundreds of handshakes, conversations, good lucks and thank-yous. His physical fitness had served him well, but it was the mental drain that proved most tiring. Constantly having to be pleasant, feigning interest and enthusiasm, dragging up a constant façade of cheerfulness and positivity. Being Mr. Nice all the time wasn't his strong suit. The set piece speechmaking sessions had been his favourite experiences, particularly when the occasional heckler had surfaced. The enemy had shown its face and had to be shot down; Somerton the soldier was in his element. The same competitive feelings readily surfaced in chaired debates with his opponents, the candidates representing six minor Parties; he felt he had come out on top every time. It might have been a different story if the heavyweights had been involved but, out of respect for MacKinnon, the Labour and Liberal Parties hadn't stood for election.

Alan Croudace, Ken Ogilvie and Laura Taylor had all played their part and accompanied him on one walkabout each; those outings had predictably generated more interest. It wasn't often the Prime Minister, the Chancellor of Exchequer and an aspiring Prime Minister paid a visit, phone camera selfies had been in great demand. It was clear to Somerton that Ogilvie and Taylor were keeping themselves to the fore, both claiming any bit of limelight in their quest to be Great Britain's next Prime Minister.

There were two notable events during the six-week campaign.

Jupiter

Somerton had contacted Jupiter mid-way through the second week, a day or so following completion of the first phase of the launch of Constellation MacKinnon. He had managed to persuade Croudace to allow twenty-eight of the fifty-two satellites to be launched, thereby maintaining the pattern of four per day. Every launch had gone well, every satellite was in place.

'Jack, this is a pleasant surprise, I've been following your campaign and know how busy you are. Is there something I can help you with?'

'I've got three topics on my agenda, plus of course anything you might like to raise.' *My, my, aren't we being nice to each other. I know what I want, I wonder what you're after Jupiter?* 'First up, as far as I am aware, Alan believes you've done a runner, but he still has thoughts about breaking into your laboratory area. I know you listen in on all sorts of conversations, and wondered if you had heard anything to suggest he might be making any plans to take access?'

'Not a whisper and it would result in researcher deaths and massive damage to the NRSC if he did. I confess that I've set up a number of highly explosive boobytraps; if triggered the outcome would be catastrophic.'

'Let's hope it doesn't come to that; you might blow me up and lose an ally. Second topic, we've launched twenty-eight satellites; what happens now?'

Jupiter raised a querying eyebrow, 'I assume you want to know about their current capability? Firstly, the telephone and broadband element is under the control of your NRSC research staff, and they are in the process of adapting telephone exchanges, masts etc. to the new system. And doing it very competently, I would add. You'll have to ask them for details. Similarly, they are progressing the straightforward photographic surveillance capability.'

Jupiter smiled. 'And now, regarding the area I think you are really interested in, the advanced surveillance and intervention systems. I am dealing with configuration but until all the satellites are in place it will only operate at around 30% of its capability. You need to complete the constellation as soon as possible if you want it to operate to maximum effect.'

Somerton nodded, 'I understand that but I'm afraid I can do nothing about that until Alan Croudace stands down and his successor is in place.'

'Laura Taylor is likely to be your next Prime Minister is she not?

'She's favourite, but not guaranteed.'

Jupiter smiled. 'She is almost certain to succeed. And your third topic, Jack?'

'A selfish one I'm afraid, winning the by-election.'

'You're certain to win Jack, it's a safe Conservative haven.'

'Maybe, but I want to win well. I want to win by the same margin Colin did. I want to gain the same percentage of votes he did, more if possible.'

'Tut, tut, Jack. You're asking me to rig the voting system.'

'That's exactly what I want. Colin got around 71.8% of the votes cast and I want to improve on that especially with Labour and the Liberals not contesting.'

'Of course. I'll ensure that happens, Jack. Is there anything else?'

Somerton shook his head. 'Not for the moment, but next time we converse I want to discuss world security, in particular the threat posed by North Korea, Iran, Russia and China.'

Jupiter smiled, 'The West's bogey men. I'll be happy to share what I know, but in the immediate future it's Russia you have to worry about.'

Before Somerton could asked for clarification, the screen went blank.

Bollocks, I guess I should be used to you by now,

Laura Taylor

The campaign walkabout with Laura Taylor had been an eye-opener. Not the electioneering aspect, which had been routine, it was the meeting afterwards that had created an impression. At her suggestion they had gone for dinner to a small Thai restaurant away from the main thoroughfares. After the usual get-to-know-each other questions she had questioned him extensively about national and international security and threats. She had seemed genuinely concerned, particularly about North Korea and Russia who she felt were totally untrustworthy. North Korea because its President wanted a place on the world stage and tried desperately to punch above his weight. Russia, she felt, because its President wanted to rebuild the United Soviet Socialist Republic and return it to its Stalin days. Its weapon stockpiles were being steadily increased and rivalled the combined firepower of NATO. He could recall her words. *'We have to strengthen our defence capability, Jack. We can't be totally reliant on the United States; they've carried the burden of Western defence for far too long.'*

Somerton had sought to re-assure her about the West's capability but agreed that defence investment should be increased. *I wonder what your view would be Laura if you knew the full capability of the MacKinnon constellation.* He had thanked her for giving up her time to support his campaign and said how much he looked forward to working with her. She had reciprocated and much to his surprise had added. 'You never know, Jack. If I'm lucky enough to become our next Prime Minister, I might just have a job for you.'

Election night.

The result of the by-election was announced shortly after 11pm with Somerton gaining 91% of the votes cast; none of the other six candidates saved their election deposit of £500. Disappointingly, the voter turnout was low at 42.1%, though fairly typical for a by-election.

Somerton made a short speech thanking the Returning Officer, his opponents, his supporters for all they had done to get him elected. He said he could never hope to fill Colin MacKinnon's shoes but promised he would represent the people of Harrow East to the best of his ability, whatever their political persuasion. The gathering dispersed over the course of the next hour; he had declined a celebratory party given the circumstances leading to the by-election.

By 11.30pm he was back in Gibraltar Heights, reflecting on the campaign and planning the way ahead, a glass of malt whisky in hand. His answerphone was flashing with a score of congratulatory messages, including those from Alan Croudace, Laura Taylor and, touchingly, from Chloe MacKinnon.

CHAPTER 14

'I, Jack Somerton, do swear that I will be faithful and bear true allegiance to Her Majesty Queen Elizabeth, and her heirs and successors according to law, so help me God.'

Somerton's voice rang out with pride; he truly believed in what he was averring, he was now a Member of Parliament. He stood with his right hand raised, having declined to take the oath on the Bible. His two supporters, as required by MPs elected via a by-election, were Alan Croudace and Laura Taylor. The Speaker had generously given him a slot on the Monday following the election and had also invited him to make his maiden speech immediately following his oath.

Somerton made his way to the back benches, sat down, and was immediately called by the Speaker to deliver his speech. He began, as tradition expected, with a fulsome tribute to his predecessor, regularly accompanied by outbursts of approval on all sides of the House. He went on to praise his constituency, Harrow East, with some notable facts drawn from past and present. Concluding his speech, he made a plea for the Government to strengthen the UK's defence and international security capabilities citing Russia, North Korea and Iran as countries that presented the highest risks to western democracies. He noticed that Laura Taylor turned her head and gave him her full attention when he raised the issue of defence capability.

He remained in the Commons for the rest of the session, leaving towards 10pm having met MPs of all persuasions, an experience oft repeated over the course of the week. Somerton established a routine; rise early and head for the NRSC to check out the latest security alerts, then go on to the Commons for the day's sessions. He agreed with Sir Isaac to attend a morning constituency clinic on Saturday or Sunday morning, both if there were urgent matters requiring attention. His intention was to carry out this pattern for the first month then review. He knew these arrangements weren't sustainable; his security responsibilities would not receive the attention they required. Additionally, he needed time to research and prioritise the assignments he had in mind for Jupiter.

Alan Croudace formally offered his resignation to the Queen, and as expected, Laura Taylor was chosen by her colleagues to be the UK's second female Prime Minister. On his final day as Prime Minister, Croudace asked Somerton to accompany him to his office.

'Grab a seat, Jack. How about a whisky to wish me farewell?'

'Sounds good to me, provided you have a malt worthy of the occasion.'

Croudace nodded, 'St Magdaline, Jack, your favourite.' He skipped over to a wall cabinet and returned with the whisky and two glasses, smiling as he poured. Somerton looked on sadly. *The end of an era, the SAS trio confined to history. Don't get maudlin, Jack, the friendship will go on.*

'Why not ask Jess to join us, Alan?'

Croudace shook his head. 'She's not here. She was a bit upset this morning and I told her to go home early.'

Somerton nodded, 'Understandable really; she loses Colin and now you, two big gaps in her life in a short space of time. Has she told you I'd like her to be my PA, either here or in the constituency?'

'No, she hasn't but it's a good idea; she's spoken of retiring but it would be a shame to lose her. Look after her if she decides to stay.

'Goes without saying, she's the best and she'll get the best I can offer.'

Croudace smiled, 'And how are you adapting to life as an MP? Early days, I know.'

Somerton shrugged, 'It's been OK, and I'm resigned to the fact that it will take time for me to get involved in anything meaningful, just as it was when I was working with you and Colin.'

'You might get an offer, sooner than you think.' Croudace winked.

Somerton raised an eyebrow, 'Don't be mysterious, spell it out.'

Croudace shook his head. 'Ignore me. Nothing is certain in politics, but I can say that Laura thinks highly of you. By the way, I am to be knighted and offered a seat in the Lords.'

Somerton put his hands to his head, 'Oh my God, the other place. Only kidding, Alan, that's great news and well deserved, congratulations. You'll be a welcome addition; there's not many of your quality in there. I hope I get an invite to the investiture.'

Croudace raised his glass, 'Let's drink to both of us. Who dares wins.'

Somerton clinked his glass, 'Who dares wins.'

For the next hour or so the two ex-SAS colleagues chatted about times gone by before going their separate ways.

Parliament, the following week

Laura Taylor settled quickly into her new role and on her first day in post made it clear she was taking the reins of power by making changes to the Cabinet. The current Secretaries of State retained their existing departments, but numerous changes were made to other ministerial cabinet roles and at less senior levels. Roles were combined, deadwood was removed, and new faces emerged as Laura rewarded her supporters.

Somerton listened to comments made on the changes but offered no opinions, in the main because he didn't know the personalities involved terribly well. He did want to discuss his National Security Advisor role with Laura Taylor, to whom he reported by default; his accountability hadn't been formalised when Croudace vacated the Foreign Office and became Prime Minister. Somerton wanted clarity and at his request Jess arranged an appointment with Taylor and was offered a slot at 10am the following morning.

Downing Street, next day.

Timely as ever, Somerton stepped through the door of No10 a few minutes early, and was pleased to be greeted by Jess Tate. 'Good morning, Jack, good to see you.'

'And you Jess, your first day under new management.'

'We did a bit of setting up work last week; Laura's fine, I like her, but I've not decided on my future yet. I still might decide to take you up on your offer.'

'OK Jess, I'll keep the job open until you come to a decision.'

Their conversation was interrupted when the intercom buzzed.

'That's for you, Jack; you can go in.'

Taylor lounged back in her chair appraising Somerton as he made his entrance. 'You ooze confidence, Jack; SAS is written all over you. Take a seat and listen up. I haven't got time for small talk today, every line in my diary is full.'

Somerton sat down and waited for her to go on, his face impassive.

'You are currently National Security Advisor and I want you to retain that role, but you'll have a new title, Minister for Homeland Security. You'll report directly to me but liaise closely with the Foreign Office and the Home Office. You will attend cabinet meetings. You'll be advised of your new salary in due course; give thought to what support you need. How does that appeal to you?'

Somerton stifled his surprise, 'Thank you very much, Prime Minister. I have to say that this is an unexpected honour.' *Don't lay it on too thick, Jack.*

'I did sound out Alan and he thought it was a good idea, though he did warn me you were a bit of a loose cannon, and I should keep a close eye on you.' Her eyes held a twinkle that suggested she wasn't entirely serious.

Somerton smiled. 'I think in his position I would have given you the same advice. I hope he also told you that I get things done.'

Taylor smiled. 'That a quality that is well known. One other thing, I'm giving you control of Constellation MacKinnon. I didn't get a clear explanation from Alan as to why it hadn't been launched. I sensed he was unhappy about some aspects of it. What can you tell me?'

Christ, I'm being put in the hot sea. What do I tell her. His brain was in an instant whirl. Somerton sighed, 'Well, there **were** some technical issues and, frankly, the only way to sort them out was is to launch and commission. I'm bolder than Alan and wanted to get on with it; after much debate we agreed on a compromise; a partial launch rather than the whole fifty-two.'

Taylor pursed her lips. 'I still don't quite get it but, looking to the future, what happens next?'

Somerton was on the back foot again. *Say the issues had been resolved and then the remaining satellites would have to be launched, or, say they hadn't and be asked to define their nature and what was being done to put them right.* 'Commissioning isn't quite complete, and we have to be absolutely sure, to the best of our ability, that the systems can't be hacked. As things stand the system has passed every test but it's not yet working at full capacity.'

Taylor regarded Somerton quizzingly, 'So when will it be working at full capacity?'

Somerton stifled a gulp. 'By the end of this week provided all goes to plan.'

Taylor smiled, 'Good. And then we launch the remaining satellites?'

Shit, now what do I tell her? A flash of inspiration and plausible reply came to his lips 'We could do, but I think I have to make you aware of Alan's main concern, not a concern that I share by the way. He is very respectful of the scientific prowess of the NRSC and worries in case the researchers might be able to enhance the system's capability to levels we aren't aware of.'

Taylor frowned and didn't let up. 'Meaning what exactly, Jack? What the fuck are you not telling me?'

Somerton shrugged, 'I'm not an expert but it's conceivable that they could develop a system capable of not only of advanced surveillance, but enhanced powers we haven't envisaged hitherto.'

Taylor looked puzzled, 'So what's wrong with that? Surely that would add to the UK's security capability?'

'That's how I feel, but Alan is the ultimate diplomat and is worried that our allies might be miffed that we hadn't consulted them. Added to that he is concerned that our enemies might even consider it to be a threat to their security, perhaps even an act of aggression.'

Taylor nodded, 'Another case of Ronald Reagan's Star Wars system.'

Somerton nodded. 'A bit like that.'

'And how do you feel about it, Jack? As an ex-military man and somewhat less of a diplomat?'

The moment had come, Somerton had been backed into a corner. 'Personally, I would launch. I would seek to develop the system to its maximum. The bigger the stick we have, the more weight it carries. Our allies would benefit as much as we would, the world could become a safer place. There would be a flurry of grumps around the world but they'd soon get over it if we put a shared control mechanism in place with those we trusted.'

'So, what are we waiting for?'

Somerton smiled, 'Your go ahead, Prime Minister.'

'You have my authority. And do call me Laura. We will keep these concerns strictly to ourselves for the time being. One other thing has just occurred to me. I think I should add to your security portfolio and give you responsibility for the NRSC. You would be Minister for Research and Security with full Cabinet Minister status. How does that sound?'

Somerton was elated, gobsmacked even. 'Sounds great to me; does it bring a salary increase rise?' He grinned broadly to make it clear he was joking.

Taylor laughed, 'Fuck off, Jack, you've done well enough for one day. Don't waste any time; get those satellites in the sky and develop them to the maximum.'

Somerton stood and bowed, 'Your wish is my command, count it as done. I look forward to working with you.'

As he left the office Jess Tate was waiting for him. 'You're looking very pleased with yourself, Mr Somerton. Good news?'

'I'm your new Minister for Research and Security and more than ever I'm looking for a very good PA. See you around, Jess.'

It wasn't long before his appointment was announced; congratulations flooded in. Newspapers, Radio and TV reporters all sought interviews; the next few weeks were going to be busy. His new role was way beyond anything he could have wished for but his thoughts were in turmoil. *You need to sit down and carefully think through the way forward - aims, policies, NRSC, and Jupiter - you have work to do Jack. And don't forget your constituency, Jack; Sir Isaac will be barking at your heels. Then there was Alan Croudace and how he would react when he heard the whole system was to be launched.*

CHAPTER 15

NRSC Somerton's office.

'Reggie Marsh speaking, who's calling please?'

'Jack Somerton.'

'Oh, what do you want?' The voice adopted a slightly aggressive tone.

'I understand how you feel Reggie, but what's happened has happened. It's history as far as I am concerned. Circumstances placed us in opposition but for my part, there was never anything personal.'

Marsh took a deep breath and attempted to bury his antagonism. 'I guess so. So, what is it you want, Jack? I'm pretty busy trying to sort out a job for myself.'

An ideal opening, Somerton thought. 'Maybe I can help you there. You might have picked up that I'm now a cabinet minister with a portfolio of research and security. I report directly to the PM.'

Marsh interrupted, 'Yeah, I picked that up from the newspapers, congratulations. So why are you talking to me?'

'I'm looking for a Research Assistant and I wondered if you might be interested? As I said, I've got research and security on my plate but added to that I have Harrow East matters to look after.'

Marsh snorted, 'Sir Isaac wouldn't hear of it.'

'I decide who works for me, Reggie, not Sir Isaac. Are you interested or not? I don't know what the going rate for a researcher is, but you'll get the usual plus an annual bonus of five grand if you perform well. You would be based in the House but would also have to spend time in the NRSC if required. You wouldn't go anywhere near the constituency office in the immediate future but Harrow East would be a key part of your remit. So that's it. Are you interested or not?

Marsh genuinely wasn't sure what he thought of the offer. 'I need time to think it over.'

'Sure, take all the time you want but if I don't hear from you within the hour, I'll look elsewhere.'

'OK, Jack, thanks for the opportunity; if you don't hear from me by 10.30am, you'll know I'm not interested.'

Somerton was smiling. *That went well Jack, I do believe Reggie is going to take the job, in fact I think I'll give Sir Isaac a call and let him know the situation.*

'Hello, Isaac, it's Jack Somerton; I want to run something past you.'

'Fire away. Oh, before you do, congrats on your appointment to the Cabinet; that's a big feather in your cap given that you've only just arrived on the Westminster scene.'

'Thank you, Isaac, I'm very lucky, it's an important Ministry; our country's security and research are key to the UK's ongoing success.'

Meyer acquiesced. 'Vital, I agree. It's a huge responsibility. In fact, ever since I heard, I've been wondering how it would affect your constituency commitments? I wouldn't want Harrow East to suffer.'

Somerton relaxed; Meyer had fed him the perfect line. 'Well, I'd just remind you that Colin managed, and he was Prime Minister. I assure you I'm determined that Harrow East definitely won't lose out and that's essentially why I've phoned you. I'm planning on engaging Reggie Marsh as a Research Assistant. I believe he did his job well in the past. In view of the sensitivities involved, he wouldn't be based in the constituency. He knows a great deal about Harrow East and will help me steer the right course. I know you won't be enthusiastic, but we shouldn't let personal issues get in the way of making the right decision.'

Meyer sighed, 'I agree, he's got a lot of experience, and I can see he would be useful to you, especially in the early days.'

Somerton sensed the tone of the conversation was going his way. 'As I said he would be based at this end and, if the occasion arose when he had to visit the constituency, I would check with you to be absolutely certain Debbie wasn't around. What do you think?'

Meyer hesitated before replying. 'I'm not thrilled, Jack, but you've made a good case; let's give it a trial and see how it works out. Perhaps appoint him on three months' probation?'

Balloks to that suggestion but I'll stay sweet for now. 'Thank you, Isaac; your understanding is much appreciated. Anything happening locally, you want to run past me?'

'Not a thing, Jack. By the way, I'm looking for a replacement for Marsh, I need someone to man the constituency office; I'll let you know when I fill the vacancy.'

'Thank you, that's appreciated; see you around.

Somerton sat back in his office chair. *That went well, Jack. Now for the next piece in the puzzle.* He reached for his desk phone and buzzed Eric Barker, his Security Supervisor. 'Eric, if this is a good time could you come through, please.'

'On my way, Jack.'

A few minutes passed and there was a knock on the door; Barker entered looking tense and sounding nervous. 'Nothing wrong is there, Jack?'

'Not a thing, Eric. I want to offer you a new post here at the NRSC, Security Manager.'

Barker blinked. 'Gosh, what's brought this on?'

'First things first, are you interested? There's a rise of five grand a year in it for you.'

Barker nodded eagerly, his enthusiasm spilling out. 'Of course, I'm interested; I assume you're going on to explain what's involved?'

'It's quite simple. I'm now a cabinet minister and there will be increased demand on my time; I need to know that the operation here is in a safe pair of hands. I need someone who can sort the wheat from the chaff and keep me informed of any red security alerts, plus of course, any troublesome issues arising with the surveillance team. If you want it, the job is yours.'

Barker didn't hesitate, 'I'll take it; when do I start?'

'Good. Start now by drawing up a full job description and let me see it. Then we'll talk to Human Resources and get a contract in place, all the usual terms and conditions will apply.'

'Thanks, Jack, I'll get right onto it.'

'Thank you, Eric. Now off you go, I've got a lot on today.'

Somerton wandered through to his overnight accommodation and made himself a coffee before returning to his office to look through the latest security alerts. He was halfway through the pile of papers when his mobile buzzed. 'Somerton.'

'It's Reggie Marsh, I'd like to accept your offer.'

'Good, report to me here at the NRSC tomorrow morning, 9am, and we'll run through what I expect from you.'

'See you then. By the way, how do you want me to address you? Minister or Mr Somerton.'

'Haven't thought about it, we'll discuss tomorrow.'

Somerton smiled, *Minister, hmm, I like the sound of that. Two down one to go Jack, you need someone to run the research programme.*

Somerton went down the stairs leading from his office area to the concourse at the rear of the NRSC, then walked round to the front entrance where he entered his security code and made his way into the main corridor. Minutes later he stood outside Lizzie King's open office door. Professor King, as she was now, sat at her desk, staring intently at three monitors filled with a mass of figures and symbols.

Somerton knocked gently and she looked round, recognition and surprise registering in her expression. 'Mr Somerton, what brings you here?'

'Do you mind if I sit down?'

She waved a hand. 'Be my guest. I hear you're an MP now, congratulations.'

Somerton nodded, 'I'm a little more than an MP, I'm Minister with responsibility for Research and Security which is the reason I'm here.'

King gulped. 'Gosh, I am impressed, so what is it you want from me?'

'Quite simply, I need someone to produce and head up the national research programme. I'm creating a new post, National Research Director. I need someone to assess and co-ordinate research proposals, formulate an annual research programme, manage its implementation and control its budget. I'm here to offer you the job. You would co-ordinate your colleague researchers within the NRSC and advise me on priorities. You would also meet formally with me at least quarterly to review research development and progress. I think that the extra responsibility merits a salary increase of fifty thousand pounds per annum.'

King hesitated, giving some initial thought to the bombshell offer she had just received. 'Thank you, I'm flattered of course. The money side isn't what makes me tick but sounds OK. I can see the need for the role you have in mind and it interests me but, and it's a big but, I'm concerned about how it might impinge on my own personal research.'

Somerton nodded, 'I understand your concerns, but it would increase your influence in deciding which research should take priority for funding.'

'That sounds suspiciously like a bribe, Mr Somerton.'

'That's exactly as intended, Professor King.'

King pursed her lips. 'I'm just not sure. Can I have a week to think it over?'

Somerton shook his head. 'Sorry, no can do, I need to act quickly. You can have twenty-four hours then I'll offer the job to one of your colleagues.'

'How about forty-eight?'

'Sorry, Lizzie, Professor King, or however you want to be addressed, twenty-four hours is all you've got. If you decline my offer, I have another strong candidate in mind. I'm just plain Jack by the way.'

'And I'm plain Lizzie. I don't suppose you'll tell me who you have in mind?'

Somerton shook his head, 'It's one of your male colleagues. Twenty-four hours, take it or leave it, Lizzie. I'll wait to hear from you one way or another. I'll go now and leave you in peace. Oh, by the way Lizzie, nobody could possibly describe you as plain.' Somerton smiled and winked and made his exit.

Somerton returned to his office the way he had come. *50-50 Jack, that's the best odds you can give that little session. Academics aren't so easy to push around. And just who is the alternative male candidate you baited Lizzie King with? You'll need to have someone in mind if she declines.*

Somerton started up his desktop and entered his twelve-digit access code, a mixture of numbers, letters, and symbols. A couple of minutes elapsed before Jupiter appeared on the screen dressed in his usual jumpsuit.

'Good morning, Jupiter. I trust all is going well with you?'

'All is well, Jack or should I say Minister? May I offer my congratulations and enquire as to why you sound so affable?

'Thank you. I'm being nice because I want to tap into that universe-sized brain of yours.'

'Tell me what you want to know, and I'll do my best to be of assistance; I want something from you as it happens.'

Somerton was curious but on his guard. *Jupiter wants something, please God, not young women again. I wonder if he listened in on my conversation with the PM.* 'You go first, what is it you want from me?'

Jupiter smiled, 'Quite simply, when do you intend to launch the remaining twenty-four satellites?'

Hmm, I wonder if he knows the PM has given me the authority to determine the launch dates. 'I'm working on it; you'll be the first to know when a decision is made. Alan Croudace has been offered a seat in the Lords, so he'll still be aware of all that's going on in Government. He has accepted my word that you're no longer on the scene, so the outlook is favourable, but not yet. Now to my question, is the system ready for use? I don't mean the communications side of things, the NRSC has told me that the telephone and broadband facilities are being incrementally commissioned. In just a few weeks the UK will have 100% coverage and the fastest broadband in the world, thanks to you. May interest today relates to the defence and surveillance systems.'

Jupiter smiled broadly, 'I have commissioned the twenty-eight satellites already in orbit but, without the remaining twenty-four the constellation's scope is severely limited. We need them all in operation before we can deal with multiple targets accurately and simultaneously.'

Somerton looked thoughtful, 'What I have in mind is a series of simple targets to get a better feel for capability; you could call them, demonstration projects.'

Jupiter nodded approvingly. 'That's encouraging, we're not too far apart in our thinking, Jack. When you identify your targets, we can proceed immediately. But do bear in mind the basic principle; the more satellites we have at our disposal the greater the defence and deterrent capability we have. You might want to double the size of the constellation in due course.'

It was Somerton's turn to smile, 'This camaraderie between us takes some getting used to; I'm not complaining by the way. Have you got the time to give me a more detailed insight as to what the system can do?'

'Sit back, Jack, and be ready to take notes.'

Forty-five minutes of questions and answers ensued, at the end of which Somerton's brain was alive with possibilities, but caution was also in attendance. *The more I learn, the more I can understand Alan's concerns. I wish Jupiter's finger wasn't the only one on the trigger. In the wrong hands…God, I don't want think about the possibilities.* 'Thanks Jupiter, that was very helpful. Sorry but I must go now; the Commons awaits me. I'll be in touch with my proposals shortly, I promise.'

Jupiter in his usual manner blanked the screen.

Somerton's smile grew ever broader as he reviewed his notes. *This is pure science fiction.*

Meanwhile Jupiter had a call of his own to make. 'I've just had a long session with Somerton; he's briefed Taylor and got the go ahead to complete the satellite launch, he's champing at the bit. I'm confident I'll be getting back to you with a plan of action very soon.'

CHAPTER 16

NRSC Next day

Somerton rose to greet Marsh when Eric Barker showed him into the office at 9am as arranged. First impressions were that he looked even younger and taller than his photos suggested. 'Grab a pew, Reggie. Thanks for being on time; punctuality ranks high in my book. Are you still up for the job?'

Marsh nodded. 'That's why I'm here, Jack.'

'Let's clear the air, I'm not interested in your love life or your family. Fate put us in competition, you lost. Business-wise, everything I've heard about you is positive. If you deliver on what I ask of you, you'll go to the top of the scale. Any questions, comments so far?'

'Easy one first Jack. I'd like to be a Senior Research Assistant.'

Somerton shrugged, 'Noted, I'm relaxed about titles.'

Marsh didn't let go, 'Agreed then?'

Somerton shook his head. 'Noted for the moment. Let's see if you're happy with what's expected of you. First up, you'll be my link man to the constituency; you'll organise polls, my clinics there, investigate complaints and draught letters for my signature setting out how they are being dealt with.'

'That's exactly what I did for Colin, so no problem there.'

'That's as I expected,' Somerton responded. 'Then I want you to do the kind of things you would have been on the lookout for if you were in my shoes. I'm thinking of how Government policy is going down in the constituency, what gaps are there in policies, legislation etc, that kind of stuff. You'll watch out for opportunities for me to step into the limelight with the right influencers. I'm not looking for money, backhanders or benefits of any kind, and nor will you. In essence you'll be my guide and advisor. We can both build our reputations if we work well together. I recognise that you will want your own patch, sooner rather than later, and I'll help all I can in that connection, provided you meet my expectations. I reckon you'll need help with that lot, so you can recruit your partner, Tricia Wilson, to be your assistant. She can work from home if that suits, same salary as now. Both of you will stay away from the constituency office for the foreseeable future, unless it proves absolutely necessary. And given your background, no shagging around in my time or on work premises. Learn a lesson from your recent experience; if I catch you at it, I'll cut your dick off.'

Marsh bridled for a second but something in Somerton's stare made him back off and he just nodded.

'Last on my agenda, get to know Eric Barker, the guy who showed you in, he's my newly designated Security Manager; learn what you can about global security, it'll stand you in good stead for the future.'

Marsh's eyes lit up, 'I'd really like that.'

'Finally, we'll meet formally once a week, Wednesdays 9am, when you'll give me a formal briefing. Needless to say, if anything urgent crops up, contact me, any time day or night. I'll give you a mobile number for emergencies.'

A relaxed and smiling Marsh nodded enthusiastically, 'Got it, I'm really looking forward to working with you, Jack.'

Somerton eyed him carefully, wondering if Marsh was being honest. 'I hope so; we'll review our relationship in three months' time and take it from there. One final bit of housekeeping; I have two close associates, my confidants, Eddie Black and Mike Davies. They are to be given access to anything they need to know or see, at any time. Get a message from them to me, at any time, including when I'm in the House. If you can't get me, do what they ask; is that understood?'

Marsh blinked. 'Unusual, but if that's what you require, you're the boss.'

Somerton nodded, 'We might just form a good partnership Reggie, my newly appointed **Senior** Research Assistant. You can start now or tomorrow, it's up to you. When you're in the NRSC use a desk out in the general office. Order a new one if you need your own. When you're in Westminster, as far as I know we share an office; I don't know what plans there are for additional accommodation in light of my Cabinet responsibilities.'

'Got it.' Marsh stood and extended his hand, Somerton remained seated but reached out and shook it. 'I'll start tomorrow, if that's ok? Oh, just a thought, you haven't said anything about my involvement in the research area?'

Somerton shook his head, 'That's because you won't really have a direct involvement. That's being handled within the NRSC. Now I must draw this to a close, I've got another commitment.'

When Marsh had gone, Somerton glanced at his monitor, 10.45am. *Professor King, your twenty-four hours are up, let's see what you have to say for yourself.*

Somerton attended to his emails and read through the pile of security alerts that Barker had put on his desk. He gave King some leeway but when noon arrived without contact, he knew he would have to take the initiative. *OK Lizzie, I'll pay you a visit and if you aren't interested, I'll offer the post to Alan Glen, with Maggie Hurst next in line.*

A few minutes later Somerton knocked on King's door, pushing it open when he heard what he took to be a muffled 'come in'. She looked round, surprised when she saw it was Somerton. 'Jack, what brings you here?'

'I know Professors have a reputation for being absentminded, but I did offer you a very important post yesterday and I had hoped you would have been in touch. Twenty-four hours for your decision was the deadline I set.'

King looked embarrassed. 'I know, I'm sorry; I should have contacted you. I mulled it over and decided I wanted the post, then I reflected and changed my mind, and I've dithered ever since.'

Somerton threw up his hands in frustration. 'So, tell me about your concerns; I want this matter settled now, one way or another.'

'Oh, it's nothing to do with the research side. It's really facing up to my colleagues and telling them that I'm running the NRSC.'

Somerton relaxed, 'Someone is going to have to do that sooner or later. You can be in the audience or on the stage, it's up to you. Why don't we take it a step at a time? I'll inform them I've invited you to be the Centre's Director and describe the national aspects of your role. I'll emphasise how pleased I was to be able to give the post to one of their own.'

King nodded, 'That would make it much easier, but…'

'But what, Lizzie?'

King looked embarrassed, 'Self-effacement I guess; out of the blue being put in charge of my colleagues, all of whom are every bit as capable as me.'

'But that's my decision. You can soften the blow by having a committee to assist you, a small committee, say four others maximum.'

King smiled, 'That sounds better, I can go with that.'

Somerton smiled broadly. 'We have a deal then. And if you want a fixed term, say three years, after which you hand over to someone else, I could live with that.'

King was nodding, reflecting on the option. 'I'll need to think about that.'

Somerton reacted immediately, 'Thinking time is over, Professor; I want a yes or no? What's it to be?'

King sighed, 'Alright, I'll take the job for two years with the option of a third. You'll make the announcement.'

'We have a deal. I'll email all Centre staff tonight and make an announcement in the House tomorrow. Now, subject to anything you might have to say, this is what I want from you. I want a quarterly report on progress on current and future research programmes, both Centre driven, and any Government funded external schemes. I want a list prepared in February and August each year, setting out research priorities and making bids for funding. We'll agree the final list of bids and I'll approach the Treasury for the money. Are you happy with that?'

'Yes Minister,' King laughed, 'sorry I wasn't alluding to the eighties TV programme.'

Somerton smiled, 'It made me chuckle, sadly the programme carried a lot of truth about the way government functions. I'll go now and leave you to get on with your research. Someone will be in touch to agree a formal contact with you. I'll phone you to arrange a briefing session and you can begin to educate me about research.'

King nodded with an impish smile. 'Yes Minister.'

Back in his office, Somerton reflected on progress so far. *Eric Barker had his complete confidence, Marsh and King were unknowns. Marsh certainly had the political nous, but could he be trusted? Does he hold a grudge against me? Would he fight my corner or do me down given the opportunity? Lizzie King was honest, an open book, but would she give the job her full commitment or would her personal research dilute her input. Watch this space, Jack.*

Meantime, Somerton was expecting an email from a friend and associate of longstanding, Kim Lee, a close confidant of the Hong Kong Chief Executive, Ellen Chang. Hong Kong, a British territory since 1841 before being given over to China in 1997 in accord with the 1898 Treaty, was now formally renamed the Hong Kong Special Administrative Region of the People's Republic of China.

His eyes lit up when he found the email in his inbox; the words wouldn't convey much to the casual reader, although an experienced codebreaker would probably discern that its message wasn't all that it appeared to be. The email had reached him by a very circuitous route, forwarded by a chain of trusted contacts. Tracing it back to Kim Lee was nigh on impossible. It told him what he wanted to know; another piece of the Somerton jigsaw had fallen into place. Now was the time to light a very slow-burning fuse.

'Jack, two calls in as many days. Do you Cabinet Ministers never rest.'

'Ha, ha, Jupiter, I hadn't realised you had a sense of humour. I have a number of projects I want you to set up, ready for implementation when I give the word.'

'Go ahead, Jack. I'm listening.'

'We both want to see the satellite launch completed, right?'

'You're being tedious, Jack. Come to the point.'

'The authority to launch rests with me and I have six projects and twenty-four satellites; you complete a project and in return I launch four satellites. How does that sound to you? I have in mind one project per week.'

Jupiter shrugged. 'Sounds like you still don't trust me, but in principle I can agree to that, subject to the complexity of each project and whether the depleted system has the capability required.'

'Based on the information you gave me last time we spoke, they should all be within the scope of the existing constellation, which of course will be increased by four a week.'

Jupiter nodded, 'Don't forget that each satellite has to be commissioned and re-configured to enable them to be deployed simultaneously.'

Somerton shrugged, 'I'm sure you'll find a way, Jupiter. You always do. I'm going to list the projects in the order I want them carried out. Correction - I'll list them in order of precedence but there is one which has overriding priority for which I'm awaiting an implementation date.'

'Intriguing, Jack, let's get started.'

Detailing and explaining the thinking behind the projects occupied the next twenty-five minutes. Jupiter listened attentively. His enigmatic expression exhibited not a vestige of surprise throughout the entire process.

'All achievable, Jack. I'll be in touch when I'm ready; it shouldn't take long.'

Jupiter logged out without further comment. Somerton was surprised at how co-operative Jupiter had been. It was almost as though he, Somerton, was fitting in with Jupiter's plans. *Forget it Jack, you're being paranoid. Get yourself a malt and celebrate the day's progress.*

Downing Street, next day.

Somerton attended his first Cabinet Meeting with Alan's words ringing in his ears. *Make sure you have something to say, don't be slow to express your opinion. Try to avoid getting into disagreement with any of the big guns until you get settled in.*

Last item on the agenda was Any Other Business. Somerton took the opportunity to update the meeting on security alerts, none of which were category red. He also informed the Cabinet about, what he termed, unsubstantiated reports on- line about the growing close relationship between China and Russia. These were increasing in number and frequency and there was mention of the two presidents meeting in the very near future.

Laura Taylor responded immediately Somerton stopped talking. 'That's very interesting, Jack; co-incidentally I had a call from across the pond last night and Will Kenny expressed his concerns about the alliance Russia and China seem to be building. I think I'm going to make security a standing item on the agenda.'

The meeting ended and everyone drifted away back to their departments. Somerton was making his way along the corridor when Lynda Jones, Croudace's successor as Foreign Secretary stopped him. 'Interesting report Jack, please remember to keep me briefed regularly.'

'I intend to, Lynda; the PM did brief me on the need to liaise closely with you, and the Defence Minister; it's a routine I'll be setting up this week, I promise. I'm still finding my feet.'

Jones gave him a radiant smile. 'Thanks, Jack I'm sure we'll get on well. Did you enjoy your first Cabinet meeting?'

'I did, though I wasn't sure when to challenge a view or when to support it. I'm generally very opinionated but I'm one of the new boys and didn't want to make enemies first time out.'

'Join the club, Jack. We all went through the same thought process. Sooner or later, you'll have to decide if you are your own man, or a yes man. If you challenge the PM's line too often, you'll be sacked. Go along with it all the time and you'll lose respect. It's down to each of us to make our mind up.'

Somerton thought it time to put down a marker, for better or for worse, 'I don't see myself as a career politician so my support will always be based on doing what is best for the United Kingdom. I believe that's my job and why I was elected and most certainly accords with my Oath of Allegiance.'

Taylor nodded sagely, 'Very noble of you, Jack, very idealistic; I wish you well.'

Somerton held her gaze, 'That's how it is.'
Taylor shrugged. 'Changing the subject, did you pick up the news about Vladic?'

Somerton's eyes glinted. Vladic, the old military adversary he had framed for killing Colin MacKinnon. 'No, what's he been up to? Last I heard he was in gaol in Serbia?'

'That was the case until a couple of days ago when he got into a fight and lost big time. He's currently in a mortuary awaiting burial.'

Somerton smiled broadly. 'Best news I've heard in a long time; I would have hung the bastard given the chance. I don't know why we don't have hanging as the ultimate punishment for extreme cases.'

Taylor shook her head. 'That's a no-no, Jack. It's not going to happen, See you around.'

CHAPTER 17

Walworth, London 18th February 2021

A loud, prolonged banging at the door finally penetrated the eardrums of the slumbering semiconscious Joe Willet, known to all in sundry as Dizzy. His bedroom looked like a rubbish dump; food wrappers, empty cans and dirty clothing were strewn over the floor. Bottles, boxes, and cartons crowded every flat surface. Cobwebs and their manufacturing resident spiders adorned most corners of the room. The atmosphere stunk of body odour, tobacco, booze, stale food and the unidentifiable.

Fuck it, right in the middle of a fun dream. Who the hell is that at this time of the night? It was around 9pm and he'd just flopped into bed fully dressed, including shoes; unwashed as he had been for four days. The knocking persisted and he gave up the hope that his visitor would go back to whence they came. He rolled over and guided his legs onto the floor, stumbling as he stood, trying to find his balance. His last dose of cannabis still clouded his thinking.

Joe Dizzy Willet lived in a one bedroomed bungalow, bequeathed to him by his adoring maternal grandmother when she passed away four years ago. It was probably worth a small fortune, but he had promised gran he would live there for at least five years after her death; besides, in his heart he knew that if he sold up, he'd only squander the proceeds.

It had been in good condition when he inherited it but was now suffering badly from neglect and a lack of maintenance as evidenced by the peeling paintwork and wallpaper. A bucket half full of rainwater sat in the middle of the greasy room that served as a kitchen. Outside, the gardens, back and front, were overgrown with long grass and multiple weeds.

The knocking continued. 'Okay, okay, I'm coming; keep your hair on. What's the fucking rush?' Dizzy staggered into the lounge, kicking boxes and cushions aside as he moved towards the front door. Bang, bang, bang, the door knocker was working overtime.

Please God, don't let it be the coppers. At last, he was across the room, his senses clearing, his vision coming into clear focus. He reached for the front door handle, then had second thoughts. *Who the fuck is it?* He peered through the peephole in the door, fighting hard to bring his vision into focus. *Don't recognise the bastard.* He could just make out the shadowy figure of a man but nothing to identify him. The man's facial features weren't clearly discernible in the unlit porch. *Must remember to replace the light bulb.* Caution took over, Willet took a step to his left from the door and pulled back the curtains to get a clearer view of his visitor. He knocked on the glazing to attract his visitor's attention and the man turned to face him, smiling. *What the fuck is he smiling about.*

Willet opened the window a fraction. 'What do you want mister? I had just got to sleep.'

The man spread his hand in a sort of apology. 'Sorry about that, my train was delayed. I was told you kept late nights.'

Willet's head was clearing rapidly, his latest fix was wearing off, the cold air speeding up the process. 'Sometimes I go to bed early, other times I'm up late, depends how I feel. What do you want?'

'I thought we might have a little party; I was told you were up for a good time. I brought this along to help us get to know each other better.' The visitor waved a small envelope. 'Best crack you'll ever come across, enough to put us both on cloud nine. Danny recommended you.'

'Danny Cotton? He recommended me?'

The man shrugged. 'Don't think he told me his surname. Are you receiving visitors or not?'

Willet's confidence was growing, a snort or two wouldn't go amiss. 'You provide the crack free? My services come at a price.'

'Of course, this is strictly business. I'm only in town for a night and I don't feel like kerb-crawling to find some entertainment.'

Willet nodded. 'It's fifty quid for a short time, a hundred if you stay the night, unlimited attention. I haven't had time to tidy up the place by the way, you'll have to take the place as you find it.'

The visitor was smiling now. 'Overnight sounds good to me. Open up and let me in, it's getting cold out here on the doorstep.'

Willet shook his head. 'Nope, you pass me the crack and the cash, then I'll let you in.'

'Sorry, not happy with that, you might take payment and then lock me out.'

'I can see that, but the choice is yours, pay up and come in, or piss off.'

The stranger pursed his lips. 'You're not very welcoming, I hope you're worth it.'

Willet knew he had won. 'Never had any complaints, you'll have a dream of a time. Now, do we have a deal or not?'

The visitor grunted, took out his wallet and pulled out two fifties, both forgeries but this ninny wouldn't know the difference. He passed the notes through the open window and stood back. Windsor glanced at them and stuffed them in his shirt pocket, then held out his hand. 'And the crack.'

'I'll have that with me when you open the door. Fair's, fair. I give you the money, it's your turn to trust me. I come this way once a month; I could be one of your regulars if we hit it off.'

Willet guffawed. 'If the crack's good, I hit it off with anybody. Anyway, let's get this show on the road, I'll trust you with the refreshments. Ha, ha, refreshments, that's a good one. Hold on and I'll let you in.'

He closed the window and pulled the curtain back into place, then reached forward to remove the door chain. That done he turned the handle to open the door; the catch had barely released when the door was pushed firmly into his face, causing him to stumble backwards. 'What the fuck, take it easy, you're a bit desperate mate. I'm not....' His words tapered away when he saw a second figure appear in the doorway. 'Here, I didn't reckon on two of you, it's going to cost extra.'

The conversation ended there; Man One stepped forward and punched him in the guts folding him over, moaning and clutching his stomach in agony. Both men were inside now, slamming the door closed and dragging him across the floor. Man Two was looking round. 'Where's the fucking light switch? We need some illumination.'

Willet heard the words and managed a little giggle. 'Ha, ha, got you there; the electricity was shut down a week back.'

Man Two found the light switch and flicked it up and down a couple of times. 'Damn, the bastard's right. Either that or the bulb's gone; we'll have to make do withs bloody candlelight. Hold him whilst I roll up his sleeve.' Willet struggled feebly but in vain and he felt the jab in his left arm, then nothing. The seconds ticked by and he entered dreamland, coloured stars and shapes were filling his inner vision; he was floating in space. 'Christ, that's good stuff, well worth a thump in the guts.'

The two men were hauling him to his feet. *What now?* He felt conscious yet somehow, unconscious. 'OK guys, get on with it, both of you for a hundred. Make it quick, but no rough stuff.' He was struggling to get his words out, fighting to keep his eyes open, the drug was kicking in big time, then nothing.

Man One took charge. 'He's blacked out; find a jacket for him, whilst I slip these gloves on the poor sod.' He pulled on the pair of blue woollen gloves he bought in a charity shop earlier that day.

Man Two returned having found a jacket lying on a chair in the bedroom. 'Sit him up and help me get this on.' The task completed, Man One removed the two fifty-pound notes from Willet's shirt pocket, then zipped up the jacket. A glance confirmed what he flagged up earlier on, Willet was wearing trainers. 'OK, let's get him on his feet; we're lucky he's a lightweight.'

The men took an arm each and hoisted the unfortunate Willet to his feet, draping an arm each round their shoulders. Man One grinned. 'Well done Dizzy my boy; you're going for a little walk.'

The two men dragged-walked Willet over to the door, opened it and stepped outside, after quickly checking that there was nobody around. The three of them made their way along the pavement, attempting to be in animated conversation for the benefit of any casual observer, towards their destination. Reaching the third side street, out of breath from their exertions, they were glad to see their black Nissan Juke parked just a few metres away.

Man One spoke for them both. 'Thank fuck that's over. Bundle him in and I'll do the necessary. I'll see you back at the hotel when the job is done.'

Man Two heaved the unconscious Willet unceremoniously into the passenger seat and slammed the car door shut. He gave his companion the thumbs up and walked away.

Man One straightened up his comatose victim, put on the safety belt and laid his head in sleep position against the side window. That done he pressed the start button and set off for his destination. A few minutes' drive brought him to a quiet side street where he parked up to await a text. Willet stirred and shouted out an oath but didn't waken. Man One gave a wicked laugh. *Hmm, think I'll give you another shot Dizzy; you don't realise it old son, but this is your lucky night.* He pushed up a sleeve, removed a syringe from an envelope in his inner pocket and injected its contents into Willet's right arm. That done he used a cloth to clean the steering wheel, not that he needed to, the latex gloves that he and Man Two were wearing ensured there were no fingerprints to be found.

Not too far away, Man Two sat in a red Kia watching a Pimlico apartment block, drumming his fingers on the steering wheel in time to whatever issued forth on Heart radio. *Come on, come on, what's keeping you?* Ten minutes went by. *Where are you, please show up.* Five more minutes passed, Man One and Man Two were both getting anxious, both 'praying' their efforts hadn't been in vain.

At last, their target finally appeared in the doorway of the block of flats, clearly recognisable by the porch light and street lighting. Man Two retrieved his mobile and sent his ready prepared text, a single word, **GO**.

Man One heard his phone buzz, smiling when he read the text. 'All set Dizzy, here we go.' He pulled away immediately, what had to be done, had to take place in a very short time frame. It took just three minutes to reach his destination and turn into the quiet street just vacated by Man Two. The area was upper middle class, the residential blocks owned by rich businessmen and women from all over the world. Not that most of them occupied; more often than not the wealthy owners were to be found in foreign parts.

In fact, there was only one individual in sight, a lone male in a track suit walking at a brisk pace along the pavement. Man One pressed on the accelerator the car lurched forward, accelerating rapidly. 30-40-50-60 miles per hour. The walker heard the straining car engine and glanced over his shoulder just as it swerved sharply from the road onto the pavement. The victim's mouth opened in shock as the vehicle hit him head on, hurtling him forward into the air, fatally injured. The walker's body thudded into the adjacent wall before being struck again by the car and left lifeless on the ground, blood draining from his multiple injuries.

Man One's mission wasn't complete; he bounced back onto the road, maintaining his speed as he randomly sideswiped a line of parked vehicles, smiling as he thought of the look on the faces of their privileged owners when they returned to their prestige cars. *Not a bad haul for sixty seconds' drive; I reckon you got a Roller, a Merc and a Morgan.* It was time for the finale. He stopped the car on the slight downward incline, got out undid the safety belt and dragged Willet over to the driver's seat then slumped him over the wheel. With the car engine still running, he moved round to the other side and knocked the automatic's gear change into drive. He took a quick glance around to see if there were any onlookers, relieved when he didn't spot any. He didn't stop to watch as the car slowly angled across the road, hit another parked car and stopped.

Man One could hear voices behind him, probably from windows in the distance as residents investigated the bangs of the earlier vehicle impacts but didn't choose to look round for their source. Time was of the essence; emergency vehicles in the area could well be on their way. He turned down the first side street and used his mobile to text Man Two, **ready**.

Man Two knew exactly where his accomplice would be and only a few minutes had elapsed when the red Kia pulled up on the other side of the road. Man One climbed in and the Kia carried on to the junction, pulling up briefly to look right to view the scene of the earlier carnage.

Two police cars and an ambulance were quickly on the scene; a man wearing jogging gear was pronounced dead where his battered body lay. His phone had been shattered in the impact and he wasn't carrying any identification. Minutes later, the Nissan Juke and its driver would be found, and police would form a view on what had taken place. The driver was in a coma and would be conveyed by ambulance to Guy's A&E. Another ambulance had been called to transport his victim to a mortuary. Police barriers were put in place, closing the road to traffic while investigations were in progress.

The incident made the late-night local news. *A pedestrian had been killed in a car collision; a young man was under suspicion of driving under the influence of drugs and causing death by dangerous driving.*

Back at their hotel, having a late supper, Man One and Man Two smiled, mission accomplished. Man One sent an eye signal to his companion to look across to an adjacent table which was temporarily being vacated by two young women whilst they headed off to the ladies. Man Two nodded that he understood - the car they had stolen was operated by an electronic key, obtained from what was just referred to as the *Source.*

Apparently, the Source tours cafes, shopping centres and similar gathering places watching out for opportunities to steal car keys left unguarded by their owners, The Source then doggedly follows the owner, waiting for them to return to their vehicle where the number is noted, and an address ultimately purchased via the DVLA. If the opportunity presents, the vehicle is driven away to a storage area and the number plate changed. In other instances, the vehicle will be stolen as and when required. It's a car hire service with a difference!!!

Man Two eyed the car keys left on the young women's table. *You're lucky I'm not a car thief, darling.*

CHAPTER 18

Houses of Parliament, Somerton's Office Next day
Somerton was ploughing through his emails with increasing irritation at the breadth of subjects his constituents chose to complain about; many were justifiable, many were downright trivial. Thankfully Reggie Marsh was already in full swing and dealing with most of them. Very few were flagged up for his personal attention and he welcomed dealing with these; they provided an opportunity to show the sender that their vote mattered.

He was nearing the end of his correspondence journey when there was a tap on his door; before he could respond, Laura Taylor made her way in and sat down, a grim look on her face. Something was seriously amiss; Somerton could sense it in her whole demeanour. 'I get the feeling I'm not going to like what you're going to tell me Laura. I'm not a hearts and flowers kind of guy, so give it to me straight.'

Taylor drew her breath and sought out the words, 'It's about Alan Croudace.'

Somerton's eyes widened. 'Alan, what about him? What's happened?'

Taylor's voice choked. 'I'm sorry, Jack, very sorry; he was killed in a car accident last night. I only got to hear of it this morning; I came straight here as soon as I heard.'

Somerton was stunned. *Alan dead? No, it can't be true, it must be a mistake.* He could only summon a single, toneless, hollow word. 'How?'

Taylor hesitantly reached out her hand to offer comfort but stopped short of a touch. 'Believe me, I know how painful this must be for you, Jack. Alan was out for a walk, and it seems a car mounted the pavement at speed, and he was killed outright. Emergency Services pronounced him dead at the scene; there was nothing anyone could do. As you know, he refused to have a security guard after he retired and was on his own when it happened.'

Anger welled in Somerton, brushing aside his grief. 'Who was the fucking driver? I'll kill the bastard.'

'Please Jack, this is difficult enough. The driver was a young man and initial tests have shown that he was likely to have been high on drugs at the time of the accident. The car he was driving had been reported stolen. It appears he side-swiped a number of cars before ending up on the pavement and killing Alan. He then ran into a stationary vehicle and that's where he was when the police arrived on the scene. For now, he's in a coma in Intensive Care. I don't know any more than that. I'll let you know immediately if I hear anything else.'

'Where can I see, Alan?' Somerton's tone was flat.

'He's in the mortuary at Guy's.'

The sound of the word mortuary sent a chill through Somerton. *This can't be happening.* 'I'll go there now.' He had to see his friend and share a final moment, before he was locked up in a box.

'Jack.' This time, Taylor reached out and took Somerton's hand. 'I…'

Somerton's heart tightened; his despair couldn't sink to greater depths. He feared to hear what was about to be said. 'What?'

Taylor's eyes moistened. 'I understand Alan has suffered a lot of damage. He's not recognisable; that's why I wasn't contacted until this morning. He wasn't carrying any identification; he was in jogging gear and looked like an ordinary guy going out for a run. Alan did have his phone with him, but it got shattered and it's taken a lot of work to get anything out of it. You might not want your last memory of him to be…..' Her words dried up mid-sentence.

'I'm going to see him, going to say a last farewell. On active service, he and I said last goodbyes to many comrades who weren't recognisable except by their dog-tags.'

'Your decision, Jack; I just wanted to prepare you. Tell you what. I think a bit of company might be good for you this evening. How about you join Nat and I for dinner, bring company if you wish.'

Somerton was on the point of refusing but changed his mind; it would be nice to see more of Downing Street if nothing else. 'Thank you, Laura, that's kind of you. When should I turn up?'

'We eat quite late, 7.30 for 8, how does that suit? All subject to anything that crops up in today's business, of course, though it's looking like a pretty routine day. I'll go now.'

'Just one thing, Laura. Alan's funeral, I assume we'll do something formal for him?'

Taylor shook her head. 'Nothing like Colin's funeral if that's what you have in mind. Wonderful servant to the nation that he was, I'm afraid it will be a straightforward funeral. There will be a few notables in attendance of course.'

Somerton nodded. 'I guess so; he doesn't leave any family, siblings or the like, not even a girlfriend. He has left a will, so maybe that lays out his wishes for his funeral. He gave me a copy in a sealed envelope, made me promise not to open it. I never thought I'd need to. Sounds silly, I know.'

Taylor rose. 'I'll go now, Jack. See you at 7.30. Sorry about Alan, I know you were close.'

Somerton felt strangely cast adrift when she'd gone, how could this be happening. But life had to go on and he made his way into the Chamber for the start of the day's business which began with the Speaker announcing Croudace's untimely death. A two minutes silence followed; the Commons was dumbfounded - two Prime Ministers lost to the nation in a few months. The mood of the House had changed. There was no appetite for the usual cut and thrust of debate; the Speaker suspended business for the rest of the day.

Somerton exited the Chamber immediately, nodding thanks to those who knew of his close relationship with Croudace and extended their condolences. He found a pool car and driver and set out for Guy's Hospital where he explained who he was and why he was there. He found his way to the mortuary where an attendant bade him wait whilst he, *Made Mr Croudace ready for viewing*. The five minutes wait seemed like an eternity but they passed, and he was shown into the viewing room. Croudace's body lay on a stainless-steel table. A small white towel covered his head, concealing what was left of his face; a green sheet covered his body from the neck to the ankles. A small tag tied on to his left foot announced that it belonged to Alan Croudace.

Somerton let his tears run freely, his friend reduced to this crumpled damaged cadaver. 'I don't know who did this, Alan, but if the Grim Reaper doesn't take the little sod, I promise you that I will.' He had seen all he needed to and paid his respects to a fallen comrade; there would be time enough for memories and tributes another day.

Somerton headed back to his home, rather than the Harrow East apartment. Home somehow suited his mood; he wanted to brood a little and check out Alan's Will. Settled back in his apartment, he reached for a glass and a bottle of whisky, limiting himself to a small tot, knowing he would be going out to dinner in a few hours' time. It felt unreal when he went to his safe to retrieve his copy of Croudace's final testament. The Will was brief. A Mayfair solicitor named as his Executor, his Pimlico apartment and contents to be sold and the proceeds divided equally between the SAS Regimental Association and the British Legion. He was to be cremated in his SAS uniform at Golder's Green Crematorium with an SAS presence and the Last Post sounded. His ashes were to be scattered by Somerton in the National Arboretum at Alrewas in Staffordshire. The Will referenced Somerton and specifically requested him to ensure that its wishes were strictly observed.

There was also an envelope addressed to Somerton, he slit it open and unfolded the handwritten letter enclosed.

Dear Jack,

If you are reading this, I'm afraid I've gone and popped my clogs so no more missions for me alas.

Just a few small requests I'd like fulfilled please. First up I would like you to have my medals, I know you will take good care of them.

Second could you please be responsible for sprinkling my ashes at the regiment's monument in the National Arboretum.

Finally, could you please decide who should attend the crematorium service which is to be led by a military Pastor. Limit the guests to a maximum of thirty plus of course Her Majesty if she's free (only kidding).

Brief the Pastor as you wish, there's no-one knows me better.

Thanks for the above, Jack, and for being a true friend through thick and thin.

WHO DARES WINS

Alan

P.S. No media involvement or I'll come back and haunt you.

Somerton smiled as a small tear escaped and rolled down his cheek. 'Count it done, Alan. I'm honoured.'

Later that day

Somerton arrived at Downing Street a few minutes early for the PM's dinner invite, having travelled there by taxi; a last-minute decision not to drive in case the liquor flowed over the course of the evening. Laura Taylor came down to greet him at the bottom of the stairs and invited him to follow her to the PM's residential area. She observed him blink when he entered the lounge; the décor could only be described as avant garde.

'I'm guessing you don't like the decorations?'

Somerton screwed up his face, searching for the right thing to say. 'Well....to be frank, it's not to my taste.'

Taylor grimaced. 'It's weird, takes some getting used to, but I can't bring myself to spend a small fortune on redecorating; so, we'll live with it for the foreseeable future. I doubt if Alan liked it either though he never said.'

Somerton smiled. 'Ever the diplomat.'

'Anyway, enough of that. Let me introduce you to my long-suffering husband. 'Nat, this is Jack Somerton, newly appointed Minister of Research and Security, a close friend of the late Colin MacKinnon.'

Nat Taylor extended a hand and exchanged a warm, firm handshake. 'Pleased to meet you, Jack. You have my sincere condolences.' His host was tall and lanky, mid-forties, hair neck-length with grey showing in abundance through its dark origins. His accent Yorkshire, the tone soft and unhurried. 'Let's grab a pew and I'll rustle up a drink. What can I get you? I had a lot of respect for Alan; he was one of the few politicians I felt I could trust. No offence.'

Somerton shrugged. 'You should know; you're married to one. A whisky please, malt preferred.'

Introductions over, Somerton sat down and cast his eyes around the décor, *Weird, no other words to describe it. What were you thinking of Colin? Just seems out of place in an historic residence like No 10.* His thoughts were interrupted when a woman entered the room, dressed in dark blue slacks and a mustard sweater. Somerton judged her to be in her late thirties.

Nat Taylor made the introductions. 'Jack, this is Laura's sister, Geraldine.'

Somerton stood and took the proffered hand. 'Pleased to meet you, Geraldine. Looks like you've bumped into a door.' He was alluding to her bruised cheekbone and blackening eye.

Her expression saddened. 'Oh, it's nothing; I slipped and fell in the gym a couple of days ago, clumsy me, no excuses. It's not painful now, though it was at the time.' She grimaced as she sat down.

'Looks like you've suffered a bit more than a black eye?' Somerton enquired gently.

She nodded. 'My ribs took a hit, they are tender. I guess I might have bruised, or even cracked a couple.'

Just then Laura Taylor called from the kitchen. 'Nat, take our guests through to the dining room, dinner is served.'

Somerton's eye lit up when he viewed the table where Beef Wellington, roast potatoes and green vegetables sat ready for serving. 'Don't know who told you, Laura, but you've cooked my favourite meal; don't count on any leftovers.'

Taylor beamed. 'Bless you, Jack; I suspect you might have said that no matter what I served up.'

Somerton nodded. 'Probably, but on this occasion, I promise you I really mean it.'

'Tuck in everybody, main course only. There's no starter or dessert, I'm watching my waistline. Might manage cheese and biscuits to finish if you say nice things about my cooking.'

The evening passed quickly, conversation followed the usual first-time meeting routes - where were you born - what got you into this and that - any hobbies -TV watching – holidays - thankfully all brightened up by flashes of humour and an absence of any boring dragged-out anecdotes. Despite the background of Croudace's demise, Somerton found himself enjoying the evening and readily engaging in discussions.

He made a note of three revelations. Taylor's husband, Nat, was a professor at the London School of Economics; she would be well advised on monetary policy and would be able to fight her corner with the Chancellor of the Exchequer on an informed basis. Her sister, Geraldine, had a Classics degree and was married with two children. As for Laura, she had graduated from Cambridge with a First in Politics and another in Computer Sciences. She had then followed these up by taking a Masters at Harvard University where she had met and become good friends with Will Kenny, the recently elected US President.

Somerton was the first to call it a day. 'Busy morning ahead folks, I'm afraid I must away. Thank you for a lovely evening, Laura. You've all been good company and it has greatly helped me cope with today's news about Alan. I can't cook, so can't reciprocate, but I'd be very happy to take you all out to dinner sometime soon. Nice to meet you all.'

Laura Taylor beamed. 'Our pleasure, Jack. How are you getting home?'

'I'll hail a taxi, there's plenty around.'

'No, you won't, I'll get the on-call driver to take you home.'

Somerton smiled and nodded appreciatively. 'Such is the power of the Prime Minister; I won't turn down the offer.' He glanced at Geraldine. 'Perhaps we could share the car?' He was mildly surprised when she shook her head, more so when she offered no explanation.

Nat Taylor sensed Somerton's curiosity and intervened. 'Geraldine is spending a few days with us.'

Somerton nodded. 'See you another time then.' *That's odd, doesn't stack up, two kids, lives not too far away, yet staying in Downing Street.*

CHAPTER 19

Scotland Yard, 8.30am

Superintendent Peter Bright looked haggard. Responsibility for investigating the circumstances surrounding Alan Croudace's death had ended up on his desk and he'd been on the go since receiving the call in the early hours of the morning. 'So, what have we got, Sally?'

Chief Inspector Sarah Clark was the crime scene investigator; she had been first senior officer on the scene but didn't display any of the world-weary signs of her superior. Small and thickset, her bearing business-like, she showed no signs of the pressure such a high-profile investigation would have been expected to generate. 'We have a preliminary report on the post-mortem carried out on the victim, ex-Prime Minister Alan Croudace.'

Bright sighed. 'Skip the prattle, Sally, cut to the chase; I know who the victim was.' He shook his head. 'Who would have thought we would have lost two Prime Ministers in violent circumstances in under a year; I don't know what's happening to this country of ours.'

Clark didn't bat an eye at Bright's outburst. 'Mr Croudace was struck by a vehicle at approximately 20.33, yesterday evening and almost certainly died instantly from multiple trauma injuries. He was severely disfigured and not readily identifiable; there was no identification on the body. He was wearing…'

Bright banged on his desk. 'I don't want to know what he was fucking wearing, Sally, get on with it. Save the frills for the team briefing.'

Clark glared at him before returning to her note. 'Mr Croudace's blood analysis produced no evidence of any undue substances. He had a meal…'

Bright thumped his desk again. 'I don't want to know what was in his stomach, Chief Inspector. I'm your commanding officer, not a fucking jury. Cut to the chase. Was Mr Croudace's death entirely attributable to being struck by a vehicle?'

This time, Clark responded directly to Bright's instructions. 'Yes sir, entirely.'

Bright nodded. 'Good, now we are getting somewhere. So, we have a potential murder enquiry on our hands?'

'Possibly, but more likely death by dangerous driving.'

'In my book it's murder until the driver proves otherwise. Tell me about the vehicle, I've got a Press conference shortly and I'm bound to be asked that.'

Clark nodded. 'This is where it starts to get interesting, the vehicle involved was a black Nissan Juke, stolen earlier that evening.'

Bright raised his eyebrows. 'Stolen? What do we know about the circumstances?'

Clark glanced at her notes. 'The owner says it was stolen from outside her house between 17.00, when it was parked, and 17.30 when she noticed it had gone. She called it in straight away. The key was found in the car with the driver.'

Bright rolled his eyes. 'Where else would it be found, Sally? How the hell did the driver get the key?'

'The owner doesn't know; she lost the original key, the electronic original, weeks ago. There were no fingerprints on it, or on the door handle, or on the steering wheel. In fact, the few fingerprints found elsewhere in the car are those of the owner.'

Brook shook his head. 'No prints, that's odd. Tell me about the driver.'

Clark fished out another sheaf of notepaper. 'The driver was Joseph Willet, known as Dizzy Willet and he was wearing gloves which explains the lack of fingerprints. He's currently in a critical condition in Guy's Hospital due to a massive overdose of heroin. He's not expected to survive. Willet is a known drug addict. It appears that he stole the car whilst high on drugs, went for a drive, mounted the pavement, and hit the unfortunate Mr Croudace at around 60mph. As I said earlier, death was likely to have been instantaneous.

'It appears that Willet didn't stop. The vehicle went on to side-swipe three other vehicles, before slamming into a fourth and coming to a halt. Willet was found unconscious behind the steering wheel. He wasn't wearing a seat belt and the air bags did not deploy; that's being investigated by our vehicle staff.'

Bright nodded. 'Good work, Sally, looks like an open and shut case. Murder unlikely; put the facts to the Public Prosecutor, suggest a charge of Causing Death by Dangerous Driving. Have a constable at his bedside ready to charge Willet if and when he wakes up. Does that sound OK?'

Clark licked her lips nervously. 'It does, except....'

'Except what, Chief Inspector?' Annoyance sounded in Bright's voice.

'I was coming to that, Sir. What is strange, is that Willet has never stolen a vehicle in all the time we've known him. We don't even know if he can drive; he certainly doesn't have a driving licence.'

Bright shrugged. 'We don't know everything, Sally. Sadly, lots of crimes remain unsolved and of course, there is a first time for everything. Willet is a crackhead; he was high on drugs, maybe he thought he was Lewis Hamilton.'

Clark nodded. 'Agreed, but there are another couple of anomalies. He was the driver, but traces of his blood were found on the passenger side.'

Bright contorted his face to look puzzled. 'So maybe he had a cut and reached over to search the passenger storage compartment at some stage to see if there was anything worth stealing.'

Clark continued. 'And other DNA traces of his were found on the passenger side.'

Bright pulled another face. He felt his irritation return. He was desperate for a quick result, a triumphant Press conference and a pat on the head from the Commissioner, who was herself under pressure from the Mayor. 'So maybe when he stole the car, he initially got in the passenger side and had a search round before moving round to the driver's side. Does that scenario meet your concerns? Are we done?'

Clark shook her head. 'Not quite, there's another anomaly; Willet was wearing gloves.'

Bright puffed his cheeks. 'Wearing gloves isn't a crime, Chief Inspector.'

'It was a warm evening, there was no reason for him to be wearing gloves.'

Bright glared at her, struggling to remain calm. 'For fucks sake, he knew he was going to steal a car; he probably watches forensics at work on TV, knows the procedures and wore gloves to avoid leaving any fingerprints. You're beginning to sound like a defence lawyer, Clarke. This meeting is terminated. You will present the facts to the DPP and recommend a charge of Causing Death by Dangerous Driving. You will present the bare facts and not garnish them with unfounded concerns. Is that understood?'

Clark nodded.

'Right, off you go, Sally If the DPP has any reservations get him to phone me. I want this case done and dusted today. Has the hospital been told to contact you if Willet wakes up or snuffs it?'

Clark nodded. 'The ITU consultant has been briefed and we have a constable on site.'

Bright smiled and spread his hands. 'Meeting concluded, keep me informed of any developments.'

Clark smiled. 'Will do, sir.' She turned and left the office, a happy bunny, her smile widening. She had presented the facts; she had voiced her concerns and they had been dismissed by her commanding officer. Any subsequent criticisms would land on Bright's doorstep.

Prime Minister's Office

Somerton had phoned ahead and charmed Jess Tate into letting him have an early unscheduled meeting with Laura Taylor, promising to keep it short. On arrival Jess met him in the outer doorway of her office. 'Good morning, Jack, good to see you.'

'And you Jess; how's life treating you?'

She raised her eyebrows and shrugged. 'In general, OK is the best I can say though Laura is not in good humour today. In fact, she told me off for fitting you in this morning. She's in a real grump so don't expect a smiley welcome.'

Somerton frowned. 'Oh dear, sorry about that Jess; I'll try to cheer her up.'

At that juncture the intercom buzzer sounded, and Jess took the call, turning to face Somerton as she spoke. 'Yes, he's here now, I'll send him in. Go through Jack, and please be brief, there's still an edge to her voice.'

Somerton nodded and made his way swiftly to the PM's office. He knocked on the door once and without waiting for acknowledgement made his way in. 'Good morning, Laura. Sorry to spring this intrusion on you; Jess has emphasised that I must be brief. I insisted on seeing you and I'll come straight to the point. Before I do though, thanks again for last night, a very enjoyable evening and one that helped me cope with Alan's death.' He paused briefly, noting the shadows under her eyes and her glum expression. Clearly something was amiss.

'I just felt you should be aware of Alan's wishes regarding his funeral arrangements in case you were planning anything. He wrote me a personal letter and I'm duty bound to see that it's complied with. It's to be kept simple, a maximum of thirty guests, chosen by me and it's to be military in style. SAS led in fact. I'll be contacting the SAS Association later today to secure their involvement. The service will be led by a military padre. I've come to ask you if you want an invite?'

Taylor's face saddened and her voice softened. 'Of course, I'll attend, Jack; other Cabinet colleagues will expect to be there, I'm sure.'

Somerton shook his head. 'Sorry, but I can't make it an open invitation; it's not what he wanted. I'll limit it to you, Ken Ogilvie as Chancellor of the Exchequer, Lynda Jones as Foreign Secretary, Theresa Davies the Speaker and of course Jess Tate. The remaining invites will be extended to ex-SAS colleagues.'

Taylor shook her head. 'He deserved more but if it's what he wanted, so be it. I won't try to persuade you otherwise; you've clearly made up your mind. Let me have the details in due course. I warn you though, and this is my decision, there will be a memorial service held in St Paul's later in the year.'

Somerton nodded. 'Fair enough. I know you're busy I'll get moving.' He half-turned to leave but stopped. 'Laura, tell me it's not my business if you wish, but you're not yourself today, is there anything I can help with?'

Taylor shook her head, her expression pained. 'Thanks Jack, but no; we had a bad time last night with Geraldine, a personal matter. I'll get back to normal as the day goes on.'

Bells rang loudly for Somerton as he recalled last night's dinner. Taylor's sister, married, two children, black eye, and bruised face. 'I reckon your sister has husband troubles.'

Taylor's eyes widened. 'How did you know?'

'Come off it, Laura. Geraldine moving in, no husband at the dinner, black eye, bruised face, bust ribs; it all adds up to domestic abuse. It doesn't take Sherlock Holmes to work that out.'

Taylor bit on her lip, her eyes moistened. 'I guess not. Please don't spread it round.'

'Christ Laura, what do you take me for? What's the husband's name?

'Guy Madison, why?'

Somerton shrugged. 'Nothing, just curiosity. What does he do for a living?'

Taylor rolled her eyes. 'An investor is how he styles himself. He seems to be moderately successful.'

'Why doesn't she leave him? Might bring him to his senses.'

Taylor shook her head. 'It's complicated.'

Somerton protested. 'What do you mean? She can't carry on getting beaten up; it's not good for her or the children. Surely you can see that?'

Taylor's eyes filled. 'It's my fault she won't walk out on him. He has a kind of a hold over both of us.'

Somerton went to red alert. 'A hold? What kind of hold can he have on you?'

Taylor let out a long, almost tearful sigh. 'I introduced Geraldine to Guy but, prior to that, he and I were in a relationship. Geraldine knew we were an item. It's not something we talk about, but he's threatened to sell his, *two sisters story*, to the tabloids with all the intimate details, real or imagined, if she walks out on him. He says he won't be afraid to make up such dirt as the tabloids would like to hear. It would really impact upon my political career; there's no way I would have got to be PM if the Party had been faced with lurid headlines.'

Somerton nodded. 'I understand, no further explanation required. He's a real bastard. I feel sorry for you and your sister, but I can't see how the present situation can be allowed to continue. First question – does Geraldine want to bail out of the marriage?'

Taylor nodded. 'I think she would if it could be done on a goodwill basis, and she felt the children would cope. He works from home a lot and spends a lot of time with the kids; they love him. I just keep hoping a solution will come along. There is another element to this scenario – Guy uses his in-law status with me to further his business interests. I confess that I've given him references in the past, particularly where the contract has involved a Middle East state. Out there they seem to give value to me the UK's Prime Minister being his sister-in-law. It's all such a fucking mess.' She grabbed a tissue and dabbed her eyes. 'Sorry to make you my confessor, Jack. Thanks for listening. Please don't repeat a word of this; I don't know why I've opened up to you.'

'We all need a friend sometime, Laura, and be assured not a word of our conversation will pass my lips.'

Taylor glanced at her watch. 'I'm sorry, but you must go, I have an appointment to prepare for and,' pointing at her face, 'do something about this mess.'

Somerton nodded sympathetically. 'Of course, I'm around if there is any way I can help. Which leads in to my second question. Would you like me to arrange for some pressure to be put on Madison?'

'Pressure, Jack? What kind of pressure?'

Somerton winked. 'The kind we don't talk about; I've met a lot of heavyweight personalities in my travels, some of whom owe me a favour.'

Taylor looked horrified and shook her head violently. 'No way, Jack, tempting as it is. Thanks for the offer. Now you really must go.'

Somerton left the office deep in thought, debating whether or not to get involved further.

Jess Tate interrupted his thoughts. 'Walking out without a goodbye, Jack? That's not like you.'

'Oh, sorry Jess, lots on my mind; I was miles away. Take care, see you soon.'

He continued to mull over Laura's situation on his way back to his office. Logic was telling him to keep out, but he didn't like wife-beaters and Taylor had done well by him; a ministerial role was totally unexpected this early in his political career.

Back in his office he used his burner mobile to call Mike Davies. 'Hello, Mike it's me. I have a job for you. I want you to find out all you can about the Prime Minister's brother-in-law, Guy Madison. He describes himself as an investor. Keep a low profile on this one, no real urgency but the sooner the better.'

Davies smiled. ''Twas ever thus with you, Jack. Eddie and I will get on his case and be in touch.'

CHAPTER 20

Metropolitan Police Headquarters

Somerton had phoned ahead and was shown straightaway to Chief Inspector Clark's office; Superintendent Bright was attending a meeting elsewhere and had offered his apologies.

'Do take a seat, Minister. Can I offer you tea or coffee?'

Somerton declined. 'Neither thanks, I don't want to take up any more of your time than necessary, plus I'm due to report back to the PM in an hour or so.'

'Understood. How can I help?'

'It would save me searching around for questions if I could see your case notes.'

Clark shook her head. 'Not allowed I'm afraid, serving police officers only.'

Somerton raised a querying eyebrow. 'I am the Minister responsible for national security. I would have thought that would have afforded me access?'

Clark's eyes narrowed, her brow furrowing. 'Are you saying there's a security issue involved?'

Somerton gave an icy smile. 'I wouldn't be here if the possibility didn't exist; nor would I be reporting my findings to the PM, and of course the Home Secretary.'

Clark's heartbeat stepped up. 'That's good enough for me though personally I can't see that there is a security strand to this case.' She pushed the case file across her desk. 'Have a read and if you have any questions, I'll do my best to answer them.'

Somerton skimmed through the photos, his stomach churning when he saw those of the lifeless, mangled blood-soaked body that had been his friend. The facts that quickly shouted out at him were threefold.

-       The air bags hadn't deployed having been disabled. The car's owner had no knowledge of them having been switched off.

-       There were no fingerprints of the perpetrator to be found anywhere on the vehicle.

-      Willet had never been known to steal a vehicle; this incident was way out of character.

Somerton leafed on through to the end, then pushed the file back to Clark. 'Just one question for you Chief Inspector. Did Willet hold a driving licence?

Clark shook her head. 'Not that we know off.'

'Don't you find that strange? A junkie steals a car but has never driven before.'

'I have to correct you, Minister. I didn't say Willet hadn't driven previously, I said that he didn't hold a driving licence of which we are aware.'

Somerton nodded. 'Fair enough. So, what now?'

'We've reported on our findings to the DPP recommending that Willet be charged with Causing Death by Dangerous Driving along with a string of other less serious charges – theft of a vehicle, no insurance, no driving licence, driving under the influence of drugs etc. It's up to the DPP now, assuming Willet survives; his condition was critical last I heard.'

Somerton stroked his chin thoughtfully. 'Thank you, Chief Inspector; you've been very helpful. I'll get on my way and leave you to it.'

Guy's Hospital

Somerton went directly to Guy's from Police HQ; he felt he had to see the man, the junkie, the accused who had ended his friend's life. Once again, he found that being a government minister was a key that opened any door. He was met at the entrance and led along a never-ending series of corridors by a young smartly dressed administrator. 'Not far now, Mr Somerton; Willet is in room four of the intensive therapy unit. I've no idea what shape he's in.'

Somerton nodded. 'We'll soon find out.' Looking ahead he could see a police constable seated in a chair reading a newspaper. By chance he happened to look round, saw the two men approaching, and immediately got to his feet.

The administrator, Hugh Brown, made the introductions. 'Mr Somerton would like to spend a few minutes with Mr Willet.' The constable, Ronnie White, glanced at the photo identification clipped to Brown's jacket then back to his face. Satisfied he turned to Somerton. 'I know who you are Mr Somerton, but can I see your identification, please? I have instructions that only clinical staff are allowed in to see Dizzy.'

Somerton detected a note of familiarity in the constable's voice when he referred to Willet as Dizzy but made no comment. He fished out his parliamentary pass which the constable made a show of examining before nodding his satisfaction. 'Thank you, Mr Somerton. You may go in, but I'll have to accompany you.'

'No problem, Constable.' Somerton turned to Brown. 'You can head off, if you wish; I'll find my own way out when I'm finished here.'

The young man smiled. 'I will take my leave if you're sure I can't be of further assistance.' Somerton shook his head and Brown left without further comment.

The constable nodded at Somerton and was about to open the door when the red light above the door began to flash and a buzzer sounded at a nearby nurse station.

P.C. White automatically raised his hand to stop position. 'Oops, bad timing, we have an emergency. Stand clear, a resus team will be here shortly. He had no sooner delivered his warning, when a white-jacketed medic and a blue-uniformed nurse came scuttling along the corridor towards them. Without a word they made their way into the single-bed room housing Willet.

Somerton addressed the constable. 'Doesn't look good.'

Ronnie White shrugged. 'It's the second time the alarm's gone off when I've been on duty; not that it matters, Dizzy won't be much of a loss to society.' Once again there was a note of familiarity in the constable's voice.

'I get the impression you know Dizzy Willet?' Somerton ventured.

'Oh, I know him alright. He's been done numerous times for drug offences, being a nuisance etc; all minor stuff.'

Somerton seized the opportunity to learn more about Willet. 'Tell me, do you think it's in character for Willet to steal a car?'

'He's never attempted it in all the time I've known him, five maybe six years. It doesn't mean he hasn't though, addicts do strange things when they're under the influence.'

Somerton acquiesced. 'I guess so. Would you describe Willet as intelligent?'

White let out a laugh. 'Intelligent? Just the reverse; he's thick as two short planks as they say. Dizzy kept himself to himself except when he was doing a bit of business.' The constable winked knowingly, 'If you get what I mean?

He wasn't much trouble, really. You seem very interested in Willet, Mr Somerton. May I ask why?'

'No reason other than he killed my best friend, who until recently just happened to be Britain's Prime Minister.'

White stiffened and nodded. 'I understand, sorry if I was insensitive, Sir.'

Their conversation ended abruptly when the door opened, and the doctor and nurse came out of the ward. 'He's a goner, Constable. Can you inform your Chief Inspector please?' With that they were gone, back whence they came.

'Will do.' White called after them. He turned to Somerton. 'That's me done here; I'll call in my report then head back to the Station. What about you, Minister?'

'I'd still like to take a look at the little bastard, if that's OK?'

PC White nodded. 'Fine by me. I won't hang around. Maybe we'll meet again another time, I'm sometimes on guard duty at Parliament. One good thing, the Country's been saved the cost of a trial.'

Windsor lay stretched out, ashen faced and still tubed up, though the monitoring equipment had been switched off. Somerton gazed at him; his emotions conflicted. This was the piece of shit alleged to have killed his friend, but was he the guilty culprit? All the pieces just didn't seem to fit, though John Law was happy; they had their man in double quick time - case closed.

Think Jack, think. If Windsor wasn't the guilty party, who else was there to blame? On the face of it, there was only one person who would appear to benefit from Croudace's death – Jupiter. But Jupiter was getting what he wanted; the satellites had been launched and more would follow. Added to that, Jupiter was very aware of the close bond between himself and Alan. Surely, he wouldn't risk a backlash from me. He knows what I'm capable of. On the other hand, as long as Alan was around, Jupiter would see him as a threat. And what if you could prove Jupiter orchestrated Alan's death, what are you going to do about it, Jack? Are you prepared to jeopardise the golden future that lies ahead to avenge your friend's death? There was no escaping the fact that Alan's death meant that the way ahead was much easier all round.

But the assassination, if that's what it was, was so crude, unsophisticated just not Jupiter's style. But what do you really know about Jupiter and what he's capable of, Jack?'

Somerton was jolted out of his thoughts when he heard a female voice. 'Excuse me, what are you doing here?' Somerton looked round to find a nurse looking at him accusingly. 'Sorry, I'm just about to go. I had hoped to have a chat with Mr Willet but I was too late.' He stepped past her and began his walk back along the corridor pondering on what had to be done.

He had to find out somehow if Jupiter his eavesdropping had picked up any talk about Croudace; any threats, any criticism. If Willet wasn't guilty someone planned and ordered Alan's death. Jupiter was essential to the success of the satellite system; I hope to hell you're not involved or I swear your laboratory will end up as your coffin.

It was time for a face to face with Jupiter but that would have to wait until after the day's business in the House.

House of Commons
On arrival back in his office, Reggie Marsh briefed him on constituency matters, outlining the actions he had taken and those he was proposing. Somerton was genuinely impressed. 'Thanks for all that, Reggie. You're going to make a good MP when the time comes. I'm lucky to have you on my team, just wish the circumstances leading up had been different.'

Marsh smiled. 'That's all put to bed, Jack. We make a good team and I hope you'll support me when the right opportunity comes along.'

Somerton nodded. 'It's a promise, Reggie. Now, have you set up any new appointments or interviews for me in the week ahead? Not that I'm looking for any, I'm pretty busy?'

Marsh grimaced. 'Just one, Jack. There's a new library opening in Harrow, and I thought you might like to cut the tape; you have first refusal. It'll make the newspapers and local TV; it'll build up your profile. Next Wednesday, 11am, so it won't interfere with your Commons routine.'

Somerton nodded. 'Sounds good, put me down for it. How about you come along?'

Marsh beamed. 'I thought you didn't want me to show my face in the constituency; Sir Isaac is likely to be there, isn't he?'

'I don't want you turning up in the constituency office just yet, though that'll come along in due course; but I reckon you've earned your attendance at other events. Sir Isaac will just have to accept your involvement – I'll deal with him. Obviously keep out of his way.'

The business in the Commons was routine to the point of being boring; Somerton sat on the front bench, nodding agreement, pointing a finger, pulling a face, whatever the moment required in support of colleagues as they made statements and responded to questions. *God, how quickly you've become one of the political fraternity, Jack.*

Gibraltar Heights.

Back in his apartment at the end of the day, Somerton switched on his computer, mulling over his approach to Jupiter as it warmed up. He entered his ultra-secure code and sat back to wait for a response, pleased when Jupiter in his usual jumpsuit filled the screen in under ten seconds.

'That was quick, Jupiter, were you expecting me?'

Jupiter nodded. 'I thought you would be in touch, Jack, in view of the sad loss of Mr Croudace. I didn't know him, I've never spoken to him, but I respected his integrity and attitude to politics. His death is a loss to the world. You have my genuine condolences; I know how much he meant to you as a friend. I've picked up that his funeral is to be a much quieter affair than that of MacKinnon's?'

'Yes, I'll be arranging a small military style funeral, exactly as Alan requested. But Alan's murder is not why I'm in touch and I know that you're not really interested in how he is to be set to rest. In fact, I suspect that you're quite pleased that the risk he presented is gone? Silenced forever.'

Jupiter grimaced. 'I think that is a trifle unfair, Jack, I don't have as much to lose as you seem to think I have. You seem to forget that I chose the UK to benefit from my scientific skills not the other way around. I can take those skills elsewhere and, I'd bet, be made very welcome. The UK, Europe, the World would be the big losers if the satellite system is not used, as only I am able to use it. I did not want Mr Croudace to lose his life – I assure you. In any case I am **always** at risk from you, Jack, as you've made clear on numerous occasions.'

Somerton's smile was icy, his voice cold. 'That will always be the case, Jupiter, but for now, I'll reluctantly accept that Alan's death was just one of those unfortunate events. He was in the wrong place at the wrong time; the victim of a low-life drug abuser. Thank you for your condolences. Can we move on to the main purpose of my contact.'

Jupiter's expression changed a little in Somerton's view. *Was it a sign of relief?* 'Please continue, Jack, what is it you want?'

An historic event was in the making but it wasn't one the world would appreciate until many months had passed. Somerton took a deep breath, even for him it was a moment to remember. 'I want to activate Satellite Target 1.'

This time there was no mistaking the change in Jupiter, his whole countenance changed, a gleam appeared in his eyes. 'I'm delighted to hear that, Jack. And what exactly is Satellite Target 1?'

It took only a few minutes for Somerton to explain precisely what was required. Jupiter's smile never left his face. 'It will be done, Jack, rest assured.'

'I have one more request, Jupiter.'

Jupiter's smile widened. 'Ask away, Jack.'

'I want to strengthen and develop our partnership, but to do that I have to have my finger on the satellite trigger as well as you. I want targets to be a joint decision and I want the system's activation to be a joint operation. I have shown that I trust you, now I want you to show that you trust me.'

'Hmm, I don't rule it out, Jack but I need time to think about it.'

The screen went blank, just as Somerton had anticipated. He had put pressure on Jupiter. *How would Jupiter deal with his request? Was his own life now at risk? When it came down to it, Jupiter didn't really need him or the Research Centre. They had both served their purpose.*

CHAPTER 21

Dover Maritime Rescue Co-ordination Centre. 26 February 2021

Barry Cleghorn looked out onto the Dover Strait, said to be the busiest seaway in the world. Not that it looked busy from where he sat. It was coming up for 11am and he was on a tea break; there was nothing more relaxing than looking out at a calm sea on what was a bright, sunny, blue-skied day. Far in the distance to the west, he could see what looked like a large container vessel; to the east, a fast approaching Calais to Dover ferry….bliss. He reached forward for his mug of coffee, a final slurp before returning to his computer station at 11am prompt, his fifteen-minute tea break over. He was in the process of swallowing his mouthful of coffee, when he heard his colleagues shout out in unison. 'What the hell's going on? What the fuck! The system has crashed!'

Cleghorn rose immediately to his feet and looked at the screens; his jaw dropping, his stomach churning when he saw that they were all blank. This was a first for him; he'd lost a screen a time or two but never a complete system crash. He looked around wondering what to do, relieved when the Shift Supervisor, Kim Watson, appeared in the doorway to her office, her attention directed at the blank screens. She displayed no visible signs of panic, in fact she calmly started issuing instructions.

'Jimmy, check out the electrical supply and the radar input.'

'Colin, tell our French counterparts what has happened and when you've done that let the Parliamentary Secretary's office know.'

'Barry, put in a call to Channel Electronics and tell them to get their best technician here pronto.'

'Christine, go through the log and get on the short-wave radio. Announce an emergency and require all vessels to reduce their speed to 5 knots until further notice.'

She bit on her biro and smiled wryly. 'Oh well, I guess it had to happen sometime; it's good experience.' *Why the fuck did it happen on my watch.*

Channel Electronics nearest technician, Eddie Grey, arrived within ten minutes and was greeted by Watson. 'Thanks for getting here so quickly, Eddie; we have a major problem on our hands.'

'So I've been told, Kim. Run me through it.'

She pointed at the multi-screen set-up. 'It's right in front of you, Eddie; the system crashed at 11am.'

'Sorry, they just said it was an emergency, no details. I'll get right on it.'

Grey set about his work, checking and re-checking every component of the system, central computer, internet connection, aerials, electrical supply and its source, keyboards, monitors, desperation setting in when he found nothing. Thirty-eight minutes flashed by; at 11.51 he gave up and reported back to Kim Watson in her office. She looked up from her desk smiling when he walked through the door.

'All done?' She enquired, confident that the answer would be 'yes', dismayed when he shook his head. 'No! You mean you can't fix it?'

'No, it's not that; I haven't the faintest idea what's going on. I checked the entire system twice and can't detect a supply fault, an equipment fault, or a signal fault; it's a mystery. I've been outside with my test equipment and the radar signals are there; they just aren't registering when it reaches your set-up.'

Watson slumped in her chair. 'So where does that leave us? This has got to be sorted.'

Grey nodded. 'Couldn't agree with you more. I've been on to H.Q, our Chief Technician and a design boffin are on their way.'

'How long before they get here?'

Grey shrugged. 'Don't know, they are coming from London.'

Watson rolled her eyes. 'Let's hope there aren't any motorway problems.'

Just then Barry Cleghorn breezed into her office. 'Well done, Eddie. You're a genius. It's all systems go as they say at mission control.'

Kim Watson looked at Grey searching for an explanation but all she got in return was a shrug. 'No idea, it's nothing I did, I can assure you.'

Watson frowned. 'It's good that we're up and working but not knowing what caused the outage is worrying. When your colleagues arrive, I want a comprehensive investigation carried out and a detailed report on my desk as soon as possible. I'll want to know what they checked, what they found, what they did and recommendations as to how to stop this ever happening again. This has happened on my shift and I'm the one who is going to be asked the awkward questions. Thank God it doesn't seem to be too busy out there today.'

Watson sighed and made her way into the control room. *Time to rally the troops.* 'Right, listen up everybody. Channel Electronics' top technical boffins are on their way and are confident they can sort this problem. When they've done their bit and you're happy with what's on the screen, reverse the calls you made earlier and advise that we're back up and working. You can add that a formal investigation is under way.'

House of Commons. Later that day.
The business of the House complete, Somerton rose to make his way out of the chamber, passing Laura Taylor and Ken Ogilvie engaged in conversation.

'Jack.' Taylor caught hold of his sleeve. 'I'd like a few minutes of your time please. Go on ahead, I'll join you shortly.'

Jess Tate wasn't around when Somerton got to the PM's office, so he sat on her desk wondering why Taylor wanted to see him. Five minutes later Taylor arrived and beckoned him to join her.

'Jess having a day off?' Somerton enquired.

'No, she's just gone into town on an errand for me. The switchboard's dealing with my calls. What do you know about this?' She reached forward two sheets of A4 notepaper.

Somerton recognised the Dover Maritime Board headline and immediately guessed the subject matter but studiously read it through to the end. 'Sorry Laura, it's a strange business but as I speak, I haven't been briefed on it. I can phone Cheltenham and the NRSC now and try to find out what they know, or I can email you a full report when I get back to the office?'

Taylor shook her head. 'I'm curious, Jack, check it out now please. If our set-up has been hacked, I want to know by whom and what we can do to stop it happening again. You can use Jess's office and I'll carry on with some business in the meantime. Join me when you're ready.'

Somerton began by phoning Cheltenham HQ, playing the innocent and asking what they knew of the incident. He hung up whilst the operative made enquiries. Ten long minutes elapsed before Somerton got a call back. 'Hello Minister, I've made enquiries and can see that the system went down at 11am and was restored an hour later, although we weren't aware of, or informed of, the problem at the time. An initial check hasn't come up with any reason for the system failure. We found no evidence of external interference, but we are continuing to investigate; I'll get back to you if anything new comes along.'

Next up Somerton phoned the NRSC and spoke to Eric Barker. 'Hi Eric, it's Jack. What can you tell me about an interruption to the English Channel Navigation System this morning?'

'We know that the system went down for an hour, 11am to noon. We know it wasn't a hardware or software failure in the Control Centre. It's highly likely that the signals to the system were somehow blocked, either by unknown persons or suffered interference due to natural causes. No evidence was found to believe the latter was the cause, no record of sun flares etc; similar systems in the area continued to work normally. We have no proof, but it does seem likely that the system was hacked by an external source. We don't know by whom or how. Sorry I can't be more helpful, Jack. We will continue to monitor the situation.'

'Thanks for that Eric. Give it another hour or so, but if there is no evidence of cyber activity or physical resource failure, revert to normal duties. There are more important threats out there.'

His enquiries complete, the expected answers received, in fact the answers he'd hoped for, Somerton knocked on Taylor's door, entered and sat down.

Taylor raised an eyebrow. 'Do take a seat Jack.' Her sarcasm barely disguised.

Somerton smiled. 'Already have done, Laura. I've checked out the Channel incident and drawn a blank. Cheltenham wasn't aware of the incident, the NRSC were aware. Both parties will investigate further and report back. The NRSC are fairly confident the system was hacked but have no idea who was responsible. I'm really concerned that this could take place and the perpetrators are able to cover their tracks so successfully. It's very worrying.'

Taylor's expression revealed nothing of what was going on in her head. 'Why is this especially worrying, Jack? Hacking is routine nowadays; most institutions have taken a hit, even the Pentagon.'

Somerton pursed his lips. 'True but it raises four questions. Number one - why the Dover set-up? Two - what motivated the hack, given it came and went in an hour? Three – how did they do it and leave no trace? Four – who was the instigator? We can't even begin to answer any of those questions. Was it a test, a warning, a threat? As your Minister for National Security, I ought to know but I don't. Hence, I'm worried, very worried.'

Somewhat to his surprise, Taylor seemed relaxed. 'It's early days, Jack. Further investigation might come up with the answers. It gives us food for thought though.'

Somerton raised an eyebrow. 'Meaning?'

'Well, you've got to admit, it's quite an achievement; the ability to switch a secure system on and off at will without trace. God knows what else it's capable off. In the wrong hands. We could do with recruiting the hackers responsible and setting them to work for us. Don't you think?'

Was it his imagination or was there a trace of a smile on her lips. Somerton nodded. 'I knew you would understand the implications of what's happened, having a degree in Computer Sciences It's very troubling, we'll spare no effort in trying to track them down; any suspicious messages on air will be followed up. What do you want me to tell the House?'

Taylor smiled. 'As little as possible; sandwich it in amongst other more interesting stuff.'

Somerton stood up and saluted. 'I expect you've got things to do, I'll head off to the NRSC.' He hesitated briefly, then asked. 'Might I enquire how your sister is?'

'Well, she's gone home for now. I just hope there's no more trouble, though I fear history will repeat itself.'

'Why don't you point him in the direction of an investment on the other side of the world?'

Taylor smiled. 'That might just be an idea, Jack. I'll give it some thought, see if I can press a few buttons in the Middle East. See you around.'

CHAPTER 22

Somerton's parliament office, Friday, one week later.
Somerton's private mobile buzzed. 'Hi, it's Mike. Are you free to speak?'

'Go ahead, Mike.'

'I'm afraid I haven't been able to come up with anything serious regards Guy Madison; some shady deals here and there but nothing involving drugs, weapons or people smuggling. He's oiled the wheels a few times, paid over a few sweeteners; all fairly minor stuff. He doesn't hesitate to introduce himself as the Prime Minister's brother-in-law and it does open doors for him. Do you want me to carry on with this or let it drop for now?'

'That's disappointing Mike, but leave it for now. Keep listening out though and let me know if anything crops up. He seems to be behaving himself; maybe he's turned over a new leaf.'

'And pigs might fly, Jack; men like Madison never change.'

'Maybe so Mike, maybe so.'

It was time to contact Jupiter again; time to set up the second target, another test for constellation MacKinnon. He went through the usual process, pleased when he got an immediate response. 'This is getting to be a habit, Jupiter.'

'What is, Jack?' Jupiter was genuinely puzzled.

'Your almost immediate response when I contact you. No matter. The Dover business went well, and I've authorised the launch of four more satellites this weekend, conditions permitting. Did you experience any difficulties with targeting the Dover set-up?'

'No problems at all, Jack. As a soldier I'm sure you know that a static target is straightforward. It's when we select multiple moving targets it becomes more difficult; that's when we need as many satellites in the air as possible. I expect you've had some questions to answer in your security role?'

'Nothing I couldn't handle, as I'm sure you're well aware, given your eavesdropping capabilities. I want you to set up

Target 2 for next Wednesday, same time, local time of course and for one hour duration, same as Dover.'

Jupiter nodded enthusiastically. 'Another static target, count it as done. I expect your thoughts are with your friend's funeral. Out of respect I would have watched the funeral but of course you haven't given any access to the media, much to their annoyance. The Press Association is furious at your ban on reporting.'

'They can bleat all they want; it was Alan's wish and that's the end of it. They can follow the gun carriage along the route and the PM is insisting on a memorial service at a future date; her decision not mine. If there's nothing else to discuss, I'll be on my way?'

Jupiter simply nodded and the screen went blank.

An hour later Somerton was about to put his laptop to sleep when a coded message came through; decoded it simply said, *Arrangements in progress, not long now.*

The Royal Military Chapel. Sunday 1 March
Knowing how much his friend admired military pomp and ceremony, Somerton had arranged for Croudace to lie in state in a closed coffin in the Royal Military Chapel in Birdcage Walk from where it was ceremoniously carried to an adapted gun carriage by Somerton, Eddie Black, Mike Davies and three serving SAS soldiers. The carriage, drawn by a military jeep then set off for Golder's Green crematorium. The procession comprised six SAS military vehicles and two Rolls Royce cars, service personnel in the former, politicians in the latter.

Somerton, in his SAS uniform, travelled with Laura Taylor. They sat in silence; Somerton deep in thought, Taylor recognising that he didn't want to converse.

The service at Golder's Green was formal and short, words spoken only by the Army padre. No eulogy, no hymns. Only the Last post sounded by a bugle; pomp and ceremony would have to wait until the formal memorial service.

The ceremony over, those present returned to their vehicles for their journey back to their respective bases. Again, there was silence between Somerton and Taylor during the journey back to

Downing Street, interrupted only by Taylor. 'A simple moving service, Jack, but I just feel he deserved more.'

'It was what he wanted, Laura. I hate funerals; they remind me of all the things I should have said and done whilst he was with us. It seems to me that funerals are for the living, not the deceased. It's the living who get the feelgood feeling, not the dead. Ach, forgive me, I'm not in the mood for conversation; I can't stop thinking that, in no time at all, I've laid to rest my two closest friends.'

New York; Wednesday 4 March 2021

The controllers in the Power Control Centre for New York City subway were full of banter about basketball, baseball, college football and politics. So far it had been a trouble-free morning. The midtown Manhattan building controlled the power supply and train movement for one of the biggest underground traffic systems in the world. It was 11am, the morning rush hour was over, controllers were either drinking coffee or making it; the chief controller, John Popovic, was smiling. And then, it all went wrong; the lights went out plunging the control room and all ancillary areas into darkness. Fortunately, the battery-fed emergency lighting came on immediately. Somebody muttered. 'Useless back-up, we'd be better off with fucking candles. John Popovic's smile was gone, a look of bewilderment filled his face as he looked up at the now shadowy map of the underground track and signalling system. The map was dead, the signal and track occupancy indicator lights extinguished. 'What the hell's going on? Why hasn't the emergency generator kicked in? What a fucking disaster. Where's the technician?'

'Right with you, John. I'm headed to the generator room right now; looks like the changeover system has failed. I'll do it manually.' Sam Allen's voice was calm, matter-of-fact; panic served no useful purpose.

Popovic nodded, re-assured, a measure of relief setting in; it was going to be OK. 'Quick as you can, Sam.'

'Dave, phone the Subway Director of Operations, explain what's happened. Tell him all trains are to reduce speed to 10 miles per hour until further notice. Trains are to travel under caution to the nearest station and on arrival wait there for further instructions.'

Dave Crosby nodded. 'On it.' Routine was boring. He was happy to be involved in an emergency.

Popovic sat back to give some thought to his next course of action. *Now where the hell is the Emergency Procedure Manual* He couldn't recall when he had last seen it, never mind having to use it. A search of the control desk drawers brought a negative result. 'Anybody seen the Emergency Procedure Manual?' He peered round the room....every head shook.

'Damn.' Popovic rattled his desk. 'It has to be somewhere. Everybody get looking and be quick about it.'

'John.' Popovic looked round to see Dave Crosby extending the phone in his direction. 'The Operations Manager wants a word with you. It seems everything is running normally on the track; no problem with signalling or anything else. He wants to know if he can let the trains carry on running to timetable.'

Popovic closed his eyes in exasperation. *How am I supposed to know what to do in an unprecedented situation? Where the hell is that Manual?* 'Gimme the phone.' He covered the mouthpiece. 'What's his name?'

'Ted Grimshaw.' Crosby dropped his voice to a whisper.

'Hi Ted,' John Popovic speaking. 'We're doing all we can this end. The control system is dead, and the emergency generator hasn't kicked in; a disaster all round. I'm sorry but there's not much I can do at the moment. The technician is working on the generator. I know the disruption this is causing but my instruction stands; maximum speed 10 miles per hour and all trains to stop at first station on their route until further notice.'

'But...' Popovic cut Grimshaw short as he began to protest. 'Sorry, no buts, Ted, this is Control Room, the buck stops here. You have my instructions.' He glanced at his watch. 'This conversation timed at 11.10.'

Just then Sam Allen returned, his expression a mix of puzzlement and apology. 'We have a mystery on our hands, John. There's been no interruption to the power supply to the Centre; that's why the generator didn't start up. But the System Panel somehow won't let the power through. I confess I have no idea why or how that can happen. I've been in touch with the electricity supply authority, and they don't believe me. Their Chief Technician is on his way, should be here shortly.'

Popovic glanced at his watch 11.15. 'So, is there anything you can do?'

Allen nodded. 'I'm going to check out the panel electronics, but I've done it already and found nothing, so I don't hold out much hope.'

Popovic shrugged, already wearied from the tension. 'OK, keep me posted.' He flopped back in his chair; all he could do was wait and hope.

At 11.18 he got the call he had been expecting, one he wasn't looking forward to. He picked up the red phone; he couldn't remember ever having used it, the one reserved for the top brass. 'Popovic speaking.'

'Toni Agostini.' Popovic heart sank; it was the Mayor.

'I know why you're ringing, Mr Mayor; I assure you we are doing all we can, this situation is unprecedented.' He attempted to go on, but Agostini cut him off. 'I don't want your excuses, Popovic. Get it fixed pronto, that's why we pay you.'

'Mr Mayor, I assure you ...'

'I don't want fucking assurances, I want solutions. The city is at a standstill so get it fixed. Phone me every fifteen minutes to report on what action you've taken, got it?'

'Yes, Mr Mayor, will do, you have my word.....'

Agostini slammed the phone down. Popovic gave him the rude one finger salute and went in search of Sam Allen. He found the technician meticulously checking the control panel circuitry. 'Any luck?'

Allen shook his head. 'Nope, everything is OK so far.' His face lit up when two technicians from the electrical supply authority walked in and introduced themselves. 'Frank Ismay, chief technician and this is our cleverest technician, Terry Sweeney. Give us a rundown on the situation from the start.'

Popovic motioned to Sam Allen. 'Brief them on where you're up to; I'll go back to my desk and await the next haranguing from the Mayor.' Just as he was leaving a young woman arrived. 'Hi, I'm Sue from Traffic Control, who do I deal with?

Popovic sighed. 'I guess that's me. John Popovic, I'm the Chief Controller but Sam is best placed to explain what's taken place.' He took another glance at his watch, 11.32, time to phone Agostini. Back at his desk he picked up the red phone and at precisely 11.33 he phoned the Mayor. He took a deep breath when he got through. 'Mr Mayor, Popovic here. I'm sorry but there is no change in the situation, except we now have four technicians working on the problem.'

Agostini grunted. 'I've been told that trackside everything is working normally so why can't the trains be allowed to carry on.'

'That's an absolute no-no, a train collision has the potential to result in dozens of deaths and I'm not prepared to risk lives for the sake of some inconvenience.'

'And what if I instruct you to restore normal running, what then?'

Popovic gulped, it was showdown time. 'I'm sorry Mr Mayor, I would be duty bound to refuse.' The stand-off was left hanging when Agostini slammed down the phone. Popovic sighed and shook his head. *There goes my job.* But for now, all he could do was wait and pray for heavenly intervention.

The minutes ticked by slowly, Popovic pondered on what he would do if he got the elbow and carried on mentally exhorting God to intervene. His prayers were answered at noon precisely when the lights came on and the panel burst into life. 'Thank you, God. Thank you, techies.'

'Dave, phone the Operations Manager and tell him to resume normal service.'

Popovic lifted the red phone, this time triumph had replaced trepidation. 'Hello, Popovic speaking.' It wasn't the Mayor, a junior had taken the call, 'Sorry the Mayor is busy.'

'Can you please inform him that I called to tell him that the subway service is back and running.'

The junior was dismissive. 'He's on site so he probably knows that.'

'Just do as you're told and let the Mayor know I called him.'
Somerton's parliament office.
Thousands of miles away Somerton, courtesy of CNN had been following the events in New York on his laptop. It was time to put his security hat on and phone Eric Barker at the NRSC. 'Eric, what do you know of this business in the New York subway?

'Not a lot, we're monitoring it closely. It's another hack but we haven't been able to track down the source.'

'Keep trying and let me know of any developments.' *Now do I wait for Laura to phone me or should I head for Downing Street. Hmm I think I'd enjoy a stroll.*

Downing Street.

'Hi Jess. Sorry to turn up unannounced but I need fifteen minutes with Laura, it's about the New York subway scenario.'

'Is that the best you can come up with? I'm beginning to have suspicions about you two.'

Somerton clasped his heart. 'You've guessed, now can I see her?'

'Let me check.' A short conversation ensued. 'You can go through, ten minutes, max.'

Prime Minister's Office

'Sit down, Jack and give me your take on New York; I've heard the media version.'

'It's exactly what happened at Dover; an unexplained power failure. It's another hack by an unknown source. It's happened on a Wednesday and again it lasted from 11am until noon. There was no warning or threat, and no claim of responsibility afterwards. It's weird. I don't know about you, but I don't believe in co-incidences; these two events are linked. Someone out there is demonstrating how clever they are. That much seems obvious but, in absence of any demand, I've no idea what they are seeking to achieve.'

Taylor clasped her hands. 'Unless it's purely a demonstration, a test perhaps? A precursor to future blackmail? Leaving that aside, who are the likely suspects?'

Somerton smiled. 'No prizes for guessing that it could be Russia, China or even North Korea, though I doubt if the latter has the expertise. There's nothing more I can add.'

Taylor's brow furrowed. 'You don't seem to be concerned that someone out there can disable key systems whenever they choose and do so without leaving a trail.'

'I am concerned, Laura, and sooner or later our guys will track them down.'

I hope so. Keep me posted. I wish I had that kind of weapon at my disposal, don't you?'

'And what would you do with it, Laura?'

Taylor laughed out loud. 'I'd take over the world of course and make it a better, safer place. I hope you would want to do the same, Jack' Her eyes locked with Somerton's inviting a response. When none came, she glanced at her watch. 'Sorry, Jack, you have to go.'

Somerton stood up and started to leave then stopped. 'How's your sister?'

'She is fine for now and there just a chance Guy might be heading off on a business trip. Thanks for asking. Have you got designs on her?'

Somerton smiled. 'I have designs on all attractive women, Laura., including present company.' He winked and strode towards the door, but a sudden thought occurred to him. 'How did you get to hear about the New York situation?'

'Will Kenny mentioned it during a telephone call. What makes you ask?'

Somerton shrugged. 'Curiosity, just plain old curiosity.'

CHAPTER 23

'Can I speak to Mr Guy Madison please?' The pronunciation was perfect, public schoolish, but with just a hint of an accent.'

'You're speaking to him. Who's calling?'

'My name may not mean anything to you Mr Madison, my name is Hassan Bashar. I act for the Crown Prince Mugrin bin Abchilayin. Your name was passed to me by the British Ambassador. I understand that you are related to Prime Minister Taylor.'

'That's correct; I'm married to her sister. Does that matter?'

'Indeed it does Mr Madison. I'm looking for someone of standing to act on my behalf; someone who can be relied upon to be discreet.'

Madison's interest grew, there was a hint of money in the air, serious money. 'Act on your behalf, in what way exactly?'

Hassan hesitated. 'I'm looking for someone to act as a middleman; a purchasing agent might be a better description.'

Madison was wary but more interested. 'What kind of purchases?'

'I do not wish to discuss the Prince's business affairs on the telephone. Would you be prepared to come to Jeddah for two or three days to discuss my offer in depth and in absolute privacy?'

'I'm interested Mr Bashar, but I don't want to incur unnecessary expense or waste your time and mine. I mean, I might not like what's on offer.'

'I fully understand your position, Mr Madison, I share your opinion. Come over and we will meet all reasonable expenses. You will occur no costs whatsoever. I will book your flight and hotel for two nights whether we can agree a contract or not.'

'Could you give me some idea of what I could expect to earn if we took this forward?'

'That's something we would have to discuss; there would be a significant retainer involved. I should add that I would like to meet you within the next few days.'

Madison had one of those light bulb moments; he already had several business interests in Jeddah and this was an opportunity to pursue them cost free. 'Well, it all sounds a bit nebulous, Mr Bashar, but I'll take your word it will be worthwhile. So, here's the deal – you will book and pay for the flights and a five-star hotel – I want Business Class travel and a car put at my disposal whilst I'm in Jeddah. I will travel over the day after tomorrow and I'd like three nights in Jeddah, if possible, please.'

Bashar chuckled. 'You drive a hard bargain, Mr Madison but I'll accept your conditions. Your flight tickets and hotel details will arrive with you tomorrow. I look forward to meeting you.'

'And I you Mr Bashar. Don't forget the car, good quality of course.'

'But of course, goodbye.'

Bashar delivered on his promise, flight tickets and hotel details arrived the following morning by Royal Mail special delivery. Madison would be flying out of Heathrow the following day on the 12.30 Saudi Airlines flight to Jeddah. Madison's eyes lit up when he saw that he was flying business class as agreed. The six-hour flight would land in Jeddah at 20.30 local time given the two-hour time zone difference. He would be met at the airport by Bashar and chauffeured to the hotel. *Oh what it is, to be the PM's brother-in-law; you have your uses Laura. OK Guy, get your finger out, you have some arrangements to put in place.*

Madison called two business associates arranging to meet both on the day after his arrival. That done he made the call uppermost on his mind. 'Hello Ketifa, it's Guy, how are you darling?'

'Missing you, when am I going to see you?'

'That's what I'm calling about honey. I'll be over tomorrow for three nights; it would be nice if you could keep me company.'

'Of course, I can darling; just tell me when and where.'

'I'll be booking into the Jeddah Hilton, the hotel overlooking the Corniche. We can go for a walk along that wonderful beach before we settle down for the evening. It'll be nearing 10pm by the time I get there so you might have to wait in the lounge. Get yourself a drink and put it on my bill. Can't wait to see you, must go, bye for now.'

Those arrangements made, he texted his wife to advise that he would be going away to Jeddah for a few days on business and gave her no option. *'You'll have to be around for the kids.'*

Jeddah International Airport

Madison disembarked the Saudi Airlines airbus twenty-five minutes ahead of schedule and made his way along the air-bridge to the Customs and Immigration Control area and proceeded to Immigration.

The official examined Madison's passport, making sure that the photograph was that of the bearer. 'And what is the purpose of your visit to Jeddah, Mr Madison?'

'Mainly business, with a bit of sightseeing.'

'How long will you be in Jeddah?'

'Three nights.'

'Enjoy your stay, Mr Madison, you may pass through.'

Madison made his way quickly along a corridor to the Arrivals Hall looking along the line of waiting welcomers, searching in vain for a hand-held notice bearing his name and cursing himself for not asking Bashar for his mobile number. *Shit, what's happened? I hope Bashar has got the date right.* He glanced at his watch, relaxing a little when he saw it was only 8.30; Bashar probably wasn't aware the plane had landed early. Just then a small, middle-aged, bespectacled Arab joined the front line of the welcoming brigade and held up a sheet of A4 with the name Madison in bold black lettering.

Madison strolled forward hand extended. 'Mr Bashar?'

'Mr Madison, delighted to see you. Sorry I'm a little late, traffic problems. Let's get out of here. I trust you had a good flight?'

Madison nodded. 'Uneventful, but very comfortable in business class, thank you. And I would add, the food and drink were excellent, thank you.'

'I'm pleased to hear that. There's a car and driver waiting for us in the car hire area. I'm afraid I can't spend any time with you at the hotel, the Prince has given me another task to perform.'

Madison concealed his annoyance; this wasn't a good start. Although on reflection he'd have more time with Ketifa. 'So, when are we going to discuss our deal, Mr Bashar?'

'Please call me Hassan. We can discuss our deal as we travel to your hotel. I'm disappointed I won't be joining you for dinner the food is excellent there, and of course it's all charged to expenses. Ah, here we are.' He pointed at the white Land Rover Epoque.

Madison whistled. 'Wow, one of my favourite cars.'

Bashar smiled. 'Alas, it doesn't belong to me, it's one of the Prince's many vehicles; bullet proof glass, darkened window, armour plate etc. Not quite a James Bond car but very nearly. Please get in and we'll be on our way; leave your bag for Nabeel.'

The driver, a large swarthy Arab got out of the car and muttered something in Arabic. 'He wants to put your bag in the boot, Mr Madison.'

'Sure. Call me Guy please.'

Settled in the car, they set out on the journey to Jeddah; traffic was heavy in the airport area and progress slow. Madison quickly lost interest in the external view; he'd seen the industrial buildings and high-rise dwellings on numerous occasions.

'The scenery isn't attractive Guy. Shall we discuss the deal I'm offering? You will be replacing our previous contractor who proved to be dishonest and was swindling money from the Prince. He is currently in gaol awaiting trial and won't be getting out...ever.'

Madison stiffened. 'Is that a veiled threat?'

Bashar smiled. 'Only if your intentions are dishonourable, Guy. Enough of that, let's talk about the deal. You will receive £60,000 per annum, paid monthly as a retainer, plus 5% of the value of all purchases made on the Prince's behalf. I can assure you these will be substantial, His Highness has very expensive tastes. You will be sourcing the finest of wines, whiskies, liquers and other commodities.'

'Do these other commodities include narcotics, precious metals or girls? I apologise for being blunt, but I want to know what I might be getting into?'

Bashar looked thoughtful. 'No girls but occasionally narcotics and precious metals. Maybe even a work of art.'

'And how do I get these goods to the Prince? Transportation is always a risky area.'

Bashar smiled. 'That's the easy bit; you simply deliver the goods to the Saudi Embassy in London from whence it will be forwarded to Jeddah as diplomatic baggage.'

Madison nodded. 'It all sounds very doable but why bring someone in like me; surely someone on the Prince's staff could handle this?'

Bashar nodded. 'Of course, but sadly there are many hierarchical politics in the Saudi royal household. Mistrust abounds, betrayal is an ever-present risk. Some of the purchases would not be thought appropriate, so it's best an outsider is recruited. Preferably one of some standing, like the Prime Minister's brother-in-law.

Madison nodded, though he didn't quite see the logic. 'And the financial side of the business. How will the goods be funded?'

'You will have a credit card and a debit card, each with a high enough credit limit to serve any purchase. A copy of all statements will automatically go to the Prince's accountant.

Madison raised an eyebrow. 'That's a very trusting arrangement?'

Bashar nodded. 'Trust is important but be assured, death or life-long imprisonment is the penalty for dishonesty. So, are you interested or not?'

'I'll think about it overnight and let you have my final answer in the morning. But for now, I'm pleased to accept your offer. I've lost track of where we are, how much further is it?'

'Not far now, in fact I think we have arrived.'

Madison was puzzled, but he had been distracted during the journey, and had no idea where he was. There was no sign of the hotel, or the Red Sea that it overlooked. His puzzlement increased when the driver turned into a driveway and stopped behind a dark-grey Land Rover Discovery. 'You do like your Land Rovers, Hassan.'

Bashar got out and motioned Madison to follow. 'This is as far as I go. I must attend to my other duties. I'm afraid you will have to change vehicles. Nabeel will get your bag.'

Maddison hesitated for a second or two then got out.

The two men stood facing each other whilst the driver recovered Madison's suitcase. Bashar smiled. 'Are you married, Guy?'

'You know I'm married; I'm the Prime Minister's brother-in-law, that's why you offered me the job. Remember?'

Bashar put his hand over his mouth. 'Silly me, of course you're married. Your wife's name is Geraldine and you beat her up regularly, do you not?'

Madison tensed. 'Who told you that?' Fear was kicking in. 'Who are you?'

Bashar smiled as he drew an automatic from a holster inside his jacket. 'I'm your executioner Guy; your wife's avenging angel.' He chuckled as he pulled the trigger twice.

Nabeel stood watching, a smirk on his lips.

'Don't stand there gawping, Nabeel. Gather him up and get him in the car. Wrap him in a blanket or something; make sure you don't mess up the vehicle. One more thing Nabeel. If his body is found, you'll find yourself in serious trouble.'

His instructions given Bashar climbed into the Epoque and drove away towards Jeddah.

CHAPTER 24

Gibraltar Heights 17th March 2021

Somerton rarely watched television, but Target 3 had been activated and he wanted to check out how the situation had developed over the course of the day. The target, Munich Air Traffic Control, got a mention in the evening news; there had a complete electrical failure at 11am local time. The outage had lasted for one hour precisely with all the anticipated disruptions resulting – flight diversions – flight cancellations – flight delays – disgruntled passengers and airlines. The earlier radio and TV reports had been brief, later versions had been beefed up with the number of flights affected and passenger numbers involved. The lack of a known cause had generated a storm of criticism; there had been no mention of a cyber-attack.

Later in the evening one bright reporter had posed the question Somerton had hope for – 'Was there a link between three recent events, Dover, New York and Munich?' The reporter, Jill Castle, had pointed out that in each case the electricity failure had occurred at noon local time and had lasted for one hour. In all three cases the power failure had occurred on a Wednesday. Castle had suggested that the biggest co-incidence of all was the fact that the cause of the failure was unknown. It appeared likely that all three systems had been hacked by an external source. She had gone on to point out that the three countries involved were all Western democracies and members of NATO. She had ended her piece by suggesting that it seemed likely that the protagonist was an eastern country with Russia, China, North Korea, and possibly Iran, the prime suspects.

The programme had no sooner ended when his work mobile buzzed. 'Jack, it's Laura. I've been watching BBC World News, so no prizes for guessing that this call has been prompted by Jill Castle's report. I'll have to make a statement in the House tomorrow and you'll have to be ready to answer the deluge of questions that will follow. Join me in my office tomorrow and we'll formulate our approach to Castle's assertions which, I have to say, have a ring of truth about them. I don't suppose you have anything you want to share with me, any revelations?

'Sorry, Laura, there's nothing I can add. I agree that the characteristics are identical and, as I've said before, I don't believe in co-incidences. All I can tell you is that we are working all out, both at the NRSC and Cheltenham to identify the hacker. The same goes for the other members of the Five Eyes; Canada, Australia, New Zealand and the States are as much in the dark as we are.'

'OK, Jack, let's leave it for now. Get a good night's sleep and be in my office at noon for a snack-lunch and discussion about where this is business is leading us.'

'Will do, bye.' Somerton sighed. *That's the million-dollar question Laura, just where is this heading? Setting up the demonstration targets is the easy bit, Jack, what's the end game and who's going to kick it off?'*

Prime Minister's office Next day.

Somerton exchanged his usual dose of banter with Jess Tate then made his way in. Taylor motioned him to sit and moved forward to remove the cling film from a plate of sandwiches. 'Tea or coffee, Jack?'

'Tea please, strong no sugar.'

Taylor looked weary, shadows showing under her eyes. Somerton opted not to remark or offer any sympathy; if she was tired, she would know it and sympathy wouldn't change anything.

'So, what have you got for me, Jack?'

Somerton carried on chewing his mouthful of tuna sandwich and made a circle with his thumb and forefinger. 'I'll answer any Parliamentary questions as you instruct me to but nothing new, sorry. All three centres have been subjected to a cyber-attack, that's certain. The level of scientific know-how is impressive in the extreme. But we are no further forward when it comes to identifying the guilty party. I'm really sorry I can't be of more help.' Somerton summoned up a look of dismay. 'I feel I'm letting you down, and the Country for that matter. The only comfort I can offer is that the Americans and Germans haven't come up with anything either.'

Taylor shook her head. 'No, Jack, you're not letting me down. It's just that whoever is doing this, is cleverer than we are at this moment in time. Seems to me that's the way it is with technology; a never-ending neck and neck race to get ahead of the game. And it's not just you, I might add. I spoke with Will Kenny earlier and he says his people haven't got anywhere either. Maybe the research bods could help? Get them on to it; pull out all the stops; we need to find out who is responsible.'

Somerton nodded. 'Of course; I'm as frustrated over this as everyone else. I'll hypothesise if you want me to.'

Taylor looked and sounded glum. 'If that's the best you've got, let's hear your thoughts.'

Somerton took a deep breath. Sooner or later Taylor would have to know the truth but not yet. 'I'll state the obvious and confirm your conclusion. We are dealing with superior technology. The shutdowns always start at 11am prompt local time and last for one hour precisely. The three centres are all western democracies so it's logical to assume that these cyber-attacks originate in the East. The purpose of these attacks is to demonstrate to the West how easy it is to take out key facilities. I think these demos are a precursor to further action, the nature of which we can only guess. It could involve permanent disabling of key installations, it could be economic blackmail, it could be all out war. The end goal would be to subjugate the West.'

Taylor nodded. 'That all makes sense; you and Will Kenny are on the same wavelength. He rather jokingly added that these cyber-attacks have all occurred since the MacKinnon Constellation was launched. He even went as far as asking me if this was a UK strategy to rule the world.' She locked eyes with Somerton and waited for a reply.

I wonder if you know more than you're saying, Laura? Somerton laughed. 'Sorry it's not on my agenda, Laura, but it's not a bad idea. The ultimate commonwealth of nations, an empire like no other. I seem to recall you mentioning you wouldn't mind having that kind of power last time we met.'

'You're damn right I would. This world of ours could benefit from some kind of overarching body running it, one with the power to bring the extremists to heel. Enough of that, let's get back to the real world. Will Kenny raised the issue of these

Russian military exercises taking place on Ukraine's doorstep; his people think that they are a pre-cursor to an invasion. His intelligence sources have heard that it's a view held by most of Russia's generals and is an open topic of conversation over there. Week by week, Rostov adds to the military deployed there. The number of tanks and missile launchers on site increases daily.

The general view is that when Rostov has the right level of military resources in place, he'll cross the border into the Donbas region. Will's people reckon it's a matter of weeks not months before Russia invades. As to motives, we both agree that Rostov hankers after an old-style USSR. The West let him take Crimea, despite all our huff and puff we did nothing. An invasion would inflate his ego, a new USSR would be his legacy. Will and I agree he must be stopped but Will won't put troops on Ukraine soil; he's afraid it could start World War 3 and could lead to the use of nuclear weapons. Rostov has outmanoeuvred us every step of the way and it's time the West hit back. Russia supplies a big percentage of Europe's oil and gas, so he has their big players by the balls. It seems that all the West is left with are financial sanctions and they are painfully slow to take effect.'

Somerton nodded. 'I can see all that; I guess there is only one short term solution.'

Taylor's brow furrowed and she looked deep into Somerton's eyes. 'And what might that be, Jack?'

'Take out Rostov.'

Taylor waved her hands dismissively. 'And just how would we do that, Jack? And if we could, the Russian high command would see it as blatant aggression by the West and World War 3 would follow.'

Somerton eased back in his chair. 'I guess so. Maybe we have to hope that one of his cronies sees him for the madman he is, and he's taken out by one of his own people. It's all a bit of a Catch 22. So not having got very far with that, what's next?'

Taylor replied immediately. 'Get your bags packed; you and I are going to New York on Thursday of next week.'

Somerton smiled impishly. 'Business or pleasure, Laura?'

Taylor ignored the sub-text. 'Will Kenny and I are agreed that one of us has to address the United Nations and I drew the short straw. We will also be having private discussions regarding

Ukraine and general security issues. You can engage with your contacts over there and get to meet more of the White House hierarchy; maybe get a tour of the Pentagon. We might just have a three-way session with Ukraine's President Zelensky.'

Somerton's eyes widened. 'I would have thought you would be taking the Foreign Secretary and the Minister of Defence?'

'They've got other commitments; someone has to mind the shop whilst I'm away. I want them to be on hand to deal with any issues related to Ukraine in my absence.'

'How long will we be over there?'

'We fly out Thursday early and fly back late Sunday; we're going to be busy. I'll feed back to the House on Monday. That's all I have for now, Jack; keep this cyber business top of your agenda, it's worrying.'

Somerton nodded. 'Will do. Let me have our flight details as soon as you have them. How's your sister these days?'

Somerton thought Taylor looked a little cagey. 'She's fine at present. Last I heard the beast is heading over to Jeddah for a few days; I must confess I nudged a little business in his direction. Are you sure you haven't got designs on my sister?'

Somerton smiled, winked, and tapped his nose. 'I'll be off now, see you in the Commons. I'm sure we'll be bombarded with questions.'

Taylor grimaced. 'Questions with precious few answers, I fear.'

Jess Tate's face lit up when Somerton appeared. 'Well?'

Somerton squinted. 'Well, what Jess?'

'What about those beautiful sandwiches I laid on for you?'

Somerton shook his head. 'Would you believe it, Laura must have been ravenous, there was only one left when I got there.'

'Really, that's ridiculous; you should have asked for some more.'

Somerton tutted. 'I'm afraid the offer wasn't made. Must go, duty calls.'

He decided to walk to the Commons and clear his thoughts on the way; he had a lot of thinking to do following his conversation with Taylor.

Somerton's London apartment

Somerton was tucking into a late evening supper when his private phone bleeped. The text message was short *Urgent, check your emails*. Urgent or not Somerton opted to finish his Thai takeaway before heading over to his computer and keying in his access code.

The message was encrypted and longer than usual; it's content alarming. He would have to meet with Taylor again first thing in the morning. His mind was in a turmoil as he picked up the phone to contact Taylor.

'Hello Laura, sorry to disturb you this late but I need to talk with you again tomorrow morning.'

'I'm intrigued, Jack, tell me more.'

'I'd rather it waited until tomorrow, I need to check out its authenticity; run it past a few sources before I see you.'

Taylor pointedly emitted a noisy sigh. 'OK, Jack, I understand though you've probably spoiled my night's sleep.'

'Oops, sorry about that, I wasn't thinking clearly. See you in the morning.'

Somerton knew his source was completely reliable but felt he had to contact his sources on the Five Eyes, to find out if they could confirm what he had just learned. He also wondered if Will Kenny had been in touch with Taylor. He spent the next two hours in discussion with intelligence sources around the world. He didn't reveal the content of the information he had received which made enquiries difficult, but in the end, he drew the blank he hoped for and was satisfied that he, and only he, knew what was about to take place.

CHAPTER 25

Prime Minister's office, early next day

'OK Jack, what have you got for me? I had a very restless night's sleep wondering what you had come up with; let's have it.'

Somerton paused and chose his words carefully. 'One of my sources emailed me last night, fully encrypted I hasten to add. Such was the important nature of the information, I felt I had to personally check it out with our Five Eyes colleagues to see if they had picked up anything similar. And I can tell you they haven't.'

Taylor's impatience broke through. 'Spare me the spin, Jack, cut to the chase. What is this news that kept me awake half the night?'

Somerton chuckled. 'Patience Laura, I'm just anticipating what you'll ask me when I tell you what's happening. My source tells me that your friend Vladimir Rostov is flying off somewhere to meet up with his opposite number in China, and it's just possible, that our little fat friend from North Korea will be invited to the party. As I said, I believe my source 100%, notwithstanding our transatlantic cousins knew nothing about it.'

Taylor eased back in her chair, her thoughts translating just what the implications were of this bombshell. 'So, what's your take on this, Jack?'

'Let's put it this way; you, at very short notice, decide to fly out to address the United Nations and meet up with your friend Will Kenny for a chinwag having seen Russia building up its armed forces on the Ukrainian border. I'm Rostov and I get to hear about your plans it's not unreasonable for me to conclude that the USA and the UK are planning to put troops on the ground in Ukraine. It's not unprecedented. Blair and Bush invaded Iraq if you need reminding. I am right, aren't I?'

'No.' Replied Taylor vehemently.

Somerton shook his head in disbelief. 'You honestly don't think it's a reasonable conclusion for Rostov to reach? Come off it, Laura. Look me in the eye and tell me the possibility won't be discussed by you and Kenny. It would be remiss of you both **not** to discuss the possibility.'

Taylor demurred. 'It's an open agenda, either party can raise any topic they wish.'

Somerton smiled. 'Yeah, sure Laura. Go on, tell me you won't raise the possibility if Will doesn't, which I think is unlikely. Not that it matters one way or another, it's what Rostov thinks that matters; put yourself in his shoes.'

Taylor nodded. 'I suppose so, Jack. But in any event, now that we know he's meeting in secret with China, and maybe North Korea, we have no option but to prepare ourselves for the worst scenario. I wish the bastard would have a heart attack; the world would be a safer place.'

'So, Prime Minister, do I inform the Five Eyes about this? We would be expected to share intelligence of this nature?'

Taylor shook her head. 'If you do, everybody will get to know, including Rostov. He'd probably cancel the meeting and leave us open to all sorts of allegations, including attempting to justify an unprovoked attack on Russia. Say nothing at this stage; I'll discuss the situation with Will Kenny and we'll agree a way forward.'

Somerton shrugged. 'You're the boss, it's a fifty-fifty call. Just remember what happened when the West sat back and did nothing about Russia's annexation of Crimea. Now, what time do we fly out tomorrow?'

'We fly out from RAF Mildenhall, take-off 3am; get there for 2.30pm at the latest.'

Somerton gasped. 'Christ, what an ungodly hour! Why don't we fly out at a decent hour and get a good night's sleep in a hotel in New York?'

'The RAF says it's more secure and MI5 agree, so 3am it is. Keep me updated if anything further emerges regards Rostov. Feel free to take him out if you get the chance; hire those hackers that have caused so many problems recently if you can track them down. Time for you to go, I've got another meeting in ten minutes.'

NRSC Somerton's office

Somerton put in a call to Jupiter. *He claims to know everything, let's put him to the test.*

'Hello, Jack, nice to hear from you at a civilised hour. How can I help?'

'I expect you've been listening in on my conversation with the PM, so you probably know what I'm going to ask. Have you heard anything about Rostov meeting up with Jing Chen in the next day or so?'

Jupiter shook his head. 'They've been planning to meet for some time now, but I wasn't aware that a meeting was imminent.'

'My source tells me that they are meeting up tomorrow; I don't know where exactly. Could you give this priority and check it out? I'm told Rostov will fly out of Moscow tomorrow around 11am local time.'

'If, such a flight is planned, I'm certain I'll be able to identify it.' Jupiter locked eyes with Somerton. 'And if I do, what then?'

Somerton held his gaze. 'Target 4.' This time Somerton didn't wait for a reply.

Chalovsky Air Base.

Lieutenant-Colonel Volkov made his way into the standby pilot's lounge unannounced, looking round the room as those present rose instantly to their feet. The customary 'at ease' didn't follow the show of respect, time was at a premium; security had dictated that no orders had been given in advance. 'Lieutenants, Petrov, Popov, Leukor, Zaitsev and Lenkov, report to your aircraft immediately and stand-by for imminent take-off under my direct command.' Volkov barked out his command, then turned and strode out of the room.

As soon as he was out of earshot Andrei Petrov swore loudly. 'Fuck it, fuck it. It's my wife's birthday, we were going out tonight.'

Ivan Lenkov shushed him. 'Ssssh. Bad luck Andrei, but we are here to serve the Motherland.'

Petrov rolled his eyes. 'Of course, Ivan, you are absolutely right, and what an honour it is.'

Fifteen minutes later the five pilots and Lieutenant-Colonel Volkov, all members of the Rossiya Special Flight Detachment, sat in their SU-57 Stealth Fighter Jets awaiting take-off instructions. Only Volkov knew the nature of their mission. Not that it was much of a mission; the flight was low-risk and routine.

He would give his pilots their orders once airborne, and then impose radio silence.

Sheremetyevo International Airport

A black Mercedes-Benz S600 Pullum-Grand drove through a secure access to the airport under the watchful protection of its small fleet of escort vehicles and the waiting armed guard. The occupants of the elite vehicle couldn't be seen through the black bullet-proof windows, but everyone knew it was the President's car. The Mercedes continued its journey, stopping a few metres short of the steps into the Ilyuskin IL-96-300PU four-engine, wide- bodied aeroplane that served as the Presidential aircraft.

Security guards immediately exited the escort vehicles and began looking round for potential security threats, not that there were likely to be any on a runway far from the airport buildings.

Vladimir Rostov smiled as he stepped onto the tarmac where five of his closest advisors were lined up to greet him.

Sergei Shogiv, Minister of Defence

Valeri Gerasimov, Chief of General Staff

Nutai Patrushev, Secretary of the Security Council

Sergei Naryshkin, Director of Foreign Intelligence Services

Sergei Lavrov, Minister of Foreign Affairs

They all knew why they were there. The West was strengthening its alliances. Previous members of the USSR had joined NATO, others were waiting for an invitation. Russia was under threat; it was essential for the Motherland to build new alliances. Rostov regarded China and North Korea as natural allies.

Rostov nodded to his inner circle, smiling and exchanging greetings, motioning for them to follow him onto the plane. They all knew the importance of what lay ahead, perhaps a turning point in East-West relations. Vladimir Rostov was determined to leave behind a historic legacy, a new USSR. The planned annexation of Ukraine, starting with the Donbas region, would mark the beginning of a new era for Russia. He wouldn't refer to the invasion as a war, doing that would inflame the West and worse, might not be well received by his own people It would be a special military operation, a rescue mission for pro-Motherland residents marooned there when Ukraine left the USSR.

Even as Rostov walked along his short line of cronies, six SU-57 stealth fighter jets were taking off; once airborne they would sweep around Moscow, their flight path and timing carefully co-ordinated to rendezvous with the Presidential plane. Only then would they learn of the nature of their mission and ultimate destination; Novosilrsk Totmachevo Airport, just four hours flying time due east of Moscow.

Lieutenant-Colonel Volkov was issuing commands; Popov, starboard front – Lenkov, starboard rear – Zaitsev, port rear – Novikoff, lower – and finally completing the enclosure of the Ilyuskin – Petrov, upper. Volkov himself would fill the remaining position – port forward. His pilots had all been informed that this was a Rossiya Special Flight, providing an escort for the President and given the latitude and longitude coordinates for their destination. They were to follow him, in formation, proud in the knowledge that they were guarding the President.

Rostov and his associates were settling down. No alcohol was to be served on the outbound flight on the President's orders; there were to be no slurred words and alcohol charged breaths around the conference table. Clear heads were needed for the meeting that lay ahead with the People's Republic of China's President, the enigmatic Jing Chen whose other titles included General Secretary of the Chinese Communist party and Chairman of the Central Military Commission. Jing Chen had so far stopped short of offering support, instead citing 'the need to uphold the principle of indivisibility of security' and 'oppose the building of national security based on insecurity in other countries.'

The president's aircraft ascended to an altitude of 25,000 feet, where it levelled out and set course for Novosilirsk Airport, its airspeed around 550 miles per hour. Novosilirsk had been chosen because it lay roughly half-way between Moscow and Beijing. The entire flight would be over Russian territory and afforded Rostov an additional layer of security. He nodded contentedly, inwardly relieved when his fighter jet escort took up its protective shield. He hadn't seriously considered himself at risk of attack, but nevertheless it was a comfort to know that six of the world's best aircraft and pilots were dedicated to his safety.

Two hours into the flight, approximately halfway and about to pass over the Ural Mountain range, tea and sandwiches were being served. The tactics for the meeting that lay ahead had been discussed and agreed. Everyone would be following the same script from the moment the sextet took their places round the table. When their tea-break was over they would go through the same points one more time; everyone would be well rehearsed in their role.

For Andrei Popov, flying in the upper position, and his fellow pilots, there were no sandwiches. No slices of cake, no cups of tea, and he was beginning to feel peckish; the mission had been sprung on them and he hadn't had time to purchase even a bar of chocolate. He was looking forward to reaching their destination where his first port of call would be the canteen. Being included in the President's escort was an honour, or so he had been told at length by his commanding officer, in reality it was boring. Still the scenery was improving; the Urals lay ahead, beautiful, majestic mountains; perhaps in the future he would have a climbing holiday and maybe climb the highest peaks, Mount Narodnaya and Mount Kapursk.

His daydreaming was rudely interrupted when his plane went into a sudden unexplained dive; he pulled back on the altitude control – nothing, the aircraft didn't respond. In desperation he wrenched the controller back and to the right, seeking to spin away and regain altitude – nothing. The aircraft wasn't responding, he knew he was doomed. Knew he was destined to collide with the President's plane. In seconds he would be dead along with the President and the cream of the Russian political hierarchy.

The SU-57 crashed into the Ilyuskin immediately behind the wings - the main cabin area of the fuselage – the explosion was massive – flame filled the airspace. The tangled mass that had once been the Presidential aeroplane was heading for its final destination, the heights of the Ural Mountains. The Presidential party knew nothing about the impact, death had been instant; in the brief seconds left to them the pilot and co-pilot could only look in horror as their plane plummeted to earth, crashing into the lower SU-57 flown by Igor Novikoff on the way and causing another thunderous explosion.

The explosion rocked the remaining four fighter jets. Lieutenant-Colonel Volkov was in a state of shock, his mind numb, his subordinates seeking orders, reminding him that he was in command. How could this have happened? Was Andrei Popov a traitor, an assassin in the pay of the West? No, he couldn't be, he was a loyal Russian, a boy recently married. No, it must have been a mechanical failure. All these thoughts flitted through in seconds; he was in command, the mission was over, his orders were awaited. 'All aircraft return to Chlalovsky Air Base. Hello Control, Volkov speaking. There has been a collision, the President's plane and two of our escort aircraft have been lost. I have instructed my pilots to return to base. The SU-57 pilot responsible for the collision was Lieutenant Andrei Popov. Please inform the Kremlin. I will reconnoitre the crash scene and ascertain the latitude and longitude coordinates for the rescue operation. Over and out.'

Volkov's thoughts were already turning to the aftermath. He and his pilots would be arrested, and an investigation would follow. He felt sick. He wasn't to blame but he would forever be associated with this disastrous mission; his career was effectively over.

Thousands of miles away, Jupiter sat with a satisfied expression on his face; Constellation MacKinnon had performed perfectly, as he knew it would. This exercise had proved that it was mankind's greatest weapon. No, not a weapon, a deterrent. He sniggered. *Whether it was a deterrent or a weapon was dependent upon whether you were the wielder or the recipient.*

New York John F Kennedy Airport

The VIP RAF Voyager, the Airbus used by the Royal Family and Government Ministers, was on its descent flight path to JFK when the news came through. Taylor and Somerton were just finishing a light breakfast when their respective phones bleeped.

Somerton glanced at the text. 'Target 4 completed successfully.' He hit the delete button immediately lest Taylor caught sight of the message and got curious.

'Oh my God,' Taylor uttered an uncontrolled exclamation, 'He's dead. My prayers have been answered, he's dead.'

Somerton feigned curiosity. 'Who's dead, Laura?'

'Rostov, Jack! Rostov's a goner, and better still, his inner clique of hardliners with him.'

Somerton summoned up astonishment, jaw dropped, eyes wide. 'Rostov? I don't believe it! What's happened; some kind of disaster?'

Taylor continued reading the text. 'This is a text from Will; the news has just come in. They're not sure, possibly a mid-air collision between his aircraft and an escort plane. The Ruskies are investigating but, for now, calling it a tragic accident.'

'We can make a bit of capital out of this, Laura. Get on to Downing Street; get the team to put some fake news out there. 'Was Rostov assassinated by a dissident pilot?'

Taylor frowned, disapprovingly. 'Why do that?'

Somerton smiled. 'Because it will cause confusion. It will bolster dissident activists and dismay Rostov's followers. And it doesn't cost anything to get a conspiracy theory going; the Press will love it. Better still, give some thought to blaming China; they must have known the flight details. See if you can get your friend Will Kenny to join in.'

Taylor shook her head, a smile on her lips. 'You're a mischievous bugger, Jack. But I'll mention it when I speak to Will.'

CHAPTER 26

United Nations, New York

The British Ambassador, Sir Edward Clarendon, was there to welcome Taylor and Somerton at the airport, although Jack knew he was only a bit player in this moment of history. He felt uncomfortable when he found himself surrounded by newshounds and flashing cameras. *What on earth do they do with all those photographs?* The formalities over, they were driven away in a Rolls Royce fitted out with its little Union Jack flags, escorted by two NYPD cars. Their destination was the British Consulate General in Dag Hammarskgold Place where they would freshen up and be briefed on sensitive current local affairs.

'I didn't book us into a hotel, Jack; we're both invited to join Will Kenny in Washington for the next two nights. He's laid on a helicopter for us, so travel isn't a problem.'

Somerton put on a false frown. 'Let's hope we don't meet the same fate as friend Rostov.'

'Oh Jack, please don't even think in those terms, I can't imagine anyone over here wanting to take us out of the game.'

Somerton winked. 'It would put an end to that *special relationship*, if you get my drift.'

Taylor frowned and snarled in response. Enough of that fucking innuendo Jack, please.'

Somerton shrugged. 'I look forward to meeting the President and getting a tour of the White House, but I wonder if I could be excused the second night. I've had an invitation from Chloe MacKinnon to spend the night at her place in Washington. I'd like to meet up with her, Abbi and the kids; it's important to me.

'Of course, Jack, I wouldn't want to stand in the way of your *special relationship*, wink, wink.'

Somerton gave a wry grin. 'I guess I deserve that.'

Taylor smiled. 'I'll arrange for an embassy car to take you there and bring you back. She glanced at Sir Edward who had watched the exchange with a mixture of curiosity and amusement. 'You can fix that up Ted?'

Of course, Laura, no problem. You can do me a favour in return. If you get the opportunity, say something praiseworthy about the United States and its historic ties and support for the UK. It's old hat I know, but it is worthwhile.'

Taylor laughed. 'The special relationship is flourishing, Ted, and the speech is already written though I'll have to make some changes in light of the Rostov incident. I also need to check out one or two matters with Will. What we have to say to the United Nations must be closely aligned. Now if that's all, I'd like to lie down for the next couple of hours?'

Clarendon nodded. 'Understood. A car is on standby to take you to the UN, leaving here at 10.30 for your 11.30 address to the Assembly. With regard to that, the Secretary General is going to request the Assembly to stand for a minute's silence in respect for the demise of the Russian President and his colleagues.'

Somerton bit on his tongue. *Two-faced bastards; one day Rostov is the devil incarnate, next the world is praying for him, bollocks to that.* He was about to speak up when, to his surprise, he saw Taylor shaking her head. 'No can do. Will Kenny has instructed the US delegation not to take part, and that Ted is my instruction to you.'

Sir Edward 'Ted' Clarendon face filled with anxiety; he hesitated and pursed his lips. 'Laura, I have to caution against that; it will cause a lot of lasting ill-will in some quarters, especially so in the East. It will make it very difficult to rebuild relationships in the future.'

'Assuming we want to, Ted; Russia is the aggressor, it's they who will have to take the initiative when it comes to rebuilding relationships. And there were no Russian representatives invited to Colin's funeral, they won't expect much from us.'

Clarendon shook his head in exasperation. 'What about a compromise. We respect the minute's silence, but don't stand.'

Taylor shrugged. I can live with that; I wasn't planning on waving a flag or singing Land of Hope and Glory. Our delegation will remain seated and twiddle its thumbs for a minute. Inform the Secretary General accordingly. I'll let Will Kenny know what we're doing, you can talk to your European counterparts and any other allies. You haven't got long. Ted, best get started.' She yawned and rubbed her eyes. 'Gosh, I need a lie down. What rooms do we have?'

United Nations, General Assembly

Taylor stood at the rostrum, looking around confidently, waiting for delegates to settle. Somerton sat behind the UK's Security Council representative along with the rest of the delegates. His thoughts were inevitably drawn to Colin MacKinnon visit there in September 2020, and the subsequent events that led to his assassination. A lot had happened since then, but nothing had really changed.

The Secretary General introduced Taylor and motioned her to begin.

'Ladies and Gentlemen, my address to you will be short. The words I had written, have perhaps, been rendered unnecessary by the death of Vladimir Rostov and his cohort. I say, perhaps, in the hope that a new Russian regime will no longer pursue the territorial aims of its predecessor.

'I will quote the wise words of Jing Chen when referring to his long-standing foreign policy principles of what he termed 'territorial integrity' and 'non-interference' and China's fundamental belief that we should all respect, 'the sovereignty and territorial integrity OF ALL COUNTRIES.' She thumped the lectern with her fist in unison with her closing words. These are values held by NATO and the western democracies. We have much in common. Let us build on these shared values and create a new tomorrow, free from war, from poverty and free from subjugation. I'll close by quoting words written over two hundred years ago by the great Scottish poet, Robert Burns.

Man's inhumanity to man makes countless thousands mourn.

'Today this very day, the actions of some, bent on territorial and monetary gain, I'm very sad to say, still makes countless thousands mourn. 'I ask all of you.' Taylor turned and looked directly at the Russian and Chinese delegates seated at the Security Council table to bring about the end of evil doing on this wonderful planet Earth. Again, I'll quote the words of Burns when he wrote of his hope that,

It's coming yet for all that and all that
That man to man, the world over
Shall brothers be, for all that.

'Ladies and gentlemen, let's all work together for that better world, and brothers be. We have the means to make this happen, and happen it will. I tell you now, this is not the empty rhetoric of the past, it will happen.

The applause was mild and there were few who did not participate, most thought that Taylor's words, were indeed, empty rhetoric.

Somerton's thoughts turned to the MacKinnon Constellation. *Could this be what Taylor had in mind? Did she see it as a means of controlling the world's destiny? But how could she? She doesn't know about its full capability, or Jupiter. And if she had some inkling of its power, who's finger did she see on the trigger? Hers, or that of her obedient servant, Jack Somerton?*

Taylor and Somerton walked straight through the waiting crowd of photographers and reporters lying in wait outside the UN, ignoring questions and refusing to stop to strike a pose for the massed cameras. The shouted questions were universally clear; what did she mean by what she said? How did she intend to fulfil its intentions? Taylor's only answer was a smile.

Once settled in the vehicle the driver set off for the Downtown Manhattan Heliport where a waiting Sirkorsky VH-Sd White Hawk helicopter stood waiting for take-off, courtesy of Will Kenny.

Somerton sat back to enjoy the ninety minutes flight to Washington and asked for some clarification from Taylor regarding her speech to the Assembly. 'You piled on the rhetoric back there, Laura; you set yourself up as the world's peacemaker-in-chief. Now, much as I admire you, I think you've taken on a very large bite of the unachievable.'

Taylor smiled sweetly, exuding a quiet confidence. 'We'll see, Jack. This world has got to change and we're going to make it change.'

Somerton arched an eye. 'We?'

Taylor nodded. 'That's right, **we**.' She made no effort to and turned her attention to some parliamentary papers.

Conversation over, class dismiss, thought Somerton and didn't pursue the matter. Instead, he looked out of the helicopter at the everchanging scenery below. One building took his attention and he invited Taylor to share the view, but she seemed reluctant to share his appreciation. 'You seem a bit uptight, Laura? I'm guessing that you're not comfortable with heights.'

'I'm not as a matter of fact, but what really gets me is that I don't think anything resembling a helicopter should be able to fly. Those blades, those whirling wings just shouldn't be able to keep us airborne. Now if you don't mind, I've got some reading I must catch up with before I meet up with Will.'

Somerton saluted. 'Yes, Ma'am. Whatever you say, Ma'am.'

Taylor gave him a look that could kill and brought the interchange to a close. 'Don't push it, Jack, you're good at what you do but not irreplaceable.'

The helicopter made good time and landed, with barely a bump, five minutes ahead of schedule, on the front lawn of the White House. A few hundred metres away, a well-built man wearing a padded air force jacket was striding towards them as they descended the helicopter steps. Somerton noted that Taylor's whole demeanour changed instantly. 'It's Will, he's coming to meet us.' There was undoubtedly a trace of excitement in her voice.

A couple of minutes later Kenny was with them, greeting Taylor with a hug and a kiss on a cheek whispering something in her ear that Somerton couldn't hear. He then turned his attention to Somerton, extending his hand, a strong grip, a few shakes, eyes taking in his visitor's appearance. 'Pleased to meet your acquaintance, Jack.' A pronounced New England accent, speech quite clipped, no traditional American drawl.

'And I you, Mr President. I'm honoured.'

'Please, call me Will on these informal occasions; other times I'm afraid it will have to be Mr President. Let's head for the Hacienda Blanca. My guys will bring your luggage. When you've settled in, and you've met Pam, we'll have afternoon tea on the rear patio.' He smiled and added. 'Freshly baked scones, cream, jam and of course, English tea served in fine china. After that you'll get a tour of the White House, then you can take a break and get ready for dinner. I've invited my two daughters to join us for dinner. How does that sound?'

Taylor nodded. 'Perfect, Will.'

'And you, Jack?'

Somerton gave a thumbs-up. 'Sounds great to me, I'm looking forward to it.'

Kenny raised a finger. 'Just one more thing; there is to be no discussion about world affairs, political gossip or the like this evening; we can do all that stuff over breakfast tomorrow morning. Tonight, is about family and friends. Is that OK with you both?'

This time, Somerton got in first. 'Best news I've had all day.'

Taylor nodded. 'Yes, though the day started with some good news, I have to say.'

Kenny put his finger to his lips with a smile. 'Ah, here's Pam.'

The President's wife joined them, blonde flaxen shoulder-length hair, slim athletic build and wearing a white trouser suit and a pair of flat blue trainers.

Absolutely stunning, thought Somerton. *Maybe I'm wrong about Laura and Will having some kind of relationship.* He looked on as she and Laura exchanged a warm embrace. *No signs of rivalry.* Pam Kenny then turned to Somerton. 'No prizes for guessing that you are the distinguished Mr Somerton.'

'You flatter me, Pam. It's my privilege to meet America's First Lady.' Somerton made a slight bow.

Pam Kenny smiled sweetly. 'I've heard differently, Jack, but enough of this mutual back-scratching. Get settled in and then we'll have tea and scones, baked by my own fair hand, so make sure you enjoy them.'

'I certainly will.' *You've made a lasting impression on me Pam.* Somerton relaxed, he hadn't known what to expect but both Will and Pam seemed very nice, feet-on-the-ground kind of people.

Settled round an ornate dark-green wrought iron table placed below a trellis with hanging branches of wisteria and laburnum in full blossom, and looking out across a well-manicured striped lawn, Somerton felt he was in the midst of an English stately garden. The chat was light-hearted and social, though Somerton sensed that he was the main focus.

'I know all about your distinguished SAS career, Jack. You achieved the rank of major, you earned a chest full of medals and commendations, but I don't know anything about your origins.

Tell us a bit about yourself.' Will Kenny made the enquiry whilst he poured second cups of tea all round.

'Not much to tell really, I don't know much about my origins. I was deposited, Moses-like, in a wicker basket late on Saturday night, mid-January, in a church, in Gretna Green. I was only days old, thankfully well wrapped up. The local vicar found me when he came to carry out a Service the following morning. Gretna Green is in Scotland, close to the border with England, so I don't know the country of my birth. A couple from Dumfries adopted me, and I became Jack Somerton. Shortly afterwards they moved south to Nantwich in Cheshire, so I've lived in England for most of my life. Sadly, they were both killed in a car accident when I was thirteen; I was shuttled around various foster parents in the years that followed. By all accounts, I was a difficult child. I joined the Army as a cadet when I was sixteen, the regular Army when I was 18, was accepted into the SAS when I was 21. The rest as they say is history.'

As Somerton's story proceeded, Taylor looked on amazed, occasionally shaking her head. Pam Kenny was first to speak. 'That's a rather sad story, Jack, I'm sorry.'

Somerton shrugged. 'No need Pam, it's history, long time gone, I can't remember the last time I spoke about my childhood. I honestly don't think I would change anything. I'm happy, proud even, of where I've arrived in life. Think of it, a good military career, a successful businessman. And now, I'm a cabinet minister sitting on the White House lawn with the President of the United States and the First Lady. The journey that brought me here began in the Old Parish Church in Gretna Green. I reckon I'm one of the lucky ones. Now, how about another scone? They're so good, I reckon you could open a tea shop in England, Pam and make a fortune,

Idle chat continued until Will Kenny took his leave. 'Apologies folks, I have to go. The Oval Office calls, sorry to butt out. Pam will give you the guided tour of the White House and the grounds; feel free to ask questions, she knows more about its history and former occupants than I do. I'll see you later at dinner. In between times I fancy you'll want to freshen up and maybe snatch a bit of shuteye. What time is dinner, darling?'

'7.30 for 8, drinks in the lounge. Try not to be late, please.'

CHAPTER 27

The White House

It was nearing midnight when Taylor climbed wearily into bed, hoping to clear her mind of the following day's business. Memories of the past flooded into her head, of how chance had brought her to this point in her life. How the pieces had fallen into place and led to her becoming Prime Minister of the United Kingdom.

She'd always wanted to be a politician; had taken degrees at Cambridge in Politics and Computer Sciences. A strange mix most of her contemporaries had said, but she saw them as a blend of past, present and future; even back then, she could see that life was going to be increasingly dependent on computers.

Having graduated from Cambridge she had decided to put her political aspirations on hold and study for a Masters in Computer Sciences determined to gain an insight into machine learning. By the end of her studies, she was more convinced than ever that the future would be guided, controlled even, by Artificial Intelligence or Machine learning, whatever it was called. Fortune had shone on her and she had secured a place at Harvard, that illustrious American University, some argued the best in the world.

She was starting to feel drowsy, smiling as she recalled the night when she, along with others, had been invited by her college to address a group of around fifty invited guests; congressmen, senators, professors and notable business men. The topic was, **'What does the future hold?'** as seen through the eyes of four Masters graduates including herself. She was the sole female to stand behind the lectern that night, primarily because she was from the United Kingdom.

Nothing said at the meeting was to be repeated outside the college walls, similar to the UK's historic Chatham House rules. The college Principal had introduced her simply, *'Ladies and gentlemen, our final speaker tonight hails from across the pond...I give you Laura Taylor from the United Kingdom. The lectern is yours, Laura.'*

Her heart rate had stepped up a notch, she had felt it pounding but had determined not to show a vestige of nerves, she might never get another chance like this.

Good evening, ladies and gentlemen, I'm honoured to have this opportunity to address you all. I'm going to begin by stating my personal ambition… she paused and looked around, *I want to be Prime Minister of the United Kingdom.* That had brought smiles all round and a goodly number of, you'll-be-lucky raised eyebrows throughout the auditorium. *But of course, that's not what I'm here to talk about, my subject is the United Nations, or rather, the reform of the United Nations I want to see a United Nations that's fit for purpose. I give you one statistic, there are currently over one hundred UN vital humanitarian resolutions being ignored, millions of innocent people are suffering as a result. And what can the UN do to bring resolve these violations?* She had looked around, seeking an answer she knew she wouldn't get. *I'll tell you in one word… nothing; zilch is the term you would use on this side of the Atlantic.*

Quite simply, wonderful institution that it is, it isn't fit for purpose in the modern age. Sceptical looks, head shakes and shoulder shrugs were visible on many but not all those present, the statistic had struck a chord with a good proportion of the audience. *I want to change that situation, I want the will of the World as represented by the UN to be implemented no matter the Country involved, great or small, be they a Republic, a Democracy, a Dictatorship or a Monarchy. We are one world and we're making a mess of it; we won't get a second chance. In short, ladies and gentlemen, in the future I hope for, I want to give the UN a big stick so that it can enforce its Resolutions, I want its catalogue of unfulfilled promises to be consigned to history.*

There was a buzz around the room, smiles and smirks but to her relief quite a number of heads nodded their approval.

She had spoken for around fifteen minutes, winding up with… it's our planet, our future, if we care about humanity, we require the authority, and the means to exercise of control over corrupt and abusive ruling bodies. I stress we have to have the means, a deterrent, call it what you will; words are not enough. We need to recognise that the current situation cannot be allowed to continue and act now.

There had been a round of polite applause; the Principal had glanced at his watch. 'Dinner awaits us so I'll take three questions only and then call the meeting to a close.' He scanned the room; Taylor had thought he looked vaguely surprised to see so many hands raised.

'Professor Rothwell, your question please.'

'Miss Taylor, it sounded a bit like you were harkening back to Great Britain's colonial days, telling everybody how to live their lives. Is that the case?'

'Not at all Professor, I would have no wish to occupy another country, although we did leave behind some good values, some former colonies of our have done rather well for themselves, including the United States. What I want is a quick and ready means of sanctioning a regime where it is irrefutably harming its people or the planet, nothing more, nothing less.'

'Thank you, Professor. Senator Sully, your question please.'

'The implication,' the Senator paused for effect then continued in his southern drawl, 'is that you, or whosoever, is wielding this undefined power of yours, will claim to know what's best for everyone else. How do you respond to that.'

'Not me Senator, although it's a claim made by many politicians especially when they are on the hustings. The power I envisage would be invested in a Body set up by the UN; it, and only, it would determine the action to be taken.'

'Thank you, Senator.' The Principal looked around the room and pointed to a young graduate. Your question please.'

The rather good-looking young man had smiled and posed his question in a new England accent reminiscent of the late President John F Kennedy.

'I personally agree with the sentiment expressed in your presentation, Miss Taylor, and hope that over time the arrangements you envisage come to pass. Perhaps all those present will look back on this occasion and recognise that it is the young who had the better vision of the future. Your aims are good but how do you see them being fulfilled, what kind of instant sanctions do you envisage?'

She had known the question would come, known too that she didn't have an answer. 'I'm sorry but I can't answer that question, I don't have the knowledge. But that doesn't mean there isn't an answer waiting to be found. The answer lies in science, in satellite surveillance linked to some sort of punitive electronic interference where necessary. Think of President Reagan's so-called star-wars concept; take a look at what we rely on, electricity, communications, transport, weaponry and find a way of disabling them remotely. You can be certain that out there somewhere, there are scientists working on the concept as I speak. Let's hope they are friendly to the aims of democracy.'

There had been gasps around the room, some had branded it dictatorship by any other name.

The Principal had been anxious not to promote any further controversy. 'Ladies and gentlemen, the meeting is closed. Thanks to all of you for making the session so interesting. Please make your way to dinner. '

As the audience filed out, she had drawn many glances, some friendly, most hostile. Only one had stopped to talk to her, the young graduate who had posed the final question.

'That was brave of you Miss Taylor; whatever anyone else may think, I think you hit the nail on the head. The West has to get its act together and quickly. Alas we aren't at the same table but I'd like to hear more of your thoughts and share some of mine; would you be free for dinner tomorrow evening, my treat.

She had accepted and after dinner had ended up in his bed; their affair had blossomed and had continued until the end of the year when they were both awarded their Masters. They had fallen in love and he had asked her to marry him and move to the States. She had been torn and nearly heartbroken to decline.

'I meant it when I said I wanted to be the UK's Prime Minister some day and I can't do that if I live on the other side of the Atlantic. I love you dearly, Will and want to be your wife. Why don't you come to the UK?

I can't Laura, I want to become the President of the USA someday; the present has brought us together, the future forces us apart, but come what may you'll always have my love.'

The young man was Will Kenny; he had married, she had married but their love for each other had never died.

CHAPTER 28

The White House, next day

Dinner the previous night had been sheer culinary excellence, whoever did the cooking deserved a Michelin star; the helpings were generous as they always are in the US. The Kenny daughters, Rose and Jennifer, aged 20 and 18 respectively were a delight. They both rivalled their mother in the glamour ratings and were excellent company. Rose confident, a born extrovert and humorous; Jennifer quieter but also funny with some great one-liners. Rose was studying to be an architect and was also an accomplished piano player. Jennifer intended to study criminal law and had ambitions to be a Supreme Court Judge. She played guitar and liked to sing folk music but declined to give a performance when invited by her sister.

As requested by Kenny the conversation remained light-hearted throughout the evening and never flagged for an instant. For probably the first time in his life Somerton experienced a sense of missing out by not having any family of his own. Neither of the girls had visited the UK or Europe but intended to do so in the near future. They were thrilled when Somerton offered them the exclusive use of one of his London flats any time they chose to visit.

'Oh, thank you Jack, that's very kind of you. We'll take you up on that offer and start making plans. Won't we Jennifer?' Rose looked excitedly at her sister.

'Absolutely, looking forward to it already.'

Somerton smiled broadly. 'That's settled then, just say the word and the flat will be at your disposal.'

He hadn't learned anything new about Kenny or his wife over the course of the evening; he'd spent an hour on Google before leaving London had learned all he needed to know. Although Kenny did mention that his brother Pete was a member of Delta, the US Army's elite special operations detachment. 'You and Pete must have many things in common, I'll try and get you both together next time you are over.'

Somerton nodded. 'I'd like that. Delta is highly respected throughout the world, none better.'

'Except maybe by the SAS, eh?' Asked a smiling Kenny.

'There's very little to choose between them, I'm obviously biased having served in the SAS.'

Breakfast

Somerton and Taylor coincidently met up with each other in the corridor on their way to breakfast.

'Sleep well?' Taylor enquired.

'Like a log, went off to sleep the minute my head hit the pillow. And you?'

Taylor grimaced. 'OK I guess, had a lot of politics whirling round in my head. And I got a late text from Geraldine worrying about Guy. She hasn't heard from him since he went to Saudi. He's usually very good at keeping in touch with the kids but they haven't heard a dicky bird.'

Somerton held back a 'no great loss' comment. 'Why don't you use one of your embassy contacts to check things out for you?'

Taylor sighed. 'I thought of that but there's a chance I could end up being asked awkward questions. I'll leave it for now. Ah,' She stopped at a door, 'I think this is it.' She pushed open the door and was greeted by Will Kenny. 'Good morning both, hope you slept well.' He didn't wait for a reply before explaining that Pam offered her apologies, she wouldn't be joining them. Apparently, she had received a call asking her if she could fill in for one of her friends who had taken unwell and couldn't attend a college event somewhere in the area.

'Have a seat.' He waved a hand at a table in a floor to ceiling windowed alcove looking out onto the side lawn. 'This is our favourite room for breakfast. It's a help yourself; I think you'll find everything you might fancy over there.' He pointed towards a table laid out with juices, fruit, cereals and half a dozen heated silver tureens. 'I assume you both want coffee?'

Taylor made her way over and opted for fruit and muesli. Somerton despite still feeling the effects of the previous night's feast helped himself to two fried eggs, bacon, hash browns and toast. 'I'm not in the least hungry but who can resist the smell of a fried breakfast.'

Whilst breakfasts were consumed, chat was intermittent and confined to praise for the Kenny daughters, the quality of last night's meal, holiday plans and even the weather. Will Kenny poured another round of coffees and opened proceedings. 'Shall we make a start? Have either of you heard from your sources since last night? I made sure you had a phone with a scrambler fitted in your bedrooms so you could keep in touch with back home.'

Taylor pursed her lips. 'I called Downing Street, but only domestic matters were raised Nothing of interest internationally except a bit about Rostov but I'm sure we'll come to that later.'

Kenny looked at Somerton. 'And you Jack, anything on your front?'

Somerton shook his head. 'I didn't use the scrambler, don't trust phones away from home. I got a few coded texts about the Rostov situation which I'll refer to later on.'

Taylor shot daggers at him, and Kenny frowned. 'I feel quite hurt, Jack, you're my guest and I am an ally. What's the problem with using the phone?'

Somerton stood his ground. 'Don't take offence Will, it's not personal. I don't trust any phones, not just those in the White House. I'm the UK's national security advisor, I know what can be done to listen in on telephone lines, scrambled or otherwise, with or without your knowledge.

Kenny shrugged. 'Not a good start but have it your way. OK, let's move on. First up the new regime in Russia. My people tell me the hawks and doves are finely balanced, it'll be days before they sort out a replacement for Rostov and then the successful candidate will have to pick his team. There is no mention of a frontrunner at this stage. Anything to add, Laura?'

Taylor shook her head. 'My lot have made a similar assessment. We just have to hope that they end up with someone who isn't another megalomaniac.'

Somerton chipped in. 'It won't make any difference who takes over. Russia is a dictatorship and dictators always resort to power when persuasion fails.'

Kenny shrugged. 'So, we know what the problem is. What do we do about it, Jack?'

'A no-brainer for me. Stay strong, increase military exercises and presence in the countries bordering Russia and invite them to join NATO.'

Taylor shook her head. 'Don't you think that will be seen as a hostile act and feed their paranoia?'

Somerton nodded. 'Of course, but think about what will happen if we do nothing. Crimea is an example, the West did nothing, Rostov moved in. We sat back and wrung our hands. Result? Rostov judged us to be impotent.'

Kenny's response was unequivocal much to Somerton's surprise. 'I'm in your camp, Jack and I'll be convening a meeting of NATO allies to promote that approach. I'll also be encouraging NATO to increase its membership and I don't give a shit what Russia or China think. They can carry on and form an eastern bloc.'

Somerton looked at Taylor, anticipating her to disagree or at least contribute but she just smiled. He was further puzzled when Kenny didn't prompt her to comment. 'Looks like we are all on the same wavelength, let's leave that topic and turn to the series of cyber-attacks that have taken place over course the of the last six weeks or so. All Western targets, Dover, New York, Munich, all three serious but not disastrous. We need to find out who is behind them. We don't seem to be getting anywhere on this side of the pond. Any progress on your side, Jack?'

'Not a whisper, Will. Whoever is behind it is clever, a genius. What's so strange about these attacks, is that they only last an hour, and nobody is laying claim to them. Hackers usually have a clear motivation, often money, or occasionally just to show how clever they are and claim their moment of fame. We have to assume the attacks originated in the East and we've targeted their satellites but found nothing. It's a mystery.'

Kenny leaned forward. 'Maybe that's why we haven't come up with anything.'

Somerton didn't follow. 'What are you getting at, Will?'

Kenny locked eyes with Somerton. 'What I mean is maybe the source doesn't lie in the East, maybe it's based in the West.'

What are you up to Will? I get the feeling you're testing me out. And you're keeping very quiet Laura. Somerton shook his head. 'I can't see that. Who do you have in mind?'

'I don't have anyone in mind, but friend, or foe, I'd like to meet with them. Whoever it is has access to the greatest intervention system in the world. It's everything I've ever dreamt of.' Kenny paused and smiled. 'I have to confess that my prime suspect is your UK Research Centre; year after year you've produced world-beating inventions. Frankly I'm surprised you haven't produced such a system, maybe you have, and are keeping it secret? What doesn't fit with that is all the targets being in Western democracies.' He engaged Taylor. 'You're not planning to take over the world, Laura?'

Taylor laughed. 'Wish I could. I'm very much the new kid on the block; I wish our Research Centre had invented it.' A smile played around her lips. 'If I had control over such a system, I'd be over the moon.' She turned to Somerton. 'What do you think, Jack?'

'You know my answer, Laura, I'm a hardliner, brought up on military operations; I would use it against an aggressor in every way available to me.'

Kenny intervened. 'But we don't have it, so what do we do about it, Jack?'

'The only thing we can do Will; keep searching the internet for clues. I'll get my team to redouble our efforts.' Somerton was starting to feel under pressure. *Should I come clean, reveal all, yes or no. I'm not sure the timing is right.*

Kenny pushed back in his chair. 'I guess if it's based in the Eastern bloc, we'll experience its full might sooner or later. Maybe that's why China is so bullish of late. On the other hand, if it's in the West or in neutral hands, I want the system under our control. I'll buy the system if that's what it takes; whatever the price and I'm talking billions.'

Somerton looked at Kenny. 'And assuming for the moment, we were to acquire the system, just what would you do with it Will?' You too Laura?'

Taylor answered first. 'Easy. I'd use its power to make this world a better place, just as I said in my speech to the UN Assembly.'

Kenny concurred. 'That's exactly it. What else would you expect, Jack?'

'The goal is exemplary but a rather grandiose concept. Everybody wants a better world, of course they do. The problem is, everybody's idea of a better world differs.'

Kenny shook his head. 'You're being a purist, Jack. We have to have faith in ourselves and our beliefs. We know democracies work best. We know the lifestyle in the West is generally better than elsewhere. We know that equality is a valid goal in every aspect of life. If we had the power, we would set about spreading those criteria throughout the world.'

Somerton resisted. 'And if other nations don't agree with our values, what then?'

Kenny's expression was one of disbelief. 'You're ex-SAS, Jack; what did you do when something got in the way of a military operation?'

'I took it out, Will, what else would I do?'

'Then you have your answer, Jack. You eradicate the problem. I think maybe we've taken this as far as we can for now. We got a kind of accord. Agreed?'

Taylor smiled and nodded enthusiastically. Somerton nodded but had a feeling he had to some extent been manipulated.

Kenny stood and thrust his hand forward for Somerton to shake. 'I have to be getting back to the Oval Office shortly and I expect you want to be heading off to meet up with Chloe MacKinnon. I'll get the car brought round for you straightaway.' He moved over to the telephone and issued the necessary instructions.'

Somerton looked on, a smile playing on his lips. *School's out, I'm being dismissed.* 'Thanks for your hospitality, Will, it's been a wonderful experience. I hope we meet up again soon, maybe if you visit the UK?

Kenny nodded enthusiastically. 'You can bet on it, Jack, it's been a pleasure.'

Somerton turned to Taylor. 'See you at the Embassy tomorrow.'

CHAPTER 29

Washington DC

A light-grey Cadillac stood waiting for Somerton when he left the White House. He had asked to leave by the front door, just something he wanted to do, another memory to keep. Kenny and Taylor hadn't seen him to the door so there was no waving goodbye. The chauffeur, a grey-haired, smallish, coloured man took his small suitcase and put it in the boot then opened a rear door and invited Somerton to get in.

'Thank you, but would you mind if I travel in the front with you? I'll get a much better view of Washington?'

'Lordy me, I ain't ever been asked that before.' The chauffeur hesitated briefly. 'Can't see the harm, it's bullet-proof glass and steel-armoured all the way round.'

'Are you expecting us to be attacked?' Somerton endeavoured to sound serious.'

'Oh, my Lord, not at all, Sir, but we sure do have to be careful. There are crazy people around nowadays.'

Somerton nodded sagely, remembering he was a government minister. 'There certainly are. Sorry, I don't know your name?'

'Thomas Jefferson Hammond, called after the great man himself, folks call me TJ. Now where exactly are we headed for?'

'108 P Street NW. Do you know it?'

'I sure do, it's not far. But instead of going straight there how about I drive you around a bit, get to see the place?'

'That would be a bonus, Thomas, as long as you don't have to get back.'

'Another twenty minutes or so won't matter, I'm not going to show you all of Washington, just a few bits. Here we go.'

Somerton sat back and enjoyed the ride. For a man in his sixties TJ didn't hang around, Chinatown, the Senate buildings, The Mall, The Holocaust Memorial were all introduced before crossing the Potomac River to Arlington National Cemetery and heading north to P Street.

'Won't be long now, Mr Somerton. What do you think of Washington?'

'Loved it and it's made me want to come back for a holiday. You certainly know your way around.'

'Should do, lived here all my life. I know every street and avenue like the back of my hand. You could say I have *the knowledge* like them London cab drivers of yours. We're now on Pennsylvania Avenue headed for 29th Street. We'll be there in less than five. It's a nice area, overlooks Rose Park. Are you over here for long?'

'Sadly no, we fly back to England tomorrow.'

'108 you said, just coming up now.' TJ pulled up in front of a three-storey red-brick federal style mansion complete with a white-columned portico entrance. *Very nice Chloe, not a bad pad. You've set yourself up nicely.*

'Thank you, TJ, I'd invite you in but it's not my place. Here's a twenty to have a drink on me.'

'Very kind of you Mr Somerton.' TJ handed over Somerton's overnight bag, tipped his brow, got back in the car and drove off singing.'

Somerton stood for a moment appraising the building, noting there were no vehicles to be seen, concluding that the drive and garages probably lay behind the brick wall on the right of the house.

Chloe Mackinnon must have been watching out for his arrival; the front door opened, and she stepped out with a broad welcoming smile, her arms outstretched. He moved forward quickly to greet her, a quick hug, and a brushed cheek the best he could manage. His conscience didn't let the moment go unpunished. *How does it feel embracing the woman whose husband you killed, Jack?*

'Jack, it's so good to see someone from home.' Chloe gave him the once-over. 'It's not been that long since we last met but you look as fit as ever.'

'Thank you, Chloe. I feel good, but the bones are beginning to creak. I have to say that you look as stunning as the day I was first introduced to you, and I mean that.'

She smiled. 'The wonders of modern cosmetics and carefully tailored clothes, Jack.'

'Well, whatever the reason, it looks good on you.'

'Enough of the flattery, come in and we'll have a cup of tea, English breakfast of course, or coffee if you prefer. You can tell me how you're getting on as a Member of Parliament. I never thought I'd see the day when Jack Somerton would turn to politics for a career. Colin told me you were very critical of politicians of any persuasion.'

Somerton nodded. 'And I still am, but love them or hate them, they choose the country's destiny, they control our lives, directly and indirectly. I will do my best to be a good one, as were Colin and Alan. Whether I succeed or not will be for others to judge.'

'A very profound statement, Jack, I do believe you're mellowing. Sorry, I forgot to offer my condolences; Alan's death and its manner were shocking; I know how close the three of you were. You'll catch up with Abbi and the kids later; I'll warn you now, we don't talk of the past. We're settled here, we look to the present with maybe just half an eye to the future. You're only with us for one night, I believe.'

Somerton sighed. 'Sadly yes, this is a business trip arranged by Laura Taylor at very short notice. I abandoned the President just to meet you guys. Kenny seems a reasonable sort.'

Chloe Mackinnon smiled briefly. 'Reasonable? Is that the best you can come up with, Jack? It sounds......guarded?'

Somerton felt slightly embarrassed that his lightweight assessment of Will Kenny had been noticed; she could be a staunch supporter for all he knew. 'Short acquaintance, Chloe, I'll make my mind up over time. You know what, I'd like to steer clear of business chat and just enjoy the short time we have together; avoid discussing religion and politics, isn't that what they say?' I'm looking forward to meeting up with Abbi, Maggie and Murray. The kids must be well into their teens?'

'Maggie is 19, Murray 18, both at Georgetown College. Maggie is studying for a degree in Mathematics, Murray wants to be a chemist. They are both bright kids.'

'They're bound to be if they take after you; you have two first class honours degrees if I recall correctly. And what about Abbi?'

'Abbi is working with the Federal National Mortgage Company, otherwise known as Fannie May. She's a Transaction

Manager and doing very well; in fact, she's already in the running for a promotion.'

Somerton blinked. 'Well done, Abbi, but Fannie May, you're kidding me. How did it get a name like that?

Chloe shook her head. 'Nope, I'm serious, I've got no idea how it came about.'

Somerton laughed. 'When we've had our tea, if it's OK with you, I'd like to see more of Georgetown. I've heard it's both charming and historic. I'm happy to call a cab if that makes it easier.'

Chloe gave him the thumbs up. 'That's great, no need for a cab, we can walk to the area I'd like to show you.'

'You're in charge. Oh, I should say that I took a chance and booked us all into the 1789 restaurant tonight, I'm told it's good; 7 for 7.30 if that's OK.'

'Oh, you shouldn't have, Jack, I would have cooked us a meal. The 1789 has a good reputation, though I've never been there. Take your bag up to your room, top of the stairs, second door on the left. I'll text the others and let them know what we're doing.'

Later

The pair made their way into Rose Park and strolled south towards Georgetown's Waterfront Park. Once there they toured the retail outlets along the riverside promenade and gardens.

Somerton felt good, politics seemed very far away. 'This is a delight, Chloe, good choice; it's very easy to feel at home here.'

After a couple of hours, they stopped at a café and had a coffee and donut on the rooftop terrace. The café overlooked the Chesapeake and Ohio Canal beyond which was the Potomac River. The sun was shining, the temperature in the mid-seventies, perfect for Somerton. The thought came to him that this was the most relaxed he had felt for as long as he could remember. He looked at Chloe, wishing she wasn't who she was, wishing this was a first date and he could make a play for her, but sadly that was something that could never be.

'A penny for them, Jack. What are you thinking about, you were miles away?' Chloe broke into his thoughts.

'Oh...just how good life can be sometimes. Look,' he pointed to the canal, 'let's go for a boat ride. I haven't been for one in years.'

'Sounds good to me, we'll need to be quick, I think they're getting ready to sail.'

P Street residence.

Back in P Street, Somerton was given a tour of the house. It was as impressive internally as externally, six bedrooms, exquisitely decorated and furnished, many paintings and ornaments; it had it all. Chloe explained that it was a family heirloom, one that would never be sold. Available only to family members for holidays and business trips, it was often unoccupied. A trusted retainer ensured that it was maintained to a high standard.

'Beautiful place you have here, Chloe, do you think you'll ever come back to England?'

Chloe sighed. 'I don't know, Jack. You know how it is with kids, they settle at college, they make friends, they form their own community and before you realise it, home is no longer home. The longer we are here, the more America becomes home. It's a subject I don't raise. Abbi is picking them up from college to make sure we can all have a chat before we go out.'

Thinking of Abbi and the kids brought another flood of guilt; Abbi's husband David had been killed on his orders. She had nearly been crippled for life. *How can you look them in the eye, Jack? Why in Heaven's name are you here?*

Fifteen minutes later they arrived; the moment had come; the remorseful feelings were set aside and he smiled broadly when Abbi and the kids walked into the lounge. Abbi moved forward instantly and gave him an enthusiastic hug and a kiss on the cheek. 'Wonderful to see you, Jack. You're looking good.'

'Thank you and can I say you look gorgeous, and that's an understatement. He turned to the two young adults. 'Hello Maggie, good to see you again.'

She immediately extended a hand. 'Good to see you too Mr Somerton.'

Somerton grimaced. 'You can cut out the Mr stuff, I'm Jack and none of this handshaking, let's have a high five.' Maggie looked pleased and they smacked palms.

Murray although only 19, was already two inches taller than Somerton, and his athletic build signalled regular gym visits. He responded with a high five and a broad smile. 'Cool, Jack.'

Somerton's tension eased; it was going to be OK. 'Right introductions over with, let's sit down and fill me in on life in Georgetown.'

1789 Restaurant.

They took their places round the reproduction oak antique table in the French styled restaurant; the décor wouldn't have been out of place in Paris.

'Do we all like champagne?' Enquired Somerton looking round. 'I'll order a bottle of white and a bottle of red to go with the meal, or beer, whatever you prefer.'

Maggie was first to speak up. 'Yes please, I love champagne though Mum doesn't usually let us have alcohol.'

'Oh dear, looks like I've broken the rules.' He looked apologetically at Abbi. 'Sorree.'

Abbi smiled and shook her head. 'It's a special occasion, we can let our hair down.' Then added, 'within reason,' with a warning glance at the kids.

The food was French cuisine at its best with the chef's modifying traditional recipes to suit the American palate. Conversation flowed throughout the evening, anecdotes abounded, college friends discussed, holiday plans were debated and even a few jokes told. Somerton felt part of a family, envied the feeling of togetherness the Mackinnon-Singleton family projected. For a few brief seconds he regretted never having married, never having children to raise. *Get a grip, Jack, you're getting maudlin.*

By the time the evening ended, everyone could be classified as merry; a bottle of Bollinger, one of Sauvignon and one of Medoc had been laid to rest. Somerton called for the bill and asked for a cab to be called though the kids tried to persuade him to walk back through the local student nightlife high spots. The limitless energy of youth was overridden by Chloe and Abbi with Somerton tactfully shrugging and displaying feigned disappointment.

Somerton smiled. 'Another time, I promise.'

The taxi journey was less than fifteen minutes, but the effects of the food and alcohol began to hit home in the warm cab; the odd yawn or two escaped Chloe and Abbi and even Maggie's eyes closed briefly. Murray and Somerton talked about sport in general but mainly the former's venture into American Football.

Back home Chloe offered a nightcap and the kids eyes lit up. 'Not for you two, you've had more than enough booze to last you a year. Off to bed, you've both got sport in the morning.'

Murray gulped. 'Oh gosh, I'd forgotten; we have an away match and I've got to be there by eight.'

Maggie nodded. 'Me too, I've got a swimming relay changeover practice We've got an inter-college competition tomorrow evening and our Coach says we need to sharpen up.'

Somerton declined a nightcap, mainly because he doubted Chloe would have any of his favourite malt whiskies. 'As for me I think I'm still a bit jetlagged, I'll retire to bed if you ladies don't mind?'

Chloe chuckled. 'Not at all Jack, I was hoping you would; I'm worn out, it's well past my bedtime.'

Abbi shook her head. 'I don't know, poor old fossils the pair of you, can't stand the pace.' She burst out laughing. 'Only kidding, I'm ready for bed; I've had a busy day.'

Maggie stepped towards Somerton and to his delight gave him a cuddle and a kiss on the cheek. 'Thank you for a very nice evening, Jack. I'll probably be gone before you come down to breakfast.'

Murray was next, offering up a high five. 'Same for me Jack, it's been great. hope it's not long until we meet again.'

Abbi was next in line with a longish hug and a kiss on the cheek. 'You really mustn't leave it too long till next time.'

'Same goes for me, Abbi. Next time you are in London, look me up.'

Chloe stood watching. 'Off you go, Jack, I'm going to lock up. Thank you for a lovely evening. I'll see you in the morning for breakfast but don't show face until eight at the earliest.'

'Orders received and understood. It has been an evening to remember, brings home the value of family. I wish…if only…'

Chloe's eyes misted over. 'Don't go there, Jack, the wound is still too raw. At times like that I miss him terribly.'

CHAPTER 30

Next morning
Somerton woke around 7am and spent an hour on his laptop going through situation reports from the NRSC, followed by those from Reggie Marsh regarding parliamentary and constituency business. The latter were routine items and Marsh had them under control. *Well done, Reggie, you're a star. I must remember to take you out for a meal when I get back as a bit of a thank-you.* There were four red security alerts notified by Eric Barker, all of which were being dealt with. Predictably there was nothing further reported on the source of the cyberattacks that had hit Dover, New York and Munich. Somerton smiled. *I have to hand it to you Jupiter, that's a helluva system you've created.*

The Russians remained mystified about the mid-air collision that had resulted in the death of their President. It was early days in the investigation, but they had not found any evidence of a malfunction. The entire fleet of stealth SU-57 fighter jets had been subjected to rigorous ground checks and a number of randomly selected aircraft were undergoing maximum duration flight testing. The authorities were increasingly coming to the view that their leader had been assassinated by Lieutenant Andrei Popov for reasons as yet unknown.

Somerton glanced at the time on his laptop, 8am, it was time to go down to breakfast. He had heard noises and voices of people moving around and saying their goodbyes and had held back not wanting to intrude on family rituals. In truth he didn't like goodbyes and didn't want to resurrect the feeling of family togetherness that had stirred in him the previous night.

Chloe was sitting in the breakfast room reading a newspaper when he entered.

'Good morning, Jack. I hope the departures didn't wake you up?'

'Not at all, Chloe. I slept like the proverbial log and took the opportunity to have a lie in; this is a late start for me. How about you?'

'I slept well and there was no need for me to get up, but I like to see them off; time moves on and the kids will fly the nest soon enough. I'll enjoy my family for as long as I'm able. Now, what can I get you for breakfast?'

Somerton patted his tummy. 'I'm still full since last night, just coffee please; black, no sugar.'

Chloe smiled. 'I know the feeling, but I'll bring you some toast anyway. Have a look through the morning paper in the meantime.'

The Washington post was full of interest articles, especially those related to the political scene. Will Kenny was popular but was being urged to take a firmer line with China and the Kremlin. In between articles Somerton looked out onto the garden watching birds going about their business, thinking how peaceful and quiet it was compared to where he lived in London.

'Here we are.' Chloe returned with a rack of toast and a tray of assorted marmalades and honeys. 'Tuck in and I'll pour the coffee.'

'Thanks, Chloe. I can't promise to eat it all. I enjoyed last night; a lovely family occasion.' He noticed that she had placed her mobile on the table, open, ready for contact.

'Did you ever consider getting married, Jack?' The question came out of the blue, taking Somerton by surprise.

He shook his head. 'Not seriously, I thought about it a long time ago but concluded it wouldn't be fair on my partner. My life was on the line daily in the SAS, never knew where I'd be posted or how long I'd be away for. Then when I left the army, I got caught up establishing my security interests in the Middle East which required me to be out of the UK for long periods. It just wouldn't have been fair.'

Chloe pursed her lips. 'I can see where you're coming from, but Colin managed, as have many others.'

Somerton shrugged. 'I guess so, maybe I made the wrong call'

Their conversation was interrupted when Chloe's mobile bleeped and the screen showed a white van waiting for entrance at the driveway doors.'

'A delivery, Jack; I'll check it out.'

Somerton nodded his approval. 'I approve, Chloe, your security system linked into your phone, full marks.'

She smiled and left the room, closing the door firmly behind her leaving Somerton pouring himself a second cup of coffee. He could hear voices but switched off and reflected on his return trip to the UK. He was sure Laura Taylor would carry out a post-mortem on their meeting with Will Kenny and there were questions he wanted answered; it would be an interesting flight. Hopefully she would brief him on what was discussed after his departure.

Was the timing right to tell her everything he knew about Constellation Mackinnon and perhaps even the existence about Jupiter. How would she react when she knew the whole story? His deliberations ended when Chloe returned, looking serious. 'Jack, come with me please, there's someone I'd like you to meet.'

Somerton looked at her, his expression seeking explanation, but she just rushed ahead beckoning him to follow. He took a last swallow of coffee and rose to his feet. *What are you up to, Chloe.* She stopped half-way along the corridor, outside the door he recalled was the library.

'In here, Jack.' She stood back and ushered him in.

Somerton's curiosity grew. *The plot thickens, what's going on.* He shrugged his shoulders and strolled in surprised when Chloe left and closed the door behind him.

Floor-to-ceiling bookshelves covered every wall with barely a space for new arrivals. Only a small window broke the mass of multi-coloured book covers. But it wasn't the books that took Somerton's attention, it was the man seated in an armchair to his left – ex-President Brian Overton, a Democrat. Another man stood looking out of the window. *Security guard.* Thought Somerton.

'Oh my God, Mr President, words fail me. It's an honour to meet you. I can't believe this is happening; Chloe hasn't breathed a word. I can't believe this is happening.'

Overton smiled. 'Take a seat, Jack and drop the formalities; we have a lot to discuss and not much time. This isn't a social call but before we go any further let me introduce my accomplice for this clandestine encounter; you would call it a black op.'

He extended his arm towards the other man who turned on cue.

Somerton's heart rate hit the ceiling. He shook his head in disbelief. 'I don't believe my eyes, what's going on?' The man facing him was none other than George Kingston, a Republican ex-President, who extended his hand though there was no welcoming smile. Somerton stepped forward to shake hands. 'Mr President, an honour. I'm dumbstruck; I've met three Presidents in as many days, I'm overwhelmed.'

Then the penny dropped, Somerton's analytical brain clicked into action. These two ex-leaders of the USA weren't presenting themselves to Jack Somerton, per se, they were on a mission. He had something they wanted.

Somerton looked from one to the other, his thoughts a whirlpool, but realisation dawning – A Republic-Democrat alliance – two ex-presidents arriving in secrecy in a closed van – the constellation targets – Rostov's death – his meeting with Kenny and Taylor – they were all linked with a common thread he couldn't see.

Somerton's bewilderment was obvious to Overton and he spoke first. 'Take a seat, Jack, you too, George. There's no time for pleasantries, Jack, we both have other commitments, our time is short. We're out of front-line politics but still in the public eye so we can't disappear for long. We're going to dive straight in, the reason for us being here will become clear as we go along. He looked at Kingston 'Do you want to lead, George?'

Kingston shook his head. 'You were always better with words than me, carry on.' He turned to Somerton. 'Just be assured that Brian speaks for both of us.'

Overton paused a second. 'I'll begin by laying out what we know, Jack, just so you won't be tempted to withhold any facts when it's your turn to respond. Firstly, we know about Jupiter and his unparalleled genius. We also know about his proclivities and what you did to satisfy them.' Somerton felt himself shudder. 'We know all about Constellation Mackinnon and its wide-ranging capabilities. We know that the constellation was the source of the Dover, New York and Munich cyber-attacks. I might add that I admire your target strategy, setting the scene with the initial attacks in the West.'

Somerton's eyes were widening by the second. 'How long have you known? And come to that and how did you get to know in the first place?'

Kingston waved his hand dismissively. 'You don't need to know our source. We haven't got long; let Brian finish what he has to say.'

Somerton stifled a blunt response and just nodded; they were holding the aces.'

Overton took up where he left off. 'We also know that the Rostov incident was planned by you and carried out by Jupiter at your direction.' Kingston mumbled something under his breath that sounded like, 'A great fucking day for democracy.'

Somerton hadn't taken to Kingston and couldn't resist a jibe. 'Please don't interrupt, George, let Brian finish.' The ex-President shot him a hateful look but said nothing.

Overton resumed his delivery. 'We know that you, Will Kenny and Laura Taylor met together the day before yesterday to agree what happens next.'

Somerton shook his head. 'Not exactly, we met primarily to discuss what Russia was up to along the Ukrainian border.'

Overton smiled and shook his head. Kingston was more direct. 'Balls, if you believe that, we're wasting our time.'

'George,' Overton raised his eyebrows gave his colleague a reproving look, 'let's take this a step at a time, please.'

Kingston nodded and waved his hands in acquiescence. 'Carry on.'

Overton's brow creased in thought for a few seconds. 'I'll come back to Will Kenny's vision of the future and feed you another fact. 'Your close friend, ex-Prime Minister Alan Croudace's death, didn't result from an act of dangerous driving. He was deliberately killed to prevent him speaking out about the capabilities and ownership of Constellation Mackinnon. The men behind the operation were two retired members of US Special Forces.

Somerton reacted immediately, leaping to his feet. 'Give their names; I'll kill the bastards.'

Kingston turned on him. 'Sit down and fucking listen; you're no innocent when it comes to killing people, even your closest friend.'

Overton spread his hands. 'Calm down, both of you.' He glanced at his watch. 'We've got less than ten minutes left. We don't know the detail of the latest Kenny-Taylor discussions, but we know that their goal is to use the satellite system to establish a world-wide system of sanction and control. Expressed crudely it will be a case of 'do it our way or else' no matter how they try to sell it. The next two targets are North Korea and China. You are calling the shots at this stage. Those are your targets, is that not so?

Somerton nodded, aghast at how much they knew. *They had a well-informed source, Surely, not Jupiter?*

Overton continued. 'Having demonstrated the system's capabilities, would you accept that Kenny, aided and abetted by Taylor, will seek to promote a worldwide regime that decides on the standards of existence for everyone?'

Somerton wondered why he was being asked the obvious. 'I think in general terms that might be the case and, personally, I think it has the potential to make this a better, safer planet for everyone.'

Overton nodded. 'Lofty aims but can you guarantee, that no matter who is in charge of the satellite system, it will always be used to good intent....**always**?'

Somerton knew he couldn't offer any guarantees, but he wasn't going to give in easily. 'Well, of course there's always a chance it could end up in the wrong hands, but that's true of any weapon.'

Overton paused. 'But this isn't any old weapon, Jack, is it? And, in your own words you've acknowledged that you can't guarantee how it might be used in the future. Here's another revelation for you. Jupiter, real name Joseph Svetinsky, is no longer in the UK acting under your direction. He is now in the USA, based in Fort Kenny, a secret operations centre known only to a select group. He was a Russian dissident who defected to the States with the help of the CIA. His potential was recognised by a small group of military chiefs hellbent on establishing a world order. They developed a long-term strategy to achieve this through Jupiter's genius. They wouldn't have been able to work safely under the radar over here so the idea of roping in the UK emerged. With regard to Svetinsky, his immune system is deteriorating; he hasn't got too long left in this world, a year, maybe less, will see him out.'

Somerton shook his head. 'That's a shame. Whatever you think of him, his scientific inventions have been of great benefit to the world. He'll be great loss.'

Kingston cut in. 'Brian, time's moving on. We need to tie this up.'

The moment of truth had arrived, Overton searched for the right words to convince Somerton. 'Listen carefully, Jack and search your conscience. It's a fact that all through history, leaders have thought they knew what was best for the world they lived in; they sought to impose **their** standards believing all would be well. All through time those with power have sought to dominate – the Pharaohs, the Romans, Hitler, Stalin and your own British Empire for that matter. The Brits at least saw the light eventually and pulled back, settling for a highly respected commonwealth of nations. The West has made serious mistakes; the Iraq War, Afghanistan are recent examples of peoples not wanting to accept the values, or the history, or the religion of others, imposed upon them. Do you appreciate what I'm getting at?'

Somerton's mind was swamped with the revelations but what Overton was saying made sense. It was coming home to him that he should give serious thought to the possibility of changing camps. Maybe Alan Croudace had been right all along. Reluctantly he was forced to concede the point being made. 'I guess you're right, I can see that, but you're both respected, both ex-presidents, why don't you speak out?'

Kingston responded instantly. 'Because we don't know friend from fucking foe. We don't know who to trust anymore, that's why we snuck in here in secret. We can't even be sure of our own staff. We could be taken out any time and end up in Arlington. Our assassination would be blamed on the Russians, or the Chinese or some Arab extremist.'

Overton nodded. 'That's the truth of it, Jack.'

Somerton didn't go along with the proposition entirely, but he felt conflicted, something about Will Kenny just hadn't rung true. 'So, what do you think I can do?'

Overton and Kingston looked at each other for seconds before the former finally spoke. 'We don't know, we're in unknown territory. Use your knowledge, your experience and your insider status to find a way. Get in touch with me through Chloe Mackinnon if we can help, but remember we are closely watched most of the time.'

Somerton nodded. 'Understood. I'm not making any promises but you've given me a lot to think about. The world is in a fucking mess and the science we have now might be its saviour. Both Laura Taylor and Will Kenny seem to be well-intentioned. In the short term, I'll start by asking one of our research people if there is a way the Constellation could be taken out of service. We use it for telecoms and have access of some kind, so there might be a way of neutralising the deterrent facility. At the moment Jupiter told me that the system's effectiveness is limited by the number of satellites.'

Overton nodded. 'We have said all we can it's up to you what path you follow going forward. You've referred to Kenny and Taylor but are you sure **they** are in full command of the situation? There are lot of military big shots on both sides of the Atlantic wanting to flex their muscles. Are they keeping their heads down for the moment, waiting for the right opportunity to take command? We just don't know. Don't let your guard down Jack, even our inside source doesn't the total cabal membership. '

Kingston tapped his watch, thrusting it in front of Overton. 'We gotta go Brian or we'll be missed.'

Overton nodded. 'Don't be fooled by anything Taylor might say; she's about to announce a trade deal with the US to produce 250 more satellites. Meantime, Kenny meantime will be manufacturing a further 150 under licence to the UK for Uncle Sam. They are really stepping up the pace.'

Somerton gulped. 'I have two questions that need answers before you go.

Obama raised his eyebrows. 'Go on.'

Somerton drew breath. 'Easy one first, I want the names of the two guys responsible for the death of Alan Croudace and the name of your inside source of intelligence.'

Kingston shook his head immediately, leaving Overton to respond. 'Can't tell you our source, Jack. We don't know if we can trust you.'

Somerton shrugged. 'That answers my second question. My guess is you don't trust me but you've got nowhere else to go. You've taken a big risk; I could report this meeting to Kenny and Taylor. But you can rest assured I have no intentions of doing that, I promise. You've given me a lot to think about.?'

Another glance between Kingston and Overton, the latter nodding and shrugging.'

Overton pursed his lips. 'Be very careful, Jack, I beg of you. We'll talk this over with our inside source and if he's willing to work directly with you; it makes sense. If he's happy with the proposal, he'll get in touch with you direct.

Somerton sighed. 'Thank you, but I want the names of Alan Croudace's killers.'

Overton shook his head. 'I know very little about them, other than their names which are Moran and Sweeney. Who they directly report to, or where they hang out, I don't know. If I do learn anything further, I'll get back to you through Chloe with the information.'

Somerton nodded. 'Thank you, Brian.'

Kingston interjected. 'Right, we're out of here, we're five minutes late already.'

A sudden thought struck Somerton. 'One more thing.'

Both men stopped and looked at him.

'Chloe doesn't know about me, about what I did?' Overton shook his head.

'And she must never be told, promise me.'

Obama nodded his head. 'She won't hear it from me.'

Somerton looked at Kingston. 'And you George?'

His reply was laden with anger. 'I promise I won't tell her but, not for your sake, Somerton. I just feel she's had enough shit in her life without adding to it.'

Keen to avoid adding to the obvious hostility between the two men Overton grabbed Kingston by the arm and led him away.

Somerton looked after them, sadness on his face. *You're right about that George, one hundred per cent.*

Chloe Mackinnon was still in the breakfast room when Somerton returned there seeking another cup of coffee. 'Sorry to spring that on you, Jack. I met Brian a few days ago at a college event and mentioned you were coming over. He asked to meet you in private. Said it was of national importance and very hush hush. I of course agreed, I could hardly refuse. I had no idea Kingston would be there though.'

Somerton felt drained, felt a weight of responsibility he wasn't sure he could carry. 'You did the right thing, Chloe it is of national importance, he didn't exaggerate. At this moment in time, I don't know if I can help but I'll give it my best shot.'

Chloe understood and put a hand on his cheek. 'Colin felt that way sometimes, but a solution always came along when he put his mind to it. Do you want to talk about it?'

'I can't Chloe, not even to you. My head's full, I need to get back to the White House. Would you mind calling me a cab, while I pack my bag?'

'I'll run you over, Jack.'

Somerton shook his head. 'I'd rather say my goodbyes here.'

'Whatever you say.'

Minutes later they said their goodbyes on the doorstep. Somerton gave her a long, loving hug; he wasn't sure when he'd see her again.

CHAPTER 31

Return flight to England

Somerton and Taylor exchanged only cursory comments on the way back to John F Kennedy airport, both were engrossed in thought or perhaps just saving conversation for the flight. However, Taylor gave forth with one bit of good news. 'You'll be pleased to know that we'll be landing at Gatwick, Jack. It seems that one of the Royals is flying off to Jeddah, an anniversary of some kind or other apparently.'

Somerton gave a thumbs up. 'Great, much quicker journey home from there than from Mildenhall. Perhaps you should ask them to keep a look out for your dear brother-in-law.'

Taylor shot him a steely look. 'There's nothing dear about him as you well know. Since you've raised the subject, I can tell you that Geraldine is quite worried about him; she's hasn't heard from him since he left the UK.'

'He's probably bunked up somewhere with a girlfriend. Who knows what he gets up to when he's let off the lead.'

'Just like you, Jack?'

'Never been on a lead, Laura.' He raised an eyebrow and let a smile play about his lips. 'What are you like when you're let off the lead, Laura?'

'I won't dignify that question with an answer, Jack.'

Somerton shrugged. 'Your choice.'

The VIP RAF Voyager Airbus stood gleaming on the runway at JFK and they were boarded without ceremony; there was no-one to see them off unless you counted the Ambassador's chauffeur. Somerton took a last look over his shoulder and saw the Rolls pull away before he reached the top of the steps.

Somerton had thought out his game plan carefully, but he was keen for Taylor to set the ball rolling and once they had been served coffee and were on their own, she duly obliged.

'What did you think of Will, Jack?'

'On short acquaintance I found him good company and somebody I could do business with. And the same goes for the whole Kenny family.

Taylor nodded. 'Yes, nice people all round. Will wasn't too sure about you.'

Somerton was taken aback. 'Really, sounds like I've let you down. Maybe I was too cautious about the future, but I wanted to hear the argument from the President's viewpoint. With due respect to you, he is generally regarded as the Leader of the so-called free world. I was playing the role of Devil's advocate to some extent. Having thought about what he had to say, I'm convinced his aims for the future are spot on. Our satellite system gives the Western democracies the upper hand and we must use it to maximum advantage. We must press on with the next target and demonstrate its full capabilities'

Perhaps it was his imagination, but Taylor seemed to relax, the tension in her visibly drained away. 'I'm so relieved to hear you say that, Jack; it would have been very difficult for you to remain a Minister if you had come out against our vision of the future.'

'There was never any danger of that Laura, I was being cautious, testing the water. Don't forget it's the first time I've met the guy, I know very little about him. We share the same goal, though we might have different ideas on how to get there. But believe me, I'm completely committed to the Kenny-Taylor alliance whatever form it takes. I'll be setting up the North Korea and China targets when I get back.'

'Remind me what the targets are.'

Somerton shook his head. 'I haven't finalised the arrangements yet; there are various options to consider but I can assure you they will hurt. Ideally the attacks should bring big headlines, but you know how secretive those countries are and I want to make sure the whole world gets to know of their failures.'

Taylor nodded. 'Our boys will see that the events are well publicised.'

Somerton nodded. 'I'm sure they will, but the events must be very visible; we can't leave any scope for our Far Eastern friends to deny they took place.'

To his surprise Taylor squeezed his hand. 'I'm so relieved to know that you're on board, Jack.'

They sat back for a while, Taylor with a trace of a smile, apparently happy with what she had heard; Somerton preparing in his mind the next phase of his discourse.

'Laura,' Taylor turned to face him, concern showing at the serious tone of Somerton's voice.

'Yes?' Caution sounded in Taylor's voice. 'Go on, you have my full attention. I get the impression you are about to say something of importance.'

'Now that we've cleared the air and I know where we're headed, I think it's time I came clean about the satellite system. I think you should know how it came to be invented and the genesis of the UK's remarkable performance in the world of research.'

Taylor leaned back. 'Go ahead, Jack; to say I'm intrigued would be an understatement.'

Somerton took a deep breath. 'Pin your ears back and prepare for a story known only to Colin Mackinnon, Alan Croudace, myself and one other person, a scientific genius known as Jupiter.' Somerton studied Taylor's expression as he spoke, her reaction was minimal, but it was there. *She knows.*

He proceeded to explain Jupiter's origins, about how the NRSC researchers gained their knowledge and the kidnapping of many young women without mentioning his role. Taylor listened attentively without interruption or questioning. He went on to explain Mackinnon's views on the satellite system and how he had hoped it could be used to peacefully create a new world order but that Croudace had been vehemently opposed to the launch and had threatened to go public.

At that point Somerton paused, waiting for questions from Taylor but none was forthcoming. 'Alan's concerns, and mine to a degree, was the inescapable fact that Jupiter controlled the satellite system. We were, and remain, totally reliant on his cooperation. Jupiter could go rogue at any time and there's nothing we could do to stop him. Colin trusted Jupiter and argued that he had never let us down. Alan argued that trust could be breached and that we knew nothing about Jupiter, a worry I shared to a great extent. Colin asked me to kill Alan and to my discredit on the spur of the moment I agreed. I thought the end justified the means, my SAS training I guess.'

Taylor displayed no sense of shock; instead, just calmly asked the question Somerton was prepared for.

'So, given all that, why didn't you kill Alan, he was the risk? Am I guessing right when I assume you killed Colin? Why did you do that?' Not that I'm complaining I've done rather well out of his demise.'

Somerton's insides were churning with shame, but the game had to continue. 'My initial intention was to kill Alan but when I thought about it further, I decided that the only way to keep him quite was to ensure the satellites weren't launched. Colin on the other hand would have insisted that the launch went ahead. It was the greatest dilemma I have ever faced and, to be honest, there was a streak of self-preservation running through it. Alan didn't know that women were being kidnapped to serve Jupiter, but there was a risk it would all have come into the open if access to Jupiter laboratory had resulted from the exposure of his existence. My role in the kidnappings might have come to light and I would have ended up in goal, as would Colin.'

Taylor regarded him intently. 'Go on, Jack. Explain your logic, why kill Colin?'

Somerton didn't need to pretend to be ashamed or sad, the feelings flooded in and displayed themselves in his expression. 'By killing Colin, I shut Alan up, the satellites weren't launched at the time, but remained available. I set out to convince Alan that Jupiter had scarpered and we could launch the satellites safely and benefit from their telecommunications capability. Over time he was persuaded and agreed we could launch in phases; that's where we are up to as I speak. Sadly, a drug-soaked nobody killed Alan and the whole scenario changed overnight.' *Your turn, Laura, tell me who really killed Alan. Or maybe you don't know. Maybe Will doesn't tell you everything.*

'In the meantime, I've built up a good relationship with Jupiter and we can now do whatever we want with his cooperation. I'm trying to persuade him to let me have direct control over the satellite system but he hasn't agreed yet. Not a day passes that I don't feel guilty, Laura, and I shall wish till the day I die, that Colin hadn't been the price paid for this brave new world we hope to create in the future. I'm determined to do all I can to further this dream as his legacy, so that his sacrifice hasn't been in vain. I just pray the full story never gets told.'

Taylor went quiet, clearly deep in thought.

'Got you thinking, Laura, haven't I? Oh, there is one more thing I should mention before you and Kenny get too ambitious. The satellite system doesn't have the capacity to attack and control on multiple fronts; it will need to be expanded considerably to fulfil your aspirations to control the world.'

Taylor smiled. 'That's being taken care off, Jack. I'll be announcing a contract for the manufacture of 250 satellites for the UK and the President will arrange manufacture of a further 150 in the States under licence. At the end of the day, we'll have over 450 satellites at our command, more than enough to achieve our goals. While that's taking place, we'll be developing our strategy, we'll be identifying further targets, we'll be escalating the magnitude of our attacks and making it clear that we hold the destiny of the world in our hands.'

Somerton nodded. 'And when you say 'we', are you alluding to you and Kenny?'

Taylor shook her head. 'Not exactly Jack, we can't act in isolation; you'll be involved along with others on both sides of the Atlantic, key military figures are on board.'

'Will yours truly get to meet all the players, both Brits and Yanks? I feel strongly that in any walk of life teams perform better when they grow together. The best strategies evolve from the best teams, two world wars proved that time and time again. We need a clear strategy to deal with every eventuality that this bold venture will throw at us. There will be a lot of resistance from many countries who will fear a loss of independence and see your efforts as a blatant takeover.'

Taylor nodded. 'What you say makes sense; I'll talk to Will about us all getting together.'

Another thought struck Somerton. 'By the way, you should know that Jupiter can listen in on conversations taking place in your office, my office, and I suspect, anywhere else he chooses. So, be careful what you talk about.'

Taylor shrugged. 'We have to trust him; Jupiter is a member of the team. There's no need to worry about eavesdropping provided you are committed to furthering the strategy.'

Somerton nodded. 'That makes sense, I'll be a more relaxed going forward; not that we have a strategy I'm party to.'

'Enough, Jack, I've got the message; I'll speak to Will about developing the strategy.'

'There's one more issue, Laura, and it's important. Referring to Jupiter, we have all our eggs in one basket, if anything happened to him, I can't see how we could proceed. With that in mind, I have to tell you that Jupiter has confessed to me that his immune system is damaged.'

Taylor's face showed genuine concern. 'You're right, it is a major concern and we're dealing with it.'

Somerton raised an eyebrow. 'Dealing with it?'

Taylor bit on her lip. 'My turn to confess. I knew all about Jupiter and his immunity problem. His immune system is more than damaged, it's in irreversible decline, he's dying. He's only expected to live for another year or so. He left the UK some months back and now operates out of a high security centre in the US.'

Somerton sighed. 'He'll be a great loss when he leaves us. Thank you for sharing that bit of information with me; I shan't mention it when I next speak to him.'

CHAPTER 32

London

Somerton got to the NRSC early next day and buzzed Eric Barker to join him in his office.

Minutes later his Security Manager knocked and breezed into the office. 'Good morning, Jack, welcome back to civilisation. How did your trip to the States go? I expect the shock news about President Rostov was on the agenda?'

Somerton grinned. 'Let's say he got a mention, but nobody expressed their regrets or sent a condolence card. I got to meet President Kenny and his family, all nice people. He's an impressive guy with great vision and I look forward to working with him in the future. He's determined to expand NATO and increase investment in Defence.' Somerton knew that Jupiter might be listening in and was signalling his support for Kenny.

'And how are things with you, Eric?'

'Busier than ever, Jack, the web is flooded with fake threats nowadays in addition to the genuine stuff. I think creating fake news is a full-time occupation nowadays. There are four genuine serious threats that we know off, but nothing to trouble you with at this stage.'

'Are you sure? I'm happy to look at them if you want me to.' Without waiting for Barker to reply he reached forward for the four files and at the same time passed Barker a hand-written note headed, DESTROY WHEN READ

Eric,

I'm probably being paranoid but I'm not talking aloud about the matter I outline below until I've swept the office for bugs. Believe it or not, one was found in the Oval Office!

I want you to run a check on two ex-US Army Special Forces operatives. They are believed to have gone rogue and may have visited the UK at any time since the beginning of February. There is even a suggestion that they may have been hired to kill Alan Croudace. I'm keeping an open mind on that possibility.

Their names are Sweeney and Moran. I want you to run a check on all incoming flights to the UK since 1st February, two yanks travelling together, most likely in their forties. I want to know their address or addresses in the States It's a bit of a tall order, don't drop everything to do this, just give it time when you can.

Obviously keep this to yourself.

Thanks,

Jack

Somerton knew he'd have to continue to indulge in the subterfuge from time to time knowing he could be overheard by Jupiter; he would have to be ultra-cautious now that he had joined the Kenny-Taylor group. He handed the security files back to Barker. 'Thanks for those alerts, Eric. Keep them under surveillance and get in touch with me immediately if there are any developments of concern. I don't suppose anything has emerged about the Dover, New York and Munich incidents?

Barker sighed and shook his head. 'Sorry, Jack, we've explored every avenue and come up with nothing, not a single lead. None of our friends have had any success either. It's a monumental fucking mystery.'

'Don't worry, Eric, our friends on the other side of the pond have drawn a blank as well. Put it on the backburner for now and let's see what comes along. I can't believe there won't be more of these incidents; someone somewhere is trying to make a point. I'll let you get back to your desk now.'

Barker nodded and took his leave.

That seemed to go well, Jack, next up...Jupiter.

It took a few minutes for Jupiter appear and it seemed to Somerton that he looked tired, almost drained, which reflected what Laura had just revealed about his health.

'Good morning, Jupiter. How are things with you?'

Uncharacteristically, Jupiter shrugged. 'OK I guess. What can I do for you?'

'If you don't mind me saying so, you neither look good nor sound good.' *I wonder if you'll say anything about your declining health*

'I'm fine, Jack, tired I guess; things have been manic here.'

Somerton let the denial pass but noted that Jupiter and said 'here' which tied in with his relocating to America. 'I want to activate the North Korea targets this Wednesday. China will follow as soon as possible thereafter. You'll be pleased to know that I've authorised the launch of the remaining satellites, so all fifty-two will be at your disposal by the end of this week.'

Jupiter's eyes lit up. 'That is good news, Jack. I'll come back to you with the details for the North Kores attack when I've looked at what is necessary. Fortuitously, your timing might be perfect.'

'What do you mean' Somerton had no idea what Jupiter was alluding to.

'I'll explain when I've done a bit more research. I just need to confirm that what I've heard is fact and not just rumour.'

'Come on, don't be so secretive, out with it.'

Jupiter didn't budge. 'No, you'll just have to be patient.'

Somerton stifled an expletive. 'Have it your way. I'm signing off now, get back to me when you've done your research.'

Gibraltar Heights

Somerton was sitting comfortably in his lounge, reflecting on the day's parliamentary business when he got a call from Jupiter on his laptop.

'Good evening, Jack.' Jupiter sounded brighter than he had earlier in the day. 'I can confirm that we'll deal with North Korea on Wednesday as you requested, although timing will have to remain flexible in view of the logistics involved. And we should be able to deal with China on Saturday or Sunday if the satellite launches go to plan. I'll let you know Friday at the latest.'

'That's great news. Sounds like you've pulled out all the stops. When we put China to bed, we'll give some thought to next steps.'

'Get in touch when you're ready. I'll leave you to come up with some ideas when you've had your discussions.'

Discussions other slip by Jupiter. On the spur of the moment Somerton decided to play the innocent. 'Discussions? What discussions?'

Jupiter shook his head. 'None in particular. I just assumed that you would obliquely sound out your political or military colleagues about possible targets.'

Somerton nodded. 'You're right, I might just do that. You don't have anything in mind perchance?'

Jupiter shook his head. 'I think we've concluded our business and I'm still not feeling too good. Goodbye for now.'

NRSC Next morning

Eric Barker joined Somerton shortly after he arrived. 'Here's today's alerts, Jack. I think you'll find all the information require.' He winked and touched the side of his nose.

'Thanks Eric, I'll go through them and get back to you with any queries.'

Somerton opened up the Alert Folder and found what he expected, a hand-written note from Barker with the information he'd requested.

Jack,

Messrs Moran and Sweeney flew out of New York on a late flight on 16th February, landing at Heathrow early next morning. I have the flight details if you need them. As of now I haven't ascertained where they stayed whilst they were here, but I can if it's important. They flew back to New York on the 19th. The address they used was 125 N14th Street, Newark.'

Somerton clenched his fist. 'Gotcha.' *Arrived 17th, Alan killed 18th, fly back 19th. Bastards, your days are numbered, it's just a matter of how and when.*

Barker's note went on. Moran and Sweeney Also travelled to Jeddah on 19th March.' That's all I've got for now. If you need more info, let me know

Somerton pulse rate went up a notch as he began to put all the pieces together, slowly forming the likely scenario. *Sweeney and Moran are probably professional hit men or maybe deep undercover special operatives trained to do what they're told and ask no questions. You took out Alan for sure. Looks like you then returned to New York and were given another assignment, and I reckon that was to deal with Guy Madison who has mysteriously disappeared without trace. Nineteenth March fits well with*

Madison's trip to Jeddah. I reckon Will Kenny, with or without Laura's knowledge, got you pair of bastards to take out Madison.

Somerton was sure of his conclusion but made a mental note to ask Taylor about Madison next time they met up.

CHAPTER 33

NRSC Tuesday

Somerton headed to Lizzie King's office; she had the lead in co-ordinating research, if anyone could help it would be her. He knocked on the door, entering when he heard a muffled *come in.*

'Jack, this is a surprise.' She stole a look at her calendar. 'I'm not late with a report or whatever, am I?'

'Not at all, Lizzie; I'm conscious that national research is part of my remit and wonder if you could spare the time to take me round and introduce me to some of the new researchers. I never did get to meet them all.'

She stared at him, puzzled, wary even. 'I'm….' He mouthed the word *please* and put his hands prayer fashion below his chin the pointed outside to the corridor. King was puzzled but recognised that Somerton must have a reason for his request and duly complied. 'Of course, Jack, that's a lovely idea.' She stood and followed Somerton out into the corridor and whispered. 'So, what's going on, Jack?'

'Sorry about this but I'm just back from the States and spent some time with their CIA people and they claim that hackers have the capability to listen in on conversations if there's a computer source nearby.'

King nodded. 'I believe so, but who is going to want to listen in on what we have to say. I think you might be a touch overcautious.'

Somerton nodded. 'Let me explain further. They also believe that unfriendly foreign powers have the ability to interfere with satellite signals and performance. As Minister for national security that's a major concern. It's just possible that they could use our satellites to attack other systems. I'd like to talk with your cleverest satellite and communications researcher.'

King furrowed her brow. 'I'd have my doubts about that theory, Jack but I'll take you to meet Jason Robertson; he hasn't been with us long but he's a real whizz kid believe me. Follow me.' She set off along the corridor with Somerton close behind, took a right and pointed at a blue door. That's where he cocoons himself. Do you want me around or not?'

'Yes please, Lizzie. He'll feel more comfortable if you're present, I'm sure.'

King knocked on the door and walked straight in. Robertson had earphones on and stood in front of a large whiteboard covered in symbols and was so engrossed wasn't aware of their presence until King tapped him on the shoulder.

'Jason, you have a visitor looking to tap into that huge brain of yours.'

Robertson turned round sharply. 'Professor King, sorry I was miles away, didn't hear you come in.'

King smiled reassuringly. 'Perhaps take your headphones off, and meet Mr Somerton, Minister for Research and National Security. He's our boss, so be nice to him and make a good impression.'

Somerton offered his hand which was somewhat nervously shaken by the young researcher. 'How can I be of assistance Mr Somerton, er Minister.'

Somerton was about to reply when King intervened, pointing at the computer. 'Let's begin by showing Jack the electronics workshop where you carry out most of your work.' Robertson looked puzzled unsure how to respond.

Somerton took King's cue. 'Good idea, lead the way, Lizzie.'

King led the way to a workshop full of instrumentation, cable electronic components and a large central work bench. Robertson looked around awkwardly not sure what was expected of him.

Somerton took the lead. 'Professor King has rightly brought us where we can talk privately, Jason and what I have to say will be new to her. Our conversation is to remain strictly between the three of us. It goes no further. Is that clearly understood.'

Robertson expression became even more worried. 'Oh gosh, really, of course, if you say so Minister.' The words stuttered out from a young man worried about what was expected of him.

'I do say so, it's important, top secret even. You can only discuss anything that subsequently arises when you're in a secure area with no computers nearby, and only, I emphasise **only**, with Professor King or myself. I have responsibility for National Security, and I've just returned from a trip to the States where I met the President and the Head of their Central Intelligence Agency. A potentially serious situation has arisen.'

Robertson's eyes widened but he said nothing. Lizzie King's attention was now fully engaged.

Somerton allowed a few seconds for his remarks to sink in before going on. 'During one of my meetings the CIA revealed that one of their satellite systems had been hacked with serious outcomes for their security surveillance installations, I'm paraphrasing, they used technical jargon beyond my ken.

My thoughts of course went to Constellation MacKinnon which is essential to our country's communications capability. It also had me wondering about the components used in the assembly of our satellites. I don't know where they are sourced or if they could be tampered with at the manufacturing, assembly, or operational stages. In short, I want our system checked out discreetly to determine if it's been interfered with? And finally, I want to know what is the possibility of shutting it down in an emergency?'

Robertson shrugged. 'You could always blast it out of the sky; that would shut it down.' He gave a little laugh.

Somerton frowned. 'That would be an extreme measure, don't you think? And just how would we explain shooting down our own satellite system? We'd look rather foolish don't you think? Our reputation would take quite a knock and the hackers would know we were on to them. I want this done discreetly. I was thinking of hackers what hackers do; using radio signals or something similar.'

Lizzie King nodded. 'Understood, Jack.' She stared at Robertson, inviting him to respond.

Robertson clenched his hands together and licked his lips, clearly feeling pressured. 'I need time to think about this. If there is a protagonist out there, they would probably allow for detection and would be able to neutralise any signals we transmit. I'll need to look at the circuit drawings, check out the components and, ideally, witness the assembly process.'

Somerton nodded. 'Sounds good to me, Jason. So, summing up, I want you to check if the system is comms only; are there any unexplained components, and, can a means be found to shut the system down. I want you to drop what you're doing and find the answers. Discuss anything technical with Professor King; she has my mobile number if I need to be involved.'

'I'll need a set of up-to-date circuit diagrams?'

King intervened. 'There's a set locked away in the vault. I'll get them when Jack's finished with us.'

The young man rubbed his chin. 'It would be ideal if I could open one up and take a look inside the casing.'

Somerton shook his head. 'That would be difficult. They are all due to be launched this week; it would look very suspicious if I put the date back just so we could look belatedly look inside a satellite. I'll see what I can do but don't count on it. It might be a bit of a pain but could you please report progress to Professor King on a daily basis, please.'

Jason nodded. 'Not a problem.'

'Thanks, Jason, I'll be on my way and let you get started.'

King caught Somerton's eye. 'A word before you leave, please.'

Half-way along the corridor, King stopped to address Somerton. 'This sounds serious, Jack, I get the feeling I'm not being told everything.'

'It is serious, Lizzie, very serious. And you're right, I can't tell you the whole background at this time but I promise I will when I'm able. Sorry.'

The Grey Goose Pub. Later that day.
Somerton, Eddie Black and Mike Davies sat huddled together in the furthest corner of the pub; the private room had been booked for a darts competition when Somerton had phoned earlier.

The guys were keen to talk about Somerton's experiences as an MP and his trip to America whilst they grappled with the generously filled sandwiches provided by the landlord, Andy Swift. Food consumed and the first round of beers downed, Somerton signalled Andy for refills. When the landlord had duly provided, Somerton furtively looked round to make certain that no-one was within earshot. Davis observed the action and leaned forward, whispering conspiratorially 'And now we come to the undercover operation, the reason Major Somerton has convened this meeting. He smiled and raised his voice. 'So out with it, Jack, you're clearly on edge. Just why are we here?'

Somerton drew a breath and came out with his prepared storyline. 'I can't name my source, but I've found out that Alan's death wasn't an accident. Let's just say for now that there were American business interests involved. There were those who didn't like the way he put a halt to a government contract to manufacture satellites and they decided to take him out of the game. They were of the belief that his likely successor, Laura Taylor, would look more favourably on a contract, given on her long-term friendship with Will Kenny. They decided Alan should have an accident and engaged two retired special ops guys to do the deed.'

Black and Davies were stunned; Davies thumped the table and uttered a string of expletives. Black let his colleague's wrath die down, then posed the obvious question. 'What are we going to do, Jack? We've got to exact revenge and the sooner the better.'

Davies spat out the words. 'We're going to crucify the bastards, that's what we're going to do. Who are they and where do they hang out?'

Somerton spread his hands and put a finger to his lips. 'Joey Martin and Chris Sweeney. They live together at 125N14th Street, Newark. I don't know anything about their relationship. So, I have their names and their address but what I'm lacking is a contact over there who could take care of this situation.'

Black spoke up. 'Are you asking us to take this on?'

Somerton shook his head. 'I want to avenge Alan's death, and my preference would be to take them out personally, but I'm too closely watched nowadays. Ideally, I'd like to commission someone in the States, but my profile has gone up quite a bit over there, a consequence of my new role and recent visit, so I have to tread carefully.'

The group went quiet for a few seconds then Eddie Black broke the silence. 'I have a cousin in Newark, he's ex-Paras. He might be able to give me a steer in the right direction. I hasten to add, this job is not his kind of thing, but I'm happy to take a trip over and check things out.'

Davies chipped in. 'I'm happy to tag along and watch your back.'

Black shook his head. 'Much as I value your company, Mike, I think on this occasion it would be best if I travel alone.'

'I feel I'm coming up short on this one, but I will meet any costs involved, sky's the limit on this one.' Somerton felt guilty, Alan was his friend, he should be the one pulling the trigger.

Black shook his head. 'We can talk about money another time if needs be, I'm doing this for Alan and the Regiment.'

Somerton nodded. 'Understood. Another drink and we're done.'

Two heads shook in unison and Black spoke up. 'Don't feel like it now, Jack. This all comes as a bit of a shock; I feel that I just want to get back home.'

Somerton acquiesced. 'Fair enough. I'm indebted to you both; I don't know what I'd do without you two at my side. Keep me posted.'

CHAPTER 34

North Korea Wednesday

President Lee Jong-Un accompanied by his two leading missile programme professors, Hwang Ji-Hoon and Paek Sung-Ho, were being chauffeured along the main highway in the North-West of the country. The President's car was closely followed by his usual entourage of security and military vehicles. Their destination was the missile launch centre on the outskirts of Touchang-ri not far from the city of Dandong.

The President was genuinely passionate about all things scientific and chatted animatedly with the Professors about the latest developments in missile technology. He was excited. Today was going to be a big day; two launches were planned. Once again, he would demonstrate to the West, and his two allies in the East, Russia and China, that his country was not backward when it came to missile technology. Ever determined to gain the world's respect, he had publicly announced his intentions to develop his country's nuclear capabilities.

His small but impressive motorcade drove through Dandong; its main thoroughfare lined dutifully by cheering school children and their teachers. Kim smiled and waved, convinced it was a genuine expression of their love for their leader. From time to time the professors summoned up a praiseworthy comment to feed Lee's vanity.

The journey was near its end; Lee's excitement mounted as his motorcade entered the site and he saw the military security personnel saluting him as he passed through the steel gates. His limousine came to a halt directly outside the control centre where he was welcomed by the Launch Director, Choi-Jeong Chan. Their timing was perfect, there would be very little waiting around. He had visited many times in the past, there would be no guided tour or introductions to staff unless that is, one happened to be an attractive young woman.

Once inside he could see the missile launch installations in the distance. Two rockets stood ready for launch about two hundred metres apart. Professor Hwang Ji-Hoon stood to one side waiting for the President's instruction to begin the countdown. Lee turned and nodded, his signal that the launch procedure could begin. The Professor scurried away immediately to the Launch Director who was seated on a raised platform. The Director in turn called to one of the twenty or so assistants seated in a line of desks, each gazing at their monitor screen and instrument panel.

Lee's eyes were now rivetted on the huge wall-mounted screen, waiting for the rocket to set out on its journey. Seconds later the Short Range Hypersonic HW ASONG-17 fired into life, quickly gained altitude then began to level out. Kim beamed as the missile disappeared into the distance and was in the process of patting Professor Hwang Ji-Hoon on the back when he heard shouts of concern from the controllers. Lee returned his attention to the main screen, aghast when he saw that the missile had performed a u-turn and was heading back towards the launch pad area, maybe even the control centre itself. Lee's momentary anger at the launch failure turned to anxiety and his eyes sought the Launch Director who was bent over two of the control desks talking feverishly to the controllers. All their lives were now at risk. The director gave the only order he could...*self-destruct immediately.* A second or so later the missile exploded in mid-air showering the countryside below it with metal fragments.

Lee jumped up and down in a fury, swearing at all in sundry. The West would publicise his failure and mock his capabilities; he could visualise the media headlines. Somehow, he had to retrieve the situation; blame and retribution would have to wait, but he couldn't risk launching the second land-based rocket in case it ended with the same outcome. He turned to Professor Paek Sung-Ho and ordered the submarine launch to proceed immediately. The Professor bowed and hurried away to issue instructions to the launch team. He knew better than to counsel Kim to delay the launch until an investigation had been carried out.

Ten minutes later Professor Paek Sung-Ho returned to Lee and confirmed that the launch could proceed. The President nodded curtly and gave his attention to the seascape that now filled the large TV screen. Nothing happened for a few minutes then to loud cheers a missile emerged from the waves and rose into the air…50metres…100metres….at which point the rocket flames died and the KW-23 short range ballistic missile fell back into the sea. The submerged GORAR/SUNPO submarine had moved away and was undamaged and thankfully no lives were lost.

Lee danced up and down in a rage, his arms waving aimlessly, a stream of vilification streaming from his mouth. He shook his fist relentlessly in the faces of the two unfortunate professors. He would be a laughing stock, his Chinese and Russian allies would question his competence. Suddenly he ceased his harangue. 'Do we have another missile on the submarine?'

Professor Paek Sung-Ho nodded slowly. 'Yes, Comrade President but it might be wise to undertake an investigation to determine the cause of the failure before we attempt another launch. There is a possibility of sabotage or external interference.'

Lee dismissed the Professor's advice. 'Nonsense, launch immediately.'

The Professor moved away to the control desks to explain what had been decided, reluctantly brushing away their protests, inviting them to give their advice directly to the President if they had the courage. Their faces expressed their concern but none dared to approach the President.

The preparations took fifteen minutes, at the end of which Paek informed Kim they were ready to launch. Lee waved a hand. 'Get on with it.'

5 - 4 - 3 - 2 -1 Lee's eyes were glued to the screen, watching anxiously for the missile to emerge from the ocean. Seconds passed and there was a huge explosion, the sea exploded skywards like a massive geyser, the submarine status display went blank, debris fell back into the sea.

Lee stood mouth agape as realisation took hold, more than one hundred and sixty lives, a submarine and three missiles lost in barely an hour...a failure of mega proportions. He glared at the professors, the director and the controllers and drew his finger across his throat. 'You have all failed me, you have failed your country, you have failed yourselves….you will rue this day for the rest of your feeble lives.'

The little dictator stamped away, dreading the mocking headlines and media comment that lay ahead.

Westminster

Later that day, business finished, Laura Taylor beckoned Somerton to follow her into a side room.

'What news of the North Korea business.'

Inwardly Somerton was fuming, the loss of lives wasn't planned, the submarine explosion rendered the mission a failure in his eyes. 'I didn't manage to speak to Jupiter, but he sent a message to my laptop not long ago. He took out one ICBM followed by a short-range missile launched from a submarine and then things went badly.'

Taylor pursed her lips. 'How so?'

'It seems the submarine attempted a second launch and the missile exploded on board with predictable results; the vessel disintegrated with the loss of all those on board. God knows how many lives were lost, well over one hundred and fifty, maybe as many as one hundred and eighty. I'm not at all happy and intend to have it out with Jupiter when we link up.'

Taylor looked surprised. 'I don't get it, Jack, they were North Korean military, potential enemies. Why are you so concerned? Good riddance, I say.'

Somerton stared at her. 'I'm fucking annoyed because these targets were to be a warning, a demonstration of what was possible, not a killing exhibition. Families will be torn apart; North Koreans will hate the West. President Kim will tell his people *this is what you can expect from the West.*'

Taylor shook her head. 'I don't agree. Maybe it wasn't meant to explode on board. Can we leave it for now. Just the big one left. Has Jupiter come up with a date?'

Somerton despaired at her attitude but controlled his anger. 'No date has been set as yet. Jupiter is trying to tie it in with a visit by the Chinese President. We'll just have to bide our time. I'll inform you as soon as I hear anything concrete.'

Taylor nodded. 'Fine. Have you got anything lined up after China?'

Somerton shook his head. 'Not a thing. Look, I'm the new boy and these are early days, but we need a strategy, a game plan, call it what you will. We have to know where we're headed. We can't go on acting on an ad hoc basis. We've shown the world what's possible and we need to work out how to capitalise on our success.'

'I agree, Jack, and I'll do what I can, but Will's in the driving seat. Without the US on board our powers are limited. I can only push so far.'

Somerton hesitated. *How hard do I push?* 'Maybe so, but he invited you to the party, he wants the UK on board. He could press on without us, but it seems to me that he doesn't want this to be seen as purely a US venture. You must play that card, Laura; push for a meeting of the entire leadership from both sides of the pond to devise a strategy. Will has the final say, of course, but we all need to sign up to a step-by-step pathway to our chosen destination, just like Eisenhower led the Allies in World War 2.'

Taylor sighed and looked uncomfortable. 'Leave it with me, I'll take your suggestion up with Will. I'm sure all our military people would agree with you.'

'That's another thing that irritates me. I don't even know who's involved from the UK side.'

'We've deliberately kept our activities under wraps but I'm coming round to your way of thinking; a grand assembly would be useful. Leave it with me.'

A thought occurred to Somerton. 'Changing the subject, what's the score with your brother-in-law? Has he surfaced yet or is he still on the missing list?'

Taylor shook her head quickly. 'Not a word heard from him since he left. Geraldine has mixed feelings and is accepting of the situation, but the kids still ask for their dad. I just don't understand it; for all his faults he idolised his kids. I find it hard to believe that he would run out on them. It's a real mystery.'

Somerton nodded. 'It is indeed a mystery. If he'd been kidnapped, you would have heard from his abductors by now.'

'I keep pressing the Embassy, but they are as puzzled about his disappearance as I am. I don't see what else I can do except keep the pressure on.'

CHAPTER 35

Constituency Office, Harrow East Thursday
Sir Isaac Meyer brought the constituency committee to order; he had an announcement to make. The meeting had been called at short notice and not everyone had been able to attend, but sufficient to form a quorum. He looked round the table with genuine sadness, not a full house but the usual stalwarts were there. 'Good morning, everyone, thank you for attending at short notice. I'm sorry to spring it upon you, but circumstances dictated.'

Eight faces looked at him expectantly, this wasn't the confident buoyant Sir Isaac they were used to, something was amiss.

'I'm afraid I'm resigning as Chair with immediate effect.'

There were several gasps, this wasn't the announcement they had speculated on since receiving the summons to the meeting.

'It's a health matter. My wife, my dearest Ruth, learned a few days ago that she has Motor Neurone Disease and I've decided to devote every minute of my time to her welfare. I'm giving up on politics and we're going to enjoy ourselves to the maximum whilst she is still able to live something approaching normal life. On a happier note, my daughter Debbie has just got engaged and there is a wedding in prospect.

'As for the present, you need to elect an interim chairman and I suggest that Mary Roberts, my current deputy takes over with immediate effect. She has agreed to do his. Will all in favour raise a hand.' Still somewhat bewildered, eight hands, including his own, were raised.

Sir Isaac looked round the table for the last time as chairman, his eyes moistening. 'Unanimous. Mary, congratulations, I now formally pass the chair and the management of this meeting over to you.' He stood and attempted an unconvincing smile. 'I'm going now; the news about Ruth has been devastating and I'm not in the mood for sympathy, or much else for that matter.'

Mary Roberts spoke quietly, her voice sombre but firm. 'I'm calling the meeting to order. We will respect Sir Isaac's wishes for privacy at this time. We will all have the opportunity to express our thanks for his leadership and friendship on another occasion.'

Sir Isaac nodded, appreciative of her understanding. 'Thank you, Mary, I'll depart now and leave you to it. Oh, by the way, I'll get in touch with Jack Somerton and let him know. I haven't told the staff; I'll leave that to you. Please give them my thanks and tell them I'll speak to them all in due course.' Meyer turned away and left the room; there was only one place he wanted to be and that was with his beloved Ruth.

Outside in his car he phoned Somerton, tutting when he was put through to voicemail. He left a brief message explaining the situation and invited Somerton to get in touch if he needed to. He was still driving home when Somerton returned his call. 'This has come as a shock Sir Isaac. I'm very sorry to hear about Ruth, you must be devastated; but medical advances are happening almost daily, let's hope some new treatment emerges. I wish you both all the best in the circumstances. It's been a pleasure working with you, albeit our acquaintance is of short duration. If ever I can be of any assistance don't hesitate to get in touch.'

'Thank you, Jack. There's nothing more to be said at this time so I'll say goodbye and wish you well in the future. And please keep in mind, Minister you may be, but never forget your constituents, the people who voted for you.'

The call ended, Somerton sat back and reflected on what had transpired; Sir Isaac wasn't a friend in the true sense of the word, but his heart went out to him in such painful circumstances. *Life can be a real bastard at times.*

The news reawakened his thoughts to his personal business interests. His role as a Member of Parliament and a Minister were increasingly demanding; politics were rewarding but could consume every waking moment. He was finding his new life interesting and motivating, but it left very little opportunity to deal with his own business interests. *It's time to stop thinking, Jack, it's time to make decisions.*

'Hello, Barry, it's Jack Somerton, I have a mission for you if you'll take it on.' Barry Jones was a trusted venture capitalist who, over the years, had helped Somerton to transform his security business, Metronos, into a company worth millions of pounds.

'Of course, I'm interested, fire away, Jack.'

'I want to sell my business, lock stock and barrel. I have no wish to retain any interest in Metronos whatsoever.'

'Might I enquire as to what has brought about your decision. Is there anything I should know about before I put out feelers?'

'There's nothing going on under the surface I assure you. I'm enjoying my new role in politics and demands on my time are growing. It's obvious that I can't devote the time to Metronos that I should.'

'Hmm, you could always appoint someone to act for you and retain ownership.'

'Thought of that. Whoever I appointed would inevitably come to me for views and decisions, I'd never be completely free. Besides I don't trust anybody to manage the company as well as I have and I'd constantly be watching over them. I want you to sound out the market and let me know what it will sell for. Be as discreet as you can; I've told no-one of my intentions.'

'OK Jack, I'm not sure it's a good decision but I'll do what I can to get you a good deal. I'll need a copy of last year's accounts and any pending contracts.'

'Thanks Barry, I'll get them hand-delivered to you later today.'

NRSC Later

Somerton was on a roll; it was time to tidy up his life, simplify it and focus exclusively on politics. He decided to enquire about the possible acquisition of his rented Gibraltar heights apartment. He'd never liked paying rent, it always seemed like money down the drain, no return on investment. If the price was right, it would be a good investment.

'Hello, Fletcher of Harrow, Estate Agents. Might I ask who is calling please?'

'My name is Somerton, I rent an apartment in Gibraltar Heights. I'd like to speak to Guy Fletcher please.'

'Certainly, he free, I'll put you through.'

'Hello Mr Somerton, Guy Fletcher. While I remember, congratulations on getting elected and on getting a Cabinet appointment. How can I help you? I hope you aren't experiencing any problems with Gibraltar Heights?'

'Not at all, I'm happy there. In fact, I'd like to buy my apartment.'

'I'm not sure the owner would be prepared to sell.'

'Understood Guy, but I'd like you to get in touch with the owner and find out. If it's not for sale, I'll probably vacate and look for something to purchase elsewhere. And just to sharpen your interest, I'll pay you a fee of 1% of the purchase cost.'

'Our normal charge is 2%.'

'This isn't a normal deal, Guy. All you're being asked to do is phone the owner and find out if he'll sell and at what price. I'm busy otherwise I'd track the owner down and deal direct.'

Fletched backed off. 'You win, Mr Somerton. I'll get in touch with the owner and get back to you.'

'Thank you, Guy. Use your charm and remember to tell them if they don't sell, I will vacate and leave them with an empty property again.'

'I'm sure I wouldn't have any difficulty renting the property, Mr Somerton.'

'Yeah, sure Guy, like it took you six months last time. Do your best and get back to me as soon as you can.'

Somerton glanced at the clock; time was moving on and he wanted to speak to Jupiter before he headed off to the House.'

Somerton got through to Jupiter immediately. 'I'm pressed for time, Jupiter, but there are two matters I want to raise. Firstly, have you had a chance to set up the China attack.'

'Some progress, Jack, all the signs are that I'll be able to activate Target 6 on Saturday. I'm not absolutely certain as I speak, the Chinese are very secretive. I probably won't know until Saturday if I can go ahead. It'll be a last-minute affair, but I am set up to proceed. And what else is on your mind, Jack?'

'I'll come straight to the point, Jupiter. I was very unhappy with the North Korean business. You were not asked to destroy a submarine with the loss of all those lives. It was an unnecessary and appalling outcome. We are trying to show the world what we're capable of, not alienate it. We've given our enemies a golden opportunity to declare how cruel and unprincipled we are.'

Somewhat to Somerton's surprise, Jupiter looked almost crestfallen. 'I'm sorry, Jack, it wasn't my wish that things worked out as they did, I assure you.'

'So, who's wish was it then?'

Jupiter bit on his lip and took a few seconds to respond. He shook his head. 'It was my doing, Jack, I'm to blame. I apologise, it just didn't go to plan. The submarine launch came as a bit of a surprise. I didn't have much time to act and got it wrong. Sorry.'

Somerton couldn't be certain but there was something in Jupiter's tone than didn't ring true. *Best leave it, Jack. Jupiter is under orders, he's the blame-hound for now.* 'You're right, I'm being unreasonable, I guess it was a difficult call, in the heat of the moment. It's a shame though, hopefully there will be no repetition when you take on China, the stakes are too high.'

Jupiter appeared to relax. 'You have my word on it.'

CHAPTER 36

China Saturday

Jing Chen, sixty-eight years old, President of the People's Republic of China was on his way to the Joint Battle Command Centre twenty kilometres north of Beijing. The President had decided to undertake a routine inspection of the facility and meet with military leaders and control staff, genuinely seeking to show the latter that he cared. The Centre was located in what were ancient caves, skilfully transformed into one of the world's most advanced military operational centres. It was now the 'brain' of the People's Liberation Army and monitored activity across China's five battle zones, not that anyone believed China would ever be invaded.

His limousine came to a halt at the head of two lines of one hundred soldiers, all standing rigidly to attention. Jing Chen walked slowly down the middle of his guard of honour, closely followed by the Army, Navy and Air Force generals his expression enigmatic as always, glancing left and right as he made his way towards the five battle zone chiefs waiting to accompany him on his tour. The Centre Director would lead him round the facility, making introductions, giving explanations and pointing out new features.

It was raining lightly, so the visitors didn't linger, making their way indoors without delay. The President and his entourage were led to a dining-room, his eyes lighting up when he saw the food spread out on the large mahogany table. All his favourite foods were there; a rare smile momentarily lit up his face and he clapped his hands with pleasure as he moved to his seat at the head of the table. He reached forward for his silk napkin and that's when the unthinkable happened. The lights went out, the six ornate chandeliers installed especially for his visit, became no more than ornaments. The emergency lighting came on immediately, and a scowling Jing Chen transferred a delicacy to his plate. The Director cringed with embarrassment. 'Forgive us,

Comrade President, this has never happened before and will be resolved speedily, I'm sure.'

Jing Chen chewed thoughtfully and took another delicacy from the silver salver in front of him. He looked along his military staff who sat stony-faced. 'Pray tell me comrades, what would you be doing if the Republic was under attack and its Control Centre was suffering a major malfunction? The five looked at each other; such were their ideological beliefs it was an event they didn't anticipate would ever occur. The Air Force General spoke first. 'We have a back-up Control Centre that could take over and the Air Force has the ability to operate independently if required. Such an incident would not go unpunished; we would immediately mount an attack on our enemies.'

The Naval General nodded. 'The Navy also has the capability to act independently; we would do whatever was necessary to deal with the enemy.'

The Army General shook his head. 'Our military services could indeed operate individually but co-ordination would be difficult.'

Jing Chen addressed the Centre Director. 'You have heard the Generals. Why are you sitting here eating; why are you not investigating the cause of this failure?' The chastened man immediately rose from his chair and bowed. 'Of course, apologies Comrade President, I will investigate immediately.'

Jing Chen continued eating but his thoughts were on recent *events power outages in England. America, and Germany. Rostov's death, the debacle in North Korea. It was too much of a co-incidence.* Ten minutes passed before the Director returned, his face lined with apprehension as he addressed the President. 'My humble apologies, comrade, I do not have an explanation for what has happened. Our best technicians are investigating; the problem with be resolved shortly, I promise you.'

Jing Chen looked at the unfortunate man with disdain. 'You have just told us you have no explanation for this occurrence. How can you promise it will be resolved shortly? Do not treat me as a fool.'

The President stood and wiped his lips with his napkin and threw it onto the table. The military personnel rose to await their

President's instructions. 'I forecast that this power interruption will last precisely one hour. I am leaving now but you will all remain and work together to determine how you would co-ordinate the defence of the Republic in circumstances where its Central Control Centre was not operable. You will submit your report to me by noon tomorrow. You,' he pointed at the Director, 'you will give the military every assistance in their endeavours; you will also seek to determine the cause of this power failure and how to prevent a re-occurrence.' He waved his hand towards the laden table. 'Distribute this food to the staff immediately, compliments of their President.' He smiled inwardly. *His meal had been spoiled; he was not going leave the magnificent food behind for his military companions. They had work to do.*

Prime Minister's Office Monday
'Good morning, Jack,' Laura Taylor was smiling, 'tea and biscuits are on their way. Good news for me I think?'

Somerton nodded. 'Just heard from Jupiter, his timing was perfect. President Jing Chen was visiting their main battle control centre when its electrical supply was cut for one hour. No news about the President's reaction but I'm confident he would have been furious. I think we can safely assume that he knows there is a threat to China's national security, source unknown and for that matter not only a threat to China but to any country on the planet. He'll be wondering what the future holds. It's a thought I share with him.'

'Meaning what exactly?'

Somerton was about to reply when Jess Tate entered carrying a tray with the promised refreshments.

'Good to see you, Jess.'

'And you, Jack. She glanced at Taylor. 'Shall I pour, Laura?'

Taylor shook her head, a smile playing on her lips, 'No, leave us to it Jess, in the interests of equality of the sexes, Major Somerton will do the honours.'

Somerton grinned. 'I knew she gave me the job for a reason. See you on the way out, Jess.'

Tate winked at him and left the two politicians to their business. Somerton lifted the teapot. 'Milk first I presume?' The serving tasks completed Somerton returned to their conversation.

'Going back to where I left off, I'm wondering where we go from here. We've done the demos but we're now in a vacuum. The major players in the East, and in the West, must all be on red alert; my lot certainly are. I'm certain the demos were successful, but we need to follow them up before all sorts of alliances start to be put in place. We need that meeting we spoke about to put together a strategy, otherwise it's down to you and Will to come up with one. I've got some ideas, but they need to be debated and tested.'

Taylor nodded vigorously. 'Good news on that front. Will is amenable and is going to talk to his people and get back to me. But what are these ideas of yours?'

Somerton touched his nose. 'I'm keeping them to myself until I get an invite to this meeting.'

Taylor frowned. 'Really? Have you forgotten who you're speaking to?'

Somerton smiled sweetly. 'How could I possibly forget?'

Taylor waved her had dismissively. 'Oh, have it your way. Sometimes you're can be real pain in the arse, Jack.'

'That's part of my role in life. Changing the subject. Is there any news from your brother-in -law?'

'No, but Geraldine and the kids are slowly coming to terms with the fact that they might not see him again. It's months now since he went to Saudi.'

Somerton thought it was time for a test. 'I've had a wild idea, which I'll share with you if you want.'

Taylor nodded, warily. 'Go ahead.'

'He disappeared suddenly. I'm guessing he didn't gather up all his stuff; just took enough for a few days. No photos, no treasured possessions.'

Taylor's eyes narrowed. 'All true, Jack, go on.'

'You may not like this suggestion, but did you discuss your sister's situation with Will Kenny? You're obviously very good friends. I'm wondering if maybe Will got his people to arrange for Madison to disappear?

Taylor grimaced. 'You're in fantasy land, Jack.'

'Could be, but you did discuss it with him, didn't you?'

Taylor acquiesced. 'As it happens, I did mention it to Will. He was very sympathetic but that was all.'

Somerton shrugged. 'Maybe, but Madison's disappearance did take place after you spoke to the President. Still, it's probably a co-incidence, although Will does have black op people at his disposal, and they don't ask questions. No matter, whatever happened, it's a good result. I'll go now and leave you in peace. I look forward to that strategy meeting.'

Taylor nodded. 'I'll be in touch as soon as I hear anything, either way.'

When Somerton had gone Taylor checked the time; it was noon so 7am in Washington. Will Kenny was an early riser, she needed to call him.

'Good morning Will. Just a quickie if you've got a moment.'

'Good morning, Laura, a quickie is never long enough with you. What gives.'

'I've just had a meeting with Somerton, and he suggested that you might have had something to do with my brother-in-law's disappearance. I wasn't sure if he knew something or was just fishing. I told him the idea was fantasy but thought you ought to be aware what he's thinking.'

'Well now, I can't think how he could possibly know anything. I briefed my guys directly, made it clear even their superiors were not to be given any details. They know better than to disobey a Presidential Directive. I'm pretty sure it's guesswork on his part. But, if he's found out somehow, maybe Mr Somerton has outlived his usefulness?'

'I'd like him around for a while longer, Will; he's good at what he does. But if needs be I'd be prepared to let him go.'

'We'll leave it for now. Whilst you're on, I've raised the question of the early strategy meeting with my people, and they agreed it would be useful. We're looking at dates; I'll be in touch in due course. In the meantime, keep an eye on Somerton.'

On his way out, Somerton had stopped to have a word with Jess Tate. 'How are you these days, Jess? Are you settled with Laura, or can I hope maybe you'll join me?'

Tate displayed genuine concern. 'Oh Jack, I'm sorry, I should have told you. I've decided to stay with Laura. We get on well and to be honest I kind of like being in Downing Street at the heart of power. Sorry.'

Somerton smiled. 'No problem, honestly. It must be special being the PM's personal assistant, rather than helping out a mere Minister'

'Be off with you, Jack.'

Somerton glanced to the side, at a blinking red light. 'Looks like your boss is busy.'

Tate nodded. 'She put a call in to Will Kenny as soon as you left the office.'

Somerton smirked. 'Ah good, she must do all she can to strengthen the special relationship; it knows no boundaries, you know.'

Tate raised her eyebrows. 'I can't imagine what you're getting at, Jack.'

Somerton left Downing Street and started out on the short walk to the Houses of Parliament. *You had better watch your back, Jack old son, don't be biting off more than you can chew, Will Kenny would be a dangerous enemy.*

CHAPTER 37

Two weeks later
It was one of those weeks when things happened, pieces fell into place, Somerton's thoughts were beginning to see the route ahead. The future and where it was leading him was becoming clearer.

The first piece of news came from Barry Jones regarding the sale of his security business, Metronos. 'Hi Jack, it's Barry, I have news for you, good news.'

'Good to hear from you, Barry. I always make time for good news, let's have it.'

'I've poured over your accounts, taken some discreet soundings in the market, and I reckon that in today's climate it's worth more than £21 million.

'That's encouraging, but as we all know projections are just that, projections. The market is volatile, and tomorrow's projection will follow whatever mood the market finds itself in on the day.'

'All true but that's where the good news come in. I have interested parties lined up to make a bid if you're serious about selling. SES, Worldsec Systems, Amecsafe and Valiant are all interested in acquiring your set up. They would want to take over all existing contracts, assets, and more importantly existing staff. There would be no redundancies. They would also want you to be available on a consultancy basis for a year, and you would have to undertake not to set up in competition for at least five years. These are fairly standard conditions of contract for a deal like this.'

'Have any of them come up with a firm offer, in money terms that is?'

'Not yet but I'm certain any offer made will be not less than £20 million, not more than £25 million.'

Somerton thoughts raced; a moment of truth had arrived. 'OK, go for £22 million, half of anything over that is yours in addition to your fee. I want the staff guaranteed at least two years employment or salary in lieu; that's not negotiable. As to the companies, forget SES which I recall is a Chinese organisation. Amecsafe is based in the States, Wordsec is European, Valiant is British and first in line for me.'

Jones paused for a moment. 'How would you feel if I got together with some investors I know and took over the business? I would aim to raise £22million. I would seek to retain and build the company and my fellow investors would be based in the UK, a mix of British, American and Japanese. I would retain the name Metronos. Where did the name come from, by the way?'

Somerton laughed. 'It's an anagram of Somerton.'

'I'd be the major shareholder though I can't guarantee for how long. I would definitely want to be able to call on your advice for a year or so.'

'OK, Barry, we have a deal, £22million and subject to the other conditions I mentioned. There is one proviso and it's a big ask, I want you to complete the acquisition within four weeks. And of course there would be no fee for selling it to yourself.'

'Christ, that's a big ask. What's the rush?'

'That's the timescale I'm working to, it's personal. Do we have a deal or not?'

Barry Jones emitted a huge sigh. 'Done. I'll push things along as quickly as I can, four weeks is a tough deadline though. I can't promise I'll meet that deadline.'

'Do your best, I can't promise I'll go ahead if you don't meet the deadline.'

'I'd better not hang about then, speak later, Jack.'

Somerton smiled, Barry was on the hook, he'd deliver.

NRSC

Somerset knocked on Lizzie King's office door, entering when he heard a muffled reply.

She looked up from her desk and smiled warmly. 'Hello, Jack. wat brings you here?'

He raised a finger to his lips to remind her not to refer to the satellite system. 'I'm looking out for a young researcher to introduce to the Security Committee, and I thought Jason would impress. Don't mention this interest to him; I haven't set up the meeting yet. And of course, it's always nice to talk to my favourite professor and see how the annual research programme is coming along.'

King smiled. 'You'll be pleased to know that the programme is coming along nicely and will be ready by the end of the month. I have to say that I'm enjoying my new role and, more importantly, my colleagues seem to be happy with me. How are you finding politics, Jack? I confess I still can't quite picture the SAS's Jack Somerton as a Minister of the Crown.'

Somerton laughed. 'I know what you mean, but I'm determined to make a success of it and, who knows, I might even get to be Prime Minister someday.'

King looked thoughtful. 'Following in your colleagues' footsteps might not be such a good thing?' She bit her lip. 'Sorry, I should never have said that.'

Somerton winced. 'Let's not go there, it's still raw. Is there anything I can help you with?'

King shook her head. 'Not at the moment, thanks.'

'Lizzie, I haven't got too long, so I'll make my way to Jason's, you needn't join in if you're busy.'

King looked relieved. 'I'm up to my neck in work so I'll take you up that offer and skip this visit, if you really don't mind. Jason is along the corridor in room 18.'

Somerton knocked on number18 and entered when invited, again holding his finger to his lips to signal secrecy. 'Good morning, Jason, Professor King suggested I called in and said hello. I'm looking for a young researcher to make a presentation to a parliamentary group looking for an insight to AI and thought you would be ideal. And, I wondered if you might like to show me over what you're working on.'

'Certainly, Minister.'

'Thanks for the respect but please call me Jack. I feel like a vicar when people address me as minister.'

'I'm working on the weight and size of vehicle batteries; all kinds, car, bus train you name it. They're currently way too bulky and heavy. We need to make them more compact and lighter. And they must be rechargeable in a fraction of the time otherwise the electric car isn't the future we hope for. Maybe we should be focussing on hydrogen propulsion, I'm not sure.'

'That sounds just the kind of work the group would be interested in. good luck with it. Is there by chance any hardware you can show me, I'm a hands-on guy and like to see things in the real.'

Robertson took his cue. 'Sure. I was about to go to the workshop when you arrived, follow me.' Once in the workshop, Robertson look the lead, 'First up, Jack, I've checked out my office and I'm absolutely sure there are no bugs in there.'

Somerton shrugged. 'I believe you, maybe I am being paranoid but nevertheless I'll be happier if we stick to our current precautions.' *You don't know how clever Jupiter is, young man.* 'Now what have you found out about our satellite system?'

Robertson shook his head. 'Not a lot. I've examined the circuit drawings carefully and for the most part everything appears to be straightforward and what one would expect of a communication system. The circuitry is certainly innovative, but I can understand how it works.'

Somerton seized on his words. 'You said for the most part, what do you mean by that?'

'There are components I can't explain and the only way I can find out what their function is, is to open up a satellite and look inside. I've investigated where they are constructed, and it appears there are three companies involved in the production of the circuit components, another does the casing, and a fifth company does the assembly. A company called Flightsat, just ten miles from here, does the assembly. I phoned and asked if I could visit the factory, but they said I didn't have the necessary clearance. So that's it, Jack. If you want me to take this further, you'll have to get me the necessary clearance.'

'That might raise questions. Leave it with me. I'll give it some thought and see what I can come up with.'

Somerton returned to his office, taking time out on the way to meet up with Eric Barker to talk through current red security alerts. A call to Mike Davies went to voicemail. 'Sorry, not available, leave a message and I'll return your call.' Next up, he tried Eddie Black. 'Eddie it's Jack. I have a job for you and Mike. I haven't been able to get a hold of him.'

'He's been a bit pre-occupied of late, almost secretive. Tell me what you want done and I'll get a hold him.'

Somerton spent the next ten minutes explaining his requirements.

'A piece of cake, Jack, leave it with us.'

He hadn't long finished his call when his mobile buzzed. 'It's Guy Fletcher, Mr Somerton. I have a price for you re Gibraltar Heights. The owner is asking £3.25million. Before you say anything and we get into haggling mode, I'll tell you the bottom price. £3million plus £100k for me. It's a good price believe me.

'We have a deal Guy. Get the seller's solicitor to send me a draft contract and I'll deal with it. And tell those involved not to linger or I'll go elsewhere. I think we're done all we can for the moment. Thanks for your efforts this far, goodbye for now.'

CHAPTER 38

Satellite Assembly Centre Abbotmere, Kent
As requested by Somerton, Reggie Marsh arranged for him to visit the SAC. The civil servant on site had been resistant initially but when invited to explain his refusal to Somerton or phone the Prime Minister, he had finally agreed whilst protesting. *I can understand the Minister's interest, and personally I have no objection, but my orders are clear. ONLY ESSENTIAL VISITORS, and this visit doesn't really sound essential.*

Somerton pondered on travelling in a chauffeur-driven Westminster pool car to impress the locals but, if his plans worked out' it would be best not to have a driver in attendance. It was around 10am when he drew up at the barrier across the access road, two armed police officers approached and asked for identification which Somerton duly provided. The barrier lifted and he was directed to drive forward into an eight feet high steel paling enclosure where he was invited to get out of the car and enter a small wooden building. Inside he was required to empty his pockets and pass through an airport-type scanner. Somerton noted that whilst this process was taking place his car was being searched and an underbody check carried out.

The process completed, clearance was given and his possessions returned with a warning that the taking of photographs of any kind was forbidden. The staff were tight-lipped throughout and made minimal response to any comment made by Somerton. The steel gates at the far end of the compound swung open and Somerton drove along the two hundred or so metres drive to the SAC noting the pole-mounted security cameras installed every forty metres or so.

His first impression of the building was how small it seemed given its importance. The Director, a tall slim middle-aged clean-shaven man, stood in the doorway smiling. *At last, a sign of welcome.* thought Somerton. The SAC Director waited patiently whilst Somerton looked around taking in his surroundings. A few minutes elapsed and when he felt he had Somerton's attention he stepped forward, hand extended in greeting. His handshake was warm, eyes friendly, a smile on his face. 'Welcome Minister, Chris Chesterton, I'm the Centre Director, and can I say I'm both delighted and surprised you've chosen to visit us; you're only the second parliamentarian to have visited us since we began production. Given the importance of what we do I thought we would have generated more political interest.'

'Call me Jack please. Might I ask who the other politician was?'

A brief look of sadness crossed Chesterton's face. 'The late Colin Mackinnon. I can recall him very clearly; a warm friendly disposition and genuinely interested in the assembly process. He asked lots of questions and really wanted to understand the underlying science. Of course, you knew him better than anyone else.'

Somerton nodded, guilt flowing in as it always did when Colin was mentioned. 'I hope I can live up to the precedent he set.'

Chesterton smiled. 'Let's find out, shall we. Follow me.' They walked a short distance along a corridor to a door where he scanned his identity card, then punched in a code and motioned Somerton to enter. 'The entry code is changed weekly, much to the annoyance of some of our staff.'

The door led to a long corridor, glazed from floor to ceiling along the left-hand side, behind which Somerton could see what looked like workshops or laboratories. On the right was a line of doors presumably leading to offices, stores and toilets. 'The glazing is bullet-proof by the way, not that I'm expecting any intruders.'

Chesteron began by outlining the assembly process. 'Each satellite is comprised of four sections; each section is manufactured in a different laboratory. Units one and two are delivered on the same day, unit three on request, similarly unit four. Any questions?'

'Just one. Where are these laboratories located?'

'I'll give you a list before you leave. They're all private UK laboratories; four of them, London, Norwich, Bristol and Dumfries.' Chesterton walked a little further along the corridor and stopped. 'This is laboratory A. As you can see, there are two staff.' Behind the glass partition there were two figures dressed in white polyester protective clothing; both wore nylon gloves. 'The clothing is to protect the electronic circuitry from contamination.'

Somerton smiled. 'So, there is nothing noxious or explosive involved in the process?'

Chesterton laughed. 'No, it's all perfectly harmless. He knocked on the glass and the two occupants made their way over. 'This is Mr Somerton, Minister for Research and Security. He's visiting us to see what we get up to. The woman on your left is Jill Calder, her colleague is Ruth Cummings. Both are Cambridge University graduates.'

Somerton, the politician surfacing, duly responded. 'Pleased to meet you both and thank you for the work you're doing; it's vital to the Country's economy and security.'

Cummings nodded. 'I bet you've used that line a time or two.'

Somerton couldn't repress a laugh. 'Only every day, but it's well meant on this occasion.'

It suddenly occurred to Somerton that despite the armoured glazing their conversation had been perfectly audible. Chesterton noted his confusion and explained. 'We're wired for sound to minimise the need to enter and exit labs. The labs incidentally are air conditioned to the highest possible standard.'

Somerton nodded. 'I can see that they are joining up units 1 and 2 both of which contain a multitude of coloured cables and circuit boards. I can't see any circuit diagrams. Unless they're blessed with infallible memories, how do they know which wire connects to which?'

Chesterton explained. 'That's where another layer of security comes into play. The monitor display gives wire by wire assembly instructions when the unique code of each satellite unit is entered into the computer. The entire assembly process takes about eight hours. On completion of stage one, that is joining up Units I and 2, Lab A will inform Lab B; each enters their connecting door code and the bench with satellite assembly is wheeled through to Lab B where the process begins again.'

Somerton was impressed. *Very cunning, Jupiter, so that's how you keep control.* 'That's sweet. Very secure, top marks.'

Chesterton waved goodbye to Calder and Cummings and led Somerton on to Lab B. 'It is a secure system but the staff find the process a bit tedious. They are highly qualified and skilled, but I reckon we could train anyone to carry out the assembly. The pay is good though and they all have more demanding work back at their universities.' He moved further along to Lab B and tapped on the window. One of the two technicians came over. 'This is Andy Wilson, and his colleague is Alice Mitchell. Mitchell looked up when she heard her name mentioned and waved. 'This is Mr Somerton, Andy.'

'Ah, our Paymaster. Pleased to meet you.'

'How do you find the work, Andy?'

'Do you want a diplomatic or truthful answer? If the former, I would say it's interesting and innovative; if the latter it's boring, repetitive almost robotic, Still, it's well paid and I'm happy. I recognise that the work is essential and just get on with it.'

Chesterton frowned. 'OK Andy, you've had your grouse. Back to work and earn what we pay you. As you will have guessed Jack, the process of wiring in Unit 3 is identical to that for Units 1 and 2. The bench transfer is the same as previously. Let's move on to Lab C.'

The immediate difference Somerton spotted was that Lab C only had one technician who Chesterton waved over. 'This is Connie Wishart, and this is Mr Somerton, Minister for Research and Security.'

Wishart, a twenty something petite redhead, smiled broadly. 'Good of you to make the time to come here and see what we do, I'm sure you're very busy. I hope your visit is proving worthwhile?'

Somerton smiled. 'It's a very impressive set-up and I really do appreciate all you are doing for our Country. How do you find the assembly process? I can see there isn't much variety.'

'I'm happy with what I do. It is repetitive, but it isn't stressful and I've plenty of interests away from here. Now, I don't want to appear rude, but unless you've got any other questions I really do need to get on with my work, I've got a deadline to meet.'

Somerton shook his head. 'No questions, Connie, nice to have met you.'

Chesterton led them to Lab D. 'This is where final assembly, testing and commissioning takes place. The end product by the way is a satellite which measures 1.5 metres by 1 metre and 0.3 of a metre depth. The completed assembly weighs approximately 30 kilogrammes. There are two technicians involved, Ted Cunningham and Zara Fairchild. I'll call them over, but I warn you they aren't very social. He knocked on the partition several times before one of them finally looked up and gave a perfunctory wave. The other glanced across and nodded.'

Somerton grinned. 'I guess they're not well disposed towards Government representatives.'

Chesterton shrugged. 'I have no knowledge of their political affiliations. They keep themselves to themselves; I'm not sure if even they like each other. I would leave them to it if I were you. So, you have the picture. If there's nothing else you want to see let's head to my office for a cuppa if you've got the time.'

Somerton shook his head. 'It would be welcome but I'll decline, thank you; I've got things to do back at the ranch. Just two questions though. Firstly, the staff; are they full time?'

'No, they all work on a sessional basis. They are all university based and have research commitments. I have a pool of people I trust and select from who is available.'

'And the finished product, what happens to the satellite?'

'We have a secure storage unit where they await collection and transfer to RAF Mildenhall for helicoptering to the Saxa Vord Spaceport in the Shetlands. They are usually dispatched in batches of four. Of course, being in charge of the launch programme you probably know that. The pick-up takes place around 7am.'

Somerton nodded. 'And who is the carrier?'

'Most times it's an RAF vehicle but occasionally they use a private carrier.'

'Could you show me the storage area please?'

Chesterton looked puzzled but didn't question the request. 'Follow me, it's at the end of the corridor.' Access was via another card swipe and code button entry. 'Only myself, and Ted and Zara, the final assemblers, are authorised to enter this area.' The internal LED lighting came on automatically as the door swung open. A trolley stood in the centre of the floor. The left-hand wall of the store was shelved; three satellites sat ready for collection.

'Thanks for that, Chris. I've seen all I need to. It's been a very satisfactory and informative visit.'

'It's been a pleasure, Jack; I'll walk you to the car.'

Chesterton led the way outdoors where Somerton felt certain they couldn't be overhead and asked the question he'd been desperate to ask.

'Chris, I know security can obsess me at times, but there's one question, I have to put to you. With regard to the satellite assembly, are there any components you think are strange, inexplicable even?'

Chesterton held Somerton's gaze for some seconds, wondering what had prompted the question. 'As it happens, the answer is yes. There are three sealed components that we have wondered about. Several of our team have raised the issue, prompted by scientific curiosity though not security concerns. I just fend them of with the usual 'need to know' national security justification.'

It was the reply Somerton had anticipated. 'And where in the assembly process are these components situated?'

'They are all in the fourth unit.'

'Could they be in any way dangerous?'

Chesterton scratched his head. 'I doubt it. In fact, I had to tell Zara off recently, I caught her in the middle of testing one of them. She reckons it didn't appear to do anything. I told not to be ridiculous. I stress though she never tampered with the components or attempted to open them up.'

'And what company or companies supply these components?'

'I did check that out with the Dumfries set-up, Scotec, and they told me the components are supplied by Washington Electronics, an American company.'

'American,' Somerton echoed, his expression thoughtful. 'I don't know about you, but I'd rather they were manufactures in the UK. It's not a good idea to be totally reliant on another country for anything essential to homeland security.'

Chesterton nodded enthusiastically. 'Couldn't agree more. But my hands are tied. I have no authority to access these components or determine who supplies them.'

Somerton smiled. 'I could argue, on the basis of National security, that I have authority. In fact, I could argue that it was my duty.'

'I couldn't possibly argue with the Minister.'

Somerton had a dilemma, could he trust Chesterton. 'Suppose I suggested that I borrow a section containing the American components and took it back to the NRSC for testing. How would you feel about that?

Chesterton grimaced. 'It would be highly irregular but, as I've said, who am I to argue with the Minister. My problem, would be how to explain it to the staff. Hmm, thinking about it though, I guess I could smuggle one out without being seen. I'd need to think about how to do that.'

'Chris, I'm going out on a limb discussing our concerns with you, but there is a genuine security issue involved here so let's give it some serious thought. Could you smuggle it out and get it into your car? A single satellite unit isn't too big or heavy, you could almost wrap it up in a lab coat.'

Chesterton smiled. 'I'm beginning to feel like a naughty schoolboy. You would have to get the unit back to me within 24hours if we are to maintain the current launch programme.' His brow furrowed. 'Oh dear, it's just occurred to me that it might be fitted with a tracker we don't know about.'

Somerton spread his hands. 'That's a risk I'm prepared to take. I don't think we should do the changeover here; I suggest I drive off and stop in a layby a couple of miles from here and meet you there. I'll aim to get it back to you in 24 hours if possible; I'll give you plenty of notice if we get behind schedule. Just remains for us to exchange telephone numbers and talk in riddles if we make a call. Thanks for your help on this Chris, I won't forget it.'

CHAPTER 39

Satellite Assembly Centre, Abbotmere, Kent.
As advised by Chesterton, Somerton pulled into an off-road layby about two miles north of the Centre. His was the sole vehicle present, luck was on his side. He fiddled around with the radio channels before settling on Smooth. Rod Stewart was belting out Maggie May, followed by Ozzy Osbourne singing a song he didn't know. Half an hour, around seven songs and a bucketful of DJ chat later, a cherry-red Rover appeared in his rear-view mirror and pulled up beside him.

Chesterton got out and immediately went to the car boot and opened it. The two men didn't even greet each other, both resolved to get the changeover completed as quickly as possible. The satellite installed safely in Somerton's car the two men said their goodbyes.

'Thanks for this Chris; if I'm asked, I'll recommend you for a knighthood.'

Chesterton guffawed. 'I shan't hold my breath, but it's a nice thought.'

'Now what time do I have to get this back to you?'

'The RAF are due here at 11am tomorrow but with two hours assembly time involved I doubt if that gives sufficient time for the NRSC to carry out its investigation. I was thinking of delaying the RAF pick-up by 24 hours and if you get it back here by noon tomorrow it will work out nicely.'

'Are you sure that won't cause a problem?'

'Not for us but I don't know how it will affect the launch arrangements.'

Somerton pursed his lips: he didn't want to delay the launch. Let's plan on me getting it back to you for 6am tomorrow morning. Any change to that and I'll let you know.' *You're going to be busy, young Jason.* 'Chris, I stress that what I'm doing is highly confidential and not on record. There's more involved than I've told you, all based on suspicious exchanges on the web. I'll explain in the fullness of time.'

'I understand, Jack, my lips are sealed.'

'Right, I'm out of here; see you tomorrow.

Chesterton nodded and the two men shook hands, both looking worried. Somerton climbed into his car and drove away deep in thought.

NRSC

Thankfully the journey back to the NRSC had gone smoothly; traffic had been light, roadworks no existent, even the traffic lights had gone his way. He pulled into his reserved parking bay at the rear of the building shortly after 2pm and made his way in. The door to Jason Robertson's office was wide open but there was no sign of the young researcher. Somerton's spirits sank. *Shit, don't tell me he's having a day off.*

'I think he's with Professor King.' A young female voice. Somerton wheeled round and found himself addressing a petite slim curly-haired brunette. 'I don't think we've met.'

'We haven't though I know who you are, Minister; Kelly Wright, I've only been here a month, my specialty is bio mechanics.

'Nice to meet you, Kelly. A very interesting area; I quite fancy being a cyberman.'

She smiled. 'Really. You would miss out on some of life's best moments.'

'On second thoughts, I've had a quick change of heart. Nice to have met you. I'm sorry but I must hurry, maybe we'll chat for longer another time.' *Why am I not twenty years younger?*

King and Robertson were deep in conversation when Somerton joined them. He knocked gently and, as was his custom now, signalled them to come out into the corridor.

'Still in hush-hush mode, Jack?'

'I have to be, Lizzie, believe me. I need to borrow Jason for the next twenty-four hours; I have a job for him.'

Robertson's mouth dropped open. 'Twenty-four hours? Cripes, I've never worked that long on the trot.'

'I hope it doesn't take that long; ideally, I'd like the unit back by 4am tomorrow morning. Having said that it can take as long as is necessary; if it takes longer, so be it, I'll have to delay the launch by a day. Not desirable but not a disaster. Follow me out to the rear of the building, both of you. Chat idly as we stroll along.'

Lizzie King rolled her eyes but made no comment.

Arriving at his parking bay Somerton went straight to his boot and pointed at the unit which had been wrapped in brown paper by Chesterton. 'Here it is, the mystery unit.'

'Gosh, I can't believe I'll get to work on a TS2 satellite.'

Lizzie King stood shaking her head. 'I hope you know what you're doing, Jack and we don't all get tried for espionage or theft or whatever.'

'I can't explain the whole story to you or anyone else, Lizzie. I wish I could share what I suspect. There are three unexplained components inside this section of satellite, and I need Jason to check them out and explain their function to me. You've still got the circuit diagrams, I presume?'

Robertson nodded. 'I have to warn you that I will have to open these components and might not be able to re-assemble them.'

'That's a risk I have to take. So where do we take this? Somewhere where you won't be observed.'

Robertson shrugged. 'The workshop isn't in use, but anybody could enter at any time though I suppose I could lock myself in. The safest place I can think off is my flat; it's not far away.'

'Have you got all the necessaries there? Tools, instruments etc.'

Robertson nodded. 'I certainly do, I'm a real electronics nerd.'

Somerton looked at King. 'I propose to deliver this to Jason's place, as of now, if that's OK with you.'

King spread her hands. 'Carry on.'

Robertson gave Somerton his address and without further conversation, he got into his car and drove off.

Robertson looked at King. 'I guess I'd better get on his tail.'

King nodded. 'And probably put your foot down on the way. Knowing Jack, he won't hang about.'

Somerton got to the flat in twenty minutes. Robertson arrived less than five minutes later and led the way in, Somerton followed carrying in the cardboard box with the satellite unit.

'I'm on the ground floor so no stairs to climb you'll be pleased to know.'

The satellite unit set up in Robertson's mini lab Somerton took his leave, handing the young researcher a card with his private number written on the back. 'Phone me on this number, anytime of the day or night as soon as you have anything to report, and I do mean **anytime**. If you can have it ready by 4am, that would be a huge bonus. And Jason, thanks and good luck. I can't stress how important this is.'

Houses of Parliament
'Hello, Prime Minister's office, how can I help?'

'Well, you could come away with me for the weekend.'

Tate burst out laughing. 'Behave yourself, Jack, you know you don't mean it. And don't forget all these conversations are recorded.'

'Oh my God, I forgot, my infatuation is exposed; I'll tender my resignation immediately.'

'OK, Jack, you've had your fun. What is it that you really want?'

'A quick word with Laura.'

'No can do, Jack. She's got the Finnish Ambassador with her, preparing the ground for next week's meeting with her Prime Minister. All I can do is tell her you phoned and ask her to phone back. Can I say what it is you want to talk about?'

'Nothing desperate, I just want to tell her I'm taking a few days leave.'

'She'll be about twenty minutes with the Ambassador.'

'No problem, she can email or phone when she's ready.' I'm at the NRSC for the next couple of hours catching up on security issues.'

Somerton made a mug of tea and put a call into Jupiter who was slow to respond. He was reaching for the off button when the screen came to life.

'Hello, Jack. This is an unexpected pleasure, what can I do for you?'

'You know I've asked for a Summit Meeting to devise an outline strategy for our campaign? I want to run an idea past you, and I'd prefer if it was kept between us at this stage. I want to be certain you can handle it, assuming it gets the go ahead. I wouldn't want to embarrass either of us with the unachievable.'

'Sounds interesting, what do you have in mind?'

'It involves ten static targets, all in the same country. I want to scare the living daylights out of our friends in China.'

'I'll bet you're talking nuclear power stations, Jack. It's difficult, but it is manageable, as long as all satellites are in orbit. Is there anything else I can help with?'

'Nope, I just wanted to make certain. Have you got anything you want to raise with me?'

'Not a thing, Jack and if we're done, I'll sign off. I've got a lot on today.'

That all went routinely, Jack. He showed no sign of being aware that one of the satellites had been hijacked. You'll still need to come up with a believable explanation for the possibility that there will be only three satellites instead of four in the final launch.

Somerton was still reflecting on the days ahead when Taylor got through to him.

'You wanted to talk to me about some days off. Not a problem though I do like having you around where I can keep an eye on you. I'm being nosey but might I enquire as to where you'll be?'

'Sure. It's something I should have mentioned earlier but forgot. When I was over visiting Chloe MacKinnon, I got an invite to her daughter Maggie's birthday celebration. It's the one she's having for her college friends and relatives on Chloe's side of the family. They were keen to have me along, so I accepted. I was pretty sure you would give it the OK; it will only be three days max.'

'Hmm, sounds like you and Chloe are getting chummy.'

'Not in the way your mind might be working. I'm fond of her but the purpose of my visit is Maggie's birthday, full stop.' Somerton introduced a touch of annoyance in his voice.

'Don't get ratty, Jack, you can go, of course you can. When is the party taking place? I've persuaded Will Kenny to organise the grand assembly you've been so keen on and if it clashed, you would have to forgo your birthday celebrations. Key diaries are being looked at and the agreed date will be non-negotiable.'

'I would fly out this coming Friday and fly back on Sunday, ready for work on Monday, if that's OK with you?'

'That shouldn't be a problem but keep your diary as flexible as possible. I have a feeling this big meet will happen very soon.'

That went well, lucky me. If she had declined my request, it would have been very tricky.

The afternoon session in the Commons had proved interesting. A group of Tory MPs, led by the redoubtable Max Penrose and army veteran Tom Tideswell, had raised a number of defence and security issues some of which had been directed to him. Added to that, his phone had vibrated causing his tummy to squirm when he saw it was from Lizzie King requesting urgent contact.

As soon as the session ended, he stood, bowed to the Speaker and hurried back to his office in two minds whether to phone her from his office or head to his London flat where he could guarantee privacy and not being interrupted. Added to that he didn't want to risk being waylaid in the Commons. He quickly bundled his outstanding papers into his red box and made his way to the car pool to engage a driver to run him home.

GIBRALTAR HOUSE

It was just leaving midnight when Lizzie King answered his call. 'Lizzie, what news do you have for me?

'Are you sitting down?'

'I am now, sounds ominous.'

'Not ominous, Jack, more mysterious. Inexplicable really. Probably the one outcome I would never have guessed at. Neither Jason nor I can come up with an explanation for what he found when he opened up the satellite components.'

Somerton drew a deep breath and steeled himself for whatever was to follow. 'You have the undivided attention of a very worried man.'

'Those three components have one thing in common, Jack.'

'Out with it, Lizzie, my heart rate is up 50% already.'

'Brace yourself. They all do precisely nothing, Jack, absolutely nothing.'

Somerton's emotions were a jumble of surprise, disappointment, concern. 'That can't be. They must have some function.'

'Jason and I are as flummoxed as you are, believe me. He carried out every conceivable test on the components and found nothing. He then opened one of them up and found that the multitude of cables passed straight through. The casing is nothing more than a sham. He carried on and opened up the other two components with the same result.

'The components do nothing, Jack. I can't think of no reason why they are there. What the hell is going on, Jack?

'I honestly don't know, Lizzie, but I intend to find out. Please, please, not a word to anyone. When I get an explanation, I promise I'll share it with you.'

'You have my word on that, and I'll ensure Jason keeps it to himself. I can't wait to learn why fifty-four very successful, very expensive satellites are housing dummy components.'

'Me too. In the meantime, get Jason to put everything back as it was as quicky as possible and let me know when he's finished. I'll collect it from his place and get it back to the Satellite Assembly Centre. Somerton texted Chris Chesterton immediately. *Can we meet at the layby tomorrow morning as early as suits you?* The reply was brief, *6am.* Somerton replied with a thumbs-up emoji.

Somerton sat back to think about what he'd just learned. His initial surprise was replaced by puzzlement. His puzzlement was replaced was with anger. His anger replaced by disappointment. Colin and he had been subjected to a giant deception; they were just pawns in the game. The US had always held all the cards, the UK nothing more than a supporting act. Jupiter hadn't acted under Colin's direction nor was he acting under his. Will Kenny is the puppet-master and always had been. There had never been a true partnership. Somerton felt like tearing his hair out, his plan lay in tatters.

His intention had been to ask Jason Robertson to either build a device that could block, or better still, control the mystery components. The latter option would have rendered them unusable without UK involvement. The former would have put the UK in complete control. *Fuck it, fuck it, fuck it. What now? He had to come up with an answer and had to do it before the Summit Meeting. There was one solution of last resort, one that might now have to be implemented or Colin's life, Alan's life, the young women abducted for Jupiter would all have been in vain. Fuck it, fuck it, fuck it. The bastards aren't going to win, I swear it.*

Somerton collected the satellite unit from Jason Robertson's later that evening.

'I've put the component casing back together as best I can, but if anyone examines it closely, they'll know it's been opened.'

Somerton shrugged, that was the least of his problems. 'I guess so, but they might just assume it had been accessed in America for quality control purposes Thanks again for your efforts, Jason and keep this revelation to yourself. I'm going to drop by in the morning around 4am to collect it and then carry on to the Satellite Assembly Centre. You can leave it in your entrance hall with the door unlatched; there's no need for you to get up at that unearthly hour.'

Robertson nodded. 'I'll set the alarm for 4am and meet you in the foyer. I'm pleased to have been of help though I would like to know what this is all about. It just doesn't make sense. I'm sorry it's not the result you hoped for.'

Layby next morning.
True to his word the young man watched out for Somerton and was waiting for Somerton when he arrived a few minutes after 4am. The route to the SAC was virtually deserted at that time in the morning and Somerton's foot was on the accelerator all the way. He was pleased when he saw that Chesterton's car parked in the layby as arranged. The two men wasted no time making the changeover.

'Thanks for all you've done, Chris, it's appreciated. I have a revelation to make.' Somerton explained the situation to Chesterton and was taken aback when he showed no surprise. 'You're either very good at controlling your reactions or you already knew these components were fake.'

'I had my suspicions and carried out checks of my own but came up with nothing. Everything I tried suggested they didn't have any performance-changing capability. I parked my findings because I couldn't come up with any reason why this could be the case. What's going on, Jack?'

Somerton shrugged. 'I really don't know but I'm determined to find out; you'll be among the first to know when I do. I won't

249

let this drop, I promise. But I stress no-one else must know of this discovery until I've completed my investigation. Everything must proceed as normal until I have all the answers. I'd like you to get this last satellite ready for launching at the earliest opportunity.'

Chesterton glanced at his watch. 4.19am 'I'd better get going and get back to the Centre and get this unit in place in time for the staff coming in at 8am. The RAF are due carry out a collection at 11am today, it's going to be tight. The launch is scheduled for tomorrow as you know.'

Somerton shook his head. 'To be honest, I'd lost track of the launch schedule.'

The two men shook hands and drove away with very different thoughts going through their heads. Chesterton wondering why Somerton didn't appear to be in any hurry to expose the findings, and Somerton thinking about where this deception and farrago of lies was going to lead. He also knew that if his investigation was discovered his own life would be at risk.

CHAPTER 40

Washington Friday

The flight from London's City airport to Washington was routine, travelling First Class in a British Airways 707 was no hardship. The food was satisfying, the drinks unlimited though Somerton restricted himself to a single glass of an English sparkling wine he'd never heard of. The main attraction of travelling First was a fully reclining bed and the relative quiet; he wanted to be well rested when he landed. Somerton selected a couple of films to keep him awake until shortly after midnight by which time sleep would be knocking on the door.

The films didn't quite provide the engagement he hoped for; his mind kept drifting back to Constellation MacKinnon. The question he couldn't answer to his complete satisfaction was why did the US need to involve the UK in the first place? Jupiter's explanation of the UK's historic standing attracting him had sounded plausible but now that it transpired that he wasn't a refugee fleeing Russia, it just didn't hold water. The US had it all, the most powerful military force in the world, a large proportion of the world's most advanced weaponry and the genius Jupiter possessed. The UK had long-standing links with Europe and the Commonwealth and that had some value; the so-called, *Special Relationship,* only kicked in when it suited both parties. Was the UK simply there to be thrust into the debate if the situation got troublesome? A sort of ally on stand-by? *There must be more to it than that, Jack.* He could only come up with one answer. There was a *Special Relationship* but it wasn't one borne of history; it was much more recent. It was the Will Kenny – Laura Taylor relationship, a duo seeking to rule the world.

Despite a whirlpool of thoughts in his head, he eventually fell asleep wondering if the MacKinnon family, now his adopted family, would like the gifts he had bought them. He couldn't remember the last time he'd bought anyone a present.

His flight touched down at 8.15pm, ten minutes early, and with only hand luggage, it wasn't long until Somerton was standing in the queue for a taxi. He had insisted on not being picked up at the airport, arguing that the flight might be delayed or late and the inevitability of hanging around in the terminal.

Within minutes he was settled in the back seat of the taxi and instructing the driver to 108 P Street NW.'

'I know the area well, sir; it overlooks Rose Park, one of the most sought- after areas in Washington.'

Somerton wasn't in the mood to chat so responded by agreeing and letting the driver know he had visited the city a few weeks ago.

MacKinnon residence.

He alighted from the cab and took a quick scan of the area, not a soul in sight. *Relax, Jack, they're not out to get you, not yet anyway.* The night sky was clear and filled with stars, the temperature mild and not a breath of wind. Somerton took a deep breath. *Perfect, just perfect.* He turned to face the house just as the porch light came on, Chloe MacKinnon stepped out and waved. She seemed to skip down the steps her face lit up with a smile, her yellow and blue floral dress swirled around her. 'Hi Jack, great to see you. Thanks for coming all this way, Maggie really appreciates it. Let's go inside, lovely evening as it is. I left the kids putting the kettle on, though you can have something alcoholic if you wish. How are you feeling?'

Somerton gave a weak smile. 'It was a good flight and it passed quickly. I got some sleep, I think, but in truth I feel a bit travel weary. Work has been hectic of late. Hopefully I'll wake up fully refreshed tomorrow morning.'

Chloe nodded. 'I'm sure you will.'

At that point Maggie and Murray appeared, the former stepping forward to give Somerton a hug and a cheek kiss. The greeting tugged at his heart and, somehow, he felt he was home. 'Great to see you, Maggie, soon to be birthday girl.'

Murray reached forward a fist. 'Welcome, Jack.'

Somerton took the cue and bumped fists. 'Good to be here, Murray. Feels like this is my adopted second home'

Chloe interrupted. 'You're in the same room as last time, Jack. Do you need to be shown or can you remember?'

Somerton smiled. 'Wasn't too long ago, I'm sure I can find my way.'

'OK, go put your bag in the room, freshen up if you feel the need, then join us for tea, or coffee if you prefer.'

'Coffee, black please.'

Chloe nodded. 'Anything to eat?'

'If it's no trouble, just a slice of toast, any colour will do.'

Somerton made his way upstairs, unpacked his bag and splashed some cold water over his face, then made his way back downstairs. The MacKinnon family, *his* adopted family, were seated round the kitchen table. Maggie immediately got up and poured him a black coffee and popped two slices of bread in the toaster. 'Thanks, Maggie.' He reached forward and handed her a package. 'For the birthday girl; And since I may not be here for your birthday, this one is for you, Murray. And last, but my no means least, this one is for you, Chloe.'

A chorus of 'thank yous' sounded simultaneously, followed by 'you really shouldn't haves'. Somerton raised a hand as they were about to open the wrapping. 'Please don't open them until I fly off to the UK.'

Maggie frowned. 'But why not?'

Somerton grimaced. 'Humour me, I'm a bit odd. I don't want to witness your disappointment if you don't like them. Indulge me please.'

Chloe came to the rescue. 'Very odd, Jack, but we'll go along with your wishes. Maggie, I think the toast has popped up.'

Somerton was relieved; the gifts were good, generous in fact. Watches for all three, an Audemar Piquet for Maggie, a Breitling for Murray and a Patek-Phillipe for Chloe. All top of the range but he had no idea what their individual preferences were, or even if kids bothered with watches nowadays. 'Now, tell me what's been happening since I last saw you?'

They chatted until nearly midnight at which point, Somerton failed to stifle a yawn. 'Sorry folks, it's been a long day.'

Once again, Chloe took command. 'Bedtime everybody, especially you Mr Somerton. We want you in good form for tomorrow. And, as it happens, these two have commitments in the morning followed by a hair appointment for Maggie in the afternoon. Which means that you and I are free to do whatever takes our fancy.'

'You know what, Chloe, I'd like to do exactly what we did last time and go for a walk round the park. I really enjoyed that outing. Will I know anyone at Maggie's birthday party?'

Chloe shook her head. 'I doubt it. Though there is a member of the army community you might get on with, a Major Ed Swanson, an old friend of mine. I'll make the introduction. The majority of the guests are Maggie's college mates and Murray has a few friends coming. Yours truly has invited a few oldies so I don't feel too out of place.'

Somerton laughed. 'I wondered why I was asked.'

Chloe smiled. 'We'll make a good match. Maggie has laid on the college rock band to provide the music, so we can have a dance if you're up to it.'

Somerton smiled wryly; dancing wasn't his thing. 'Who could resist such an invitation?'

Maggie chipped in. 'The band has a good vocalist, and they play a variety of old and new. They'll get you on the floor, I'm sure.'

'I'm not very good, I warn you.'

Chloe chipped. 'Nonsense, it's not rocket science; I'll guide you round.'

'I'll hold you to that, Chloe. You'll regret every moment you're on the floor, I warn you.'

'We have a deal. Now, bedtime everybody.'

Next morning

Breakfast over, Chloe and Somerton set out on their walk ending up in a rowing boat on the river around noon.

'You row really well, Jack.'

Somerton smiled. 'Back in the day my life depended on it at times. It's surprising how quickly you can develop a skill when the adrenaline valve opens up.'

They spent the next two hours on the river trip, admiring the flora and fauna and riverside willows, excited when they caught sight of a kingfisher. Afterwards they made their way to a nearby café for a light lunch. 'I enjoyed that sail, Jack. Believe it or not it's something Colin and I never got round to.'

'I know the feeling; when I look back, there are gaps in my life I wish I had filled; and probably never will now.'

Chloe looked at him closely. 'Do you think you'll ever marry, Jack?'

Somerton shook his head wistfully. 'I doubt it, though I can see all the advantages of a good marriage, especially one with kids like yours. They must keep you young at heart. I guess it's too soon for you to even begin thinking if you'll ever remarry?'

Chloe's eyes moistened; her expression saddened fleetingly. 'I confess I do get lonely from time to time but I think remarrying would be a step too far. What Colin and I had was very special. At this moment I can't imagine ever letting another man into my life.'

Somerton nodded, eyes near to moistening. 'I can understand how you feel.' *And I'm the bastard who took him out of your life. I pray to God you never find out that I killed Colin.*

Chloe glanced at her watch, eyes widening when she saw it was 3.30. 'Gosh we'd better head back. I've got to do my hair and help Maggie get ready. By the way the party is being held in the college function room. We'll need to be there to greet the arrivals, say 6.45 at the latest. The party officially kicks off at 7. I reckon there'll be around forty guests in total. Food is a help-yourself buffet. We adults will keep the students under control best we can; only joking they are a good bunch of kids. There will be plenty of opportunity for you to talk to Ed Swanson, best done outside on the terrace I think.'

Somerton nodded his face tensing at the prospect.

Chloe saw his reaction and put her hand on his. 'It's serious, Jack, isn't it?'

'Very serious, Chloe. I'm sorry I can't talk about it. I'm really looking forward to the party, and, by the way, your hair already looks great.'

CHAPTER 41

The Party

Somerton and Murray lined up behind a reception table, ready to offer the guests a drink; Maggie and Chloe stood near the entrance to provide a welcome. Both were dressed in long figure-hugging evening dresses, Chloe's a deep red, Maggie's an emerald green. Both wore matching high heels and jewellery, mother's gold, daughter's silver. Somerton wasn't a flash dresser, but he'd had checked out his apparel with Murray and got a thumbs up approval. Murray was wearing a multi-coloured abstract design tee-shirt and baggy bright yellow trousers.

As the guests arrived, Somerton was struck by the contrast; nearly all the girls had opted for stunning eye-catching dresses whereas the boys, in the main wore relaxed gear; there wasn't a suit in sight.

Chloe made a point of introducing Somerton to the eight older guests she had invited, five female, three male. He wasn't formally introduced to the students though he exchanged banter with those who expressed an interested in his presence. Partnerships and groups formed and eventually drifted away from the bar area to the waiting tables and chairs set up round the dance floor.

Drinks were free for the first hour, then the college bar opened for service and guests had to purchase their own. The buffet was set up adjacent to the bar and made available around 8pm to coincide with band's arrival. The musicians set up in record time and quickly got into their rhythm. The kids flocked onto the floor, singing, dancing arm-waving, hips gyrating; the party was in full swing.

Somerton glanced at his watch 8.50. *Where the hell are you Swanson? Please don't let me down.* Chloe must have noticed his concern and came over to join him. 'Don't worry, Colin, Ed will turn up. I'm sure of it. Later on, I'll detach myself from the older guests and partner you for the rest of the evening if you'll have me. How does that sound?'

Somerton smiled and relaxed. 'Those are the best words I've heard all evening.'

'In the meantime, let me get you a drink. I seem to recall you like Scotch.'

'Thank you, sounds perfect. A malt if they've got it, please.'

Five minutes later she was back at his side, a glass of amber liquid in her hand. 'Sorry, no Scotch but I got you a Jack Daniels. I hope that's OK?'

'Of course.'

Suddenly her face lit up. 'Ed's just arrived.'

Somerton followed her gaze to a tall, ruggedly handsome, forty something man who stood at the entrance area looking round the room. She waved and Swanson smiling broadly, made his way over to join them.

Chloe gave him a hug and brushed cheeks then stood back. 'I was starting to get worried you weren't going to make it.'

'Sorry Chloe, a last-minute emergency which I was fortunately able to delegate.'

'Let me introduce you to Jack Somerton, a friend of long-standing. He's ex-military so you two have that in common.'

The intros made, the handshake complete, Chloe took charge again. 'Follow me to the bar Ed and I'll get you a drink.'

'Thanks Chloe, I could do with one. See you around, Jack.'

Relieved that Swanson was here, Somerton sidled away and started up a conversation with one of the older couples, friends of Chloe's from Connecticut. All the usual social questions followed. How do you know Chloe? How long have you known her? How long are you over for?

The guy explained that he owned a small building company and boasted about some of his so-called celebrity clients. He then enquired as to Somerton's interests. Somerton replied that he was ex-army, deliberately avoiding any mention of being ex-SAS or a Member of Parliament. He reckoned that that would have prompted a deluge of questions. He was rescued when the man's wife heard a song she liked and dragged *darling* onto the dance floor.

He turned away just as Chloe returned. 'Hope you're not being asked too many probing questions, Jack; an English accent always arouses interest. When you see Ed leave, give him five minutes then follow him. You'll go out where you came in, take a left to the end of the building, then turn right, and follow the line of the building opposite. This will bring you to a small courtyard where you'll find him waiting for you. Ed, rose up through the ranks in the Marines.' She smiled. 'Promise not to fight too many battles. But as of now, until Ed departs, I want you on the dance floor.'

'It must be my lucky night; I'm getting to dance with the best-looking woman in the room. I warn you again, I'm not the world's best dancer, in fact I'm pretty hopeless.'

'Shush Jack, flattery not required. Ah, this is an Elvis Presley medley requested by me. You don't dance to this you just smooch.' Chloe took Somerton's hand and led him onto the floor. The strains of Don't filled the hall; the vocalist doing his best to capture the King of Rock and roll's romantic tones.

'It's a lovely song, Chloe, though I'm not sure if the kids will enjoy it. It's way before their time.'

'You think so? Take a look around you Jack.'

She was right, the floor was filling, the youngsters not missing an opportunity to hold each other close.

'Happy to be proved wrong and even happier to follow their example with your permission.' He drew Chloe closer but not too close. He was struggling with his emotions. He couldn't even begin to let his feelings surface. Chloe laid her head on his shoulder and they moved slowly along in time with the music. As the song progressed, he fought against his growing feeling of love; a love that could never be. The song ended and Somerton made to let go her hand, but she resisted.

'It's a medley, Jack, you'll have to put up with me for a little longer. Ed will have to wait.'

The haunting lyrics of Presley's Are You Lonesome Tonight came through the speakers. Somerton held Chloe's eyes for few seconds. 'Ed can wait all night as far as I'm concerned.'

Chloe snuggled closer, muttering. 'Well, maybe not that long.'

The medley finished with, It's Now or Never, Somerton mood swaying between guilt and desire. *You've got to get out of here, Jack.* Thankfully, the mood was broken when the song ended and the singer announced it was time to step up the pace and the band broke into a rousing rock song that Somerton didn't know.

Chloe pulled away. 'Thank you, Jack, I'll let you go and catch up with Ed now. Good luck. We'll dance again before the end of the evening? Please, I don't get to dance much these days?' She looked at him, raising an eyebrow, asking the question.

Somerton smiled and nodded. 'Wouldn't miss it for the world, Chloe.'

They left the floor together, Chloe wandering across to some friends, Somerton walking quickly towards the exit.

Swanson was seated on a wooden bench on the far side of a courtyard, smoking a cigarette which he stubbed out when he saw Somerton. 'A filthy habit I know, but I still enjoy a drag from time to time.' Swanson remained seated, looking at Somerton intently. There was no way of knowing what was in his thoughts; maybe like Somerton, he was weighing up the risks even at this late stage. Both men were strangers to each other, both were having to trust each other, either or both might be putting their lives on the line. Swanson had the backing of ex-Presidents Overton and Kingston but for all they knew he could be a double agent. And for that matter they had no worthwhile reason to trust Somerton; they knew very little about his motives or how close he was to Laura Taylor.

Somerton opened the conversation. 'Thanks for meeting with me Ed, I recognise that you're taking a helluva risk. From what I've learned your bosses wouldn't take kindly to anyone who gets in their way.'

Swanson nodded and shrugged. 'It sure would be easier if we knew exactly where we were heading with all this. Sometimes I wonder if maybe Will's right, Brian and George might have got it wrong, but in the final analysis I'm putting my trust in their judgement. There has to be limits to power, lines have to be drawn.'

Somerton shrugged. 'I guess so, Ed, but speaking for myself I've never been backward at crossing the line when needs be.' Somerton was gently testing Swanson, trying to find the scope of his commitment. *I wish I knew what was best.*

Swanson acquiesced. 'I know where you're coming from Jack, I've crossed a line or two when I've had to, when there was no alternative but only when there was no alternative. Snatches of conversations I've overheard suggest there are people at the top of the military with one goal and one goal only, and that's world domination. Bear in mind that Will Kenny won't be in office forever, nor will Laura Taylor, unlike the military chiefs who'll be around for a long time. And they can ensure that their successors are likeminded, make sure that only those who share their views get promoted. The way I see it, we are in the last chance saloon.'

Swanson was earnest, convincing, but was he genuine? Could he be trusted, the stakes were high, too high to take any risks. Somerton decided to string Swanson along. *Having a deterrent was no bad thing, tyrants only bowed to superior force, the Cold War had proved that. Were Kenny and Taylor making the right call? Why does life have to be so fucking complicated?*

'So do you have any thoughts on how we go about this, Ed?'

'No, I don't, Jack.' His expression glum, his brow furrowed. 'Sorry. I've thought long and hard but haven't come up with any worthwhile ideas. I'm well placed but I'm also closely watched, even being here is a risk.'

Somerton went quiet for a minute or two. 'Maybe we ought to wait to see what comes out of the forthcoming Summit meeting before taking this any further. Hear what the top echelon has to say.'

Swanson shook his head vigorously. 'No, no a thousand times no; I've heard them all at various times, they are all hell bent on ruling this planet.'

Somerton nodded, though his inner self still wasn't fully convinced. 'Talking about the meeting, do you know when it will take place?'

'Last I heard, it was going to be two weeks hence, either Saturday or Sunday. I'll know tomorrow; it's my responsibility to set up the security arrangements, Kenny will want them to be as tight as can be.'

Somerton nodded. 'Understandable. Do you know the meeting venue?'

'That I do know. It'll be held at Fort Kenny, and it will be an all-day affair. Very few will have heard of Fort Kenny and even fewer have any idea of its purpose.'

'What plans do you have for security, Ed?'

'The usual procedures. You'll be picked up and driven to Fort Kenny. The Fort has a high-level security fence, CCTV cameras everywhere and it's got more guards than the Pentagon and Fort Knox put together. You'll be checked through perimeter security and then everyone from Will Kenny down will go through a scanner. Your pockets will be emptied, your phone will be confiscated. You will then go through to the conference area, the door to which will be closed and locked behind you. Once inside you will be in a toom full of concealed cameras and microphones. I'll be in the security control room keeping an eye on proceedings. I'll witness everything you do on a series of monitors, and that includes the toilet areas. Nothing will be recorded; Kenny doesn't want the proceedings of this meeting on record. And one other thing, I'm suggesting no laptops be taken into the room. Everybody will be issued with one and if they are making a presentation involving visual aids, will have to bring a flash-drive with them.'

Somerton smiled. 'That all sounds good, I'm sure your lord and master will be impressed.' He glanced at his watch. 'I guess I should be making my way back to the party before folks wonder where I've got to.'

'Say goodbye to Chloe for me, I think it's best if I don't be seen following you in.'

'One last thing Ed, do you have a burner phone number I could have? I think we need to be able to contact each other. I have one and change its number regularly.' He handed Swanson a card. 'My number is on there, memorise it and destroy the card please. Text me anytime night or day, call only if absolutely necessary.'

Swanson scratched his head. 'I don't have a burner phone Jack.'

'Get one, soon as, and text me with your number. We have a lot of thinking to do over the next week or so.' The two conspirators shook hands and Swanson headed off to the car park.'

Somerton returned to the hall and spotted Chloe talking to some friends. He made his way over and joined the group. Chloe smiled. 'Where have you been Jack.'

'Went outside to get some fresh air. I think I'm still fighting off jet lag'

Chloe smiled. 'Not long now, Jack, it's getting late for we oldies. I have an announcement to make then maybe we could have another couple of dances before we go home?'

'You've got my vote, go to it.'

Chloe made her way to the stage and signalled them to stop playing at the end of the current medley of rap music. When the band finished, she beckoned the lead singer, Charlie Kool, to her side and explained what she wanted to happen. She took the microphone and looked around the dance floor, smiling. 'I'm going to say a few words then the seniors amongst us might take our leave. First up – are you having a good time?' Cheers rang out all round the hall.

'Great, now what about a huge round of applause for our wonderful band.' When the applause died away Chloe smiled broadly. 'Thank you all for coming, it's been a pleasure having you here. What I want from you now is a rousing rendition of Happy Birthday for my lovely daughter, Maggie.' She nodded to the band who started to play and everybody joined in, singing loudly and enthusiastically. When the song and cheering died away, Chloe took to the microphone again. 'We're now going to have a couple of old-time classics so I can have a last dance before I head back to the ranch, good night and God bless.'

She stepped down from the stage and made her way to Somerton. 'So did you do as I ask, Jack?'

'Of course.'

'So don't keep me in suspense, out with it. What have you requested?'

'Wait and see, you'll know both songs, I'm sure.' Somerton gave Charlie Kool the thumbs up, and the band started playing She, an old-time Charles Aznavour favourite. Chloe sighed. 'Good choice, Jack. 'Her head on his shoulder they began to dance, Somerton wondering if maybe she was a little bit tipsy. Rightly or wrongly, he held her close, wishing history could be wiped out, knowing they could never be more than friends. The song ended and, with barely a pause, the singer began to sing My Way, not with the magic of Sinatra, but with sincerity.

Chloe took her head from his shoulder. 'This song is very you, Jack but I don't suppose you know it was one of Colin's favourites.

'I didn't, I'm sorry if it upsets you.'

She shook her head. 'Not one bit, Jack. I just hope the words aren't prophetic.'

Somerton looked at her puzzled.

Chloe grimaced. 'I was referring to the words, *and now the end is near.*'

Somerton shook his head and pulled her close again. 'I just thought it was appropriate for the end of a wonderful evening. Who knows when we'll get the chance to dance with each other again?'

'You're not going all romantic and slushy are you, Jack?

'Alas, I could never allow myself to do that, Chloe.'

She held his gaze for a moment. 'No, I guess not, but thank you, Jack, it's a dance I'll keep in my memory for a very long time.'

There wasn't much conversation in the taxi on the way back to Chloe's place; even the driver seemed to sense it was a time to be quiet.

The journey over, Chloe led the way into the house, immediately kicking her shoes off. 'That's a relief. Do you fancy a coffee or maybe a nightcap?'

Somerton shook his head. 'I think I'll go straight to bed. Thank you for a lovely evening, Chloe.'

'What time's your flight?'

'I have to be at Dulles for 3pm. I've booked a cab.'

'Oh Jack, you shouldn't have. I would have dropped you off.' Her voice held genuine disappointment

Somerton shook his head. 'I hate airport partings; we'll say our farewells here. Maybe go for a walk in the morning?'

Chloe looked disappointed but shrugged. 'Whatever you think best. Shall we say 9.30am for breakfast. The kids won't be around I'm afraid, it'll be well past midday before they surface.'

He leaned forward and kissed her gently on the cheek then made his way up to bed.'

Next morning
Breakfast over Chloe drove them to the Smithsonian where they spent a couple of interesting hours followed by lunch in the café. Conversation ensued but somehow it lacked the spark of spontaneity. Maybe both felt that last night's unspoken feelings had been a step too far. The last port of call was a walk around Arlington Military Cemetery where Somerton found himself surrounded by memories of past conflicts. So many young lives sacrificed in pursuit of freedom and democracy. Maybe some sort of world order could provide the answer; maybe, maybe, maybe, that damnable inconclusive word. *Maybe Kenny and Taylor's new world order could put an end to the loss of so many young lives in times to come.'*

What path should he follow? Could the US-UK alliance bring peace to this troubled planet? Would China, Russia and North Korea get the message or would they simply resort to the ultimate power struggle, World War Three. Somerton gazed around the graves. *We must find a way to stop this happening.*

'Penny for them, Jack' Chloe interrupted his thoughts.

'Just being here makes me ponder on what the future holds, Chloe.'

'I meant to ask before now, but how did your meeting with Ed go.'

'It was helpful, but we didn't reach any conclusion. He's a good guy though and I'm happy to work with him. We've arranged to keep in touch.'

Chloe sighed. 'I'm truly sorry we can't share what's troubling you; I dearly wish I could help.' She glanced at her watch. 'I think we should be getting back. I'm sure you have packing to do.'

Somerton smiled. 'Yeah, that huge suitcase of mine.'

Chloe laughed. 'I forgot you only had a carry-on bag.'

Later.
The farewells were brief. Murray with his customary fist tap. 'Nice seeing you, Jack, I hope it's not long till we meet again. We guys must go out on our own next time, and I'll show you round the hot spots.'

Maggie seemed to hold back, and Chloe stepped forward to give Somerton a hug and a peck on the cheek. 'Don't leave it too long, please; we'll all miss you.'

Maggie moved and put her arms round Somerton's neck. 'Thanks for coming to my party. Mum spoke for all of us, come back soon.' She kissed him on the cheek, then whispered in his ear. 'I disobeyed orders. I opened my present. I love my watch. I'll be the envy of all my college mates. Thank you so very much, you've been far too generous. I'll treasure it all my life.' She stood back, her eyes moistening.

Somerton fought back his emotions; tears weren't far away. 'Thank you all for having me. I look forward to the next birthday. I'm not the soppy type but I mean it when I say, you're the family I never had.'

That said, he turned on his heel and walked down the steps to the waiting taxi. His last view was of the trio waving goodbye.

CHAPTER 42

The return flight to London was uneventful, though Somerton's mind worked overtime throughout the flight; attempts to sleep rejected by the constant working of ideas. A ghost of a plan had transformed into a workable solution. How could the power of the satellite system be harnessed to benefit mankind? It was a question he couldn't begin to answer until he met all the players, knew their thinking, knew their goals. Brian Overton, George Kingston, and Ed Swanson had presented a pessimistic view, but he wasn't ready to discard the concept of a satellite sanction system until he knew more. Will Kenny and Laura Taylor were key, as was Jupiter, the brain behind the system. *You'll have to plan for the worst, hope for the best, Jack.*

His thoughts were briefly interrupted when his phone vibrated; a text from Laura Taylor requiring his presence at 8.30. *Thank you, Laura, just what I needed, an early start.* Fortunately, the flight was on time and touched down five minutes early at 6.25. Customs were nowhere to be seen and the new passport scanning system meant he was seated in a taxi on his way to his London flat shortly after seven. The taxi driver agreed to wait for Somerton to dash to his flat, shave, quick shower, freshen up and change into a formal suit. *Take as long as you like guvnor, you're paying.'* A look of excitement crossed the cabbie's face when Somerton returned and told him his destination was No 10.

'No.10, blow me! I'll get you as close as I can, but security is tight around there. So, what are you up to guvnor, if you don't mind me asking?'

'I have an appointment with the PM at 8.30.'

'Gosh, I'd better get a move on. You're an MP, are you?'

'Yes, Harrow East.'

'Don't suppose I can ask what you're seeing her about at this early hour?'

Somerton laughed. 'You can ask, but you won't get an answer.'

The cabbie shrugged. 'Oh well, fair enough. I'll let you gather your thoughts'

The rest of the journey took place in silence and Somerton almost fell asleep.

After the usual security formalities, Somerton was allowed through the steel gates and strode purposefully along Downing Street to No10. The street was deserted; no public, no protestors and happily, no baying hordes of media people. The famous black door didn't magically open immediately and he had to wait a few moments before he was recognised and invited to enter.

It was 8.20 when he walked into the outer office, smiling when he was greeted by Jess Tate. 'Welcome back, Jack. A good trip?'

'A bit rushed but Chloe and the kids made me very welcome, and the party was fun. They all asked after you; they know how Colin thought the world of you. Chloe especially sends her love.'

'How is she nowadays?'

'Happy enough I guess, given the circumstances, but she's not quite the Chloe of old, a bit lonely I thought. It's taking time to get absorbed into Washington life and she doesn't rule out coming back to the UK but I think the kids will take precedence. They are growing up fast and love the Washington scene, so I have my doubts she'll come back, certainly not before the kids fly the nest. She asked me to tell you that you would be very welcome to visit or holiday there anytime.'

Tate smiled, 'I might just take her up on that offer.'

The door to the PM's office opened and Taylor stood appraising the duo. 'I thought I heard voices. On time as always, Jack, not even a transatlantic flight gets in the way.'

'I just mentioned your name to the pilot, and he put his foot down. It must be great to have so much influence.'

'Yeah, yeah, thank you Jack. Coffee for two please, Jess.'

Taylor sat down behind the famous desk. In a formal mood thought Somerton.

'How was the trip, Jack?'

'Thoroughly enjoyed it, everything on time and to plan. It was great seeing Chloe, Maggie and Murray.'

'Maggie's birthday party I recall.'

'Yeah, we had a great celebration; she's a lovely girl.' responded Somerton.

Just then Jess Tate entered with the coffee. 'Would either of you like biscuits?'

Taylor shook her head. 'No thanks, Jack is sweet enough as he is.'

Somerton smiled dutifully. 'Ha, ha, ha.'

'So how did the party go?'

Somerton was puzzled. *She gets me here for 8.30 and then asks about the party; I can't believe she's interested in my social life. What she up to?*

'The party was held at Maggie's college, there were about fifty guests, forty kids, ten oldies. There was a rock band with a lead singer called Charlie Kool. We danced the night long, and sang Happy Birthday to Maggie. As far as I know a good time was had by all.'

'Meet anybody interesting?' Somerton went to red alert; this was starting to feel like an interrogation. *She knows I met Swanson.*

'There were a couple of very attractive ladies, alas escorted by their husbands or I might have been asking you if I could extend my leave. Other than that, there were some interesting characters amongst the students, male, female, trans, the whole spectrum I would say. Oh, nearly forgot, I was pleased to meet a fellow soldier, an old friend of Chloe's. an ex-US Marine, so we had plenty to talk about; Ed Swanley, no that's not right. Ed Swanton, something like that. He was a Major General, outranked me, but we had a great deal in common and shared our combat experiences, not often I get the chance to do that nowadays. Sadly, he was younger and more handsome.'

'What's he up to nowadays?'

'He's got a desk job, somewhere in the Pentagon, I think. I was more interested in his military exploits than his ability to hold a pencil. I'm surprised you're so interested in my social life, Laura. Are you checking up on me? I am available if you're interested, though I thought you were already fully committed.'

Taylor smiled and seemed to relax. 'Not at all, I'm just showing interest in a valued colleague.'

'Steady now, don't lay the praise on too thick. Now, please tell me why I've been summoned to your office at 8.30?'

'You'll be pleased to learn that the Summit meeting has been arranged for Sunday, two weeks hence; that's the earliest date we could come up with. I'll let you have the flight details in due course. We won't all travel together for security reasons. We'll use a number of carriers, Queens flight, RAF and commercial. We don't want to be seen travelling together, it would raise too many awkward questions. Return flights will be staggered.'

Somerton nodded. 'A good idea, as your security supremo I approve.'

Just one more thing. Will is enthusiastic about your China project and asks if it could go ahead as soon as possible?'

Somerton smiled. *Good old Will, maintaining the charade right to the end.*

'I'll get right on to it and let you know later today, but I stress we're in Jupiter's hands. He didn't foresee any problems last time we discussed.'

Taylor leaned forward on her desk, seemingly satisfied. 'Have you got a date in mind?'

'I thought Wednesday around midday. Given they are eight hours ahead we can sit back and watch the scenario evolve on TV on Wednesday afternoon. It will be interesting to see how Jing Chen reacts. I'll keep you informed as soon as I've talked it through with Jupiter.' *I'm sure Will Kenny has already given you all the details, Laura, but the game must go on.'*

'Thanks for that, Jack. I'll let Will know. That's all I have for you, so you're free to go unless there's anything you want to raise?'

'There is just one thing. Where is the Summit Meeting being held?

Taylor shook her head. 'I asked but Will wouldn't tell me; it's a top secret set up.'

Somerton smiled. *Why don't I believe you?* 'Can't fault the security.'

'You'll be fully committed this visit so don't make any plans to visit Chloe this time round.'

Somerton nodded.' Fair enough. I'll cut along now, I've got some catching up to do, constituency business and preparation for this afternoon's Commons session.'

That evening.

Somerton was wearied by the end of the day's business in the Commons. The Speaker had called on him to make a statement on a number of security and research matters at short notice. Questions had followed from all sides of the House and it had been a tough session. Still, he had enjoyed the cut and thrust of debate and found it quite exhilarating at times. He must have performed well; Laura Taylor gave him thumbs up as he left.

He took a few kebabs back to Gibraltar Heights and quickly scoffed them, keen to get in touch with Jupiter before retiring for the night. The genius must have been on standby and answered his call almost immediately.

'Hello Jack, welcome back.'

Somerton was shocked by his appearance, Jupiter looked haggard, almost frail.

'My God, Jupiter, are you ill? You don't look at all well.'

Jupiter sighed. 'Usual problem, Jack, I'm having a problem with my immune system. I'm waiting for the results of some tests. How can I help?'

'Sorry to hear that. I hope you feel up to tackling the China Project at short notice? We can defer if you think it will be too much, though ideally, I was hoping you could trigger it Wednesday around midday.'

Jupiter managed a weak smile. 'Presumably so you can have all day to gloat as you watch the media breaking the news.'

'Precisely. You know me too well. There's a big meeting coming up, as I'm sure you are aware, and how China reacts might have bearing on the discussions.'

'Of course. I wish I could be there.'

Somerton smiled. 'I've got no doubt you'll be there.'

Jupiter's voice sharpened. 'What do you mean, *I'll be there*?'

Somerton smiled at Jupiter's discomfort. 'As a fly on the wall of course, how else? I know you can listen in on any gathering, anywhere in the world if you choose to. That's the case, isn't it?'

'Of course. If that's all you have for me, I'll shut down and get started on programming.'

'Before you go, so there are no mix ups, could you just go through the names of the ten power plants involved.'

Jupiter frowned but he pressed a button somewhere and the names came up on the screen. 'Satisfied?'

Somerton looked them over, nodding when he saw they were all listed. 'Perfect thank you. And will you do them all simultaneously or sequentially?

'Two sets of five.'

'One final question, please. Just explain in simple terms what you'll be doing. I want to understand the process.'

Jupiter's eyes narrowed. 'You're very curious tonight, Jack.'

Somerton nodded. 'Humour me, please. I never know what questions Laura Taylor will throw at me.'

Jupiter screwed up his face and waved a hand dismissively. 'Very well. There has to be a balance between electrical demand and power generated. The means of controlling demand are the reactor control rods. The rods control the desired state of the fusion reactors by insertion and retraction. Lose control of the rods and you lose control of the reactor. Left unchecked, a nuclear disaster would result which would be greater than Chernobyl.'

'Thanks for that, Jupiter, I feel better now I have full insight into how you will handle the attack. I assume you'll take the situation to the very brink. There's much more at stake here than any of the previous projects. And most importantly, I hope you're confident of retaining control of the rods.'

Jupiter stared at Somerton, anger blazing through. 'I've never let you down, have I? I feel quite insulted. Of course, I can guarantee retaining control of the rods. Satisfied?'

'Apologies. I can see I've upset you. I guess I'm nervous. This is by far the biggest project we've tackled; the risks are enormous. Apologies again and thank you. We can sign off now.'

Jupiter's screen instantly went blank.

Somerton sat back shaking his head, speaking to himself. 'All that power vested in a mere 54 satellites; the US could render the whole of China radioactive at the drop of a hat. God knows what they could do with five hundred satellites.'

Somerton had two more bits of business to execute. Ed Swanson had acted promptly; his new burner phone number had been sent to Somerton during his flight. He texted a series of questions and sat back to wait for a response. Twenty minutes passed and he received he answers he'd hope for. His plan had taken another step forward.

Next up he contacted Mike Davies and Eddie Black to set up a meeting at the Grey Goose, the following evening at 7pm.

CHAPTER 43

Tianwan Nuclear Power Station

Han Bai yawned and looked at the wall clock, 11am; he had been on duty since 6am, seven hours of his twelve-hour shift left. As it always did the demand for electricity grew as the day progressed and the reactors would soon be operating at about 70% of their capacity. Cheng scrutinised the reactor status display on his monitor, his eyes widening when he saw how active the fusion reactors had become. He fingered the slider to lower the rods in Reactor One then paused to observe the output display, puzzled when he saw it continue to increase. If the current rate of increase continued, they would go critical within the next fifteen to twenty minutes.

Han had been a controller for three years. He had a goodly amount of experience, but was beginning to be seriously worried. He fingered the slider again, seeking to achieve maximum control rod insertion, horrified when it had no effect. The reactor's output continued to increase; the indicator bar was at the point of moving out of the green safety zone towards the red danger section.

He reached forward and buzzed the Chief Controller who answered immediately; Han hurriedly explained the situation and Jiang immediately slammed down his phone and left his office, running to the desk where Han was now on the verge of hysterics. Jiang reached forward and jiggled the slider to no avail; it had reached its limits. The reactor indicator arrow had entered the red section. In another ten minutes the reactor would be in a critical state and the situation irretrievable.

Jiang couldn't bring himself to raise the alarm and signal an evacuation, but he couldn't think of an alternative course of action. The red phone on the desk seemed to be staring at him and he knew he had to report the situation to Beijing, something he had never had to do in his career of twenty years.

Reluctantly he picked up the phone, glancing one more time at the indicator gauge. The arrow was a quarter of the way through the red section and still creeping upwards. He considered putting evacuation in progress but decided instead to report to the Director in Beijing.

It took a full five gut-wrenching minutes before his call was answered, by which time the needle was half way into the red danger zone. The Director, Xia was not his usual calm self and, before Jiang could even begin to explain the nature of his call, the Director shocked him by stating that the nuclear power stations at Taishan, Sanmin, Haiyan and Ningde were nearing critical. He informed Jiang that it appeared the control systems had been hacked by an outside source. Jiang was instructed to exercise his own judgement as to whether or not to instigate evacuation. The Director broke off the conversation to talk to his Deputy who was shouting something in the background. The phone went silent, and Jiang was left to his own devices. The arrow was now more than half-way into the red. There was nothing more he could do; Jiang reached past Han and activated the evacuation procedure. The power station filled with sounds of claxon horns in every corner of the building. Staff immediately went into panic mode and the scramble to the exits began.

The power station wasn't the only location in a state of high alert; an evacuation alert was automatically initiated in every community or village within a ten-mile radius of Tianwan. Evacuation had also commenced in Sanmin and Ningde. Local dwellers were in a state of frenzy, some gathering up possessions, others racing to their cars; schools and factories were being evacuated. People were terrified, they knew that radiation was a death warrant.

National Nuclear Power Station Control Centre, Beijing

Director Xia looked at Deputy Director Yao, fear etched in their expressions. They couldn't give advice; they didn't know what to do. The situation was unprecedented and completely out of control. Much of China was doomed. Two more phones were ringing; five power stations had reported their reactors were nearing critical status. Evacuations had been put in place, a disaster was in progress

At that moment he didn't realise that a further five power stations, Fuging, Yangjiang, Quinshan, Hongyanhe and Lufeng, had also been put on the path to critical condition.

All local controllers had been given the same advice by the National Director – Lower all control rods to maximum – Continue to observe reactor output gauge – Give order to evacuate only if absolutely necessary – Remain on station for further instructions.

Local controllers were cursing, trust the Centre to give useless advice and pass the buck - fuck them, they were miles away and not immediately at risk.

Beijing Central Headquarters.

President Jing Chen had been alerted to the power stations situation and had summoned every conceivable source of advice to his conference room; his best scientific, technical, computer, political and military advisors were all in attendance, thirty off them, plus administrative staff and of course his public relations people. News would get out and they would have to find a coat of gloss to put on this disastrous occurrence.

Heated discussions were in progress, questions were being asked all round the room, most of which couldn't be answered. The blame game began. It must be the West but who in particular? The military wanted to hit back but who and how. Everybody had an opinion but who was right.

The President banged on the table and achieved instant silence. He was very angry and it sounded in his voice. Gone was the enigmatic expression and soft tones. 'This is not a war it, is a potential disaster for our country.' I have eight questions requiring answers and **you**,' he waved his hand round the room, 'have to come up with the answers.'

1.   Who is responsible for hacking our Nuclear Power Stations?

2.   What is their motive?

3.   How many casualties will there be, power station staff and civilians?

4.   What areas of our country will be radioactive when the power stations explode, as they seem destined to do?

5.   How to we cope with the loss of the electrical power lost?

6.   What will be the effect on our Country's economy?

7.   What industrial, farming and environmental losses can we expect?

8.   What arrangements will have to be put in place to house and care for the evacuees?

When we know the answers to these questions, we can then decide what, if any, revenge we can take?

A sea of blank faces looked back. 'As I thought. You have no answers. We must instruct all power stations to evacuate immediately. The Army must start evacuating all affected areas.'

The Chief of the Army, Li, raised his hand. 'Evacuate to where comrade President?'

Jing reacted furiously. 'Start thinking for yourself, Li, use your fucking brain if you have one.' Gasps of astonishment went round the room; such a reprimand was unprecedented.

At that moment the President's personal red phone rang. Jing considered ignoring it but on reflection picked it up. Bad news or good news it had to be heard. He listened intently, nodding from time to time, a sigh of relief escaping from his lips. 'Keep me informed.'

Turning to his advisors he addressed them stonily. 'The reactors at Tiaman, Taishin and Sanman are still critical but are starting to slow down. Disaster might be averted. The situation seems to be returning to normal. It seems the hackers are sparing us a catastrophic ending.'

Tension in the room visibly eased, only a few whispered conversations ensued.

Jing stood, he had everyone's full attention. 'Everyone is to remain seated. No-one is to leave until we are certain all ten nuclear power plants have returned to normal.'

An hour passed, then another; there was little conversation; everyone was inwardly considering their answer to the President's question. Finally at 1.35pm Jing received the last of a series of calls confirming that normal operating conditions had been restored at all ten power stations.

'You may depart comrades, but you will all re-assemble in the Grand Meeting Room tomorrow morning at 8.00am. We will address the questions I raised earlier today. Those of you involved in public relations must do everything possible to prevent news of this incident getting to the Western media, though I fear your efforts will be in vain. Think long and hard comrades; we are dealing with an unknown enemy, perhaps the most powerful the world has ever seen.'

The Grand Meeting Room 8.00am the following morning.

Jing sat at the head of a large green marble table watching as his underlings took their place. The atmosphere was tense, most stared straight ahead, their expressions impassive. Few had slept well, all worried by what the morrow would bring; Jing did not readily forgive failure. Their careers were at stake maybe even their freedom.

The President invited his Head of Security to speak first.

'Comrade…. Comrade President,' his words stumbled out, 'we know that yesterday the controls of our nuclear reactors were hacked at 11am approximately. We know…'

Jing thumped the table. 'We all know what happened yesterday, Comrade. This is not a history lesson, tell us what you have found out that is new to our ears. Who was responsible for the attack?'

The unfortunate man bowed his head and mumbled 'We have not been able to determine who carried out the attack. We think that the attack may have been satellite initiated. We worked through the night and continue to investigate, comrade President. I humbly apologise for the inadequacy of my reply.'

Jing waved him to sit down and turned to the senior military representative. 'Comrade Marshall, have you been able to discover anything regarding these attacks?'

'No, comrade President, but we are certain this is an act of aggression by the West. All military services are on full alert and are preparing plans to revenge this blatant attack on our country.'

Jing frowned. 'And exactly who would you attack? Europe, the United States, India or perhaps the whole of NATO simultaneously? Your solution, it seems, would be to begin World War Three; don't be ridiculous. Have you devoted any resources to the formulation of an evacuation plan for all affected areas around all our nuclear power stations?'

'No, Comrade President. Surely we must avenge this…..'

Jing slammed his fists upon the table. 'You're excused, go back to your office and begin to formulate evacuation plans without further delay. Do you not recognise that a similar attack could take place at any time? Perhaps even as you sit here proposing a World War which would only add to our difficulties and do nothing to resolve our current crisis.'

The President then turned to his public relations team. 'Comrade Wen what is the Western media saying?

Wen shook her head sadly. 'The incident is headlined all round the world, Comrade President. The narrative is very accurate though they do not speculate as to who is responsible.'

The chief of the military, Marshall Lu, thumped the table. 'The West is well-informed because the West is responsible for this outrage. We must seek vengeance.'

Jing rose to his feet. 'I told you to leave Comrade Marshall, do so now and take all your military colleagues with you. That is an order.' Lu stared balefully at the President but knew better than to disobey. He nodded respectfully and signalled all his colleagues to follow.

Jing nodded at his PR Director to continue.

'Thank you, Comrade President. 'We have issued a statement confirming that there was a major cyber-attack which threatened our nuclear power stations. We stated that out security and technical staff had dealt with the interference within two hours and that the stations are now operating normally and safely. We declared that we have added additional security to prevent a similar attack in the future. We have also suggested that every country in the world should review the security of its nuclear power stations. I indicated that we would be happy to give assistance if requested. I trust this is satisfactory Comrade President?'

Jing nodded and gave a semblance of a smile. 'A worthy statement, thank you, Comrade Wen.' The young woman sat down. She knew her statement would be well received; she was after all, one of the President's mistresses and the statement had been prepared by him.

The President rose to his feet. 'The attack on our nuclear power stations was a warning; it is not a declaration of war. You will all continue to work on the questions I set out yesterday and we will gather here one month from today to report on progress. Our scientists will spare no expense in trying to determine how this attack was instigated. China must develop greater and better technology; our science must match and exceed those of other nations. We must not be left behind in. We must be able to respond to these technological threats or our entire future is hostage to those who have this unbelievable scientific capability at their disposal.'

Gibraltar Heights

Somerton had purchased a range of daily newspapers, British and American; his television had been on since 6 am and his desktop was set to Reuters. He wanted a broad range of opinion on the satellite attack. Every source had its expert, its retired ex-military commentator giving their view. Government officials worldwide were expounding what it meant for society.

The previous cyber-attacks were cited by some; links were made, theories given, some closer to the mark than others. Opinion agreed on one matter – whoever carried out the cyber-attack had the world's most dangerous weapon and was a potential danger to all. There were reports on You tube, Instagram, Twitter and other web sources that extra-terrestrials were preparing to raid Planet Earth.

Not for the first time in recent months, Somerton's thoughts were in turmoil. The same old paths were trod, the same old answers born again. *Armageddon or Valhalla, where was the World headed? Was it on a path to global peace and prosperity or was Doomsday approaching? Who was making the right call, the Overton-Kingston alliance or that of Kenny and Taylor?*

Somerton put in a call to the NRSC. 'Hi Eric, no prizes for guessing why I'm calling. What do we know about the latest cyber-attack?'

Barker sounded apologetic. 'In a word, Jack – nothing. We've been on the case since the news broke. It is satellite originated, that much we're certain of, but which of the thousands in orbit, we haven't a clue. We would have to be scanning the right area at the right time to have a chance of identifying it and that's unlikely to happen.'

'Keep on it; if anything turns up, even speculatively, let me know.'

Further calls to Cheltenham and his opposite numbers in the Five Eyes alliance brought similar responses. It was exactly what he expected and what he had hoped would be the case. He had to assume that Constellation MacKinnon, a recent arrival on the scene, would have been checked out by China and Russia. It was a new constellation and, due to the timing, would understandably be highly suspect. But not a single accusation had been made. Jupiter must have some means of screening the signal.

The House of Commons Later that day

Somerton saw that Taylor had a look of self-satisfaction when she took her seat on the Front Bench. *You love the headlines, don't you Laura?* She got a grilling when the Speaker called Prime Minister's Questions, but held her own. Somerton was also placed under pressure, especially by the Opposition, citing the cost of security investment, and yet he had no idea who had mounted the cyber-attack. His pride was hurt when one of the Opposition suggested that maybe he wasn't up to the job. He had leapt to his feet and pointed out that there wasn't a country in the world who knew who was responsible.

Taylor had winked at him as the left the Chamber and whispered. 'Well done, Jack, I think we won every round. I'm really looking forward to the Summit meeting now that we've demonstrated just how powerful our system is.'

Except that it's not OUR system, Laura, it belongs to the States with Jupiter its sole controller.

Grey Goose Pub Later that day

Burgers eaten, pints down, recent headlines explored, and chit-chat exchanged, the trio settled down to business, Somerton explained what he wanted of Mike Davies and Eddie Black. 'You'll be well rewarded when this is over. You can act individually, or jointly, agree your own detailed plan of action when you get there. Spend what you need; I have an American Express card for each of you and there's a couple of grand cash in each of these envelopes. I haven't booked flights or hotels; travel separately, use different airlines if possible and fly into different airports. Take every precaution, keep under the radar every step of the way.'

A few questions followed but Jack's tone was clear, nothing was to get in the way of the mission's achievement; in military terms, it was code red.

They had a final pint and toasted success before leaving, all three in a sombre mood.

CHAPTER 44

Outside the Grey Goose
The three men said their goodbyes. Somerton watched, as first Eddie and then Mike, were driven away; not for the first time thinking back to his SAS days when you knew your enemy, knew what your mission was and were confident about how it was to be achieved.

His taxi drew forward. 'Good evening, guvnor.' Somerton smiled and climbed in, settling comfortably into the back seat, automatically fastening his safety belt.

The driver looked over his shoulder. 'Where to, guv.'

Somerton fancied a bit of a walk to clear his head before he bedded down for the night. 'Anywhere near Grosvenor Square, I'd like a five-minute walk to stretch my legs.'

'Sounds like you've been celebrating?'

Somerton nodded, 'Sort off, just meeting friends and talking about old times.'

'Nothing better. I think I recognise you from somewhere, guv.'

'Could be, I'm an MP, Jack Somerton.'

'Gotcha, security wallah or something like that?'

'Got me in one.'

The driver touched his forehead. 'Right, we're on our way, I'll drop you off in Bolton Street and you can walk from there, it's not too far. I'll just call that in.'

Whether it was the food or the booze, or the stresses of the day, Somerton suddenly felt tired and closed his eyes; he would sleep well when he climbed into bed that night. Not for the first time his thoughts drifted to Chloe MacKinnon and his last trip to Washington. *Why, oh why did you have to be married to Colin. Oh Chloe, another time, another place and it could all have been so different.* He forced her out of his thoughts, she just couldn't be part of his life, not now, not ever but there was a part of him that just didn't want to accept that. *Don't yearn for the impossible, Jack. Oh Jack, oh Jack you might just have fallen in love.*

He opened his eyes and looked out of the cab; traffic was light even for that time of night. 'The roads seem quite tonight.' He offered the driver.

The cabbie nodded. 'Can't explain it, it's been quiet all day; you're only my fifth or sixth fare, usually I would expect double that number. I'm hoping it will get busier when the theatres and restaurants start to empty.'

Somerton glanced out, uncertain as to where he was, certainly across the river. The taxi slowed as the cabbie signalled and turned into a quiet residential street. Very few of the windows were illuminated, their absentee owners on their travels, or at home in their Middle or Far East mansions.

Random thoughts prompted by the rich neighbourhood flooded in. *How on earth did I, an abandoned child end up in Grosvenor Square? Not quite rags to riches, his adopted parents had been working class but comfortably off. And here I am a former SAS Major, a millionaire business man, a cabinet minister and now sharing control of a satellite system that has the potential to make the world a better place. And who knows, if I'm around long enough I might get a shot at being Prime Minister. And there was Chloe. Enough, Jack.'*

'Hello, what's he want?' The cabbie was slowing down, Somerton looked forward and saw a policeman step of the pavement, smiling, with hand raised, signalling the driver to pull over. 'What have you been up to, guv? This is a first time I've ever been pulled over.'

Somerton smiled and sighed, he just wanted to get home. 'Only one way to find out.'

The driver nodded and brought the cab to a halt. He rolled the window down. 'What's the problem constable?'

The copper was smiling broadly as he drew a pistol from his pocket. 'No problem at all man.' The cabbie's last action was to raise his eyebrows as he saw the gun. Two shots rang out, two bullets smashed into to the unfortunate cabbie's head, knocking him back into his seat. His life extinguished he toppled sideways onto the passenger seat.

Somerton threw himself to his left reaching desperately for the door handle, a reflex action, a waste of time but he had to try to escape his inevitable death. A shot rang out shattering the window the bullet slamming into the cab body just above his head. He grasped the door handle and pulled, surely the guy wouldn't miss a second time.

'You're wasting your time Somerton, there's no escape; death is on its way.' The accent was American, the tone calm, almost clinical.

Two more shots rang out in quick succession. Somerton flinched, this was it, two life-ending bullets but nothing…nothing. In disbelief he pushed himself up and turned to face the shattered window expecting to find himself looking at the barrel of a gun, and he was, except it wasn't in the hands of his attacker.

Instead, it was being held by a motorcyclist who was looking down at the body of the rogue policeman clutching his chest, blood frothing from his mouth. The motorcyclist pointed his gun at the dying man and fired another shot into the killer's head.

The motorcyclist raised his visor and, Somerton could see he was black. 'You OK Mr Somerton?' The accent, soft, another American, but this one spoke with genuine concern sounding in the voice.

Somerton thoughts were racing, an attempt on his life, why, who? How had they known where to find him? It looked like the cabbie, or somebody in the cab company, had to have been in on the ambush, but who was the paymaster? And his rescuer, his real-life guardian angel, how had he come by the same information?

His rescuer's voice broke into his thoughts. 'We should get out of here Mr. Somerton, they might have a back-up. Can I give you a lift to your place?'

Somerton was beginning to think rationally, he opened the door and got out of the cab. 'I owe you my life, how can I repay you. How come you knew about this attempt on my life?'

The motorcyclist shook his head, his face anguished. 'Difficult for me, Mr Somerton, I can't say too much; what I've done is an act of betrayal but I couldn't let you die. I'm in black ops and by chance overhead two of the team talking about coming to London to take you out before some big meeting. I don't know who gave the order but you can bet it's somebody very near the top. As soon as I heard, I took some leave and flew into Manchester ahead of them, hired the bike and set out for London. I couldn't risk flying into Heathrow, I had to cover my tracks best I can. I've watched your back for the last couple of days. I don't know who gave the order but whoever they are, they're very close to the White House.

He looked round anxiously. 'We really do have to get moving, there's another guy on the loose somewhere; you'll have to be very careful hereon. We really do have to get moving; get on the bike and we're out of here.'

Somerton shook his head. 'I'll have to call this in. I'll give you time to get clear; there's no way I could explain your presence. Best thing is for you to give me your gun and I'll sort this out. But I still owe you big time, I can't just not show my appreciation somehow. What's your name for a start? 'Do you have any idea who's behind this?'

'My name is Mike, Major Somerton but that's the only question I can answer; this is all well above my pay grade. You can have the gun, it's not traceable I assure you.'

'Thanks Mike, you saved my life one hundred per cent.' Somerton took the gun and made a note to clean of prints. 'Please, how can I begin to repay you, now or in the future, I can't just let you walk away.'

'Sorry Jack, you have to. Maybe sometime in the future our paths will cross again, but for now, I gotta go. In any case you don't owe me anything, you repaid me a long time ago in Africa You knew me as Mikki then. Without another word Somerton's rescuer pulled down his visor, revved up his motorbike and drove away.

Somerton thoughts spun backwards in time, to the Central African Republic, to the Vladic atrocity, settling finally on a young boy he'd rescued. *Mikki? Was it really you from all those years ago? A real-life fairy story.* He smiled briefly. Fate has an odd way of repaying its debts. Maybe the world isn't such a bad place after all.

Somerton cleared his thoughts, there were things to be done, first he used a tissue from a box in the cab and gave the gun a good wipe to clear away Mike's fingerprints. Next, he fired another shot into the back seat of the cab to make sure he had some gun residue on his hand in case he was tested. Finally, he phoned the Metropolitan Commissioner who he'd met on numerous occasions, and explained that an unknown, dressed as a police constable, had tried to assassinate him.

'I'd like a quick clean-up operation and I'm putting a D notice on this as of now. If you have to cover it up, blame it on an accident, a pedestrian hit by a taxi driver following a heart attack. Do whatever you think best I want this kept out of the media until I say otherwise. I'll be speaking to the PM when I'm gone from here.'

'Unconventional to say the least, Minister, but I'll comply with your wishes for now. Where exactly are you?'

'I'm in Bolton Street, very near Grosvenor Square where I live. I'm leaving the scene as soon as we finish our conversation. I have to start the process of finding out who's behind this and what their motive is. We'll speak later, in the meantime thank you for your co-operation.'

Before setting off, Somerton bundled his attacker into the back seat of the cab along with the gun he'd used. That done he hurried away, keen to get back to the sanctuary of his flat; he had some serious thinking to do. He had all the pieces but how did they fit together.

CHAPTER 45

Gibraltar Heights

Back in the relative safety and comfort of his flat Somerton poured himself a large whisky and switched on the TV, tuning into the news channel; he needed to be aware if the media had learned anything of the incident. It was only a matter of time until the information leaked out; Government departments were like a sieve. He needed to relax, clear his thoughts of the sheer shock of the attempt on his life. He wanted to figure out who was responsible. And how the taxi driver got involved, how come he was killed if he was complicit. Who had started the ball rolling…Jupiter, Laura Taylor or Will Kenny. Or perhaps even Ed Swanson?

'Ed Swanson?' Somerton voiced the name aloud. He instinctively trusted Ed, but it was routine for those undercover types to be plausible, no matter the situation, But Overton and Kingston trusted him and so did Chloe. *What a fucking mess.* Somerton glanced at the television as a breaking news banner appeared on the screen, relaxing again when he saw it wasn't relevant.

'Laura Taylor?' *Whether she trusts me I know not, but she seems to want me on board, for now at least. And she had seemed willing to be open about the clandestine aspects of UK-US relations. I've delivered everything she's asked for, so why have me bumped off, and why now? I doubt if you know about tonight's business Laura, but being realistic, you would go along with whatever Will Kenny required.*

Somerton poured another whisky and rolled the amber liquid around the glass sniffing the aroma before taking a goodly sip. *And that leaves the obvious suspect Will Kenny.*

'Will fucking Kenny.' Somerton almost shouted the name aloud. *I sensed you neither liked or trusted me right from our first encounter but why have me taken out now? And Jupiter, were you in on this? I don't know why, but somehow, I don't think you were. Are you being naïve, Jack?*

Somerton slugged down the last of his whisky and slammed down the glass. 'Fuck it, fuck it fuck it, who the hell can I trust.' He turned the television over to BBC World News and watched for the next thirty minutes letting all the angst slowly drain away. There was still no mention of the assassination attempt, the Chief Commissioner had been true to his word this far. Suddenly he felt drained, exhausted, events had taken their toll. *'Bedtime, Jack, time to hit the pillow; tomorrow's going to be interesting.'*

Next Morning

Somerton rose early and prepared his coffee and toast, then switched on the TV to check out the news, his heart sinking when he saw a banner headline slide across the screen **Taxi driver found dead in a London street.** Minutes later the announcer reported that the driver had been found late evening in a side street near Battersea Power Station. The whereabouts of his cab wasn't known and enquiries were ongoing. The BBC understood that he had died from a gunshot wound. The public were being asked to report any sightings of anything suspicious in the area and the driver's photo was displayed; a young bearded, blond, long-haired male. Somerton breathed a sigh of relief; the story hadn't leaked as yet. *'Poor sod, wrong time, wrong place, and all for nothing.*

Somerton picked up his red phone and dialled the Commissioner. 'Good morning, Commissioner, Jack Somerton.'

'Good morning, Minister. I'm guessing you've seen the news about the London taxi driver death and his missing taxi. Looks like he was hi-jacked on his way to pick you up, shot in the process and his vehicle stolen. It is the same taxi that was involved in the attempt on your life, so your cabbie was in on the attempt to assassinate you. Why he was killed is a matter of conjecture, most likely to eliminate the chances of him being caught and revealing all he knew about the plot. Neither the killer or the driver have been identified as yet. We've run their fingerprints and photos through our data base but so far, we haven't had any success. We'll involve Interpol and our American colleagues later today but it all risks the news getting out. The gunman does have a Stars and Stripes tattoo so he could well be a US citizen but it's hardly conclusive. The bullet that killed your taxi driver and the vehicle's owner were fired from the same gun. The bullet that killed your would-be assassin as you know was fired from the weapon you left in the taxi; it's standard US army issue but also used by many other services throughout the world.

'An associate of mine gave it to me a year or so ago, I do have a number of weapons from my SAS days and I am licensed to carry a firearm.'

'Hmm, well we're managing to keep this quite so far but I can't guarantee that news won't leak out sooner or later. Is there anything you would like to share with me at this time?'

Somerton hesitated briefly. 'I'm afraid not, Commissioner, sorry. I am making my own enquiries and I promise to report back with my findings. In the meantime, the D notice remains in place.'

The Commissioner sighed pointedly. 'That's disappointing, I'll respect your wishes for now but I reserve the right to consult the Prime Minister if I consider it necessary.'

'Of course, that's your prerogative, Commissioner. I will in fact be phoning Laura Taylor when I end this call. I'll sign of now if there's nothing else you want to raise. Your co-operation is appreciated I assure you.'

Somerton pursed his lips and reflected on the conversation, *Progress of sorts I suppose, now who do I call next? Laura or Jupiter?* His decision made Somerton moved over to his computer and keyed in his Jupiter code. A few minutes elapsed and he was on the point of giving up when the screen lit up. Jupiter looked worse than ever, skeletal, haggard, exhausted, the expression on his face crestfallen, down heartened; a beaten man.

Somerton was shocked. 'My God, Jupiter, sorry to say it, but you look worse than ever. What's happened to you, if this is a bad time, I can phone later?'

Joseph Svetinsky sighed, shook his head. 'I haven't slept well recently. My immune system or lack of it is playing up, I'm not in a good place. Can you be brief please, there's things I have to do, sorry.'

'I'm sorry to hear that, I hope you can get back to your best soon. I will come straight to the point. Someone tried to kill me last night, most likely an American Special Services operative.

My taxi driver was shot and killed. Fortunately, I was armed and was able to kill my attacker. We're trying to identify my would-be assassin but haven't been able to do so up to now. I know you tap into political conversations everywhere, and I'm certain this was a well-planned, politically motivated operation. Have you picked up anything in recent days?

Jupiter's mouth dropped open, he shook his head, 'Kill you? Who on earth would want to kill you, Jack. You have my word that I have no wish to kill you and would have refused any attempt to involve me. What motive could I possibly have? I would have warned you if I had been aware that you were in any sort of danger, I swear. Please believe me. I haven't heard of any threat to your life. I do listen in on a lot of conversations, but I haven't got access to every single one that takes place. And for that matter I don't have the time to screen all those that I am able to record.'

Jupiter sounded genuine, clearly alarmed by the situation; Somerton was inclined to believe him. 'I believe you but someone wants me out of the picture and the most likely suspects are Will Kenny or Laura Taylor because I know so much.'

Jupiter shook his head. 'I make a point of listening in on their conversations and neither has spoken of having you executed. I would admit though that the President doesn't like you much, and doesn't trust you to follow orders. He sees you as a bit of a maverick and he's probably right about that. Laura Taylor always defends you but given their close relationship I'm sure she would comply with Kenny's wishes.'

Somerton nodded. 'I can't argue with that assessment, thanks for the run down. Can I ask that this conversation remains strictly between us, please?'

Jupiter nodded. 'You have my word, Jack. And Jack, for what it's worth, I don't trust Will Kenny. I really must go I'm feeling extremely unwell.'

The screen went blank before Somerton could respond. He sat back and pondered on his next move. *If I phone Laura, and she's involved she'll lie and deny, and if she isn't involved lots of questions will follow. Either way she'll immediately get in touch with Will Kenny. I'm vulnerable no matter what I do. If Kenny is pulling the strings, he'll surely know the operation had failed;*

his operative not having reported back. Who knows he might be arranging a follow-up attack at this very moment. It was time to meet up with Laura Taylor.

Prime Minister's Office

'Good morning, Jess, I wondered if I might have a few minutes with Laura, it's important?'

'She's got one of the civil service mandarins with her but shouldn't be much longer if you're happy to hang around for a bit. I'll buzz her and let her know you're here.'

That done she smiled and nodded. 'She'll see you shortly. I think she welcomed the interruption, gives her an excuse to conclude the meeting…not a happy one methinks.'

A few minutes passed and a forlorn-looking woman exited Taylor's office not glancing left or right, clearly mission not accomplished. Somerton got the nod from Tate and made his way into the PM's office.

'Sorry to interrupt, Laura but it is important. Who was Miss Cheerful.

'Oh, she's second in line to Sir Wilbur Smythe at the Foreign Office, claims she's being bullied. I'll get the Cabinet Office to look into it and report back. What can I do for you, Jack?

'I'm not sure you can do anything but I felt you ought to be aware there was an attempt on my life late yesterday, not far from where I live in Grosvenor Square. I was travelling home after a meal out with friends.'

Taylor looked stunned, her face creased, with what looked like genuine concern, eyes wide open. She looked shocked. 'But why? How? Who? The questions flew out of her lips. Who would want to kill you, Jack? Someone from your past, I suspect you've made a few enemies in times gone by? And how come I'm only hearing about it now?'

Somerton explained how he had put a news black-out in place whilst he investigated, and went on to fill Taylor in on the detail. Taylor listened intently her eyes widening again when he recounted the American connection.

'Your attacker was American? Surely not, they're our allies, I can't believe anyone in the States would be responsible. But one thing is for sure, henceforth you will have security in attendance when you leave this building and an armoured chauffeur driven car. I don't want any arguments from Jack Somerton, ex SAS major, those days are by. So that's the deal, either accept it or resign.'

Somerton grinned from ear to ear. 'Yes ma'am, whatever you say ma'am. I bet the media will have a bit of fun when they find out I'm being wet-nursed. but thank you for your concern, Laura it's appreciated.' Somerton stood to go. 'I was wondering if you would authorise me to carry a gun? I have one in my flat but haven't carried it on duty.'

Taylor smiled. 'I won't ask if you need any training, just be careful, Jack, I need you on my team. Things are hotting up; the top-level meeting isn't far ahead and I want you there. And by the way, I think I'd like to raise this matter with Will Kenny. How do you feel about that, especially with the American connection? He might be able to help.

Somerton nodded. 'Sure, no problem. I'll be interested to hear what he has to say.' He made his way over to the door turning back to face Taylor. 'The thought just occurred to me; you don't think Kenny could have anything to do with the incident; I don't think he likes me very much?'

Taylor frowned. 'Don't be ridiculous, Jack, Will would never do anything like that.'

Somerton shrugged. 'Have it your way, though I'd bet he wouldn't hesitate to take me out if he thought I was being obstructive.'

Taylor waved her hand dismissively. 'Go away, Jack, you're in fantasy land. If Will Kenny had any concerns about you, he'd come to me to resolve them.'

CHAPTER 46

JFK Airport New York; Early morning

Eddie Black's cousin, Finn Causton was waiting in Arrivals to greet him when he landed. It had been around fifteen years since they last met up, but even from a distance Eddie could see that Finn hadn't changed much in the passing years. His tall, muscular frame and mop of wild curly ginger hair distinguished him from those around him. He was dressed casually, jeans and a dark green roll neck sweater.

The two men shook hands. 'Great to see you, Eddie, it's been a long time.' His accent American, there was no trace of his Irish origins.

Black nodded. 'I reckon it's at least fifteen years; both of us were on active service when we last met. I still miss the excitement of those days.'

Causton smiled. 'They were good times, but I can't say I miss them; family life has brought its own rewards. Let's go and get a coffee, I know this is a flying visit, no pun intended.'

The two men settled down in a corner of Starbucks, reminiscing about times past and discussing Causton's family. 'You never married, Eddie, it's the best thing I ever did. I can recommend it.'

Black smiled. 'I'm pleased to hear it, Finn; I was never motivated to marry. I'm a loner at heart and never met a woman to make me change my mind.'

'You don't know what you're missing, fella.'

Black laughed, 'You're beginning to sound like you're running a marriage bureau. Down to business if you don't mind me pressing on; my schedule is quite tight. Have you been able to help me out?'

Causton nodded and produced a key from his pocket. 'The cabinet number is 289, in the luggage storage area in Grand Central Station. You'll find what you want in the package; it's ex-army and non-traceable. I don't need to know why you want it and I don't want it returned. Dispose of it safely and don't ever mention it again. OK?'

'Sounds perfect, Finn. I owe you one. I might need wheels; is there anybody you would recommend?'

Causton shook his head. 'Sorry, Eddie, I'm not into this kind of stuff. I left it all behind when I married Mollie.'

Black nodded. 'A sensible decision, though I still get a kick out of going on a mission. I'm not sure I'll need them anyway.'

'I don't suppose I could persuade you to come back with me to meet Mollie?'

Black shook his head. 'Best keep clear water between us on this trip in case it goes pear-shaped. Definitely next time, I promise.'

Causton shrugged. 'I'll hold you to it. Good luck with whatever you're up to, Eddie. It looks like it's not going to end well for somebody. Let's go, I'll walk you out and you can choose taxi, bus or rail into the centre, the choice is yours.'

Outside the two men said their goodbyes and Black handed him an envelope with a thousand dollars in it. 'Buy Mollie some flowers and the kids a teddy bear.'

'There's no need, Eddie.'

'I know, Finn, I know.'

Black opted for a yellow cab and asked to be taken that New York landmark, the Empire State Building. After he was dropped off, Black wandered around like any other tourist for an hour or so then booked himself into a hostel explaining that he wasn't sure how long he'd be in town. His first priority was to freshen up. A quick shave followed by a cool shower and a change of clothing and he felt renewed. Ready for business, he removed a briefcase from his suitcase then made his way out. From a nearby bookshop, he purchased a map of New York and found 4th Steet North; it was a fair walk, but he needed the exercise. Fortunately, he had taken a sleeping tablet and had slept soundly on the flight over. He felt no trace of tiredness.

Forty-five minutes later he walked past number 125, 4th Street North, appraising the apartment block as he went. Just twelve floors high it was relatively small for the area. He walked on for five minutes or so then crossed the road and walked back the way he had come to the apartment block. He took a small packet addressed to Joey Moran from his pocket and walked confidently into the lobby. As expected, there was a multi-letterbox rack serving the block. Each box was labelled with the flat and floor number, and the names of the occupants. A quick scan and he found who he was searching for, Messrs Moran and Sweeney. They occupied the pent house flat on the top floor. Predictably there was a staircase and an elevator. Black smiled when a quick look round didn't reveal a CCTV camera; its absence reduced the risk. His survey complete he crumbled up the envelope and put it in his pocket; it had served its purpose and was now destined for a waste bin when the opportunity arose.

Black checked his map and set off on his walk to Grand Central Station, one of New York's most iconic buildings. He admired the architecture as he made his way across the concourse, all the time trying to recall the names of films involving the remarkable edifice. The left luggage cabinets were in a quiet area of the station and there was nobody else in the area. He quickly found number 289 and removed the brown paper package, mildly surprised at how much it weighed. He promptly slipped into his briefcase, smiling to himself at how smoothly everything had progressed so far.

He was about to exit the Station when hunger pangs struck, and he realised he hadn't eaten for hours. *Now, what shall I have? I'm in the Big Apple so it has to be a local delicacy; you must have a burger Eddie, nothing but the best for you.* He called in at a café on the park's perimeter and studied the menu, somewhat overcome by the range on offer. 'Just a single tier beef burger with onions please and a dash of barbecue sauce. And a black coffee, one shot only.'

'A limey eh, over on holiday. We get a lot of you guys over here. There you go, enjoy the burger, best in the business though I say it myself. Coffee coming up straight away. You from London?'

Black nodded.

'I love that city, been there a few times. Have you met the Queen?'

Black smiled. 'Not recently she's been busy lately.'

'Yeah, I guess so. Here's your coffee.'

He studied his map and opted to head for the lake in the centre of Central Park. It wasn't long before he was wandering along the path to the water, all the time, marvelling at how quickly the noise of traffic died away. He glanced up at the clear blue sky thinking how lucky he was with the weather and comfortably warm temperature. He settled on the first bench he came across and sat for a moment looking at the stretch of water, idyllic. It was all so very much at odds with his reason for being in New York. *You must visit again soon Eddie.*

His hunger sated he made his way back to his hotel; there was nothing more to be done except wait. Everything was in place for what he had to do, just one thing to be checked. He tore open the package Finn had left for him at Grand Central. There it was, a Smith and Wesson SW22, and a loaded magazine, ten rounds magazine. As he had requested, there was a silencer. Black smiled, a feeling of satisfaction creeping over him; all that stood between him and his mission was the passage of time. He laid down on the bed and used the remote to switch on the TV; a quick roll through the channels and he settled on an old black and white favourite, the Maltese Falcon starring Humphrey Bogart.

It wasn't long before his eyes started to close; next he knew his wristwatch was vibrating, 7pm, time to get on the move.

Cousin Finn had carried out some surveillance on his behalf and established that Moran and Sweeney were in residence and not off on another of their undercover missions. Other than that, nothing was known about their routines. Black reasoned that like most people they would go to bed at night and get up in the morning, so 6pm to 6am was his operational time frame. He'd give it till 8pm then set out to pay them a visit.

It was around 9.15 when he climbed the stairs of 125North 4th Street, having first checked from street level that the lights were on in the top floor flat. He held two large pizza boxes in his left hand, the SW22 with silencer fitted, in his right hidden under the boxes. He rang the doorbell and waited; seconds later he heard footsteps and the door was opened by Joey Moran.

Moran looked at the boxes and shook his head. 'Sorry, wrong flat buddy.' Black pulled the trigger twice and Moran fell to the floor clutching his chest. Black nodded appreciatively at the gun's minimum recoil, then stepped into the corridor and closed the door quietly. He put the pizza boxes on the floor and waited for Sweeney to appear but gave up after a minute. The television was issuing forth a ball game commentary from a room on his left and he eased forward quickly through the open door, frowning when he saw it was empty.

He made his way along the corridor, the SW22 held ready. The first room on his left was a study come games room, to his right a kitchen-diner – both empty. Next on his right was a closed door to which he pressed his ear – silence. Next two doors to his left and right were open, both were bedrooms. Cautiously he edged forward and stole a quick glance around the room on the left – empty. He immediately swung round and stepped into the room on the right, finger on the trigger, swearing when he saw it was empty. *The bastard must be out, fuck it.*

He was resigned to waiting for Sweeney to return when he saw the clothes laid out on the bed and reasoned that his next victim might be in the bathroom. Moving forward he pressed his ear to the door, smiling when he heard the shower running. *Enjoy your last few moments, you'll be a nice clean boy when they put you in a body bag.* His mind conjured up the shower scene from Alfred Hitchcock's Psycho and he pondered on entering. *Don't be a meanie, let the poor sod enjoy his last moments, Eddie.*

Black sat on the bed, taking in the classy décor, the silk bedcover, the luxurious carpeting. *Hmm, you must be big earners. You'll miss this place when you end up in Hell. Come on for fuck's sake, you must be a sweaty bastard.* Five more minutes passed, and Black was again considering going in when the door opened.

Chris Sweeney stepped out, naked, gasping in surprise when he saw Black sitting on the bed. 'Who the fuck are you?' Then he saw the gun and knew he wouldn't be getting an answer. Black pulled the trigger and shot Sweeney in the gut, only wanting to maim, not kill. Sweeney slumped to the floor, kneeling, clutching his tummy, blood oozing through his fingers, disbelief on his face.

Black stepped towards him. 'You asked who I was. The name's Black, Eddie Black.' A pair of agonised eyes gazed at him, a mouth trying to form words.'

Black smiled. 'You don't know me, but you knew an ex-SAS colleague of mine, the late Alan Croudace. Remember the name? The guy you two goons mowed down in London. Well, this is come-back time, final curtains for you. I'm sure you know how we ex-army mates stick together. I wish I had time; I'd gladly watch you die slowly, painfully, but I'm in a bit of a hurry.'

Sweeney tried to say something but only blood bubbled from his mouth.

Black smiled wickedly. 'Sorry, you'll need to speak up, I didn't catch that; cat got your tongue? Goodnight sunshine, rest in Hell.' Black pushed the gun forward into Sweeney's mouth and pulled the trigger, unmoved by the bone and brain fragments that scattered into the wall behind.

Black returned to the corridor where Moran lay lifeless, blood pooling on the floor. He was gone, no need to waste another bullet. He grabbed hold of Moran's collar and towed him along the corridor and into the bedroom where he laid him alongside Sweeney. He carefully inspected himself for blood spatter, satisfied when none was visible. No doubt a forensic team could find some with their scientific paraphernalia, but they would they would need to find his clothing, and it was going back to London. In a TV drama they always got lucky but, in real life it was unlikely at best.

There was just one more task to complete; turn of all lights and appliances. With that done the recently deceased duo wouldn't be discovered for days.

Black gathered up the Pizza boxes then looked through the peephole in the door to ensure the landing was clear before stepping out, then started down the staircase to the ground floor, fingers crossed, hoping that he didn't meet anyone coming in the opposite direction. He strode purposefully through the empty entrance and onto the relative safety of the pavement. He took a circuitous route back to the hostel, constantly on the lookout for a large-wheeled rubbish bin in a back street. It wasn't long till he came across one where he dumped one of the pizza boxes containing the SW22. In similar fashion, a few streets away he was able to dispose of the silencer inside the other pizza box.

Back at the hostel, the young woman in reception bade him welcome. 'Did you have a nice evening, Sir?'

Black smiled. 'Lovely thank you, nothing special, just a walk around the area looking at the late-night shops.'

She nodded in agreement. 'I like a bit of window-shopping myself, never buy much mind you. Sleep well, Sir. See you in the morning; my name's Millie if you need anything.'

He had had a shower as soon as he got into his room then, put the clothes and shoes he had worn in a plastic bag he had brought for the purpose. When he got back to London he would launder and dispose of everything.

Next morning

Black studiously watched the local morning news just to be sure that, by some fluke, the bodies hadn't been discovered. He texted Somerton and Davies, no words, just an emoji thumbs up, well after all, he *was* enjoying his trip to New York.

His return flight was scheduled for early evening so he had time to kill. He took another stroll in Central Park and visited Macey's and other large department stores in the area, grazing here and there when he felt hungry. He rounded the day off with a walk along Fifth Avenue looking at the signs advertising the Broadway shows, wishing he'd had time to see one.

All good things come to an end, and the time came to head back to the hostel to collect his suitcase which he'd left in reception. Millie was there and he asked her to call a cab to take him to the airport.

'It'll be here in a couple of minutes, it's not far away.' She wished him a safe journey back to London. 'You mind and come back sometime soon, Sir.' Her smile was radiant, the invite sounded genuine, practice makes perfect. He gave her a generous twenty dollars tip and made his way out to the cab she had called for him.

Washington.

Mike Davies had flown into Washington on Saturday evening, his mission an easy one by comparison with Eddie Black's. He was simply a middleman. He had to hire a car at the airport and go straight to his hotel then await a text that would tell him where to rendezvous with a third party the following day. He would drive there, meet the carrier, collect the package and drive to another location to meet up with his contact later the same day, maybe as late as 10pm. That done, his mission would be over, and he would be free to spend a few days in Washington, drive on somewhere or return home. Somerton hadn't told him what was in the package and he knew better than to ask.

The programme went exactly to plan. The parcel, which he judged weighed 4 to 5 kilos, was handed over to the unknown contact at 10.20pm in a back street near Rose Park. The two men spoke only to say state an security code to identify themselves; Davies thought the guy seemed tense, on edge even, but that was no concern of his.

He spent the next three days in glorious sunshine and it was with some reluctance he left the city behind when he flew out of Dulles on an overnight flight back to London.

CHAPTER 47

Somerton's Parliamentary Office Tuesday

Somerton was working through some draft Bills when Laura Taylor breezed in unannounced, closely followed by Reggie Marsh, who was grimacing an apology, and spreading his hands in resignation.

'Good morning, both. Grab a seat and make yourself comfortable. Can I get you a tea or a coffee, health drink, pick-me-up, pinch of snuff, anything to keep you happy?'

'Nothing thanks, Jack. I won't take up much of your time, I promise.' She looked round at Marsh. 'You can leave us.' To his credit, Marsh ignored her and pointedly looked at Somerton for confirmation.

Somerton handed him some papers. 'Read through these papers for me, Reggie. Mark up anything significant or needs changing, please. See you later.'

Marsh took the proffered papers, gave a not-too-friendly smile to Taylor. 'Prime Minister.'

Taylor watched him leave and close the door. 'What's his name?'

'Reggie Marsh, a very bright young man, a budding MP, knows more about politics than I ever will. Definitely one for the future; proud to have him as my right-hand man.'

Taylor pursed her lips. 'Hmm, seemed a touch offish to me.'

Somerton raised his eyebrows. 'He's protecting me from intrusive visitors, not that I'm suggesting you're intrusive.' Somerton smiled sweetly. 'I wouldn't get by without him, but he's not the subservient type if that's what you're getting at. He knows his own mind, something I encourage. I've got no time for yes men or women.'

Taylor sniffed and shrugged. 'If you say so, Jack. I'm here regarding our forthcoming meeting. As far as the media and Parliament is concerned, I'm describing it as a meeting to discuss global security issues of joint US-UK interest with our opposite numbers. I will not make it known that our military chiefs will also be attending. You and I will fly out in the Queen's Flight; separate arrangements will be made for the others.'

'In other planes, I hope, at least two others, three if necessary.'

'That's hardly environmentally friendly.'

'Don't go all Green on me Laura, please. My advice is the old adage, don't put all your eggs in one basket. If the aircraft went down, or there was a terrorist incident, you would lose the cream of British military, think of what happened to friend Rostov.'

'I suppose you have a point.' Taylor conceded reluctantly. 'I'll think about it.'

'Are you going to tell me precisely who will be joining us on this momentous occasion?'

Taylor shook her head. 'No, you'll find out when you get there. We will be picked up from Downing Street on Friday and fly out of Mildenhall at 08.30. I'd like you to join me at 6.30, to allow for any traffic problems. We will stay at the White House on Friday night and be driven to the venue on Saturday We will set out at 10.00 next morning. I'm told the journey takes about an hour.'

Somerton jotted down the times. 'And what format will the meeting take?'

'As host, President Kenny will Chair the meeting and make the opening remarks, then make a short presentation. My presentation will follow. After that, everyone present will be invited to respond to whatever Will and I have to say. Everybody will be invited to make their own vision statement of what might be achieved when the satellite system is fully operational. Well done with the China business, by the way. I think Jing Chen and the whole world got the message.'

Somerton smiled broadly. 'Agreed 100%, all credit to Jupiter, he's a genius. I hope to meet him face to face at the meeting. He will be there, I assume?'

Taylor looked as though she was about to say something, hesitated, then changed her mind. 'He certainly is a genius but I'm not sure if he'll be invited to the meeting which is about policy, not science. Have you got your statement ready?'

Somerton nodded. 'Personally, I think he should be there and get credit for all he's achieved. Yes, to your question, just a few finishing touches to make. It's more of a presentation than a speech. It'll all be on my laptop when the time comes.'

Taylor drew a sharp breath. 'Oh sorry, Will has beefed up security for this meeting, you won't be able to take your personal laptop into the meeting room. This is the first time all the key players have got together and he's being super-cautious. He doesn't want to risk anyone making a recording of the proceedings.'

'I guess that's sensible, but I have some diagrams and maps I planned to refer to.'

Taylor smiled. 'I'm sure others will have similar intentions. Put your stuff on a flash drive. There will be a laptop allocated to everyone attending. They will all be wireless linked to a large screen and speakers; I'm sure you won't have a problem. You'll probably have to give up your flash drive for security reasons before you leave.'

Somerton nodded. 'That sounds fine, I always respect good security.'

Taylor stood. 'I'll go now, Jack. See you in the Commons later.' She moved to the door and was about to exit when she turned back. 'Did you pick up on that incident in Washington?'

Somerton looked blank. 'I don't really follow American news. What incident?'

'Two ex-marines shot dead in their flat. Seems they've lain around for days.'

Somerton shrugged. 'I'm surprised it made the news; shootings are ten a penny in the States.'

'I guess so, just wondered if you've heard.'

Somerton shook his head. 'Wouldn't have caught my interest, I'm surprised you got to hear of it. Any motive suggested? Robbery? Revenge?'

Taylor shook her head. 'Will mentioned it to me; he didn't put forward any motive. I'll go now and leave you in peace.'

Somerton watched her make her exit. *Testing me again Laura. I'm beginning to think you and your friend Kenny don't trust me. I wonder why that is?*

He buzzed for Reggie Marsh to join him.

Somerton motioned him to take a seat.

'Nothing wrong, is there Jack?' Marsh sounded worried.

'Everything is just fine, Reggie. I just wanted to say how very impressed I've been with your efforts, especially given our shaky start. You've provided invaluable assistance to me; you know more about Harrow East and our Party's politics than I ever will. I doubt if I could do my job without your support. I've been singing your praises to the PM.'

Marsh gulped. 'Gosh, thanks Jack. That's really kind of you, totally unexpected.'

Somerton leaned back in his chair. 'I'm off to the States with the PM on Friday; a top-level security gathering. I've got a lot of preparation to do; I want to make sure I impress our American cousins. In my absence, I want you to handle all my meetings until I get back on Monday. In fact, keep your diary clear all next week; I just don't know what might come out of this meeting. I know you must be busy, there seems to be a lot of constituency mail around these days, most of it pretty petty. I don't know how you manage to be so placatory sometimes.'

Marsh nodded. 'It's not a bad sign, Jack. Get things done and people come to you, it's as simple as that. It's our loyal voters that keep us in our jobs.'

'If that's the case Reggie, it's mostly down to you. Thanks again for all your help. I have nothing else I want to bring up so I'll let you go and get on with *my* work. I feel certain you have a good future ahead of you.'

The business of the day went well but Somerton's thoughts invariably drifted off to the forthcoming meeting. *Who would be there? What would they be putting forward about the future of the world? What part would he have in that new world? Did Kenny and Taylor trust him?*

His phone buzzed with an incoming text from Mike Davies who had just flown into Heathrow. *The eagle has landed.* Somerton smiled. *You've got a great team around you, Jack.* He replied with a text to Davies and Eddie Black. *How about a meal out with me tomorrow night? Meet me at Chateau Pierre, 8pm, my treat.*

Mike Davies responded immediately. *Can't refuse if you're paying.* Eddie Black's reply followed soon after. *Will report for duty as requested, Major.*

Somerton responded with a simple smiling emoji.

Chateau Pierre Wednesday.
Somerton, Davies and Black sat around a circular table in a private room, a bottle of Dom Perignon on ice and two bottles of Mouton Rothschild at the ready.

'Gosh, you're pushing the boat out, Jack. What's brought this on? Davies sipped the champagne appreciatively.

'It's long overdue guys You're my closest mates, you've never let me down, you're always there when I need you.'

Black grimaced. 'You're sounding soppy, Jack, I'm worried about you. You're not coming down with something nasty, are you?'

Somerton laughed. 'Not as far as I know. Your recent visits to America went well and I just wanted to say thanks.'

Black was dismissive. 'We're all SAS, Jack, as close as brothers as makes no difference. And anyway, apart from that, you've always looked after us very well.'

Somerton nodded. 'Maybe but no more that you deserve. Metronos wouldn't have been a success without your input over the years. Technical and financial expertise I can always buy at market rate but not those grey undercover projects that you guys had to undertake. With regards to Metronos, I've decided to sell the business; I'm finding life too busy now that I'm one of Her Majesty's Ministers of State. I have insisted though that you two remain on the books as consultants for the next two years at £100.000 per annum. You'll be paid via an off-shore account so there won't be any tax on earnings.'

Both men were stunned. Davies spoke first. 'I'm surprised you're selling up but appreciate that your political commitments must take priority. Another couple of years and I'll be past my sell by date anyway, so suits me. Can't speak for Eddie though.'

Black raised his glass. 'Suits me. Here's to you, Jack. We'll always be around if you need us, whether we're on the books or not.'

The trio clinked glasses. 'Anything to report on your U.S visits?'

Davies grinned and responded. 'What an arduous mission it was, can't tell you how fucking hazardous it turned out. I collected a parcel. I delivered a parcel. It pushed me to my limits. It was a piece of cake Jack. Are you going to tell us what was in the parcel?

'Nope. And what about you, Eddie?'

Black took a large sip of Champagne then gave a step-by-step account of his assignment. Just four pulls on the trigger, a dawdle, Jack.'

Somerton nodded. 'Well done, I'm sure it wasn't quite that simple.'

Davies chipped in. 'More fun than my boring little escapade. Just a pity you didn't take the second bastard out before he had his shower.'

Black frowned. 'What are you getting at?'

'Well, it would have been better for the environment. All that hot water wasted. Think green next time.'

Eddie Black sat back. 'And you and Laura are off to the States again, for another meeting, nudge nudge, wink wink. Tell me honestly, Jack, are you bedding the Prime Minister?'

'No, I'm not.' Somerton protested. 'Not that I would turn down the opportunity. I think her heart is with Will Kenny, though I don't know for sure. It's a meeting about global security and that's all I can tell you. Now let's cut the business chat and get some food on the table.'

He pressed a buzzer on the table, impressed when a waiter entered room almost immediately and orders were duly placed. Two hours later, Somerton settled the bill and the three friends got up from the table, their smiles a little floppy. Somerton put his arms around their shoulders.

'Great evening, guys. Tell you what, let's all go to the Grey Goose for a pint, what say you?'

Davies blinked. 'OK with me, what about you Eddie?'

Black nodded. 'I'm always up for a pint. What's brought this on Jack, you're not emigrating, are you?'

Grey Goose Pub

Andy Swift was washing glasses when the trio walked in. 'Just clearing up, guys, it'll be one pint only'

Somerton nodded. 'Understood, Andy. Pull one for yourself, join us if you like.'

'I'll put the drink behind the bar for another time and carry on with clearing up tonight's debris. Hope you don't mind?'

Twenty minutes and two pints later, Andy Swift ushered them out. Three very merry men stood on the pavement chattering until three taxis arrived to take them home.

Gibraltar Heights.

It was a very woozy Jack Somerton that flopped down for his night's sleep, forgetting to check, or maybe incapable of checking, his computer for incoming mail.

He woke next morning shortly after 6 am with a thumping headache; his first port of call the loo quickly followed by two Alka Seltzer tablets. His coffee and slice of toast weren't well received. *Serves you right, Jack, you overdid it last night.* He gave up on his breakfast and decided to check his computer for emails. The monitor livened up immediately and Jupiter appeared on the screen. Somerton was once again shocked at his appearance; cheeks drawn, eyes half-closed, complexion sallow. 'My God, Jupiter, what's happened to you? You look at death's doorstep.'

Jupiter nodded. 'My immune system's giving up, I haven't got long to go. I tried to contact you last night.'

'Sorry, I was out with friends. You should have tried my mobile.'

Jupiter shook his head. 'I needed you in front of your computer, there's something I want to show you on the screen.'

Somerton shook his head. 'Forget that for the moment. You need to be in hospital getting treatment. Business can wait, nothing is that urgent.'

Jupiter smiled wryly. 'A hospital is no use to me, Jack; my immune system has gone past the point of no return. I've done all I can for it, I'm near the end of the road, believe me. I'll likely be gone before this day is out, tomorrow at the latest.'

Somerton was shocked but felt a touch of sadness. 'Whatever our differences, I'm truly sorry it's come to this. The girls got you a black mark but world owes you a great debt; your inventions have changed the course of history. You are the greatest genius ever known to man. I was hoping to meet you face to face one day.'

Jupiter managed a weak smile. 'Thank you, Jack. I wanted to meet you too. I was looking forward to your trip over here this coming weekend but I can't see me being around.' Jupiter suddenly clutched his heart, staggered, and drew a deep breath. 'I'm going to take you on a little tour, there's something you must see.'

Jupiter must have switched on a CCTV camera; the screen filled with him walking towards a door where he swiped a card. A bank vault type door swung open and beyond Somerton could see a line of six huge computers to Jupiter's right and a wall of screens to his left.

'What am I looking at.'

Jupiter smiled. 'This is the real Jupiter; this is my back-up brain. What it knows, I know. These are six hyper-quantum computer processors; they are my eyes and ears, my satellite controllers. Artificial Intelligence, Jack, the world's future; we're years ahead of any other nation on this planet but we're only scratching the surface of their ability to help mankind.'

'So why show me now, why these revelations?'

Jupiter shook his head and sighed deeply. 'I'm worried, Jack. I really was sincere about what I told Colin long ago. I trusted the UK more than any other nation; you seemed to have learned the lessons of Colonialism, but now I'm not so sure. I've heard some disquieting statements made by both Kenny and Taylor. I may be wrong, but I have great concerns.

'The satellite system has great potential but only in the right hands. I'm no longer confident that this is the case. It will be something for you to judge after your forthcoming meeting; I'm putting all my faith in you to do the right thing.'

Jupiter drew a long deep breath, clearly struggling to go on. 'I'm going to switch the satellite system off and give you a start-up code. Make a note of it now before it's too late. With this code you will have sole control over access.'

Somerton lifted his mobile. 'Go ahead.' Jupiter gave Somerton a sixteen-digit code, a mix of letters, symbols and numbers.

'Be careful if you have to use the code, Jack; it will accept only three failed attempts after which it will destroy itself irreparably. Read it back to me, please.'

Somerton read back the code as requested,

Jupiter nodding as he went along. 'Perfect. The future of our planet is now in your hands, Jack, good luck. I'm going now; this might be our last meeting.'

'Wait. Before you sign off don't you think I should have the deactivation code as well?'

Jupiter thought briefly. 'Of course, forgive me, I'm not thinking clearly.' He gave Somerton the deactivation code, all the time clutching his heart. When the exchange was complete, Jupiter sighed deeply. 'I'm going to close the system down now.'

Somerton looked on whilst Jupiter ran his fingers over a keyboard, clearly entering a series of instructions. One by one the lights on the computers went out, screens went blank.

'That's it, the Constellation MacKinnon is just a communication system now. Goodbye Jack.'

'Jupiter, I'm gutted, thank you for all you've done. The world is a better place for your inventions. I promise to do what's best.'

The screen went blank.

Somerton sank back in his chair, saddened and afraid; afraid of what lay ahead. He had the codes; he was probably the most powerful man in the world, but the system was five thousand miles away. He gazed at the two codes on his mobile, shuddering at the responsibility fate had thrust into his hands.

About an hour later, just as he was about to set out for the NRSC his burner phone buzzed with a brief text from Ed Swanson. *Jupiter found dead in his laboratory a few minutes ago.*

CHAPTER 48

Washington

Somerton's flight touched down at 6.30pm on a chilly Friday evening, the sky filled with ominous black clouds. Taylor and he were met by Will Kenny dressed in what seemed to be his favoured army-like clothing; fawn chinos, a light-khaki shirt and zipped up bomber jacket. Four tough looking security staff stood nearby constantly looking around in all directions for a non-existent terrorist.

Kenny embraced Taylor warmly and kissed her on the lips, perhaps momentarily forgetting to be discreet. Fortunately, there were no photo-hungry media around. He shook hands with Somerton and motioned to his driver to load his guests' luggage. That done, they all climbed into the black-windowed limousine and set out on their journey to the White House.

'Pam is looking forward to seeing you guys again, she enjoyed your company. You made a good impression, Jack.'

Somerton's brow furrowed, 'Really? I couldn't begin to guess why.'

Kenny shrugged, and somewhat ungraciously nodded his agreement. 'Me neither, probably brain fog following too much wine over dinner. You can ask her when you see her.'

Somerton smiled. *I might just do that, Mr Bighead.*

Kenny turned to Taylor. 'I hesitate to ask, Laura, but has your sister heard from her husband?'

'Not a dickie bird, he's out of the picture as far as she's concerned. She can thank her lucky stars in my view.'

Somerton let a bit of devilment take over. 'Laura's right, he was no great loss from what I've heard. I reckon your sister paid somebody to take him out of the game. He's probably cooking under six feet of desert sand.'

Taylor frowned. 'Don't be ridiculous, Jack. She couldn't afford it for one thing.'

Somerton pouted. 'Well, he hasn't been in touch and he hasn't been seen by anybody outside the airport. Something must have happened to him. Maybe some knight in shining armour came along and did her a favour. What's your guess, Will?'

Kenny held Somerton's gaze. 'No idea, Jack. I doubt if she would have had the connections in Saudi to set up his disappearance. My guess would be that a deal went wrong and he upset somebody. The State can be lethal if you cross them.'

Somerton held Kenny's gaze and let a smile play on his lips. 'Yeah, you're probably right.' *Be careful, you're sailing close to the wind, Jack*

The White House

The First Lady came forward to greet them, dressed in a pale-yellow silk trouser suit that showed her bronze tan to maximum effect. Taylor and she exchanged brief hugs, then she turned to Somerton. 'Hello Jack, it's a pleasure to meet up with you again.' She stepped forward and kissed Somerton on the cheek, smiled and stepped back.

Somerton locked eyes on her. *You look gorgeous. I hope Will's right and I did make an impression on you.* 'The pleasure is all mine Pam, I assure you.'

'Looks like rain, let's get indoors. I'll send someone out to get your luggage. You're in the same rooms as last time, I thought that would be best. And how was the flight, Laura?'

'Restful all the way Pam; ideal really, gave me the opportunity to prepare for next week in the Commons. Some controversial motions have been put forward for debate. I was so deep in thought that Jack and I barely had a meaningful conversation.'

Somerton chipped in. 'Not quite as bad as that, Laura, but yeah, we were pretty engrossed in work for the most part.'

Pam Kenny rolled her eyes. 'Getting ready for tomorrow's big meeting I suppose. Will's been very secretive; he hasn't told me anything about it. All very hush-hush; more secure than the dark web it seems to me. Isn't that so honey?'

Kenny shrugged. 'You'll get to hear all about it in due course. Now why don't you two freshen up and join Pam and I for a light meal in half an hour or so.'

The light meal transpired to be grilled sea bass with a salad on the side, more than adequate.

'Where are the kids?' Somerton enquired. 'I was looking forward to meeting up with them again, lovely girls.'

Pam Kenny smiled. 'Nice of you to enquire, Jack. Jennifer has gone to a college sports camp and Rose is away for the weekend with her boyfriend, probably coupling as we speak.'

Her husband protested. 'Pam, please, don't embarrass me in front of our guests.'

His wife gave him a cynical eye. 'You don't think they've gone off together for the weekend just to tour art galleries? Surely you haven't forgotten what you got up to at college.' She turned to Taylor, 'What do you think, Laura?'

'Drop it Pam.' Kenny's voice was sharp. 'Rose is entitled to her privacy.'

Somerton though it was time to change the topic. 'Anything we should know about tomorrow, Will?'

'Nothing you won't know already. It's a one-off kind of meeting, maximum security, you'll be familiar with the drill. Be prepared to be body-scanned, no phones, notebooks, laptops etc. Everybody will be in civilian dress, no uniforms on this occasion. We've taken every precaution to keep this meeting secret.'

Pam Kenny put her hand to her mouth and put on an exaggerated tone. 'Oh my God, I've told all the girls about it; I bet the entire College knows by now. You'll have to charge me with giving away State secrets.'

Will Kenny sighed. 'Thank you for that, darling. What's got into you today?'

'Have a guess, darling, I'm sure you'll come up with something.'

Somerton watched the exchange and kept surprise off his face. *You are giving him a hard time, Pam, this is much deeper than the usual marriage squabble.'.*

Kenny glanced at his watch. 'It's half past nine, I vote for an early night unless any of you guys want a nightcap?'

Taylor declined but his wife nodded. 'Thank you, darling. I'll have a brandy; a large one, our best Napoleon. Please join me, Jack.'

Somerton looked from Pam to Will, then nodded. 'Sure, I'll join you Pam. I'll have a malt whisky if you've got one.'

Kenny moved across to the cocktail cabinet. Somerton thought Taylor looked a little uncomfortable. *Hmm, something going on.*

Kenny returned with two crystal glasses. 'There you are folks. Yours is on the left, Jack, enjoy.'

'Thanks, Will. I meant to ask where exactly is the meeting taking place?'

'You'll find that out tomorrow, Jack. That's me done, see you in the morning. Goodnight, darling.'

Pam Kenny just sipped her brandy and watched as her husband left the room. 'And then there were three. Surely you would like a drink, Laura?'

'I won't, thank you though. I have to put the final touches to my presentation for tomorrow. I think I'll follow Will's example and retire for the evening.'

Pam Kenny smiled, a little too sweetly it seemed to Somerton. 'Good idea, get your beauty sleep. I hope you manage to get off quickly.'

Taylor rose. 'Night Pam, night Jack, see you at breakfast.'

'Fancy another one, Jack?'

'Best not, Pam, I have to have a clear head tomorrow.'

'Do you mind if I have one?'

'Not at all, let me get it for you?'

Somerton poured her a modest brandy, turning to find that she had seated herself on a sofa. Her eyes held his as he bent over to hand her the glass.

'Forgive me asking, but are you and Will having a bad day?'

She held his eyes again. 'You could say that. In fact, if we weren't who we were, and had a strong sense of duty, I'd probably walk out.'

'Oh dear, I'm sorry to hear that. Politics can be very demanding on family life.' Somerton was genuinely understanding.

'Maybe, but most of the Presidents in recent times have had solid marriages, the Reagans, the Bushes, the Obamas.'

'But maybe not the Kennedy and Clinton clans. Men are a bit prone to stray.'

'It's a bit more than straying, Jack. You do know who he's involved with don't you?'

Somerton chose to play stupid. 'How could I, I'm on the other side of the Atlantic?

Pam Kenny laughed. 'So is his mistress.'

Somerton pointed upstairs. 'You don't mean…?'

'Right first time. Your boss, Britain's Prime Minister, Laura Taylor. They're probably at it already, they have inter-connecting rooms. Will's arrangement, not mine. Said he thought it best if he slept alone tonight, had a lot on his mind. He's been bedding her since they met at Harvard.' She gave a wry laugh. 'It really is a *special relationship.*'

Somerton was at loss for words at her directness

She reached out and stroked his cheek. 'You know what? How about I even the score and join you for a spell tonight? Get to know each other really well.'

Somerton was dumbfounded. He should say no but she was a beautiful woman and at this moment in time, very desirable. He would be playing with fire, words didn't come.

Pam Kenny smiled. 'I'll take your silence as a yes. Off you go to bed and I'll find my way to you in a little while.'

Somerton lay waiting under a light sheet, the air conditioning running silently in the background maintaining the temperature at a comfortable eighteen degrees. The only illumination was the table lamps on either side of the king size bed. Fifteen minutes passed and he was beginning to think she had changed her mind, or something had gone wrong, when the door opened. Pam Kenny slipped in quickly. She paused briefly to turn the key in the lock, then hurried over to the bed. She smiled at him, and slowly, deliberately, let her pale mauve short dressing gown slip from her shoulders and fall to the floor. She stood smiling, naked, hand on hips, inviting Somerton to gaze at her body

'My God but you're beautiful Pam, Will must be mad.'

She pulled the sheet away, climbed into bed and began kissing him, her tongue urgently searching for his. Their passion grew as they sought to please each other, their first lovemaking over almost as soon as it began. They had sex three times, saying nothing to each other, no endearments, no promises, no expressions of desire, other than the odd groan or whimper. It was clear to Somerton it wasn't about love, not even desire; their tryst was born of revenge. Not that he cared about motivation one way or another.

'Thank you, Jack. I needed that. It was just sex, nothing more, nothing less, but it was all I had hoped for.'

Somerton shook his head. 'Thank **you**, Pam. I'm glad you chose me. There isn't a man on the planet who would refuse you. Will's a damn fool.'

Pam Kenny smiled. 'Bless you, Jack. Another time, another place we could start an affair. Who knows, we might even have found love but fate doesn't always do what we wish for. I'm going now, see you in the morning. He blew her a kiss as she left the room. He lay for a while reflecting on what had happened then decided to have a shower and try to get some sleep.

Next morning

Somerton made his way down to breakfast at 7.30, surprised to find Will and Laura already there and tucking into scrambled egg on toast.'

'Good morning both.'

Kenny waved a hand at the breakfast bar. 'Good morning, Jack, help yourself. I trust you slept well?

Somerton smiled. 'Sure did, a very comfortable bed; I got off right away. Where's Pam?'

'Oh, says she's feeling tired and needs a lie in. She's not usually like this, she must have had a busy day yesterday. Anyway, she's having breakfast in bed and won't be joining us, sends her apologies. Eat up folks, we gotta be out of here in twenty-five minutes.'

Somerton smiled inwardly. *I guess she's feeling embarrassed.* 'That's a shame, do give her my best.

Taylor and Kenny sat in the back of the armoured limousine, no-one talking, all three deep in thought. Somerton noticed that the windows were completely blacked out; no-one could see in, passengers could barely see out. The driver also sat in front of a darkened glass partition.

'I presume this total black out is another security measure, Will?'

'Sure is, Jack. Folks can't see us, and we can't see where we are going.'

'Can't say I like it much, seems a touch ridiculous really. The Prime Minister of your closest ally, totally in the dark about our destination, but your lowly paid driver knows exactly where he's headed.'

'It's how it is. If things go as planned today, all will be revealed. I promise.'

Somerton timed the journey, seventy-three minutes precisely; around fifty miles maybe. He had no idea of what direction they had travelled.

Fort Kenny.

The car drew to a halt, the driver had a brief word with someone and then the car pulled away, stopping again after a few minutes. 'We're here folks.' Somerton and Taylor followed Kenny out onto the tarmac, eyes blinking in the bright sunshine.

'Welcome to Fort Kenny. If all has gone to plan everyone else should be here. I didn't want my most important guests queueing to go through security.'

Somerton took a good look around, not immediately impressed by the long single floor, flat roofed building in front of him. Security and communications looked to be well served though; there was an array of security cameras and satellite dishes and a high perimeter fence one hundred yards away in every direction. Manned security was provided by a detachment of the US Marine Corps.

Kenny led the way into the building where they were met by Ed Swanson whom he introduced to Laura Taylor. 'I believe you've met Ed.' He addressed Somerton.

Somerton nodded. 'Yes, quite recently, at a 21st birthday party, daughter of a close friend.' Nice to see you again, Ed and to see you are being kept busy. You didn't mention this set-up in our conversation.'

Swanson smiled. 'No, I didn't, did I?' He extended a hand and shook Somerton's warmly. 'Good to see you too; maybe we'll get a chance to talk later.'

'Hope so, depends what the President has in store for us.'

Somerton, Taylor and Kenny went through the security procedure; Kenny insisting on going last. All their loose possessions were placed in a cardboard box labelled with their name and put on a rack. Swanson lifted Somerton's flash drive and scrutinised it. 'I'll have to check this, Jack.'

'Be my guest.'

Swanson stepped away into a small side room, returning a few minutes later.

'All clear to go, Jack. I hope the meeting goes well. I'll be following proceedings on a screen.' He nodded over his shoulder at the room behind.

Kenny had stood to the side watching the procedure being carried out. Somerton wondered if perhaps he was looking for interaction between himself and Swanson.

'OK guys, follow me.'

He led them along a short corridor to a waiting elevator, ushering in Taylor and Somerton, giving an explanation of the layout.

'We go down three floors; lots of space is required for the numerous computer installations.' The elevator came to a gentle stop, the doors slid open, and Kenny led the way along another short passage to a steel door which he pushed open. They all filed in, the President striding ahead, taking command. Somerton noted that the door swung closed behind them.

Talking died away almost immediately and everyone present turned to look at the arrivals, those in the military making their profession obvious by standing smartly to attention. Somerton smiled to himself wondering if he was about to hear a rendition of Hail to the Chief.

The large room was full of people, mainly men, gathered in groups chatting. Dress varied from fairly casual, to suit, shirt and tie. The room was set up like a lecture theatre with a platform and a large screen out front. There was an electronic whiteboard on either side of the screen. Facing the platform were rows of small individual desks and seats laid out in semi-circular rows.

Kenny walked to the front to address the gathering. 'Let's get this show on the road. Each desk has a name card on it, US delegates on my left, those from the UK on my right.' I'll give you a few minutes to take you place then I'll open the proceedings.'

Most had sussed out previously where they were seated and quickly took their places, waiting attentively for Kenny's opening remarks. Taylor sat on a seat on the right next to the stage, Kenny directly opposite on the left.'

The President looked round, checking that every seat was occupied, then began.

'We will begin by introducing ourselves. Our UK colleagues will take the lead, followed by US delegates. When we come to presentations, a US representative will lead off, followed by someone from the UK and we will continue to alternate. I want each of you to stand and tell us, how we should use the Satellite system to improve this planet of ours. You should aim to take no more than ten minutes; I stress that we're dealing with broad principles on this occasion. There will be future opportunities to address the detail. I will give you a warning if I think you are holding forth for longer than necessary. Each of your name cards has a number which represents the running order. You'll state your name and the position you hold. I'll lead off, then hand over to the Prime Minister.

'Right, let's get this show on the road. I'm Will Kenny, President of the United States of America.' He nodded to Laura Taylor.

I'm Laura Taylor, Prime Minister of Great Britain and Norther Ireland.'

It seemed to drag on forever. Somerton quickly got bored; photographic memories excepted, nobody was going to remember every name and its face. And besides they were clearly visible on the both sides of the name tags on the desks. But the process continued, four Generals, two Admirals, two Air Marshalls. He did a quick sum in his head; there were around twenty delegates, ten to fifteen minutes each, plus Taylor and Kenny, five long hours lay ahead.

The introductions made Kenny invited everyone to get themselves a coffee, or tea if preferred, a process that took nearly fifteen minutes. 'Right, I assume those that want a drink, have one. I want all of you to switch on the laptop in front of you.' He waited a minute or so until the screens filled.

'Everybody tuned in?' He looked around. 'Good. These proceedings are being filmed so you should have me on your screens. All got that?' He looked round the room. 'Yes? Well done Ed Swanson.'

Kenny glanced at his list and looked around, then pointed at smartly dressed young woman seated at the back of the room. 'Stand up Charlie. Let me introduce Charlie Bonetti who will run the publicity campaign when we get down to telling the world what we're up to.' Bonetti smiled broadly and waved.

'Right', he looked at his list again. 'Ruth Gamotti, you have the floor.'

One by one, the politicians stood to give their view of how they thought the Satellite System should be used. Somerton was surprised, shocked in some instances, how representatives from both sides of the pond saw the world being reshaped. A theme began to emerge. Essentially, the world was to be westernised, the West was successful, the West was democratic, the West knew what was best for everyone. There were no dissenters.

When all the political speakers had made their presentations, Kenny called a halt to proceedings and invited delegates to go through a door at the rear of the stage where they could help themselves to a stand-up buffet lunch. 'You've got forty-five minutes and that includes a visit to the bathroom. I won't like it much if you're late. His expression declared that it wasn't an empty threat.'

Somerton made a point of mingling with military delegates from both sides, asking essentially the same question of each group he joined. His approach was to introduce himself, praise what had been said, support the philosophy of West is best and then ask the blunt question. *'What do we do if other nations don't go along with our strategy?'* The military responses ranged from the Brits raised eyebrows approach. *'We shall have to find a way of persuading them of the error of their ways old chap.'* to the blunt approach of the US military representatives. *'We kick their fucking asses; it's all these people understand.'*

Everyone back in their seats. Kenny took the floor again. 'Thank you for being timely. We now move into the military presentations to hear their strategy for what we do if our approach isn't being adopted universally.'

He looked at his list, 'Harry Dennison let's hear what the US Navy could do for us.'

Twelve military leaders, eight American, four British, made their statements. Their lunch time utterances were repeated openly, power was next to Godliness; the impact of the China and Rostov outcomes, were routinely quoted. One US general was very clear - W*e will have them by the balls and should squeeze hard right from day one – we've tried all that softly, softly United Nations resolution crap over the years and got nowhere. It's now or never in my book.*

Somerton kept his eyes on Kenny and Taylor throughout, saw their nods of approval, saw their smiles, Kenny even punched the air on a few occasions. His thoughts went to MacKinnon. *Surely this isn't what you envisaged, Colin?* He sighed deeply when he thought of Croudace. *You were right all along, Alan, I wish you were here now.'*

The military presentations complete, Kenny rose smiling broadly, his expression one of complete satisfaction. 'Nearly there, Jack Somerton from the UK is next up. He has led the Constellation MacKinnon satellite project from the start and I'm sure will give us his insights on the systems full capabilities. When Jack's done, Laura and I will sum up and you can all go home and dream of the bright future ahead of us. I would remind you that Constellation MacKinnon comprised just fifty-four satellites; our constellation, as yet unnamed will have five hundred. And that's just phase one. I'm aiming for two thousand over the next five years.' Somerton wasn't the only one who gasped.

'OK, Jack, the floor is yours.'

Somerton, plugged his flash drive into his laptop and took a large sip of cold water and moved forward to the podium. 'I'm going to use the big screen to show you how I see the future so make sure your laptops are on and running. I'll guide you through, as I make my presentation. I promise I'll be brief. I'll begin with a question for Will Kenny. Will, the genius behind our wonderful satellite technology is Joseph Svetinsky, code name Jupiter. Why is he not here with us today?'

Kenny stared at Somerton making no attempt to conceal his anger. 'Today is about strategy and policy not science and technology. In any case he's indisposed; we'll get to meet him another day.'

Somerton nodded. 'I hope he gets well soon; the system will be very limited without him. He's a good man.' Laura Taylor visibly squirmed in her seat.

Somerton pressed a key on his laptop. 'Eyes on a screen, large or small, please.' Most eyes went to the big screen, expressions puzzled by what they were seeing. Kenny and Taylor were staring at Somerton. The screen was filled with names. Caesar, Alexander the Great, Attila the Hun, Hitler, Stalin, Mussolini.

Somerton looked round the room. 'I'm sure you all know what they had in common. They were all men who wanted to conquer the world, they were all men who thought they knew best, all men who would stop at nothing to achieve their aims - all dictators.'

Voices were muttering in protest some louder than others.

Somerton continued undaunted. 'And, of course, there were the minor dictators Sadam Hussein, Colonel Gadaffi, Idi Amin and the like. Add to those, the idealists - the Crusaders, the Vatican, the Ottomans and my own British Imperialists.' Taylor whispered, 'Enough, Jack.' Kenny hissed. 'Get off this theme or shut up.'

Somerton smiled. 'Did you hear my Prime Minister? Did you hear your President? Did you listen to yourselves? Your message is clear - only you know what's fucking best, democracy only exists within your boundaries. If somebody speaks against you, shut them up and shut them up quick. Will Kenny lied to you by the way, Jupiter isn't indisposed, he's dead. He died yesterday and the computers that run the satellites are shut down.'

Kenny scrambled to his feet. 'Don't listen to him, I have the start-up code, it's not a problem.'

Somerton looked Kenny in the eye.

'Why did you lie about Jupiter, Will? Are you **sure** you have the start-up code, or has Jupiter pulled the wool over your eyes? Sorry Will, but you've just demonstrated that you can't be trusted.'

He turned to face the delegates, pointing around them. 'And do you know what? You lot couldn't be trusted to do what's best for humanity. You all have one solution, the *final solution*. Are those words familiar? I'm sorry - sorry for you, sorry for your families and friends, but this dream of your ends here and now.'

Somerton calmly reached forward and pressed a key on his laptop.

The room erupted like a volcano as every laptop exploded in front of its user, killing them instantly. Blood, brains, bones and body-parts scattered in every direction. There were no yells, no cries of pain, there was no suffering, death was instantaneous. The biggest headline in media history had been made in a split second.

Ed Swanson watched the carnage on his security screen, he had known what would happen, and had played his part in making it happen. Somerton had arranged for the supply of the extremely powerful PETN explosive he had inserted and wired into the laptops issued to everyone in attendance. All it took was 50-60grams in each laptop to create the carnage he had just witnessed.

A tear rolled down his cheek. 'I salute you, Jack Somerton.'

But there was no time to linger; he had a job to do. The site had to be secured. He picked up the telephone and got an immediate response. He said two words only. 'Operation Flamingo.'

A couple of miles away a detachment of Marines, ostensibly carrying out a field exercise was alerted by the call. Their armoured vehicles formed into a convoy and set out at top speed for Fort Kenny. Swanson meanwhile walked at full pace to the site entrance, the guards springing to attention when he arrived.

'Stand easy. There's been a terrorist incident below ground; a huge explosion in the conference room. I fear everyone, including the President, has lost their lives. A Marine detachment is on the way now to secure the site; only they are to be allowed access. News of this disaster must not reach the media. If it does, you will be held responsible, and imprisoned pending trial. Got that?'

CHAPTER 49

The Aftermath

Ed Swanson had acted quickly; Fort Kenny was secured from the Media and all State machinery. Somerton had asked him to enter the de-activation code and disable Jupiter's hyper-quantum computers but he had gone further; he had used some of the PETN explosive to destroy the entire installation. The threat that they posed was gone, along with their creator.

He had selflessly done what necessary for the future of mankind but he couldn't help wondering what his future was. He was responsible for security at Fort Knox and would be the first to come under suspicion; an explanation for what had gone wrong would have to be found. The situation was unprecedented, the United States no longer had a President or a Vice-President, the Leaders of the Senate and House of Representatives were gone. He was the only one in authority who knew what had taken place. He would be suspected of treason.

The United States leadership was gone, someone had to take command but who would it be? No doubt somewhere in the Constitution the answer could be found but that wasn't a problem for him to solve. He was going to pass that problem to the most senior Supreme Court judge. No-one he could think of was better qualified. He scrolled through the numbers on his mobile and made a call.

Supreme Court Judge, seventy-one years old, Amy Anderson, was speechless.

'Is this some kind of a sick hoax, Major-General Swanson? I'm afraid I can't say I've ever heard of you'

'No Judge, I swear; you can check with the Pentagon. You can also phone the First Lady; I'm sure she will confirm that the President had a meeting at Fort Kenny today.'

'That's another thing, I've never heard of Fort Kenny.'

Swanson gulped; this was proving more difficult than expected. 'It's classified as Top Secret; it's a research centre. I can appreciate your caution, but the situation is urgent. If you wish you can check out the whereabouts of the President, Vice-President and the Leaders of the Senate and House of Representatives with their Assistants and you'll find they are all attending this meeting. Please Judge, I beg you, believe me. I'm the only one who knows the scale of this disaster. The Prime Minister of the United Kingdom and her deputy are dead, along with other officials and high-ranking military from both countries. It's a terrorist disaster of epic proportions. Please, please do whatever is necessary.'

Swanson's sincerity and pleading finally won through. Anderson's mindset changed; this wasn't a hoax this was a tragedy of epic proportions. 'God save us.' her voice broke, and she went quiet for what seemed to be an eternity to the waiting Swanson whilst the Judge recovered her composure.

'You've secured the site and told no-one else about this incident. That was the right course of action. A news black-out must be put in place until new leadership is put in place in our country, and, in Great Britain. I will inform the US Secretary of State and Her Majesty's Secretary. In the meantime, you must remain at Fort Kenny. Have you called the emergency services for ambulances?

'No Judge, there are no survivors I assure you. Involving medical services at this stage would be pointless and lead to the incident becoming public very quickly.'

Anderson sighed. 'You're probably right but only if you are absolutely certain no-one has survived.'

Swanson wasn't absolutely certain, how could he be, but he didn't want anyone to come out of that room alive. 'Sadly, I couldn't be more certain, Judge.'

Whilst they conversed the Judge had accessed the internet on her laptop to make sure Swanson was legitimate. One thing in the scenario troubled her. How could the security of a top-secret establishment be breached so calamitously? Add to that the fact that Swanson was responsible for security and he was the sole survivor. These were very serious questions requiring answers. But that side of things would have to wait, America needs a head of state and so did the United Kingdom; those were the priorities for now.

Anderson lost no time in setting the wheels in motion; acting Heads of State were put in place on both sides of the Atlantic within hours. The slow process of establishing political normality began. The US and UK leaders asked each other questions that couldn't be answered. *Who arranged the meeting? What was its purpose? Why were the governing chambers of democracy not informed of the meeting beforehand? How could such a serious lapse of security have occurred?*

The only thing both countries immediately agreed on was to fly their flags at half-mast for a week; most of the world followed suit. Funeral arrangements had to be discussed and it was readily agreed both countries should act together to honour their dead. Ex-Presidents Overton and Kingston together with the UK's Acting British Prime Minister and Leader of the Opposition met and after much debate agreed on the way forward. The four leaders personally made contact with the families of those who perished and obtained agreement that there should be no attempt made to recover the bodies. The process involved would have been arduous, the end products not a sight loved ones would want to view.

The recommendation was made to declare Fort Kennedy to be a national memorial, owned jointly by the United States and Great Britain in perpetuity. The building would be demolished and accessible underground areas filled with soli and aggregate. There would be an international competition to design a monument which would be adopted by both countries. In the Unites States it would be erected at Fort Kenny. The United Kingdom's memorial would be located in the National Memorial Arboretum in Alrewas, Staffordshire.

When the news became public, the media worldwide sprang into action; the conspiracy theorists were in their element, accusations and counter accusations were rife. The blast was investigated in depth by a team of US investigators and independently by a team of UK investigators; laptops were quickly identified as the source of the explosions. PETN was identified as the explosive. Major-General Ed Swanson was the main suspect, but his service record was impeccable, and no credible motivation could be found. His movements were checked and re-checked, security camera footage was scrutinised, but no circumstantial evidence was found to incriminate him.

During questioning he played his trump card, Jupiter; a suggestion made by Jack Somerton. *I believe that Joseph Svetinsky also known as Jupiter may have carried out this dreadful crime. I suspect when he knew he was dying he chose not to leave behind the technology he invented. As to why he chose to kill all those attending the meeting, I can only guess. He wasn't invited to the meeting, perhaps he felt undervalued, unrecognised globally, perhaps he was worried about how his invention would be used. His immune system was in terminal decline, perhaps he wasn't thinking clearly; his brain may have been affected by his condition and medication.*

Ex-Presidents Overton and Kingston both vouched for Swanson's character and at the end of the enquiries the conclusion was reached that Swanson wasn't guilty. He was however removed from his security duties and offered a desk job in the Pentagon which he accepted.

Eddie Black and Mike Davies were devastated when they got the news of Somerton's death and they met to console each other. Their thoughts inevitably turned to that final night with Somerton and the parcel Davies had delivered to somebody who looked remarkably like Swanson. They had no idea of why it had been necessary to wipe out the cream of British and American Government and its military leaders, but one thing was certain, Jack Somerton had a hand it. They didn't have any answers, but they knew Jack, and his priority would have been his beloved Great Britain.

Chloe MacKinnon broke down in tears; she could barely speak even to her own family for day. She was just starting to emerge from the shock when a parcel arrived special delivery from the UK, sent by a firm of London solicitors. Accompanying the parcel was a covering letter.

Dear Mrs MacKinnon,

As you will be aware, Mr Jack Somerton sadly died in a terrorist incident a week ago and I am contacting you in pursuit of our obligations as his Solicitor and Sole Executor.

A copy of his Will is enclosed. If you require any guidance regarding its contents, please get in touch.

I will contact you in a week or so regarding your inheritance, when you have had the opportunity to give the matter due thought.

A parcel is enclosed with this letter. I do not know what it contains, I am simply following Mr Somerton's instructions and forwarding it to you.

Yours sincerely

James Agnew

Tears ran down her cheeks as she opened the package and found two black ornate boxes and an accompanying handwritten letter.

Dearest Chloe,

Looks like I've checked out.

Could you please accept the enclosed medals, Alan Croudace's and mine. Please keep them alongside Colin's – three colleagues united in perpetuity. They were, and are, my closest and most trusted friends.

You will have received a copy of my will and will see there is some provision for you, Maggie and Murray. Money is a crass way of showing the regard I have for the three of you. I love you all, you are the family I never had.

Be happy always, much love, Jack xxx

Tears continue to run down her cheeks, sorrow and shock engulfing her in equal measure as she saw the bequests made to her and her family.

Eddie Black £2,000,000

Mike Davies £2,000,000

Jessica Tate£1,000,000

Abbi, Maggie and Murray MacKinnon £2,000,000 each

Chloe MacKinnon £5,000,000

After all debts and taxes are paid the balance of my estate is bequeathed to the SAS Association

Later. Fort Kenny Memorial

A grand memorial service was held to honour those who died; representative attended from all over the world. At the end of the testimonials and the blessings a US Marine sounded The Last Post and an SAS piper played The Flowers of the Forest.

Ex-Presidents George Kingston and Brian Overton attended the memorial service, and when it was over, walked back to their cars together where they said their goodbyes. As two men shook hands, Kingston shook his head. 'You know, Brian, I never thought I'd say it but maybe, just maybe, when all's said and done, Somerton wasn't such a bad guy after all.'

www.ingramcontent.com/pod-product-compliance
Lightning Source LLC
Chambersburg PA
CBHW070429170726
48291CB00002B/423